# MARIA V. SNYDER

# Taste of DARKNESS

HARLEQUIN®MIRA®

Harlequin MIRA is a registered trademark of Harlequin Enterprises Limited, used under licence.

Published in Great Britain 2014
by Harlequin MIRA, an imprint of Harlequin (UK) Limited,
Eton House, 18 24 Paradise Road,
Richmond, Surrey, TW9 1SR

© 2014 Maria V. Snyder

ISBN: 978 1 848 45280 0

58-0114

Harlequin (UK) Limited's policy is to use papers that are natural, renewable and recyclable products and made from wood grown in sustainable forests. The logging and manufacturing processes conform to the legal environmental regulations of the country of origin.

Printed and bound by
CPI Group (UK) Ltd, Croydon, CR0 4YY

For my father—a perpetual tinkerer, who showed me the benefits of hard work and persistence. It took me a while to catch on, but I eventually 'got' it. Thanks, Pop!

# TASTE *of* DARKNESS

# CHAPTER 1

Cold air caressed my back. I rolled over, muttering at Kerrick for hogging the blanket, but stopped. Something felt…odd, wrong, missing. Opening my eyes, I confirmed the emptiness next to me. Kerrick was gone.

For a moment, I stared at the dent in the pillow. Had yesterday been a dream? Had I imagined Wynn's betrayal, Tohon trapped in a magical stasis, Kerrick's miraculous arrival, and the rest of the insanity?

No. The events replayed in my head with vivid details. The blood, the overpowering reek of dead ufas, and Wynn's poisoned knife striking Kerrick's arm. Poisoned with Death Lily toxin. I'd thought I'd sucked all the deadly poison from Kerrick's wound…but what if I hadn't?

Icy fingers of fear wrapped around my heart. I shot to my feet and dressed in record time. Kerrick's shirt, boots, and sword lay in a heap by the dying fire. Not good.

Out in the large main cavern, the rest of the infirmary staff stirred. I scanned the patients' cots on the off chance Kerrick had collapsed into one. He hadn't.

Loren added wood to the cooking hearth, poking it into a bright blaze.

I rushed over to him. "Have you seen Kerrick?"

"Nope, and we figured we wouldn't see either of you until..." His smirk faded. "Maybe he went outside for some fresh air." This in a hopeful tone.

"Without his shirt?"

"Well, when nature calls..."

"Or his sword?"

Loren jumped up. "Let's not panic, Avry."

Too late.

"Have you searched the other caverns?" he asked.

"Not yet."

"Okay, then you look for him inside, and I'll go outside. If he's not nearby, I'll ask the guards if they saw him last night. All right?"

I nodded, but dread clawed up my throat. Kerrick wouldn't be in another cavern unless he'd been too sick to find his way back to me. Gulping down the tight knot, I grabbed a lantern and checked all the other sleeping areas.

A few people grumbled after I swept the light over them, but I didn't care.

Odd squinted in the brightness, but sat up as if he'd been awake. "What's wrong?"

I explained.

He cursed. "Not only did Wynn stab us in the back, she's twisted the blade, too."

"While I'd love to plot revenge with you—"

"Yeah, go. I'll be right out."

The other caverns yielded the same results. Even the one reserved for the privy. A detached part of my mind noted the buckets needed to be dumped. However my heart kept its frantic rhythm. That was the last place inside. Perhaps...

Running back to the main cavern, I spotted Loren and Odd talking to a soldier.

"…sometime after midnight," the man said. "Don't recall if he came back or not."

Loren rounded on him. "Don't recall! You're *supposed* to be guarding us. What if the enemy grabbed him? If someone goes into the woods and doesn't come back, that's a big red flag, you idiot!"

Odd touched Loren's shoulder and tilted his head toward me. "Not helping right now."

"He was outside?" I asked.

The guard had seen him leave. I dashed out into the cold morning air. The fresh scent of moist earth reminded me of Kerrick. Without hesitating, I embraced the closest bit of foliage, seeking the vibrations of Kerrick's forest magic.

Nothing. I drew a shaky breath. Don't jump to conclusions. He could be unconscious. Odd and Loren had followed me out. Six inches shorter than Odd, Loren ran a hand over his buzzed black hair. More silver sprinkled his hair despite only being thirty-five. Odd on the other hand had let his hair grow since Tohon's surprise attack. Although saying it had grown was being generous. His dark brown locks remained close to his scalp in a fine fuzz.

"We need to search the area. Wake the others," I ordered.

They hastened inside and soon Flea, Quain, and most of the soldiers had assembled by the cave's entrance. Using one of Ryne's military maps, Loren divided the surrounding area into quadrants. The infirmary cave was located in Pomyt Realm, northeast of Zabin and east of the ruins of the Healer's Guild.

Quain growled at everyone, but he appeared healthy despite being frozen in Sepp's magical stasis only yesterday. But Flea's face remained pale and he seemed unsteady on his feet. The discovery of his ability to break Sepp's stasis had taken a toll on him.

I moved closer to him. "Flea, stay here, you're in no condition—"

"No. I'm going." Despite being sixteen, he sounded much older. And his firm gaze meant I'd have an easier time convincing fire not to burn.

Before assigning quadrants to the teams, Loren pulled me aside. "Hate to bring this up, but if he's... If we find..."

"A dead body?" Not like I hadn't thought of it a million times since I'd woken up.

"Yeah."

"Tell them to find me as fast as possible. I have the Lily map—we'll head to the closest Peace Lily and hope for the best." I glanced at Flea. A Peace Lily had saved his life and mine; it might save Kerrick's.

The strain on Loren's face eased just a bit. "Right." He shouted orders and the teams of four headed into the woods, fanning out to their assigned areas.

No surprise that Loren, Quain, and Flea joined me. I trailed my fingers along the greenery, hoping to detect Kerrick's magic. At this point, I'd pray to Estrid's creator if I thought it would help.

As a group, we moved in silent mode. Despite Tohon's current condition—frozen in stasis, because if he weren't, he'd die from the deep stab wound in his chest, a little gift from me—his army still advanced from the south. Cellina had taken over command. Just as ruthless as he was, at least she couldn't create more dead soldiers. And we'd discovered how to stop the ones in existence. So it was only a matter of time until we neutralized them all.

What if we didn't find Kerrick in time? The Peace Lilys were picky. From the little I'd learned, the person in question either needed to be a magician or have the potential to be one, and the body had to be fresh. Flea'd been dead a few hours and I had died inside the Lily.

Well, actually, the Lily hadn't brought us back to life. It'd preserved our bodies until another person touched us. I'd awoken Flea and Kerrick had saved me.

*Kerrick, why didn't you wake me? Why didn't you tell me you felt sick?*

What if the Peace Lily rejected him? Like it refused Ursan and Noelle? Although Ursan had been a magic sniffer, he'd been dead too long, and my sister, Noelle, hadn't been gifted with magic. I was the only one in my family who'd developed powers. Healing powers, not that it helped with either of them. Or Kerrick. I couldn't cure those poisoned by Death Lily toxin or infected with the plague.

The plague had killed two-thirds of the population of the Fifteen Realms. At least there hadn't been a new case in almost three years. But during its prime, over six million people had died.

Gee, not like I wasn't depressed enough. I focused my energies on the search. How far could one sick man go anyway?

The day dragged on. We made sweeping arcs through our area, but only managed to scare a few rabbits, which Loren shot with his bow. Sunlight streamed through the gaps in the trees, heating the air to a comfortable level—summer's last gasp. Fall started in eleven days.

Memories of last fall came unbidden. Around midseason Kerrick and the guys had rescued me from the guillotine. Because of his forest magic, his eyes had matched the color of the forest with warm browns, gold, and amber flecks. I huffed. His personality hadn't coordinated at all. He'd been cold, mean, and only cared about healing Prince Ryne, which had been why he'd freed me from jail.

Loren raised his hand in a stopping motion. We froze, listening. Hope surged, but died just as quick. The noise of the other searchers' passage had carried. They weren't as skilled in moving through the forest. Instead of their movements blending in with the forest's song, it stood out like an out-of-tune violin in a string quartet.

My emotions had been on an endless seesaw over the past month. First Tohon's vast army had surrounded Estrid's and he'd demanded unconditional surrender. Cellina had acted as his liaison and Kerrick's sword had hung from her belt. She'd claimed Kerrick had been torn apart by her pack of dead ufas. He hadn't. But then Ryne had sent Kerrick north to fight the invading tribes and a messenger had reported he'd died in the attempt. He hadn't.

So this was just another false alarm. Right? Kerrick was like a cat with nine lives. Three down, five left. I clung to that thin thread of hope because… Well, if I didn't, I'd shatter.

We searched all day.

When the sun hovered over the horizon, Loren called it off. "We can resume in the morning."

"You can go back," I said, "but I'm staying."

"We need to regroup and see if anyone has seen anything."

"I agree, but you don't need me for that."

Loren exchanged a glance with Quain. Close to my age of twenty-one, Quain had teamed up with Loren before joining Kerrick. Their antics had earned them the nickname the monkeys. I'd once quipped Quain was the bald monkey since no hair grew on his head.

"Avry, you haven't eaten all day," Quain said.

"Really, Quain? Is that all you got? Do you think I have an *appetite* right now?" I regretted my harsh sarcasm immediately. It wasn't Quain's fault.

He stepped closer to me. His voice dipped low. "You're not the only one hurting here."

"I know, I'm sorry."

Quain paused at that, blinking at me as if no one had ever apologized to him before. "Do you think you'll be able to help Kerrick if you're passed out from exhaustion?"

"I know my limits, Quain."

"And how effective can one person be stumbling around in the dark?"

I drew breath to blast him again, but Flea said, "I'll stay with Avry."

Flea's face had paled to bone white. The only color was the dark smudges underneath his eyes. He swayed on his feet. Talk about passing out… If I stayed, Flea would insist on staying, as well.

Sighing, I said, "You're right. I'd be useless."

Quain showed an amazing amount of restraint in not gloating over my comment. Loren raised his eyebrows, but kept quiet.

As we headed back, I walked next to Flea and took his hand. He squeezed my fingers in silent support. However, I had another purpose for linking hands. I sent him a subtle flow of magical energy. Since I'd awoken him, we had a bond. He sensed when I was in trouble, and we could share strength.

Once we found Kerrick, we'd have to figure out the extent of Flea's new magic. Was he now a death magician or a hybrid magician who didn't fit in one of the eleven categories of magic? The fact that he could break Sepp's stasis made for another weapon in our growing arsenal against Cellina's army. Funny to think of the thousands of soldiers as Cellina's now.

I slowed as Flea grew stronger.

"Hey! Stop that." He let go, shaking me off.

"Stop what?" I acted confused.

"Don't pull that on me. I didn't ask for help."

"Yes, you did. You just didn't know it." And before Flea could protest, I added, "Healer. Remember? It's what I do."

"But what if we find Kerrick?"

*What if?* Those two words had haunted me all day. And just like with Flea, Kerrick and I shared a bond. I reached for the bushes, touching the leaves. Still no ripple of magic. Yet a tightness deep down inside me wouldn't let me despair. It clung to the notion I'd been wrong about his death before. In fact, it reasoned that until I had proof to the contrary, I should assume he was alive.

"*When* we find Kerrick, I'll have plenty of energy," I said.

Back at the cave entrance, the other teams milled about, talking in low voices. From their universal serious expressions, I guessed they'd been unsuccessful.

"I'm sorry, Avry, but there's been no sign of him," Odd said, joining us. "A few of the teams covered their entire areas. Are you sure he's sick? I hate to be gross…but we didn't find any vomit. And it's hard to imagine him traveling farther if he wasn't feeling good."

"Kerrick can be stubborn," I said, hoping that annoying trait had saved him.

"He had to be sick. Why else would he be out without his shirt or sword?" Loren asked.

"All right. So he goes outside thinking he's going to throw up…then what?" Odd asked.

We'd all assumed he collapsed, but… What if he'd realized he was dying? I imagined his thoughts and feelings at that moment, putting myself in his place. He'd promised me he wouldn't die. But it was inevitable. Yet Kerrick didn't give up easily.

I gasped. "He headed to a Peace Lily!"

# CHAPTER 2

"Of course," Flea said. "Why didn't I think of that?"

And I wished I'd figured it out sooner. Sick and dying, Kerrick must have done the only thing he could—head to a Peace Lily. He'd been there when the Lily had saved my life and he'd recently learned about Flea's survival. A surge of energy coursed through me.

"Could he find a Lily at night?" Odd asked.

"Yeah, he's a forest mage," Flea said.

"Loren, where's the map you used for the search areas?" I pulled out my Lily map, but the sunlight was all but gone.

"I left it with the captain of the watch in case anyone returned and needed to find us," Loren said.

"Go get it and ask the search teams how much of their areas were covered today. Oh, and see if they encountered any Lilys and where."

"Got it." Loren dashed off.

Quain, Flea, and Odd followed me inside the infirmary cave. I knelt next to the fire and spread my map out. The locations of the clusters of Lilys had been marked on it.

Handy, except the markings didn't indicate if they were Death or Peace Lilys. For once it didn't matter, because Kerrick also couldn't tell the difference. He'd head for the closest cluster since the odds were in his favor. A hundred Peace Lilys grew for every Death Lily. However, I still needed to know if the teams had found any Lilys. Since I'd been using the map, I'd discovered it wasn't 100 percent accurate.

I paused, letting the irony sink in. Death Lily toxin killed my sister and might take Kerrick, but it stopped Tohon's dead soldiers, and had given me my healing magic. Ironic or warped? Or twisted? How about plain old sad?

Loren arrived with the information I'd requested. We consulted and pinpointed the closest Lily cluster. Half a day southwest. I remembered that group of six Lilys. One had been a Death Lily, and I'd harvested its toxin sacks. More important, five were Peace Lilys.

Standing, I said, "Let's go."

Quain exchanged a look with Loren, doing their silent monkey communication that Belen liked to tease them about. Belen. I bit my lip. No. I wasn't going to think about him right now. If I did, I'd dissolve into a little puddle of goo. And time was too critical right now.

Pushing past Quain, I fetched my knapsack from my sleeping cavern. Kerrick's clothes remained where I'd tossed them last night. I shoved them into my pack along with his boots. He'd need them; the air turned cold at nights. I wrapped my cloak around my shoulders.

When I returned, Loren and Quain waited for me with their packs. Flea sat by the fire. Two bright red patches spread on his cheeks, and his lips were pressed into a hard line. Odd stood behind him with his arms crossed. Their body language said it all.

"Here." Loren handed me a few sticks of beef jerky. "You can eat it on the way."

"Thanks." I bit into one as we left the cave. A half-moon lit the sky, giving off just enough light for us to see the trail, but not enough to see well. We traveled slower than normal to avoid tripping. Plus we kept searching for Kerrick. He might have collapsed on his way to the Lilys. I touched the greenery from time to time, seeking his magic. My heart, though, wanted action and it raced regardless of our pace.

"I'd rather you had a hot meal before we left, but I rarely get my way," Loren said.

"You stopped Flea from coming along."

"Only because Odd threatened to sit on him. Flea said he wasn't going to speak to me ever again." Loren shook his head. "I've been waiting for Quain to say that for years."

"Hey!"

I cut in before they could launch into a verbal battle. "You did the right thing, Loren. He needs to rest after yesterday."

"Yeah, but he doesn't like to miss out. And I'm with him on this one. I wouldn't want to be left behind, either."

"Why is he so tired?" Quain asked in concern. "Is it because of…me?"

"I don't remember him saving anyone else's life yesterday," Loren said.

"I know I owe him one. But what did he do to break the spell? I wasn't dead. I was just…" Quain glanced at me. "What was I? I didn't feel anything."

"You were paused. Neither living nor dead, just suspended. Sepp once explained it as a fake death."

"And now Tohon's trapped in this fake death?" Quain asked.

"Yes. And according to Sepp, Belen is, as well. He used that information to try to stop Kerrick from killing him," I said. Tohon had told me he'd turned Belen into one of his dead soldiers. I didn't know who to believe, but I knew who I desperately wanted to believe. Either way, Belen had been missing for over a month.

"Estrid and her top staff are also frozen," Loren added.

"Yeah, but it didn't matter. No offense, Quain, but Tohon had to be stopped," I said. "By taking out Sepp, no one would have been able to awaken him, or so we thought at the time. Cellina can't create more dead soldiers. In the end, by killing Sepp we'd have saved thousands of lives."

Except Wynn had hit Kerrick with her knife before he could finish Sepp off. Eventually Sepp, Wynn, and Cellina had escaped and Flea had awoken Quain.

"If it makes you feel any better, it was a very painful decision," I said.

Loren put his hand on his stomach. "Like a bad bout of indigestion."

"Thanks, I feel all warm inside." He bumped Loren with his shoulder. "So now that Sepp's still alive, what does that mean?"

Loren met my gaze. What indeed?

"It depends on Cellina," I said. "If she likes being in charge, she'll leave Tohon frozen. If she truly loves him…"

"She'll come after Avry," Loren said. "She's the only one who can heal Tohon."

Not exactly. Danny's healing magic had awoken during his adventure with Kerrick in the north. But not many people knew about him. Yet another worry flared. Had Tohon told Cellina about his experiments with the Death Lily toxin? The people who survived being poisoned with the toxin all developed healing powers. Tohon had been injecting it into children, hoping to make healers. Danny and Zila had lived through it, but I'd rescued them. If Tohon had kept it secret, all should be well.

If not… I considered. Danny remained with the northern tribes and Zila stayed with Kerrick's brother, Izak. Both were in Alga Realm, safe on the other side of the Nine Mountains for now.

"But Avry won't heal Tohon," Quain said. "Right? You agreed with Kerrick's decision to kill Sepp."

"Right. I won't."

"And we all know you can't be threatened, bullied, coerced, or bribed to heal someone you don't want to." Loren smiled.

Quain rubbed his neck. "Yeah, we learned *that* lesson the hard way."

"I'd say Kerrick had the most learning to do. Fun times."

I wouldn't go so far as to call them fun. However, those days when we'd been all together had been...nice, despite the danger. And now... Grief and sadness filled me. Would I lose everyone I loved before this war ended?

We lapsed into silence. The farther we moved away from the infirmary cave, the greater the chance of encountering an enemy patrol. The night insects buzzed and chirped.

When the sun rose, we stopped for a quick breakfast and continued. In the daylight, the monkeys searched for any signs that Kerrick had passed this way.

"Would he even leave a trail?" I asked.

"If he was too sick to do his tree mojo, he might have broken some branches," Quain said.

And I still hadn't felt a ripple of his magic. Which meant he was either unconscious, already inside a Lily, or dead. I leaned against a tree's trunk for a moment as a wave of misery swept through me. No. Not until I had proof.

Pushing away those dire thoughts, I straightened. "I'll meet you guys there. You're slowing me down." I sprinted down the trail.

They picked up their pace and we reached the Lily cluster a few hours after dawn.

"There's no sign Kerrick came this way," Quain said, examining the ground.

I shot him a nasty look.

Loren punched him in the arm. Hard.

"What?"

Ignoring them, I pulled off my cloak and knapsack, setting them down. I moved closer and studied the six Lilys. The cluster grew among the trees. Giant white man-size flowers topped thick green stalks. Thorny vines jumbled below and the scent of honey and lemons filled the air. Get too close to a Death Lily and either the petals snatched you or the vines ensnared you and pulled you in. Once trapped, you couldn't escape even if armed with a sharp knife. The thick and fibrous petals and leaves resisted punctures and tears.

Death Lilys moved fast for a plant, hissing a warning a second before they grabbed their victims. Once you were caught, it pricked you with two barbs and injected its toxin. One of three things happened next. You die, and it feeds off your flesh, spitting your bones out when it's finished. Or you don't die, it spits you out, and you suffer horribly, dying later. Then there are the very few who don't die at all and become healers. Like me.

On the opposite side, Peace Lilys wouldn't capture a person or bother anyone. As far as I know, Flea and I were the only people they'd taken. And here was another irony—Tohon used Peace Lily serum to create his dead soldiers. The serum preserved the dead body in a fake life so they didn't decompose. His magic did the rest, but I still hadn't figured out how.

"Stay away from that one." I pointed to the Lily farthest southwest. "That's the Death Lily."

"How can you tell?" Quain asked. "They all look the same."

"Death Lilys have a faint odor of anise when you get closer, and Peace Lilys smell like vanilla. If you smell anise, then you're within range of its vines."

"Oh, so anise will be the last thing you smell before you're plant food. Good to know." Quain backed up a step.

"Now what?" Loren asked.

"I'll see if any will open for me." When I had returned to the Peace Lily that held Flea's body, it had bent down and deposited him onto the ground. Perhaps one of these would drop Kerrick. Every fiber of my being hoped so.

*Please be here.*

I approached the closest and waited. *Please be here.*

Nothing happened. Not a twitch of a vine nor a rustle of a petal.

After a few minutes, I moved to the next. *Please be here.*

And the next. *Please.*

And the next. *Be.*

And the last. *Here!*

The Peace Lilys ignored me. "Please?" I said to it, hoping it would take me and explain as one had after it had refused my sister. I'd gotten the impression that the Peace Lilys were all one being with each flower an extension of it, like fingers. Same with the Death Lilys, but with another being at its core.

Still nothing.

Loren gestured to the flowers. "What's going on?"

Crushing disappointment and grief, but no need to state the obvious. "I'll see if I can find out." I walked over to the Death Lily.

"Uh, Avry," Quain said. "Are you sure that's a good—"

A loud hissing drowned out the rest of his words. In a flash, white petals surrounded me, blocking all light and noise. In the darkness, two barbs pricked my upper arms and the toxin flowed into me like a soothing elixir. Escaping my pain-filled body, my consciousness floated free and I connected with the thoughts and contented feelings of the Lily.

*Welcome back.* A surge of pride. *More?* Thinking I wanted its toxin sacks, it showed me a mental picture of another cluster of Lilys nearby.

*No, thank you.* I formed a picture of Kerrick in my mind. *Seen him?*

A flood of images hit me. Kerrick running through the woods, hunting, walking with Belen, Flea, and the monkeys, holding me in his lap, blending into the woods, using his magic. They tumbled one right after the other, threatening to drown me.

*Stop, please!* I concentrated on how he'd looked that night without his shirt, feeling sick. *Did he come here?*

*He stopped.* Sorrow flowed.

*Stopped where?* If I could just find his body, I might—

*Gone into the green.*

*Where?*

A vision of the entire forest filled my mind. It was empty. However, I refused to believe it. The barbs pulled away and the Death Lily set me on the ground. I huddled there in utter misery for a moment, then gathered every bit of strength I had left.

I still had no proof. *Gone* in Death Lily speak could mean he left the forest or was in a cave. It didn't have to mean he… No. Not going to go there. Not yet.

Quain and Loren hovered as close as they dared, their expressions hopeful.

"He didn't come here," I said, standing.

I glanced away. Bad enough to feel the grief burning inside me, I didn't need to witness that same pain reflected in my friends' eyes.

"What now?" Quain asked in a quiet voice.

"We go back to the infirmary cave. I've patients to check on."

"And Kerrick?" Loren touched my shoulder.

"We keep searching."

Taking another route back, we reached the cave after sunset. Ryne had arrived. He sat by the fire intently listening to Flea and Odd. I exchanged a glance with the monkeys.

"Did you send a messenger?" I asked Loren.

"Kerrick did when we returned from our...uh, encounter with Tohon and the others. Thought Ryne should know what happened, especially about Cellina's takeover."

It made sense. Prince Ryne led our ragtag army. He had the military savvy and strategic acumen to counter Tohon. However, he was the last person I wanted to see right now. His genius tactics had caused me quite a bit of pain and suffering over the past few months.

Before Ryne noticed me, I sent the monkeys over to the fire. "Talk to him."

"What about you?" Quain asked.

"I need to check on my patients. It's been—" my sluggish thoughts refused to add the hours "—too long."

Concentrating on the injured soldiers, I moved from cot to cot, talking to the men and women. No new casualties had arrived since yesterday. The caregivers had done a fine job of keeping everyone comfortable and the bandages had all been changed. I consulted with the head caregiver, Ginger. Her capable and no-nonsense attitude was perfect for this type of work.

The floor wobbled under my feet, and I stumbled. I stared at the ground, trying and failing to understand how it had moved. Then the room spun. Ah. Exhaustion had finally caught up to me. "Wake me if you need me," I said to Ginger.

Keeping to the shadows, I slipped into my cavern. Still empty. The guys had moved out the night before last to give Kerrick and me privacy. It was just as well. I didn't want company. Before lying down, I pulled Kerrick's shirt from my knapsack. I pressed it to my face and breathed in his unmistakable scent—spring sunshine and living green.

Tears pushed and my nose filled, but I wouldn't cry. Not yet. Not until I had proof. I fell asleep clutching his shirt tight.

"Avry." A voice shattered my dream.

With effort, I opened one eye. Ryne knelt next to me.

"Go away," I mumbled, rolling over.

"Avry, we need to talk."

"I don't want to talk to you. Go away."

"You can't avoid me."

True. I sighed. "We'll chat in the morning, before the search parties go out. Okay?"

"I've called off the search."

I sat up, turning. "What? Why?" Fury blew away the sleep fog.

He reached for my hand, but I jerked back. Ryne settled back on his heels. "He's gone, Avry."

"No. You're wrong."

"I wish I was, really I do." Ryne pushed a lock of his brown hair from his tired hazel eyes. Worry lines creased his face and he appeared much older than twenty-seven—the same age as Kerrick. "Remember that book on magicians I have?"

"Couldn't forget that." I didn't bother softening my sarcasm. His school textbook on magicians and their powers had led to Ryne leaving me behind to be caught in Tohon's nasty trap. I shuddered at the memory.

He ignored my tone. "It reports that forest mages go into the woods when they die. And their bodies disappear."

"No. Not buying it. What if they're in a city?"

"Avry, it fits. You know it. Death Lily toxin is lethal. He died in the woods and the living green reclaimed its gift to him."

"No."

"Then why can't we find his body? And if he didn't die,

why isn't he here? You know Kerrick, he would never just leave you."

"No. No. No. No!" I screamed the last one. And with that one word, all the emotions I'd been suppressing burst from my core. I collapsed as great gasping sobs pounded my body.

# CHAPTER 3

I woke in Ryne's arms. He was curled next to me. It took me a moment to remember what had led to this. Ah, yes. Ryne insisting Kerrick was gone. The suffocating pain returned, pressing my chest as if I lay under the Nine Mountains. Groaning, I rolled away.

Ryne pushed up to one elbow. "Avry, are you—"

"Don't ask. Ever." I grabbed my boots and left.

After checking on my patients, I searched for Loren. He sat with the group around Ryne. They'd probably been discussing military tactics, but I didn't care. I caught Loren's attention and gestured for him to join me. He nodded and slipped away.

His face tight with concern, Loren approached me as if I'd attack him. I would have laughed if the circumstances had been different.

"What's going on?" he asked.

"Do you still have the map with the search areas marked on it?"

"Yes. Why?" He shifted, wary again.

"I need it."

"But Ryne—"

"I don't care what he said. I'm not giving up until I have proof. Can you get it for me, please?"

His shoulders drooped, but he shuffled off to fetch it. I consulted the Lily map and located the cluster the Death Lily had pointed out last night.

Loren returned with the map and Ryne.

I glared at Loren before snatching the map. Ignoring Ryne, I scanned the search grids.

"Avry, you're needed here," Ryne said.

"No, I'm not. My patients are doing fine."

"What if more casualties arrive?"

"I'll be back by nightfall." I folded the maps and tucked them under my arm.

Ryne trailed me to my cavern and watched as I organized my pack, removing Kerrick's boots. Debating about my cloak, I left it behind and strode for the cave's exit.

"I can order you to stay here," Ryne said, hurrying to catch up.

"You can." I kept moving.

He huffed. "I can order the guards to stop you."

"You can."

By this time Loren, Quain, and Flea had joined Ryne.

"Avry, you're not going to find Kerrick. He's gone," Ryne said.

I stopped and turned. Suppressing the desire to punch Ryne in the mouth, I asked, "Who said I was going to search for Kerrick?"

They all blinked at me in surprise.

"You need more toxin sacks, right?" I asked. "Or did Wynn lie about that, too?"

"We do need more, but—"

"So what's the problem? I'm going out to collect them. Unless you know someone else who can harvest them from the Death Lilys?" I waited.

"Uh…" Ryne rubbed a hand over the stubble on his cheeks.

"All right, you can go, as long as you take the monkeys with you."

"I'm going, too," Flea said, shooting us all a stern look that dared us to argue with him. At least he had more color in his face today.

"Fine. But hurry up, we're burning daylight."

They scrambled to get their weapons and packs.

Ryne stared at me. "Don't go too far. There are still enemy patrols to the south and west."

"And we can easily avoid them. They all sound like a herd of drunken deer."

"But for how long? Wynn is working for Cellina now. She learned how to be quiet in the woods and it won't be long before she's teaching Cellina's soldiers."

Good point. And she'd learned that skill from me. Another ramification of her betrayal. However... "It's only been a couple days."

"Still worth considering. In fact, now that Cellina's in charge, it's even more dangerous to be out there. We've no idea what she's planning."

"And you knew Tohon's plans?"

"Yes. He wanted to conquer all the realms and be king. Not hard to figure out his next move. Cellina, on the other hand, is more of a mystery. Plus she has Wynn's information. We'll have to relocate the infirmary and my headquarters as soon as possible. And until I get intelligence on her movements, it's best for everyone to lie low."

If he was trying to scare me, it wouldn't work. "We'll be extra careful."

Ryne frowned.

The guys returned and we left the cave.

"Which way?" Loren asked me.

I touched the greenery, seeking Kerrick's magic. Disappointment jabbed. "East. And keep a sharp eye out."

"For what?" Flea scanned the forest.

"Lilys. Right, Avry?" Quain asked with a sad smile.

"Yes. We're searching for *Lilys*."

"*Oh*." Flea hefted his pack. "Why didn't you say so in the first place?"

Although we found nothing that first day, we continued to seek Lilys after my morning rounds each day. I harvested a few toxin sacks, but not near enough to neutralize the thousands of dead soldiers or to stop our daily excursions. Wounded arrived sporadically as Ryne's soldiers encountered Cellina's. Odd returned to patrolling with the odd squad, and Ryne relocated his headquarters. The prince's men continued to scout for an alternate infirmary site.

The burning knot of misery that had lodged in my chest consumed a little more of me each day.

After a week of Lily hunting, Loren spread the map on his lap and said, "We've covered all of the area around the infirmary. We'd have to camp overnight to reach new territory."

Quain and Flea glanced up from their bowls. They'd been shoveling food since we'd returned from our latest sweep. We sat around the hearth.

I ignored Loren's implication. "Okay. We'll bring our bedrolls tomorrow."

He paused for a moment. "But the odds of finding...er...a Lily that far away are high."

"You can stay here, Loren. I'm not giving up."

"Yeah, I figured you'd say that."

"Then why did you bring it up?" I demanded.

"Because it needed to be said. And while you don't want hear it, it's true. But if this is what you need to do...then we'll go with you. However, I plan to be the voice of reason whether you like it or not."

Flea and Quain ducked their heads. Cowards.

"I'm not giving up," I said again. Jabbing my spoon into my soup, I swirled the contents around. My appetite was nonexistent since Kerrick had disappeared.

"Okay. Do you want to go farther east or check along that stream to the north?" Loren asked, pointing to the map.

Neither place had any Lilys nearby. "Stream to the north."

"We'll need a full day to get there. How soon can you leave tomorrow?"

We spent the remainder of the evening discussing our plans.

Before I turned in for the night, I checked my patients. Most were already asleep, but one of the new arrivals remained awake. He had fallen into a ditch and broken his left leg below the knee. Ginger had immobilized it in a splint. Although he claimed he felt fine, there was no mistaking his stiff movements and tight expression.

I consulted with the caregiver on duty. "Has anyone given Private Davin medicine for the pain?"

"Yes, he drank a cup of bittwait."

"How long ago?"

"Right after supper."

He shouldn't be in pain. I returned to his bedside. Davin had been carried in this morning. I'd done a quick visual exam, spotted the broken leg and let Ginger do the rest. Perhaps I'd been too quick. Healing magic gathered in my core. When I placed my hand on his forehead, I let my magic flow into Davin.

His leg was broken in two places, not one, and he had a couple cracked ribs and a sprained ankle. No wonder a single cup of bittwait hadn't worked. I fetched the caregiver and, after he drank another cup, we wrapped his ribs and ankle and also immobilized his entire leg. I stayed with him until the crinkles on his forehead relaxed and he fell asleep.

Guilt throbbed along with the ever-present grief inside me. If I hadn't been so anxious to leave this morning, I'd have used my magic and known the extent of the young man's injuries. He wouldn't have suffered all day.

Wide awake, I lay next to the small fire in my cavern, staring at the flames. Our plans for tomorrow meant I'd be gone for two days at least. And for what? To keep my hope alive? To do something, anything, just so I could say I wasn't giving up. Stopping the search didn't have to mean I'd given up hope. Or accepted his death.

We were at war, and my patients needed me here. And I couldn't forget about my promise to Mom, the innkeeper of the Lamp Post Inn. She had done so much for me, creating my disguise so I could go undercover in Estrid's army. I'd promised her I'd keep her daughter, Melina, safe. Melina had been conscripted into Estrid's army and then sent to the monastery in Chinska Mare for not being a virgin. While Melina was safe from the war, there was no way I'd let her stay incarcerated.

I'd tell the guys my decision in the morning. At least now I'd have time to figure out a way to rescue Melina while Flea and I experimented to learn the extent of his magic.

Even after making the difficult decision, sleep still eluded me. I considered other hard decisions and wondered what Cellina would do about Tohon. She had to know I'd refused to heal him. Unless… I sat up. Unless she had Kerrick!

We'd assumed she'd retreated to safety after our encounter. But what if she'd doubled back? What if she'd seen Kerrick leave the cave and captured him? What if Sepp put him into a magical stasis so Cellina could negotiate with me? Kerrick's life for Tohon's.

I wilted. She would have sent a messenger by now. And I

wouldn't heal Tohon. Not even for Kerrick. Or Belen. If he was her prisoner, which we hadn't confirmed. Plopping back on my bedroll, I endured another bout of sorrow and wished my healing power could heal a broken heart.

In the morning, I gathered my determination. Moping wouldn't change a thing. However, actions would. I focused on the positive. For example, Flea's magic. If Belen had been touched by Sepp, we had a way to free him.

The monkeys and Flea weren't surprised by the change in plans. A sad acceptance emanated from their hunched postures. Flea bent his head so his long bangs covered his eyes.

"Don't give up," I said. "I'm not. Kerrick's the most stubborn person we know. He'll show up one way or another. But for now, we need to concentrate on Flea."

Flea glanced up. "Me?"

"Yes." I sat next to him. "We need to determine the extent of your new ability and figure out if you're a true death magician. We know you can break a stasis, but can you put someone in one?"

"I...I don't know."

"Then we'll need a volunteer."

The three of us looked at Quain.

Quain put his hands up. "Hold on. I've already gone through it."

"Which makes you the expert," Loren said. "You can tell us if Flea did it right or not."

"It's the 'or not' that I'm worried about," Quain said.

"Sepp said he can't take a life like Tohon could, but he can freeze life in a fake death," I explained.

"But how do I do that? When Quain was frozen, I had this weird compulsion to touch him. And when I did—" he grimaced at the memory "—it felt like my stomach turned inside

out. It was the same when you were in trouble. I got this…
sour feeling. But right now, I've got nothing."

"Maybe you need to concentrate on it," I suggested. "Think
about pausing his life."

"Uh, I don't like the sound of that." Quain scooted away
from Flea.

"It doesn't hurt, you big baby," Loren said.

"Then why don't you *volunteer?*"

"That's enough," I said to the monkeys. "This is important.
If he's able to do it, it'll save lives."

"I'll try." Flea closed his eyes. He twisted his shirt in his
hands. After a minute, he opened them. "Nothing. Sorry."

"Try again, but this time, put your hand on Quain's arm,"
I said. "Quain, push your sleeve up."

Frowning, Quain exposed a muscular forearm. His loose
shirt hid his powerful build, but the muscles on his neck
bulged with tension. Flea rested his fingers on Quain's arm,
closed his eyes again and pressed his lips together.

We waited.

Flea gasped and jerked his hand away. He stared at Quain
in horror.

Quain looked confused. "Did he pause me?"

"No," Loren said.

"What's wrong?" I asked Flea.

"I—I think…I'm going to be sick." Flea dashed out of the
cave.

I chased after him. He bent over a bush, vomiting. When
he finished, he sank to the ground. Kneeling next to him, I
put my hand on his sweaty forehead. My magic didn't stir. At
least he wasn't truly sick.

The monkeys hovered by the cave's entrance. When Flea
spotted Quain, he squeaked in alarm. I gestured to them,

waving them back inside. Sitting back on my heels, I dropped my hand.

"What happened, Flea? Talk to me, please."

He drew in a deep breath, then met my gaze. I almost glanced away. His light green eyes shone with pain and grief. His haunted expression looked straight through me for a moment. "You can't tell Quain. Promise me."

Uh-oh. "I promise."

"I saw his death. When, where, how. All the gory details."

"Oh, no. I'm so sorry, Flea."

He shook his head. "Not your fault. I need to learn... But I'm not going to tell him or anyone else. Not now. Okay?"

"Yes. We'll stop experimenting. Ryne has that book—"

"No. I need to know what else I can do. It's too important." He took my hand and relaxed a bit. "Touch is still okay." He gave me a half smile. "Guess I need to concentrate in order to see. And, truthfully, I never want to do it again."

"You don't have to." And at the moment, I couldn't think of a reason he'd need to. Except... "Uh, Flea. Can you at least tell me..."

"Not soon. He'll be annoying us for a while."

I sagged against Flea. "Good. I don't think I'd survive if I lost another friend."

"Me, either."

We sat together for a while. When we returned to the cave, the monkeys hustled over. Flea took a step back, but then recovered.

"What happened?" Loren asked.

"Flea threw up, but he's okay," I said.

"Why did you get sick?" Quain asked.

Flea shrugged, but wouldn't meet Quain's gaze. "I guess when I try to use my magic, it makes me sick."

A lame excuse and Loren was too smart to fall for it. But I gave him a pointed look and he dropped the subject.

Flea accompanied me during my afternoon rounds.

"Another aspect of Sepp's magic is he could tell if an injured or sick man would die from his injuries," I said.

"Isn't that what I just did with Quain?" Flea hugged his arms to his chest.

"Not quite. Quain's healthy. Sepp called death a threshold. He said he could see what caused a person to cross over the threshold and also sense if they're close to crossing. He never mentioned being able to see into a person's future. And knowing Sepp, he would have bragged about it and used it to his advantage."

"Oh."

I checked on Private Davin. Color had returned to his face. In fact, a little too much color and his breathing was ragged. Probably a fever.

"Flea, touch his hand, but don't concentrate on anything. Just see if you get a…feeling."

He hesitated then placed his fingertips on Davin's knuckles. Flea snatched his hand away as if burned. "Something…" He tapped his chest. "In here. A clot? It's not good."

Surprised, I took Davin's hand. My magic flowed into him. This time, I waited, letting it seep in, ignoring the obvious injuries. I detected a small blockage in his lungs. If left untreated, it would grow and be fatal.

"What's wrong?" Flea asked.

"It's a pulmonary embolism. You just saved his life."

"Me? No, you. You're the healer. You would have figured it out."

"I was going to give him fever powder. If you hadn't spotted it, he would have died tonight."

Flea stared at me a moment as if he couldn't quite believe

what he'd heard. "You mean, this…magic might be a *good* thing?"

"I know he can be annoying, but don't you think waking Quain was a good thing?"

"Yeah, I did, but…that was more a onetime deal. And after seeing Quain's…" He spread his hands. "Just seemed more like a curse."

"It's a gift from the Peace Lily. But I understand what you're saying. Having magic is a mixed blessing. Yes, we have power and can do things others can't, but we also have a duty to use them to help others and a responsibility not to abuse the gift."

Flea groaned. "Why does everything have to be so complicated?"

"I wish I knew. And if I could, I'd change it in heartbeat, trust me."

Before I healed Davin, I continued checking the rest of my patients. Growing bolder, Flea touched each one, reporting what he felt. Glad there hadn't been any other medical surprises, I returned to Davin.

This time after my magic flooded him, I pulled it back into me, assuming the clot and his cracked ribs to make him more comfortable. Wheezing with the effort to draw breath, I walked gingerly to my cavern. Pain ringed my chest with every step. I almost passed out from taking off my boots.

"Avry, wait." Flea carried a cot. He set it down next to the fire. "You shouldn't be lying on the cold stone ground tonight." He helped me lie on it, put my pillow under my head, and covered me with a blanket. Flea paused when he spotted Kerrick's shirt on the floor. Then he scooped it up and tucked it next to me.

"Thanks, Flea."

"You'd do it for me."

"Yeah, but you'd complain I was fussing over you too much."

He shot me his lopsided grin. "You are overprotective, but I'd be…sad if you weren't. Good night, Avry."

"Night."

When he reached the exit, I called his name. He turned.

"I'd like you and the guys to bring your bedrolls back. It's way too quiet in here."

"Will do." He saluted and left.

I drifted into a deep healing sleep. Dreams mixed with memories.

*I stood in the garden in Sogra with Kerrick behind me. He traced the scars on my back as Tohon called my name. Instead of running away this time, I turned to embrace him. But he'd disappeared. A thorny bush grew in his place.*

*Tohon laughed. "You can't escape me, my dear. I'm always with you. Unlike Kerrick, who has a nasty tendency to leave you when you most need him. Who's going to save you now?"*

*"I can take care of myself."*

*"You're sick and injured."*

*"I'm safe inside the cave."*

*"Are you sure about that, my dear?"*

A shuffling noise woke me. I peeked through slitted eyelids. Messy bedrolls surrounded the fire pit. The guys had been here, but by the tossed blankets and scattered pillows, I guessed they'd left in a hurry. Unease swelled. Drawing in a deep breath, I tested my ribs and lungs. Still very sore, limiting any extended physical activity.

More shuffling sounded nearby. I murmured and rolled over as if still asleep, managing to free my hands from the blanket. If I touched skin, I could defend myself. Too bad I'd left my stiletto in my pack.

After several minutes the slide step of boots resumed. Fear

churned in my stomach, but I resisted the urge to tense my muscles. Two, maybe three people approached. Risking another peek, I spotted a black figure nearby.

I counted the steps. One. Two. Three. I surged to my feet and lunged for the closest figure, wrapping my hands around my attacker's thick neck. A good idea, except he wore a hood that also protected his throat. In fact, the man was completely covered. Other than a thin slit for his eyes, no skin showed.

Not that it mattered now that I'd lost the element of surprise. His companions pulled me off him. I struggled and shouted for help until one of them pressed a sweet-smelling cloth over my face.

The cave spun as the sticky odor invaded my nose. My muscles turned to liquid and I giggled.

"Take her out," the man said. "I'll make sure no one follows."

Scary words, but I didn't care. Instead, I marveled as I floated over the floor. If only they'd release me, I'd fly to the ceiling. We left the cavern and snaked through the cave. Lanterns hung along the walls, casting a sickly yellow glow.

"Wow, good thinking," I said to my captors. "Using the back entrance. Did Wynn tell you to do that?"

They ignored me.

I tsked. "Didn't your mothers teach you any manners?"

We kept moving.

"Phew! What stinks?"

They shushed me, which just made me shout louder. Finally a gloved hand clamped over my mouth. My head cleared by the time we neared the back exit. Fear returned full force. Even though I dragged my feet and fought, our pace never slowed.

Panicked, I increased my efforts despite the pain in my ribs.

Nothing worked. They had me in a firm grip and weren't letting go.

# CHAPTER 4

Fresh air brushed my sweaty forehead and cleared the stink of the privy from my nostrils. Normally welcomed, fresh air in this case meant my chances of rescue decreased. Still held tight, I'd stopped struggling as the two men dragged me out the back entrance of the cave. My efforts to escape hadn't made any difference, so I'd decided to save my strength for later. If there was a later. Fear pulsed through me.

They halted to let their eyes adjust in the predawn light. Four others waited for us. All wearing black clothing and hoods that exposed no skin, like my captors. The three soldiers who had been stationed to guard the cave lay on the ground. Knocked unconscious and not dead, I hoped.

"This way," one said, gesturing. "Quickly."

We followed. After a few steps, the trees rustled. Thuds followed curses and yells. The two holding me fell forward, pushing me down as something heavy landed on top of us. Pain ringed my chest and all my breath whooshed out.

More cries sounded before the weight lifted off my back. I curled into a ball, gasping for air. Once my noisy inhalations eased, other noises of a scuffle reached me.

"Area secured," a voice said.

"Send a team to sweep the cave," another ordered.

"What's the status on the frontal assault?" a familiar voice asked.

Odd? I sat up, wiping dirt from my face. Odd stood amid a group of soldiers.

"The remaining ambushers have retreated. Should we give chase, Sergeant?"

Odd glanced at me. "No. Join the others and help with the evacuation."

Evacuation? I struggled to my feet.

Odd helped me stand. He pulled a leaf from my hair. "Are you okay?"

"Yes. Thanks. What's —"

"I'll explain later. Come on." He sheathed his sword and strode away.

I didn't follow.

Odd stopped. "You're a target, Avry. We need to get you to a more secured location."

"And I need my boots and pack." The rising sun wouldn't dispel the cold air until much later.

"Prince Ryne ordered—"

"I don't care."

"You should. If it wasn't for him, my squad wouldn't have been here to rescue you."

Interesting. "How long have you been here?" I asked.

"A couple days. He suspected Cellina would send a unit after you."

"So you allowed them inside the cave?" Had I been used for another one of Ryne's tactics?

"Uh…" He rubbed a hand over his face.

And that would be a yes. I waited.

"Prince Ryne wanted us to make sure they—"

Refusing to listen to the rest, I checked on the three soldiers who'd been guarding the cave. All alive, but with nasty bumps on their heads. Relieved, I called over a handful of soldiers and asked them to carry the men inside. They looked at Odd for permission. He fisted his hands, but then nodded.

I headed into the cave and almost ran into the monkeys and Flea.

"Told you," Flea said. "I knew she wouldn't leave."

"Why would I leave?" I asked.

"For your safety." Loren glanced at Odd looming behind me.

I rounded on Loren. "So you knew about this, too?"

"Only since one of his men informed us of their plans."

"When was this?" I demanded.

"About five minutes ago."

"Oh. Sorry."

"You should still go." Quain held my pack and boots out.

"Not until I make sure my patients are in good shape to travel."

"They are. You know that, Avry," Flea said.

And he knew it, too. Shoot. No one else had their packs. "What about you guys?"

"We'll help with the evacuation and meet you at the new site," Loren said.

"Fine." I snatched my stuff from Quain. Sitting down, I yanked on my boots then stood. I gave each of them a stern look. "You be extra careful. Okay?"

They nodded.

"And keep Flea close."

"Hey," Flea protested.

But the monkeys promised.

Before I left, I pulled Flea aside. "After everyone's packed up, can you leave a note behind?"

"For…Kerrick?"

I nodded. "Just in case."

"Yeah. I'll use our old signals from back when we were searching for you." Flea gave me a wry smile. "Never thought I'd miss *those* days."

I hugged him then followed Odd. His odd squad fanned out around us. As soon as we entered the trees, we all matched our gaits to the sounds of the forest, going silent.

As I recalled the attack, a hundred questions bubbled up my throat, but I only asked one when we stopped for a break. "Did you jackknife the ambushers?"

Odd grinned. "Yes. Seemed the best strategy. We had a few men on the ground as well because there was no guarantee they would have crossed under our trees."

"Ursan would be proud." That had been his squad's signature move, jumping down on the unsuspecting enemy from a tree limb high above. They had earned the nickname the jumping jacks.

"I don't know. I think he'd be mad we stole his idea. Although..." He gazed at me. "He'd be glad our mission was a success."

"And how exactly did you determine that?" I kept my tone neutral.

"Since they went after you, we now know Cellina plans to heal Tohon. According to Prince Ryne, that knowledge is important and will help him."

"Lovely."

"I don't know why you're being so pissy about this. You weren't in any real danger. We were there the entire time. Plus Cellina needs you alive. That should make you feel better."

It didn't. But Odd had been acting under orders. No need to vent my annoyance with Ryne on him. Instead, I asked about our destination.

"HQ."

A surprise. "Not the new infirmary site?"

"Not yet." Odd kept his gaze on the ground.

Not the best liar, Odd was hiding something. I considered. Pulling out my Lily map, I unfolded it. "Where is HQ?"

He pointed to a spot a couple days northeast of our location. We'd pass close enough to a Lily cluster to check for Death Lilys and possibly harvest its toxin. It was also outside the area we'd searched for Kerrick, so there'd be new ground to cover. And once we reached HQ, I would get to be pissy to Ryne in person.

A bright side after all.

Clouds covered the sky on the first day of autumn. A damp breeze rustled the leaves, sending a few spiraling to the ground. Most of the surrounding forest remained green, but a brush of yellows, orange, and reds tipped the trees.

Before leaving our camp, I touched the ground, pressing my palm to the cool soil.

*Come on, Kerrick. Where are you?*

No response. Not even a faint tingle. I closed my eyes as grief escaped the tight knot inside me, expanding like a bubble, threatening to overwhelm all my senses.

"Avry, you okay?" Odd asked.

"Give me a moment." My voice cracked.

Instead of moving away, Odd sat next to me. "Ursan used to tell us not to get romantically involved with anyone who fought beside you. It caused too many problems."

Opening my eyes, I glanced at Odd. Was he trying to upset me more? Or was he referring to his relationship with Wynn?

His distant gaze peered into the past. "If you look at it logically, Ursan was right. It's dangerous to be a soldier—the chances of being killed are high. Plus you fight differently because you care more about another than yourself. And you take more risks to be together."

I waited.

"I don't think Ursan ever found that…person."

"Person?" The word sounded unemotional.

"Yeah. That person you'll break the rules for. That person who is worth dealing with all those problems for. That person who's worth fighting for."

Oh. "That's a shame. Everyone should find their…person." And was he implying I should be happy that I'd found mine? That at least I hadn't died without ever meeting him?

Odd looked at me. "Do you think there is more than one person for everyone?"

"Right now, I'd say no. But in five or ten years…I might feel different. You?"

"I'm going to remain hopeful. Otherwise the future looks pretty bleak."

I mulled over his comments. "Was that supposed to make me feel better?"

"Did it?"

"I guess a little."

"I think it helped me, too." He ran his hands over the ground. "Something about being in the forest reminds me of Ursan. Don't know why." Odd stood and brushed his fingers on his pants. The dirt blended with his fatigues. "We'd better get moving. The detour to the Lily patch is going to add a few hours to our trip."

Stopping by the cluster of Lilys ended up being a good idea. Two Death Lilys grew among eight Peace Lilys—the largest cluster I'd seen in this part of Pomyt Realm. I harvested four toxin sacks and placed them in my pack.

Odd watched me from a safe distance.

When I joined him, he said, "The corn fields in Ryazan Realm had been abandoned during the plague years. The last time I saw them, the Lilys had taken over. Hundreds of acres full of Lilys. If we run out of toxin, we could travel south. We shouldn't run into any problems cutting through Tobory Realm."

"It would depend on how far east Cellina's army is. With Estrid…neutralized and most of her soldiers fighting for Ryne, Cellina could push all the way through Pomyt and into Ozero and Tobory with little to no resistance."

"True, but it's only been a couple weeks since they invaded Zabin."

Just a couple weeks? It felt like years. "And don't forget Jael. The last time I saw her, she was heading south." The air magician had tried to either kill me or use me a number of times. I'd be happy never to see Jael again.

"General Jael's scared and on the run," Odd said. "She bugged out before Tohon was neutralized. Unless she finds out what happened, she'll stay far away."

Not the way I'd describe her. Cunning, smart, and power hungry would be closer to the Jael I'd encountered. When she'd realized Estrid couldn't stop Tohon, she'd made a tactical decision to escape his trap, abandoning the army that she'd led. I suspected Jael had big plans and would return. Oh, joy.

"We can suggest a trip south to Ryne and see what the *master strategist* thinks," I said with just a trace of sarcasm.

"Can't wait." Odd's tone matched mine.

We arrived at HQ the next day. Bracing for another dank cave, I paused when we reached the outskirts of a tiny town. Amazed it hadn't burned down during the plague years, I scanned the area. At the town's heart stood a sprawling two-story-high factory, surrounded by a handful of houses and stables. The place appeared abandoned, but I spotted a few guards tucked among the buildings. As we walked toward the center, we passed a single bathhouse and inn. At least I wouldn't be sleeping on the ground tonight.

"Place is called Victibus," Odd said. "Named after the family who owned the only business in town." He gestured to the factory.

Faded letters on the side of the building spelled out Victibus Mining Company.

The door opened before we reached it. Two soldiers stepped out with swords in hand and questioned us.

Odd answered. "Sergeant Oddvar and the odd squad returning from a retrieval mission."

Annoyed, I glanced at Odd. "I'm the retrieved?"

"Was your mission a success, Sergeant?" one guard asked.

"That's debatable, Private."

"Hey." I swatted Odd's arm.

"I see," the private said, ushering us inside. "I'll let Prince Ryne know you've returned. Wait here."

We stood in a typical reception area complete with an area rug, desk, and chairs. Surprising, since the towns that hadn't burned down had been looted by the plague survivors.

I perched on the edge of one of the wooden chairs. "I hope this isn't the only entrance."

"Don't worry, there are other ways out," Odd said with a gleam in his eyes.

"What aren't you telling me?"

"You'll see."

I muttered under my breath, but Odd ignored me. Soon enough, the private returned and escorted us inside. Tall machinery occupied the main area, with screens and conveyor belts connecting them. Piles of rocks littered the floor. Some reached as high as the metal roof. I put the clues together and guessed Victibus had mined some type of stone and used this equipment to break it into smaller pieces.

After we passed the machinery, we headed to an open area where tables had been assembled and maps spread out over

them. A number of soldiers surrounded the conference tables
and Ryne bent over a map. So this was HQ. Not very impressive.

When Ryne noticed us, he gestured us closer. Wearing gray
pants, a black tunic, and black boots, Ryne looked nothing
like a prince of Ivdel Realm. Or rather like the king of Ivdel.
Even with his parents gone, he hadn't assumed the title. Neither had Kerrick. Which had changed my preconceptions of
*all* royalty being backstabbing and power hungry. Now it was
*almost all,* since Tohon and Jael matched the stereotype.

"Any problems?" Ryne asked.

"No," Odd said.

"Yes," I said at the same time.

Odd continued in a formal tone, "Cellina sent a team after
her, like you expected. We intercepted them as ordered."

"It was a little sloppy," I chimed in. "A few of our guards
were hurt. Perhaps next time you can just stab the fish hook
right through my stomach and dangle me from the trees. It'd
be more effective."

Ryne's gaze focused on me. "I see. Avry, I'd like a word
in private."

"Okeydokey."

He stared at me as if gauging my mood before turning away.

I followed him. Expecting him to lead me to an empty
corner, he surprised me by pulling open one of the oversize
loading doors. In this section of the building, large mounds
of earth had been piled. And right in the middle was a huge
hole in the ground.

Ryne headed straight for it and descended steps that led
down to an underground room.

I paused at the edge.

He glanced up. "We'll be more comfortable in my office."

Oh, no. "Your office is down there?"

"Yes, along with a number of caverns and tunnels. We could house our entire army down there if we had to."

I groaned. "The mines."

"Exactly. And the best part is, they extend for miles in all directions. Once we figure out where they go, we can use them to move troops unseen. Isn't it wonderful?"

From a military standpoint, yes, but I'd rather be outside under the stars than under the ground. My visions of spending a night in a normal bed vanished. I joined him at the bottom.

Ryne led me along a well-lit corridor. Lanterns hung every few feet and the air remained warm.

"Up here in the living levels, there's plenty of light," Ryne explained, noticing my interest. "As you go deeper, the spacing of the lanterns is wider, and the ones we haven't explored are dark."

"Living levels?"

"Yes, the miners stayed here while on duty. There's an entire cavern filled with bunk beds. It would make a good infirmary, except..."

"Except what?"

"I don't want injured to be brought to HQ, they're too easy to follow. And I don't think navigating dark tunnels with casualties is a good idea."

"So where do you want to locate the infirmary?"

"Closer to Zabin."

Not what I expected. "Why?"

"I've just received some intelligence on Cellina's troop movements." He rested his hand on his sword's hilt. "It appears the bulk of her army is retreating back into Vyg Realm."

"Why? Doesn't she have the upper hand?"

"She does. We've been harrying her northern flank, but it's caused more of a nuisance, like mosquito bites on an ufa, than any real harm."

I considered. "Is she trying to lure you down to Zabin?"

"Perhaps. She's leaving a couple companies behind to guard the town."

"Maybe she set a trap." Unbidden, memories of another trap played in my mind. Tohon had surrounded Zabin with his dead soldiers, encircling us. Ulany, his earth mage, had hidden them underneath the ground until it had been time to strike. A shudder of horror ripped through me. "Can she command the dead like Tohon?"

"I don't know. But I do know she can't surprise us with them like Tohon did at Zabin."

"Why not?"

"Ulany's dead."

"Oh." I didn't know that. Glancing at Ryne, I wondered what else he kept from me.

"We took her out when we rescued Estrid's soldiers from the trap."

The time he left me behind, again. With good reason, but still... No, I wouldn't go into that now. Instead, I asked, "Why do you think she's retreating?"

"I think she's regrouping and taking stock of her resources. Pulling back into the safety of Vyg, Cellina can coordinate her forces and plan her next move." He stopped in front of a wooden door. "That's what I'd do if I was in her position."

"All right. But that doesn't explain why you want the infirmary closer to Zabin."

Ryne grabbed a lantern from the wall, opened the door and gestured me inside. I scanned the room. Desk, armchairs, a worn couch, a single bed, and chest of drawers filled the space. This was more than just his office. The single bed snagged my attention. I wondered if Ryne had ever found that person.

He set the lantern on the desk and sat behind it. He probably didn't have time for anything other than waging war. Perhaps when this was all over.

I plopped into one of the armchairs on the opposite side. Sinking into the thick cushions, I relaxed. Nice until I remembered he hadn't answered my question. I repeated it.

He propped his elbows on the desk and rested his chin on his hands as if debating how much to tell me.

Sick of the song and dance, I leaned forward. "Enough with all this mystery, Ryne. How about a little trust?"

"I told you about Cellina."

"Not that. I'm talking about Odd's timely rescue. You could have sent me a message, informing me of your plans."

"Would it have made a difference?"

"Hell, yes!" I slammed my hand on his desk. "I wouldn't have taken on two broken ribs, weakening me. I'd have kept my stiletto handy."

He creased his brow. "But you knew there was a chance she'd send a team to kidnap you."

"I did. But I didn't know you told our guards to let them *in*. If you're going to use me as bait, at least warn me."

"Ah." He dropped his hands and pushed a few papers, lost in thought. "But what if you objected?"

"There's that trust issue again, Ryne. Let me give you an example. I really didn't enjoy dying for you, but I trusted Kerrick and his reasons that you needed to live. If you'd explained that confirming Cellina's desire to awaken Tohon was important, then I'd be fine. I might not like it, but I trust your reasons. Now you need to trust me to follow your logic."

Ryne shook his head. "Kerrick warned me you wouldn't follow orders, so I figured if I worked…around you, it'd be better."

"That was different. I didn't trust him then."

"I see." He leaned back. "What if I can't tell you for a very good reason? Will you still trust me?"

Good question. "Yes, as long as you keep me in the loop with all the other stuff."

"Agreed." He reached over and shook my hand.

"Now that's settled. What's going on?"

He laughed. "I'm planning to attack Cellina's troops in Zabin."

That explained why he'd want the infirmary closer. "Why?"

"It's a good strategic position. If I can clear them out, we'd have a stronger defense against her army."

"What if you can't?"

"Then we retreat and the offensive becomes a rescue operation."

Rescue? Ah. "You think Cellina left Estrid and her high-ranking officers behind?" Sepp had frozen them all in a magical stasis.

"It doesn't make sense for her to drag them back to Vyg. Besides, she believes only Sepp can awaken them."

Oh. Now I understood his earlier reluctance. "You need Flea to go in with the initial attack and awaken them if they're still there." It was easier to rescue people who could walk.

"Yes. And I know how…protective you are of him."

"I am. Which just means I'm going, too."

"No, you're not," Ryne said, as if that ended the discussion.

It didn't. "Yes, I am."

"It's too dangerous."

"Then keep Flea with me at the infirmary until you've secured Zabin."

"And if we can't, there will be no second chance. He has to go." Ryne held up a hand, stopping my protest. "He's a good fighter, Avry. Very capable."

"I don't care."

He fingered the light brown stubble growing on his cheeks. Dark smudges of exhaustion marked his eyes. "How about if I assign a squad with the sole purpose of protecting him during the attack?"

"That's acceptable, but I'm still going."

His demeanor changed. "I can *ensure* you stay behind."

# KERRICK

He resisted the pull. Fought the fever.

*I'm not.*

*Going to.*

*Relax.*

*I promised.*

*Avry.*

At times, he was everywhere. Every blade of grass, every tree, and each bush *was* him. Stretched across the forest, he felt every intruder, every animal, and each breeze. Pain from broken limbs and trampled grass pulsed inside him.

At times, he was nowhere. He existed in a void of light and sound. But he struggled against the nothingness and returned to the living green.

At times, he was everywhere and nowhere, teetering on the edge.

The voice of the living green spoke to him. Told him to rest. Told him to stop fighting.

Kerrick never liked being told what to do.

*I'm not.*

*Going to.*

*Rest.*

*I promised.*
*Avry.*
He resisted the pull. Fought the fever.

# CHAPTER 5

Ryne's hard expression and threat to prevent me from joining Flea failed to affect me. "Uh-huh. And who's going to help Flea when he pukes up his guts after awaking Estrid and still needs to awaken her staff of about twenty people? He won't have the strength to do them all."

His shoulders drooped. "Why didn't you tell me about that?"

"You were too busy being all 'no, you're not going and I've spoken' about it."

"And you were too busy being all defiant. You could have explained."

"I could have."

He studied me for a moment. "Except I was too busy putting my foot down instead of asking you why."

"That's what I just said."

"Yes, but without the sarcasm." He rubbed both hands over his face. "Now I understand what Kerrick had to deal with all those months. You're exasperating."

"Thank you." Kerrick's name sent a jab of pain deep into my chest, but I kept it from showing on my face.

Dropping his arms, Ryne just shook his head. "Okay, you can accompany the offensive. I'll make it work."

"Good. And just so you know, if Flea and I go, then—"

"The monkeys will insist on going, too. Got it."

Another thought occurred to me. "What happens if word gets back to Cellina that Estrid and her staff have been reanimated? Do we want to tip our hand now or wait?"

"Excellent question. I debated the very same thing. In the end, I need Estrid. Her acolytes have been effective in recruiting soldiers for her army, and there are a number of her companies that have refused to join my forces. Hundreds of fighters have fled back to Ozero Realm and we need them."

Unpleasant memories of my encounter with High Priest Chane in Mengels played in my mind. His men had tried to ambush me. "The acolytes use strong-arm methods and outright kidnapping to recruit people. Do you really want to resort to that?"

"Of course not. Which is why we need the High Priestess. Only an order from Estrid will change their methods. Plus she amassed a rather large army and could again. If Tohon hadn't used his dead soldiers to trap them, he would have had a hard time defeating them."

"But they fight in the name of the creator."

"I don't care if they fight in the name of broccoli. The goal remains the same."

True. I considered. "What happens if our combined forces conquer Cellina and High Priestess Estrid decides she wants to be in charge?"

"You mean you don't want to become an acolyte?" Ryne faked horror.

"It's those garish red robes. The color clashes with my hair." I flicked an auburn strand from my face.

"Now, now. The creator frowns on vanity."

"And on laughter, joy, music, dancing… Basically all forms

of fun. Oh, and on sex, too. The creator's a dour deity. However, you're evading the question."

"I am?"

"Ryne, talk or I'll zap you."

All humor dropped as he gaped at me for a moment. "Will you?"

"Are you crazy? I was just kidding."

"I know, but I've been curious about your healing powers. There's no record of that defensive move you've used in my book on magic. I'd like to feel it for myself."

Remembering the attack at the infirmary, I hugged my chest. "Unfortunately, it's not a secret any longer." I explained about the head-to-toe covering they wore. My magic only worked if I touched skin.

"Still it would be useful to know the extent of the pain."

"You are crazy."

"Please."

Low blow. "All right, but answer my question first or I *won't* zap you." Did I really just say that? The situation had turned unreal.

Ryne smiled, acknowledging the twisted logic. "If Estrid desires power beyond her Realm of Ozero, then I will stop her. I promised Kerrick that I would return our world to its preplague state—with all Fifteen Realms thriving and prospering. Once that's accomplished, I'll retreat to Ivdel and assume my place as its king."

A heck of a to-do list. And it explained why he hadn't assumed the title. Impressed, I studied Ryne. Intensity burned from his hazel eyes. Kerrick had utter faith in this man, which meant I did, too.

Ryne stuck out his arm. "Okay, now zap me."

I gestured toward his bed. "It would be better if you lie

down. Some people have a low pain tolerance and collapse right away."

He huffed in amusement, but followed my advice. Before I took his hand he said, "Low pain tolerance? Do you judge people based on their pain thresholds?"

"Don't worry—your manhood isn't at stake. Well…unless you break down and bawl like a baby," I teased. "Then I have no choice but to tell the monkeys and Flea."

"I'd expect nothing less. Uh…have people bawled?"

"Yes. It can be very overwhelming. Just squeeze my hand twice if it gets too severe."

"You once told me you zapped Kerrick so you could escape. How long did he last?"

Bittersweet memories surged. I'd blasted him with every ounce of strength, depleting all my energy. "I didn't escape." The stubborn, infuriating man wouldn't let go. And I hoped that exasperating quality helped him now.

"Oh."

"Yeah, I would have been impressed except I hated his guts at the time." I patted Ryne on the shoulder. "Don't worry, I don't hate you. Well, not at the moment. But if we keep reminiscing…"

"All right." He laced his fingers in mine.

Magic flowed from my core, but instead of healing, I channeled it to cause pain. Starting out with a tiny spark, I gradually increased the power. Ryne's expression tightened and he fisted his other hand. Color leaked from his face as sweat beaded on his forehead. All his muscles tensed.

He pumped my hand a few minutes after I'd reached the level most people collapse at. I stopped. Ryne lay there panting. He wiped his sleeve over his face, mopping up the sweat before it reached his eyes.

Pushing up to his elbow, he said, "Wow. That's a significant weapon you have. And as soon as you stopped, all the pain disappeared."

"That's because the magic affects your nerves, but doesn't damage them."

"Handy."

"As long as there's exposed skin for me to touch. Otherwise it's useless."

"What about that neck thing?" Ryne pointed to the base of his skull.

"That's harder to do in a fight. I need to touch the exact spot and send a burst of power. That move doesn't hurt, it just renders the person unconscious for a couple hours. Do you want a demonstration?"

"No." Ryne hopped to his feet. "I've too much to do."

"Uh-huh." I followed him from his office. 'What's next?"

"I'd like you to stay here for a few days while the patients are moved into the new infirmary site."

"Why can't I go now? And don't tell me it's not safe. No place is ever completely safe."

"I agree. But that's not the reason. During our explorations of the tunnels, we've encountered a number of exits that are blocked by Lilys. We need you to determine if they're Death or Peace Lilys." He paused. "Funny that I've mixed feelings about the results. On one hand, I hope they're Peace Lilys so my men can get in and out, but on the other, we're in serious need of more Death Lily toxin."

That reminded me. Rummaging in my pack, I pulled out the four sacks I'd collected on our way to HQ and handed them to Ryne.

"You're amazing," he said.

"I know." I smirked. "And if any of those Lilys in your way are Death Lilys, I'll talk to them, see if we can work out a truce."

"You can do that?" He sounded incredulous.

"Of course. I'm amazing after all."

He groaned. "I've created a monster."

"Why am I here?" Odd asked from behind me. His words echoed slightly.

"For protection." I peered beyond the bubble of lantern light, searching for a sign that we'd reached the end. Nothing but a solid wall of darkness.

"Protection from what? Rats?" Odd's voice held a slight hitch.

I glanced over my shoulder. "Don't tell me you're afraid of rats."

"Not rats."

"Then what?"

"I don't know…. It's creepy down here. Are you certain you know where you're going?" he asked Hogan.

Sergeant Hogan carried the lantern in one hand and a map in the other as he led us through the labyrinth of tunnels. "For the fourth time, yes. My squad has been mapping these shafts for days and this one is pretty straightforward."

"Days? Gee, I feel *much* better now," Odd grumbled.

Hogan ignored him. Smart. The quiet young sergeant was one of Ryne's soldiers from Ivdel and he had a rather no-nonsense demeanor. Unlike Odd.

Puddles dotted the uneven floor of the mine. Our footsteps sounded too loud and a heavy mineral scent laced the damp air. Having spent many days and nights in caves, I wasn't as bothered by the tight space or the tingly feeling of pressure on my shoulders. Just because thousands of pounds of dirt and rocks hung above our heads was no reason to be… Oh, who was I kidding? It *was* creepy. Odd had a point.

"This is payback, isn't it?" Odd asked me.

"Payback for what?"

"For letting Cellina's men ambush you."

"Don't be ridiculous. You were following orders."

"Somehow I don't feel all warm and fuzzy inside."

"Sounds like a personal problem."

"Cute. What was I supposed to do? Warn you?"

"Did Ryne tell you not to?" I asked.

"Yes."

"Again, you were following orders."

"Swell. And the reason I'm here…"

"Ryne wanted us to take along another person just in case we ran into trouble. And I chose you." Which I was starting to regret big-time.

"Why?"

"'Cause of your sunny disposition."

Hogan huffed in amusement. "Good one."

"Avry—"

"It's because I trust you. We've worked together, did the whole silent training together. You know, friendship-type stuff. Gee, think much?"

"Oh." Odd remained silent the rest of the way.

After some time passed—it was hard to keep track without the sun—Hogan slowed. A faint blob of light flickered ahead.

When the blob sharpened into sunlight filtered through large leaves, Hogan stopped. "Lily vines are wrapped all around the opening. We're safe here."

"Good. Stay," I ordered, striding past Hogan.

The sergeant gasped when I reached the edge of the vines.

"You get used to it," Odd said.

I stepped between the vines, trying not to harm the Lily. Exiting the tunnel, I paused, breathing in the fresh air. The sun hung low—late afternoon. We had left in the morning, not that it mattered below the earth, but Ryne had wanted my ribs to heal and for me to get a good night's sleep. As if that was possible. Dreams of Kerrick and Tohon had sabotaged my rest. At least my ribs no longer caused me pain. Just a dull ache that should disappear soon.

A handful of Lilys grew nearby. As soon as I approached, the scent of vanilla dominated. Peace Lilys. They didn't even twitch when I rested a hand on their petals.

"It's okay," I called to the men. "They won't hurt you." I searched the area, seeking Death Lilys. None.

When I returned, Hogan sat cross-legged on the ground. He sketched on a piece of parchment stretched across his lap. Working fast, he drew the landscape with a piece of charcoal.

"What are you doing?" Odd asked.

"Drawing landmarks," Hogan said.

Confused, Odd glanced at me.

"Do you know where we are?" I asked him.

"No."

"Neither does Hogan or Ryne. That sketch will help them figure out where this tunnel leads to."

Odd nodded.

"We did find a rudimentary map of the mines," Hogan said. "But it was old and doesn't show half the shafts we've discovered."

If only Kerrick was here. He'd know our location the instant he touched the forest. While Hogan worked, I wandered among the greenery, trailing my fingers over the leaves and along the rough tree bark.

Most of the Pomyt, Casis, Vyg, Sogra, Lyady, and the northern half of Ozero Realms were wooded. On a color map of the Fifteen Realms they appeared like a green belt south of the Nine Mountains. No surprise that lumber and mining were the top two resources for them. Farming dominated the realms of Zainsk, Sectven, Tobory, Ryazan, Kazan, and the southern half of Ozero. Bavly Realm extended into the Southern Desert and they sold the high-quality sand used in making glass wares.

Of course, all the trade and sharing of resources died when two-thirds of our population died. Not enough workers to plow the fields, mine the sand, or cut trees. Not enough man-power to stop the marauders and outlaws from running amok. Not enough craftsmen to provide goods and services. It had been utter chaos. A dark time when the people executed heal-ers because they blamed us for unleashing the killer among them.

I'd believed we had nothing to do with the disease, but I'd since learned the healers did indeed cause over six million deaths. They'd been experimenting with mixing Death Lily toxin with Olaine pollen as a way to heal those pricked by the lethal Lilys. Instead, it had triggered the plague.

Did all my colleagues and friends deserve to die? Or just those few who lost control of their experiment? Tough ques-tions.

And now Ryne hoped to return us to peace and prosper-ity. Or rather a semi-peace. The leaders of the Fifteen Realms squabbled like siblings over things like mine rights and border issues. Minor compared to Tohon's army of the dead.

"Avry...hello?" Odd waved a hand in front of my face.

I focused on him. His brows were pinched together.

"Something wrong?"

"Hogan's finished his sketch and wants to get moving to the next blocked exit."

We headed back, joining Hogan at the threshold.

"How many more of these—" Odd gestured to the Lilys "—do we have to check?"

Ah, the reason for his scowl.

Hogan consulted the map. "Four more."

Odd gave me a sour look. "Gee, Avry, if this how you treat your friends, I'd hate to see what you do to your enemies."

We spent the next couple days trekking through the Victibus mines. I made and discarded a dozen plans to rescue Melina as we moved through the forest. Peace Lilys blocked the next exit, but at the third one a small Death Lily grew. Not big enough to snatch a man yet, its petals reached as high as my hip.

"Is that…" Hogan backed up a step.

Odd laughed. "It's just a baby. Can't hurt a full-grown man."

"Should we pull it?" Hogan asked.

"No. It has a flower and is still dangerous." I stepped between him and the Lily. Before the plague, teams of people would cull the young Lily plants before they flowered to save lives.

"But we might need this exit."

True, but these plants had a sentient core. "Let me talk to it."

"Uh—"

"Don't ask," Odd cut in.

I knelt next to the Death Lily and extended my hand. With a high-pitched hiss, it parted its petals and grabbed my arm. Two barbs pricked my wrist. Toxin flowed in me, but it wasn't strong enough. Semi-detached from my body, I connected with the Lily's consciousness. However, the connection remained weak. I caught a glimpse of another Lily, one fully grown a few miles away.

"How do you know where it is?" Hogan asked after I'd recovered. "We don't even know where we are."

How to explain? "The Lily showed me a map of the area. Like your sketch, but in my mind."

"And you trust this?"

"Yes. And we need more toxin. It'll only be a short detour."

"But Prince Ryne—"

"Will be very happy to be able to eliminate more dead soldiers with the toxin we collect."

Hogan glanced at Odd.

Odd shrugged. "Just so you know, she's going whether you agree or not."

"You can wait here if you want. We'll be back by sunset." I hefted my pack.

Hogan tried again. "Prince Ryne ordered us to stay together."

"Then come on—you're wasting time." I strode north. "Besides, what can happen? We're in the middle of nowhere."

"Now you've done it," Odd said, catching up to me. "Never invite danger."

"How's that inviting danger?"

"Asking 'what can happen' is a challenge to fate. It's like asking fate to throw something our way."

"That's a silly superstition."

"To you."

Uh-oh. Had I hurt his feelings? I glanced at him. Instead of wounded puppy dog, his expression remained serious. I remembered Odd was from Ryazan Realm. "Is this a Ryazan belief?"

"No. Soldiers don't tempt fate. We don't brag or boast, which is different than being bold and aggressive. We aren't cocky, just confident. Well, the good ones are."

"But you brag all the time at camp."

"About stupid stuff, not the important things. You've never heard me come back from a patrol and brag about how many enemy soldiers my squad killed. Or how we ambushed them while they slept."

True. He'd bragged about stealing the last cookie from the mess tent or about dumping Ursan in the mud during a training session. Actually he'd never seemed to tire of teasing Ursan over that one.

"I understand and I'll be more careful in my...word choices from now on," I said.

"Thank you," Odd said.

We walked in silence for a while. While Odd and I moved with the sounds of the forest, Hogan didn't. He needed the silent training. The afternoon sun warmed the air and drove off the damp chill. Tipping my head back, I enjoyed the heat of the sunlight on my cheeks. We'd been overnighting in the tunnels for the past two nights. I hoped Ryne's new infirmary location wasn't inside a cave.

After an hour, we reached the Death Lily. It grew among a dozen Peace Lilys, the largest cluster I'd seen since I'd been harvesting the toxin.

I dropped my pack and approached. It snatched me in one quick gulp. Impressive. Pain jabbed my upper arms. Then I broke free from my body, flowing into the roots of the plant and joining with its soul.

Joy and contentment pulsed over my arrival. I smiled. Death Lilys didn't get many willing visitors. It wished to help me and it showed me its entire network of Death Lily plants, offering the toxin sacks from them all. A generous gift. Committing as many to memory as I could, I concentrated on the locations.

Then I asked it about not taking Ryne's soldiers.

*Show me,* it said. It desired a mental picture of every person in Ryne's entire army.

*I can't. Another way?*

No response. Perhaps I could mark the Death Lilys with paint to warn Ryne's men. But then Cellina's army would fig-ure it out, too. And I didn't mind if the Lilys ate them.

Another memory occurred to me. It wasn't nice. When I'd been a prisoner in Tohon's castle, I'd learned how to kill a full-size Death Lily. With its toxin. If I sprinkle it on the ground below the flower, the toxin would be absorbed by the Lily's roots. It would die. But just the idea... I hated it. However, it might be the only way to make those exits safe for Ryne's army.

*Seeds,* the Death Lily said.

*What kind of seeds?*

*Mine.* It showed me an image of a deer grazing under a Lily. A breeze shook the leaves and a handful of oval seeds showered on the animal's back. Eventually a noise startled the deer and it ran off, carrying the seeds. *Protect seeds. Make new.*

Understanding dawned. *If Ryne's soldiers wore those seeds, would they be protected?*

*Yes.*

*Will you—*

*Yours.*

But nothing happened. *What's wrong?*

*Others.* Another image rose in my mind. A squad of a dozen soldiers wearing Tohon's uniforms crept up on Odd and Hogan.

Alarmed, I fought to be released. *I need to warn them!*

*Too late.*

Odd spun, pulling his sword. Hogan leaped to his feet and yanked his weapon—a long thin blade. Both had daggers in their other hands. Outnumbered six to one, the fight lasted mere moments. Disarmed and forced to their knees, Odd and Hogan surrendered to the squad's leader.

Their situation was all my fault. Guilt and fear pumped in my heart.

The leader—an older man with wide shoulders and a powerful build, pointed to my pack on the ground and asked Odd, "Where is your other member?"

Odd glanced at the Death Lily. "Eaten. Damn fool got too close."

"What are you doing out here?" the leader asked.

Odd refused to answer.

*More.* The Lily showed me a large number of other squads moving east through the forest.

Not good. Did Ryne know they were here? Why were they so far from their main forces in Vyg? What was Cellina planning? The answer clicked. She dangled Zabin's strategic military position to lure Ryne south. Meanwhile she sent her forces north in the hope of sneaking up behind him.

The leader motioned to his men. They manacled Odd's and Hogan's hands behind their backs and pulled them to their feet.

"Bring them to camp. If they don't talk, we'll feed them to the ufas," the leader said.

Bad. Very bad. I had to rescue them. Right now.

# KERRICK

At first, Kerrick fought to remain inside his body and not spread throughout the forest. He concentrated on the vines growing on him. On the moist earth cushioning his body. On the dirt wedged under his fingernails.

Then he struggled to hear the wind shake the tree's limbs. The call of the birds. The rasp of air filling his lungs.

He inhaled the scent of wood smoke. The mist of pine. The faint aroma of vanilla.

Jolted by that smell, he clung to it. Memories flowed. Promises remembered. He pulled the scent toward his core, anchoring his consciousness to his body. Now he perceived touch, sounds, and smells all at the same time. Progress.

Other sensations intruded. Hunger. Thirst. Cold. Aches.

He awoke. Heart-shaped leaves obscured part of his vision. Sunlight flashed between them as they danced in the breeze. Kerrick tried to brush them away, but he couldn't move. After a bit of wiggling, he discovered the vines not only blanketed him but held him tight.

Stretching his senses, he reached for his connection with the living green. Except it wasn't there. Well, not the way he remembered it. Before, it required effort for him to draw magic from the forest. It was a conscious decision to form a link. Now there was no need to tap into the power. It already resided within him.

With a mere thought, he commanded the vines to release him. A ripping sound accompanied multiple stings of pain along his skin. As the vines retreated, cold air caressed his body, sending ripples of goose bumps.

Kerrick sat up. His stiff muscles protested. His pants had been destroyed by the roots. Blood welled from a number of throbbing cuts along his torso, arms, and legs. The vines' roots had left creases on his brown-and-green skin. He held his hands out. They, too, matched the colors of the forest. His survival instinct had probably kicked in when he passed out, camouflaging him from danger. He'd worry about it later.

He rubbed the ache at the back of his neck. Had he collapsed or had someone knocked him out? Memories swirled through a thick fog.

Slowly the events that had led to his current situation assembled. Seeing Flea. The fight with Tohon's dead ufas. Cellina and Sepp. The attack on Quain. Avry!

With a surge of energy, Kerrick stood, but he leaned against a tree as dizziness threatened to topple him. He needed food and water. How long had he been out?

He sniffed the cool air. Crisp and sharp, it no longer held the humid earthy scent of summer. A few red, yellow, and orange leaves littered the ground. Early fall. Panicked, he pushed through his jumbled thoughts, searching for answers.

Avry had stabbed Tohon. He smiled. *That's my girl.* Flea had awoken Quain. And some sergeant had nicked him with a blade treated with…Death Lily toxin. Memories of being sick made him queasy anew. Kerrick sank to a sitting position.

Had he died? Was he dead? A ghost of the forest? He dismissed that silly notion. He hurt too much to be deceased.

But how did he survive? Avry? No, she'd be with him. Plus she couldn't heal those infected with Death Lily toxin.

And then he remembered the voice of the living green. Had it saved him?

*No,* the living green said in his mind.

*Then who?* he asked.

*You did.*

*How?*

*Your magic.*

*But my magic doesn't work that way.* And the living green had never spoken to him before he'd gotten sick.

Mirth. *No voice that you'd understand.*

*But now I can.*

*Yes.*

*Why?*

*You are of the forest.*

*But I'm alive.*

*Yes. Alive like trees and plants.*

Kerrick's temples pounded. Definitely alive. But how much time had passed? The living green showed him a tree's small growth—its measure of time, but not helpful.

Concentrating on his immediate needs, Kerrick pushed all his other concerns aside for now. First he found edible berries, roots, and nuts with ease. A stream nearby quenched his thirst. As for clothing, Kerrick decided to stay camouflaged until he could slip back into the infirmary cave. He'd left his pack and the rest of his clothing with Avry.

Avry. He remembered her emotional reaction to their reunion. She had thought he'd died fighting the northern tribesmen, and then when he'd been poisoned she'd kept him at arm's length most of the night.

Did she believe he'd died again? He hoped not. Hurrying northeast, Kerrick noted the location of the various patrols and avoided them. He had awoken much farther from the cave than he recalled. As he drew closer, he slowed. No one guarded the front entrance. Not good.

He looped around to the back. Deserted, as well. Waiting proved difficult, but he didn't want to walk into an ambush. Well, not naked and unarmed.

After an hour with no signs of activity, he stepped from the forest. Or rather, he tried. A force dragged him to a stop. Pouring every ounce of strength into his legs, he managed a couple more steps. But his feet acted as if they'd grown roots and he stumbled to another halt.

The pull to remain in the forest was like no other he'd encountered. If felt as if an invisible net had been thrown over him and tied to a tree's trunk. Perhaps it was the living green's way of warning him. He drew power and the force eased. Odd. He stepped closer to the cave, but the force increased. More magic meant more distance.

Not stopping to analyze it, Kerrick gathered as much power as he could and sprinted. He had enough energy to confirm the cave had been abandoned and to find the message from Flea.

Weak and drained, he crawled from the cave toward the forest. Each inch a relief until he collapsed just past the border.

As he lay panting and spent, he'd realized he hadn't needed to use his magic to find food or to locate the soldiers. That had required no effort. Unlike leaving the forest, which required a feat of strength and considerable endurance.

The living green's comment repeated in his mind.

*You are of the forest.*

# CHAPTER 6

I had mere moments to act. Once Odd and Hogan were taken to the enemy camp, I'd have no chance to rescue them. I considered my options. One—wait until they were out of sight, drop down from the Death Lily, and chase after them. Then what? It was twelve against one.

Two—drop down before they left, surprising them. Then what? It was still twelve against one.

Three—I had nothing. What did I have? A Death Lily and a dozen Peace Lilys. But they didn't know the others were Peace Lilys.

*Vines?* I asked the Lily. *Grab the men? Will the Peace Lilys help?*

*Yes. They go.*

*Drop me down, I'll distract them while you and your friends ensnare them. Okay?*

*Yes. Taste them?*

Despite what I'd contemplated earlier, the thought of the Death Lily snatching each soldier and essentially killing him or her didn't sit well with me. *No. Please let them go after we disappear into the mines.*

Agreement pulsed.

*Thank you. Okay, drop me...now.*

The Death Lily yanked its barbs from my arms and spat me

onto the ground. I yelped as I hit hard, rolling. Disoriented for a moment, I lay there. But the voices of the soldiers returning to investigate reminded me of the danger.

I staggered to my feet as the nine men and three women stopped to gape at me. The soldiers needed to be closer to me for the vines to reach them. Hogan and Odd stood in the center of a loose circle. Odd kept his expression neutral, but an amused amazement sparked in his eyes. Hogan frowned, but kept quiet.

Swaying, I gestured wildly to the Lily. "Whoa. Did you see that?" I asked. "So fast. I just dropped my pack and…swoosh!" I hugged my arms and faked a shiver.

They moved in a few feet. The Lily's vines crept toward their boots.

My shirt had been ripped by the Lily's barbs. Blood welled. I coated my fingers with it and then thrust them out, showing them the bright red tips. "Look! It attacked me!"

"Calm down, miss," the leader said. He stepped in, but kept out of the reach of the Lily's petals. "You survived. You might live—"

"I'm going to die," I screeched. "No one lives. No one. Ohh…" I put my hands on my face and stumbled as if about to faint.

Instinctively, the soldiers shuffled a couple more feet before they halted. Good enough. Vines from the Peace Lilys snaked along the ground behind them.

"Miss, you need to move away from the Death Lily so we can help you." The leader held out his hand.

I stared at him. "Help me? There's nothing you can do."

"She's right, Vonn. Leave her," a woman said.

Vonn turned to her. "She's with them." He pointed to Odd and Hogan. "Since they won't talk, maybe she will. And we can't have her running back to her commanding officer as soon as we leave."

Blinking as if really seeing the group for the first time, I said, "You… Oh, no." I backed away.

The Death Lily hissed. Everyone's gazes jerked to the huge white petals parting above my head and not to the vines circling their ankles.

"Maybe this time it will kill her," the woman said.

I squealed in alarm and rushed Vonn. Wrapping my arms around his neck, I knocked him over. On the way down I touched the base of his skull and zapped him into unconsciousness. Other cries and yells followed mine as the eleven remaining soldiers were yanked off their feet by the vines.

They struggled and some grabbed their knives to cut the tendrils. But regular steel wasn't sharp enough to do the job. It didn't take long for them to be wrapped tight. Not able to move, they begged me to help.

His face white, Hogan stared at them.

Odd grimaced. "The Lily has enough food for a season."

I searched Vonn's pockets until I found the key to the manacles. Unlocking the cuffs, I freed Hogan and Odd.

Hogan rubbed his wrists. "What—"

"Not now. I'll explain later."

"Did you get what you need?" Odd asked.

"Not yet." I picked up my knapsack and returned to the base of the Death Lily. It bent over and deposited two toxin sacks and two seed pods into my open pack. "Thanks." I secured the flap. "Let's go before another squad finds us."

"But what about them?" Hogan asked. "We can't just leave them."

Odd agreed. "I know they're the enemy, but that's cruel."

I studied the panicked faces of the patrol. Odd had a point. And what difference did it make to tell them now versus them realizing it later? That was if they even believed me, which I doubted they would.

"Listen up," I said to the soldiers. "You're not going to become the Death Lily's next victims. Once we're well away, it will release you." I turned to Odd. "Now can we go?"

"Are you lying to them?" Hogan asked.

"No."

"How can you…" He caught my expression. "You'll explain later. Got it."

We hustled back to the tunnels. Once deep inside, I told them about the squads heading east and the seeds.

"And you learned all this from a *Death Lily?*" Hogan asked in disbelief.

"Yes."

"Death Lilys can *communicate?*" Again he didn't mask his incredulous tone.

"Only with healers. We're immune to the toxin."

Hogan glanced at Odd with a "do you believe this?" look.

"I've ceased being surprised when it comes to Avry," Odd said.

Now it was my turn to gaze at him. Did Odd mean that in a good or bad way?

"Oh, come on. You can't deny that you've been full of surprises since we've met, Sergeant *Irina.*"

He had me there. I'd worn a disguise and joined Estrid's holy army using the name Irina from Gubkin Realm to gather information. "But I had good reasons." And they benefited the most by learning how to go silent in the forest.

"I didn't say you didn't. You just keep things…interesting. Like today, for example."

Uh-oh. Time for the lecture.

"I'm torn over how to feel. If you hadn't insisted on going to that Death Lily, we wouldn't know about Cellina's plans.

But when we were captured, my thoughts about your impulsiveness weren't all warm and fuzzy."

I'd bet.

Odd spread his hands out. "I figured we were done for. The only bit of hope was that you might escape and tell Prince Ryne what we encountered. But then you dropped out of that Lily, and I thought you were insane."

"I couldn't let them take you," I said. "They were going to feed you to the ufas. Talk about cruel."

"Yeah, that would have been horrifying."

"I agree. Those poor ufas."

"Hey." Odd bumped me with his shoulder.

I shoved him back. He pushed again.

Hogan cleared his throat and gazed at us. We stopped as if scolded.

After a few minutes of silence, Hogan asked, "Who's Sergeant Irina?"

Odd's laughter echoed off the hard stone walls. "Oh, man, it'll take too long to explain. Trust me."

"Clever. She's being smart. Damn it," Ryne said, throwing his stylus down.

Odd, Hogan, and I stood on the opposite side of the conference table in the factory. We had reported in and now faced a very angry prince.

"Did you check all the exits?" Ryne asked.

"No," Hogan said. "There is still one left."

We'd headed straight back after the encounter with Cellina's squad. It had taken us a full day.

"All right. Get out of here and wait for your orders. I need to think," Ryne said.

I turned.

"Not you, Avry. Stay."

Odd shot me a smirk before he hurried away. I smoothed my expression and returned to the table. Ryne studied me as if he debated between strangling me or stabbing me. I braced for his reprimand.

He shook his head. "I don't... I can't... Here." He handed me a piece of charcoal. "There's a map of Pomyt Realm over on that desk." He gestured to the left. "Mark where you saw the Death Lilys and Cellina's troops on it."

"I'm not sure if I can remember them all," I said.

"Just mark what you can." His lips moved, but his teeth remained firmly clamped.

"Okay." Even though a question about his plans for the attack on Zabin pushed up my throat, I retreated.

I spent the night drawing squiggles for Lilys and Xs for the squads. When the sunlight shone from under the metal doors, I couldn't keep my eyes open any longer. My head pounded with fatigue and I rested it on my arms for just a moment. At least, that was the plan.

*Standing in the middle of King Zavier's throne room, I turned in a slow circle, marveling at all his expensive treasures. Tohon lounged on his father's jewel-encrusted throne, watching me with a predatory glint.*

*"So nice to see you aggravating Ryne, my dear," Tohon said with a soft chuckle. "The poor guy doesn't quite know what to do with you. You have rendered all his diplomatic training useless. You're unexpected and don't follow Ryne's notion of logic at all." He tsked. "Not that I have any good advice for him. I completely underestimated you. A mistake I won't make again."*

*"Because you can't. You're out of commission, Tohon," I said.*

*"Are you sure? I am having this lovely conversation with you, my dear."*

*"You're a result of my worries and nothing more than a nightmare."*

*"And again I ask, are you certain? Did you not consider the pos-*

sibility that one of the children I experimented on has developed healing powers?"

"They're too young."

"The ones you saw are. But I've been working with Death Lily toxin for a number of years. There could be other older survivors that you aren't even aware of."

Alarmed, I stepped closer to the dais. "Are there?"

He shrugged. "How should I know? I'm a nightmare born from your fears and desires." Tohon leered and stood. His royal robes disappeared and all he wore were his black silk pajama pants. The hip-hugging material accented his flat muscular stomach and chest. "Still like what you see, my dear?"

"Go away. You shouldn't be able to invade my dreams. And if you do have a healer, it's too soon for you to reach your castle. So you're still frozen." I concentrated on banishing him.

He laughed. "Yet I remain. Perhaps there is another reason?"

"You didn't claim me, Tohon. I fought you and won."

"True. I couldn't possess you. But I am a part of you, my dear. I've...branded you with my magic, and as long as you live, I do, too."

"Ridiculous."

"Is it? Remember the first time we met? When my dead retrieved you? I kissed your hand and since then we've been linked."

I denied it. No way. If I was linked with anyone, it would be Kerrick.

"Yet Kerrick's not here. I am."

A hand gently shook my shoulder. "Avry, wake up." Ryne knelt next to me, peering at my face in concern. "Bad dream?"

Straightening, I knocked the charcoal to the floor. I'd fallen asleep on the map I'd marked with the Lily and troop locations.

"Is there any other kind of dream?" I asked.

"Not for me."

Then we shared something in common. "Does Tohon haunt your dreams, as well?"

"No. My father does."

Surprised, I glanced at him. "But King Micah's—"

"Dead. But that doesn't seem to stop him from telling me what I've done wrong every night. He delights in pointing out my mistakes and telling me I'm incompetent."

"Sorry to hear that."

"I've accepted it as a manifestation of my insecurities. I suspect your dreams of Tohon are similar. Perhaps a way for you to express your fears."

His explanation made sense. Yet I couldn't shake the truth in Tohon's words. "Sounds very logical, Ryne. But have you really accepted it?"

He huffed. "No. I wish he'd shut up and get the hell out of my dreams."

"I could give you a sleeping draft."

"No, thank you. I have to be able to wake up if needed." He stood and examined the map. "What does Tohon say in your dreams?" he asked in a casual manner, but his arm muscles tightened.

"He gloats. He goads me. But one time he warned me."

Ryne jerked his head, meeting my gaze. "How?"

I explained about the ambush. "And he hinted that there might be older children who survived his experiments and who might be healers by now."

"Both dreams are easy to explain. You must have heard a noise while you slept, alerting you to the danger, and the idea of other healers is just your own intelligence working through the possibilities. Which we should consider. Come on." He strode over to his work table.

Curious, I followed him.

Pulling a piece of parchment and grabbing his stylus, he sat in his chair. "Let's see. Tohon helped at the Healer's Guild for a year after we'd graduated from boarding school. I suspect this was when he began experimenting with the Death Lily toxin and putting the clues together about the source of your magic." He wrote dates on the parchment. "That was about five years ago. Plenty of time for him to inject the toxin into a child."

"Except at that time, the plague hadn't spread all over the Fifteen Realms. He couldn't just inject it into a patient or child without someone noticing. Unless…"

"Unless what?"

"He claimed it was an attempt to find a cure for the plague. The healers' desperation increased as more people sickened."

"Or he had a willing subject," Ryne added. "Someone working with him?"

"Possible. But then why wasn't this person helping in his infirmary? Why didn't I meet him or her? And why did Cellina try to kidnap me?"

"All good questions. Perhaps Cellina doesn't know about this healer. Maybe Tohon kept his or her identity a secret."

"But Sepp would need to know. Are you saying this mystery healer and Sepp are working together?"

"It's just speculation."

"Based on a dream conversation."

"You did spend time in his castle, Avry. You might have noticed something while there and your dream is just making the connections for you."

"Or I could have read something in that crate Belen found in the Healer's Guild's record room." Mentioning Belen's name reminded me that I hadn't asked Ryne if he'd learned anything about Poppa Bear.

"No news." Ryne sounded as tired as I felt.

I considered our strange conversation. "Danny might know if there were older children in Tohon's castle." Except he was in Alga Realm with the northern tribes. "Kerrick told me his healing powers ignited. He should be training with me."

"One of the tribeswomen has a form of magical healing and he's working with her. He's safer there for now."

And Zila was with Kerrick's brother, Izak, and his Great-Aunt Yasmin. Four years younger than Danny, her powers wouldn't develop for a few more years. Although Danny was only thirteen; young for a healer, but not unheard of.

"Avry, go get some sleep. I'd like you to check that last exit before leaving for the infirmary," Ryne said.

"All right. Where should I spread my bedroll?"

"There's barracks on the living level in the mines."

"Beds?"

He smiled. "The mattresses are thin, but they're off the ground."

I sighed. That was the best news I'd gotten all day. Which said quite a bit about my day.


"Did you request me to escort you to the infirmary?" Odd asked. He leaned in the doorway of the barrack.

"No. I asked for Saul and his squad, but they just returned from a ten-day patrol." I folded my blanket and stuffed it into my pack.

"Saul? Even after I just spent the last seven days crawling through the mines with you. I'm insulted." A pause. "Why Saul?"

"We didn't crawl, and I thought you'd like a break. Besides…"

"Besides, what?"

"He's quieter," I teased. Saul was a man of few words.

"Fine, then I won't talk during the entire trip." Odd crossed his arms and pouted.

"You sound like a four-year-old."

"Who's a four-year-old?" Ryne asked as he squeezed by Odd.

"Odd's acting like one," I said.

"Am not!"

I spread my hands out. "See?"

"Avry, be nice. Odd's one of my best sergeants. His squad has one of the highest mission-success rates of my army."

"Ha!" A pleased, almost smug, expression creased his face.

"Now you've done it. He's going to be impossible. I'm willing to wait a day for Saul to rest up."

"I'm not," Ryne said. "We can't waste any time. News of your little incident with Cellina's patrol will eventually reach her, and one of two things will happen. She'll either recall her troops or stick with the plan. Either way, I can't send as many soldiers as I originally planned to attack Zabin or we won't be able to hold off if Cellina's northern troops engage."

"Why would she continue?" I asked. "She no longer has the element of surprise."

"True, but she still has us outnumbered. And if your marks on the map are accurate, she has already positioned her troops in prime locations. So instead of an outright offensive to re-take the city, I'm sending only a few elite squads to harry her defenders and draw them away from the manor house while you, Flea, and another squad rescue Estrid and as many of her staff as possible."

I considered his plan. "With her troops coming from the north and the ones in Zabin, won't you be caught between the two?"

Ryne stared at me a moment. "I should make you a general. That's exactly what's going to happen, but we're going to hunker down in these mines and make a nuisance of ourselves for now."

"And the rest of us?"

"The new infirmary location is near Grzebien, southeast of Zabin. There's a cave system that's—"

"I'm well acquainted with that cave." The grief inside my heart pushed against my throat. I spent about twenty days there with Kerrick and the boys. Lots of memories waited to ambush me there. Looking past the pain, I recognized the strategic strength of the location.

"Here's a map. I've marked where you, Flea, the monkeys, and the odd squad need to rendezvous with the rest of the team."

Odd moved closer to study the markings. "When?"

"Twelve days," Ryne answered. "That'll give you enough time to travel to the infirmary, check patients, and get to the rendezvous location."

"I thought you were worried about time," Odd said.

"My squads are on foot. If I had enough horses for everyone, it'd be different. But the same goes for Cellina, and I hope by the time the news reaches her and she adjusts her strategy, we'll be there and gone."

I calculated. We'd have to give Zabin a wide berth as we headed south—familiar territory for me, and I'd have at least three days with my patients. "Twelve days works for me. What about Jael?"

"What about her?" Ryne asked.

"Last time I saw her, she was in that area. She could be holed up in Grzebien." I'd no desire to run into the air magician.

"My intelligence agents report she's headed toward Dina."

Dina was one of Tobory Realm's major cities. A little too close for comfort, but better than in Pomyt.

"Okay. What if we're delayed? What's the contingency plan?" I asked.

Ryne tapped the map. "Second rendezvous point for day fourteen. If you don't arrive there, then the mission is cancelled until we can regroup. Details about the mission will be given to you when you meet up with the team. Captain Drisana will be in charge."

"How will I know it's her and not one of Cellina's spies?" I asked.

Odd nodded. Wynn's betrayal remained a raw spot in our hearts.

"Ask her what realm she's from. If she doesn't answer Ronel Realm, then it's not Drisana."

Ronel was the dangerous sea east of the Fifteen Realms. It made sense not to use a real realm, as a person had a one-in-fifteen chance of guessing it right.

"And you trust this Drisana?" I asked.

"Oh, yes, she's been with me since before the plague. Just follow her orders and the mission should go smoothly."

Odd huffed. "Follow orders? You do remember who you're talking to." He jerked his thumb toward me.

"Hey." I batted Odd's hand away.

"Do I need to provide examples?" Odd asked. "I've several."

"No need," Ryne said drily. "I'm well aware of Avry's… uh…unpredictability."

"Good save," Odd said.

"I'm sure he learned that in school," I said, matching Ryne's dry tone.

"You're right. It's one of the four *D*s we studied."

"Four *D*s?" I couldn't resist asking.

"Diplomacy, defense, deception, and disinformation."

"Ah. And which *D* were you referring to?"

Ryne handed me the map. "I'll let you figure that one out. You're a smart girl." He left.

Just as I feared, a flood of memories assaulted me as soon as I entered the cave near Grzebien. Outside this cave, Kerrick had taught me how to move silently in the forest, and we had all played a fun game of hide-and-seek to test my new skills. I'd boasted of being Queen Seeker and Kerrick had tried to trick me by hiding in a tree. But I'd sniffed him out, following his wonderful scent of spring sunshine and living green.

I wondered if the painted targets were still visible on the trunks from when Belen had shown me how to throw a knife with accuracy and heat. I'd learned survival skills, and after three years of searching for information, I'd discovered my sister, Noelle, had survived the plague and been conscripted into Estrid's holy army.

And it all had happened only three seasons ago. So much had transpired since then it just amazed me.

I checked on the patients. The move had gone well and no one with major injuries had arrived during the transition. All were settling down for the night.

When I joined the boys, I didn't need to say a word. Flea and the monkeys' expressions of sad acknowledgment spoke volumes. We huddled together around the communal campfire and exchanged information. I told them about my adventures at HQ.

"I'm not surprised she's being aggressive," Loren said. "I think Cellina's been planning to take control of Tohon's army from the beginning. Tohon didn't know about her sister, did he?"

"No, and Wynn claimed she hated him, and Cellina did sic her pack of dead ufas on Tohon," I said.

Talking until midnight, we batted a few ideas around, but no one had any more insight into Cellina's plans. Tired from seven days on the road, I spread my bedroll near Flea's.

"Can I talk to you in private?" Flea asked in a whisper.

"Sure." We moved away from the fire.

"There's a patient I've separated from the rest," he said.

"Why?" Flea's serious tone scared me more than the secrecy.

"There's something wrong with him."

"You should have told me right away. Where is he?" I demanded.

"He's not critical. He's in another cavern. It's just…"

"What? Flea, spit it out."

"I think he has the plague."

# KERRICK

Kerrick didn't know how long he lay on the forest floor. Energy returned to him in small frustrating increments. He'd only been gone from the forest for a few minutes and it had sapped all his strength and magic. Which was the opposite of how his magic worked before he'd gotten sick. Now he needed to use his power to leave the forest and to turn his skin back to its original tan color.

*You are of the forest,* the living green had said to him. *Alive like trees and plants.*

Those words scared him. Did they mean he was confined to the forest, rooted there like the trees? Was that the price for his life? He hoped not. Perhaps he just needed to regain his strength. After all, he'd been unconscious for weeks.

When he felt better, he pushed to his feet. Flea's message had been terse. *Bag in sticky pine.* Kerrick smiled, remembering how Flea hated to get sap on his hands. Quain had teased him, saying that as an ex-thief Flea should be used to sticky fingers. The boy had stared at Quain through his long bangs and replied, "Who said I'm retired?"

Kerrick found his pack shoved into the bushy branches of a white pine tree. Needles stuck to the material, and a squirrel had chewed on the leather straps. Most of his clothing, along with his weapons, money pouch, and boots had been stuffed inside. Only one shirt was missing. His dadao sword had been wrapped in oiled skins and hung from a branch.

The setting sun had cooled the air. He dressed quickly, wrapping his short black cape around his shoulders. His clothes turned the colors of the forest as soon as he donned them. Handy. A quick check confirmed his lock picks remained in place. Flea had also included jerky, travel rations, and a note. Kerrick built a small fire. Gnawing on a piece of jerky, he read Flea's letter.

Kerrick,

If you're reading this, then me and the monkeys are wrong and, boy oh, boy, I'm going to be so happy to be wrong! We all believe you're dead (again—you really need to communicate better if you're not), so does Prince Ryne, but Avry refuses to accept it and I guess she's right if you are indeed reading this.

A warmth spread throughout his chest. Avry had faith in him. Kerrick hoped she held on to it and hadn't changed her mind. He hated to think he'd caused her any more pain.

Avry asked me to write this note. She's gone with Sergeant Odd to Prince Ryne's new HQ. I'll write the location below in our old signals just in case this gets into enemy hands. Those raccoons can be devious when they want—ha-ha. Me and the monkeys are headed with the rest of the infirmary staff and patients to our new location (written below) where we're supposed to meet up with Avry sometime.

I say 'supposed to' because you know Avry. She already

disobeyed orders by searching for you after Prince Ryne called it off. And I wouldn't be surprised if she decides to keep searching and not join us until she's done. Plus Prince Ryne was really keen on her going to HQ so he might have a special mission for her there. She was all pissed off about it so he'll have his hands full—ha-ha.

I really really hope you are reading this letter! I have this magic now and it's awful. I don't want it. Have you ever felt that way? Probably not since your forest magic is useful. There's nothing useful about death.

Flea

Kerrick reread the letter. This time picking up on what Flea didn't write. A friction between Ryne and Avry? Or an attraction? Jealousy flared for a moment before he squashed it. Avry refused to believe he died. That meant a lot. He returned to the note.

Was Flea a death magician now? Too many questions without answers. He read the locations and debated his next move. Travel to HQ or south to Grzebien? Ryne wouldn't separate Avry from her patients if he didn't have a good reason.

What would be the quickest route to Avry?

Through Ryne.

He finished his jerky and doused the fire. With his deeper connection to the forest, traveling in the dark wouldn't require as much energy as before. One benefit to his new...what? Situation? Magic? Existence? Prison? Better than the alternative—death. And as Flea said: *There's nothing useful about death.*

Two days later, Kerrick crouched at the edge of the forest, studying the activity around the town of Victibus. At first glance, the town resembled any other small town struggling to recover from the plague years. Yet small clues hinted that not all was as it seemed. No children ran through the streets. Everyone walked with a purpose and didn't amble or gather in groups to chat.

A large factory attracted the most activity. Ryne's HQ, no doubt, and it explained why he couldn't detect either Ryne or Avry in the surrounding forest. During the last couple of days, he'd experimented with his range and discovered his ability to sense living creatures reached about five miles.

But right now Kerrick had to figure out how to reach Ryne. He didn't have enough energy to go that far from the forest. But would Ryne believe him if he sent a note? No. Frustration boiled. Kerrick needed to find someone who recognized him and would take a message to Ryne.

It sounded easy enough, but only after checking every single patrol for three days did he see a familiar face around midafternoon. Too bad he couldn't remember the guy's name— just that he was a sergeant and had helped Avry escape from Tohon in Zabin. A prince in Kerrick's opinion.

Kerrick rushed to intercept the squad. Not hard to do, but he scared them when he appeared without any warning. They yanked their swords out and formed ranks. At least he remembered to pull enough power to turn his skin, hair, and clothes normal.

He held his hands out, showing them he was unarmed. "Sorry, gentlemen, but I'm in need of assistance and don't have time for niceties. I need you to take a message to Prince Ryne and Healer Avry."

"And I need a vacation and a purse full of gold coins, but that ain't gonna happen," one of the men quipped.

Turning to the sergeant, he asked, "Surely you recognize me? I'm Prince Kerrick." Ugh, he hated using his title. "I believe you were in the infirmary cave when I arrived with Avry, Loren, Quain, and Flea. Remember?"

"I also remember you disappeared and the major ruckus it caused. Why can't you take the message to them yourself?" the sergeant asked.

Good question and one he'd prepared for. "I'm a forest mage and I am tracking a person of interest. If I leave now, I'll lose him. Please ask them to come here. I need to talk to them both." And hug one very tight.

The soldier who had spoken before glanced at the sergeant. "Do you want us to take him, Enric?"

"No. He's legit. I'm not sure Healer Avry's still here, but I'll relay your message."

"Thank you."

The men continued on to HQ. Unable to keep still, Kerrick walked in circles. He didn't need to remain in that exact location because as soon as Ryne or Avry entered the forest he'd know in a heartbeat.

Hours later, or so it felt, Ryne arrived. Not in the direction Kerrick'd been expecting, but from the opposite way. His life force popped up from seemingly nowhere. Strange. The prince had at least a dozen bodyguards with him. Considering he thought Kerrick was dead, he guessed he shouldn't be insulted by the soldiers.

One person was missing. Avry. Worry flared.

When Ryne approached, Kerrick drew power to appear normal and then made noise before stepping out from the bushes. Tense bodies and expressions relaxed.

Ryne grinned and rushed him, grabbing him in a tight hug before pushing him away. "You bastard, where have you been?"

"Long story."

"And why couldn't you come inside?"

"Even longer story. I'll tell you all about it, but first, where's Avry?"

"She's at the new infirmary site down near Grzebien."

Disappointment stabbed deep.

"She's going to be ecstatic."

"I need to catch up to her."

"Not until you explain what you've been up to."

Every fiber of Kerrick's being wanted to bolt. To leave Ryne without an explanation. The desire to catch up with Avry pulsed with each heartbeat. And despite Ryne's entourage of guards, it'd be so easy to disappear.

# CHAPTER 7

My heart skipped a few dozen beats. Did Flea just... "The plague? Are you sure?"

"At first, I thought he had an upset stomach. He couldn't keep anything down, but now he has flu-like symptoms—aches, pains, fever, and that unmistakable oily sweat with the sugary rotten smell." Flea's nose crinkled.

Classic stage-two symptoms. Oh, no. "Is anyone else showing signs of the plague?"

"No, but I moved him so he doesn't get anyone else sick."

A good idea. "Where is he?"

"In the back, I'll show you." Flea grabbed a lantern and led me deeper into the cave system. "I thought everyone who survived was immune to the plague."

"They are, but not every single person in the Fifteen Realms has been exposed to the disease. Ryne managed to go a number of years before getting sick." When Tohon had sent an assassin to infect him. Except Ryne's sister had been among the first wave of people to die from the plague. They'd been in Pomyt on a diplomatic mission. Why would he survive only to sicken later? And why hadn't I thought of this before?

"In here." Flea held up the light.

The soft yellow glow illuminated a tiny cavern. Lying on

a cot in the center, a young man tossed and turned. He had kicked his blankets off. A sheen of sweat coated his face. As I approached him, my magic stirred from deep inside, signaling a familiar warning. I didn't even need to examine him. He had the plague.

Fear pulsed as I remembered what I'd read about the spread of the plague. Not airborne. "Flea, did you touch him?"

"Of course. I helped him in here." He peered at me in confusion.

"Did you have skin contact? Did some of his oily sweat rub off on your skin?"

"Yeah, I did my death touch on him because he wasn't getting any better." He paled. "Am I going to get the plague, too?"

"How do you feel?"

"Queasy." He sank to the ground.

Which could just be the power of suggestion. I crouched next to him and pressed my fingers to the back of his hand. A recognizable vanilla-scented coolness pumped through him.

"Am I going to die?" His voice squeaked.

"No."

He sagged against the cave's wall. "Thank the creator!"

"You've been hanging out with Estrid's soldiers too long."

"Who should I thank, then?"

"The Peace Lilys. Their serum flows in your blood, protecting you."

"Wow. That's some powerful stuff."

I agreed. It had saved mine and Flea's life. Tohon used the serum to animate the dead. The serum and his life magic—I still hadn't figured how the combination worked. As soon as I'd learned Death Lily toxin would eliminate his dead soldiers, I'd stopped thinking about it. Too much else going on.

"Did the patient encounter the enemy before he sickened?" I asked Flea.

"Yes. Private Yuri said his squad was ambushed. He was knocked out and when he woke he was alone. He had a cut on his neck, but was otherwise unharmed."

Interesting. "Has the rest of his squad reported in?"

"No. They're considered missing in action."

Not good. As I stared at the sick patient, my thoughts returned to the puzzle of the Lilys. If this man died, his body would probably be rejected by the Peace Lilys because he had no magic. The Lilys only saved those with magic or the potential to wield it. There was a slim chance the patient had potential. If we brought his body to the Lily fast enough, it might work. But why wait until he died? We could transport him now. Except only Flea and I could be near him. I wouldn't risk anyone else.

What if I brought the Peace Lily serum to him? It might accelerate his death like it had with me. He was going to die regardless. But it might work. It was worth a try.

Excited, I straightened. "No one else cares for this patient or even comes near him. Just us. Understand?"

"Yeah."

"Good. You need to scrub your hands with soap and water before you leave this cavern every single time. Have you touched anyone else since checking him?"

Flea stood. "I don't think so. I moved him this afternoon, and then you came."

A bit of good news. "Stay here with him tonight. I'll bring back a dose of fever powder to make him more comfortable before I leave."

"Leave? Where are you going?"

"To find a Peace Lily."

★ ★ ★

I debated between speed and safety. The man had a few more days until he experienced stage-three symptoms, and the monkeys would never forgive me if I left without them. Safety won. I fetched the fever powder, soap, and a water bucket for Flea before finding my friends. Despite the late hour, Loren and Quain hadn't gone to sleep. They waited for me by the hearth.

"What's going on?" Quain demanded.

"Is Flea all right?" Loren asked.

"He's fine. There's a very sick patient that needs care," I said.

"So why all the secrecy?" Quain asked.

I lowered my voice. "He has the plague."

"Flea!"

"Shh, Quain. Not Flea. The patient."

Loren wilted and rubbed his face. "Not this again."

"Not if I can help it."

"The healers couldn't stop it before," Loren said. "And you're not sacrificing your life again."

"I've an idea." I explained about the Peace Lily serum.

Quain jumped to his feet. "Let's go."

"What about Flea? Will he get sick, too?" Loren asked.

"No." I smiled as they both accepted my answer without question. "Bring your packs, it might take us a couple days to find a Peace Lily." The map wasn't as accurate in this area and the Death Lily had only shown me its flowers.

"Should we clear it with someone?" Quain asked.

"I don't need permission to take care of my patients."

"And when Prince Ryne learns you left the infirmary with just us for protection, he'll have a fit." Loren rolled up his blanket.

"I don't care."

"Avry." Loren gave me his don't-be-stupid look. He usually aimed it at Quain, so I must be acting unreasonable.

"All right. I'll talk to the person in charge of the infirmary's security. Do you know—"

"Lieutenant Macon," Odd said, joining us. He eyed our packs. "And I can guarantee he won't let you leave with just two protectors."

"We managed with just Hogan," I challenged.

"And a dozen Lilys."

True. And if we ran into an enemy patrol, I didn't want Quain or Loren to be harmed or captured. Actually, I wanted them and Flea in a safe place like Alga Realm with Kerrick's brother. But they'd just refuse.

"Wait here, I'll talk to him." Muttering under his breath, Odd strode away.

"Do we want to dash while Odd is distracting the L.T.?" Quain asked.

"Tempting, but Cellina is after Avry. And while we can easily handle a dozen…" Loren gave us a wry smile. "If she sent her dead-ufa pack after us, we'd be—"

"Snack food," Quain finished.

Odd returned. "You can go as long as my squad goes with you. Let me guess, you want to leave now."

"Yes."

"I'll go wake them up. This had better be important."

"It is."

Odd's gaze met mine for a long moment. He nodded. "Give us a couple."

While Odd roused his men, I consulted the Lily map. East would be the ideal direction to avoid any nasty encounters with the enemy. According to the map, a cluster of Lilys grew a day's walk roughly northeast.

It seemed as if hours had passed before Odd and his squad

were ready. I led them into the forest surrounding the cave. We all went silent and the odd squad practically melted into the darkness. A half-moon shone enough light so we didn't stumble.

Odd stayed by my side. "Are you going to tell me what this is about?"

"It's for a patient."

"And it couldn't wait for morning?"

"Yes, it could, but I like to bother everyone and drag them out of bed."

"Okay, dumb question. Give me a break, I'm tired."

"Sorry. Thank you for coming along."

Odd grunted.

"I should warn you," I said.

"This ought to be good."

"You're not going to get much sleep in the next two days. A man's life is at stake."

"Yeah, I figured. I'm not *that* tired. Lead on, boss lady."

Boss lady? That was new. Was Odd being sarcastic? Or just being...well, Odd? He kept pace with me, moving with easy, graceful strides. No signs of tension. I relaxed.

No one said much as the sun rose and traveled across the sky. I spent most of the trip to the Peace Lilys mulling over a number of scenarios. If the Lily gave me its serum, should I inject it all? Or a portion? If the serum killed my patient, would my touch bring him back to life? What if the Lily refused? Tohon had harvested the serum using his life magic, stealing it from the Peace Lilys. Those he injected it into had remained dead, but the serum preserved their bodies, preventing them from decaying. One thing I did know, I wouldn't steal from the Lily.

We reached the cluster of four Lilys a few hours after sunset. In the cooling air, I smelled the familiar scent of vanilla.

None of them moved or hissed as I approached. They were all Peace Lilys.

This might be harder than I'd thought. The single time I'd communicated with a Peace Lily had been after Noelle died. I'd attacked the plant when it refused to save my sister. Remembering the vision of Tohon placing his hands on the base of the Peace Lily's flower, I copied him. Smooth and thick, the white petal was cool under my palms.

Nothing happened.

I concentrated on why I needed its serum, forming a picture of the dying patient in my mind. Suddenly the petals parted and I lurched forward as my right hand disappeared into the heart of the plant.

Barbs circled my wrist, jabbing into my skin. Ice flowed into my arm, up my shoulder and stabbed into my head.

*One only. Learn,* it said.

Then it released me, expelling my hand. I fell back. Odd and Loren pulled me to my feet.

"Well?" Loren asked.

I relaxed my grip. A single grape-size blue ball rested in the center of my palm. Except for the smaller size and color, it resembled the Death Lily toxin's sack—squishy and durable.

"That's good, right?" Quain asked.

"I'm not sure." Remembering the Lily's words, I examined it. Learn what?

"When will you know?" Odd asked.

"When I see the results. Let's go."

"No can do," Odd said. "My men are exhausted. We need a few hours of sleep or we'll be stumbling into things and making a racket."

I glanced around. His men had built a small campfire. A few huddled around it and a couple already snoozed nearby.

Loren and Quain drooped with fatigue, too, but they'd never admit it.

"All right. Four hours max. You can sleep as long as you like when we return."

Odd left to organize a watch schedule. I placed the serum in an outside pocket of my pack. Unable to resist the lure of a warm fire, I joined the others. Wrapping my cloak tighter around me, I settled next to flickering flames, using my pack as a pillow. I'd just rest my eyes for a moment.

*"How's that for proof, my dear?" Tohon asked as he led me around the dance floor.*

*I wore the green silk gown with the plunging neckline and open back. The heat from Tohon's fingers seared my skin, but I couldn't break away from him. Music filled the air like a mist, swirling around us.*

*"Proof of what?" I asked.*

*"That part of me resides in you. Why else did the Peace Lily open for you?"*

*"I needed—"*

*"It doesn't care. You placed your hands in the exact same spot I did and it worked. Proof."*

*"But it gave me its sack, I didn't steal it."*

*"Trivial details, my dear. And not worth ruining our evening over." Tohon increased his pace, twirling me in circles.*

*The other dancers blurred by. When Tohon finally stopped, we stood in the garden. My head kept spinning. Tohon hooked his arm in mine and walked me along the stone paths. When my vision cleared, I noticed the once-manicured bushes and plants were now overgrown and wild. Weeds grew everywhere.*

*Tohon tsked. "Such a shame. Look what happens when the gardener is gone."*

*"Kerrick's not gone."*

*"Then where is he, my dear?"*

Cold drops struck my face. Water ran along my jaw. The sound of sizzling matched the steady shushing of rain. I groaned and opened my gluey eyes. The others stirred, as well. Darkness remained. Smoke billowed from the wet embers.

"Ah, the joys of camping," Quain said. "Waking up in a puddle."

"Yeah, sure, it's a *puddle*," Loren teased.

"Grow up." Quain pulled his hood over his bald head.

"I'm not the one with the puddle."

"That's enough, gentlemen," I said. Every muscle in my body ached. I clambered to my feet. Rain dripped into my eyes. I yanked my hood up. Icy water splashed down my neck. Lovely.

"Welcome to the rainy season," Odd said. He swung his cloak around his broad shoulders.

Quain peered into the dark sky. "I told you the weather last year was unusually dry."

"And how does that help us now?" Loren asked.

I ignored their bickering. My thoughts returned to my nightmare as Odd gathered his squad and prepared to leave. Tohon's magic couldn't be inside me. Could it? No. I'd never heard of such a thing. Then again, that shouldn't be a surprise; my knowledge of the other eleven types of magic was limited. Perhaps it was mentioned in Ryne's book about the various magical powers. I'd have to ask the next time I saw him.

The rain continued as we traveled back to the infirmary. The darkness turned into a grayness. The sound of raindrops striking the leaves interfered with our efforts to match the noise of our passage with the forest's song. We stopped often to listen for intruders or signs of an ambush. At each stop, I touched the greenery without thought, seeking Kerrick's magic. Nothing.

While I understood the need to be cautious, my frustration over our slow speed grew as the day progressed.

It was close to midnight when we arrived. I grabbed a few supplies and headed to Yuri's cavern, ordering the others to remain behind. Flea slept on his bedroll, blocking the entrance.

He woke the instant I stepped over him. "Did you find a Peace Lily?"

"Yes, and it gave me its serum." I placed everything on the floor so I could take off my dripping cloak and toss it into a corner with a wet plop.

"Do you think it'll work?"

I pulled the blue sack from my pack. Was there even enough inside to save the patient? "I'm not...sure."

"Then talk it through. That always helps me." He flashed me his lopsided grin.

"Okay. If I inject this serum into Yuri, it'll do one of two things. It will accelerate the disease and kill him. Then I revive him with a touch. Hopefully."

"And the other?"

"It will cure him."

"Why would you think that?"

I explained the link between the plague and Death Lily toxin.

"So you think since Death counters Peace, it'll work in reverse?"

"Yes."

"What happens if Yuri dies and you can't bring him back to life?"

"Nothing. He'll be gone."

"Which will eventually happen regardless." Flea gazed at the sleeping man. "We should ask Yuri first."

"Is he lucid?"

"At times. He knows he has the plague. I thought it only fair to tell him."

"You're right. And we should ask for his permission to try the serum."

Flea woke Yuri. The young man's gaze jumped from Flea to me and back as we explained my theories. It was a lot of information to absorb.

When we finished, he closed his blue eyes for a moment. Then he looked at me. "Go ahead and do it. It's my only chance to live."

I picked up the syringe, poked the needle into the blue sack, and drew all the clear liquid into the reservoir. Tapping it, I expelled the air bubbles. Yuri's gaze never left me. He held his right arm out. Flea stood on the other side of the bed, holding Yuri's hand.

A drop of serum hung from the end of the needle as I approached. I ran my fingers along the inside of his arm, seeking the best spot.

*Learn.* The Lily's comment came unbidden. I stopped as another scenario popped into my mind. Was the serum for me? Was I supposed to heal Yuri, die from the plague again and be revived by Flea's touch?

Of all the options that one made the most sense. Had the best chance of working. Had worked before.

Why hadn't I considered it prior to this moment? Was it because it would take me twenty days to die and the pain during those last three would be the worst I'd ever experienced? Oh, yes.

I met Yuri's confused gaze. Could I endure the plague again? Should I? Others needed me as well as this young man. And we had to rescue Estrid and her staff in two days.

"What's wrong, Avry?" Flea asked.

"I figured out what I'm *supposed* to do."

"That's great. Right?" Flea's brow crinkled.

Not so great. Now I needed to decide if I should.

# KERRICK

Kerrick suppressed a sigh and invited Ryne to get comfortable. No matter how much he wanted to catch up to Avry, Ryne needed to know.

They built a small fire and sat on opposite sides as if negotiating a treaty. The guards fanned out in a wide circle around them. Kerrick explained waking in the forest and his new limitations. "That's why I couldn't go inside. I still don't have enough energy to leave for long."

Ryne hadn't said anything during his story. Now he leaned back against a tree trunk. "That's...quite a story. Avry was right again. Good thing she's not the type to gloat."

The warmth in Ryne's voice raised Kerrick's hackles. "Why did you bring her to HQ when she's needed at the infirmary?"

Ryne told him about the Lilys. "She completely disregarded my orders and put my men in danger, but I couldn't yell at her because she discovered vital information. Do you know how frustrating that is?"

Oh, yes, Kerrick was well acquainted with Avry's inability to follow directions. "I've found the best way to work with her is to explain the situation. She'll figure out the best way to approach it and you avoid the whole 'ordering her around' thing."

"I've learned that the hard way."

Kerrick laughed at Ryne's martyred expression. "What was the vital information?"

"Cellina sent troops to our north. She was doing a classic backdoor sneak, but once word of the...incident with Avry reaches her she might change tactics. Regardless of her plans, I need to protect our flank, which means we had to change the attack on Zabin to a distraction and rescue." He continued outlining his plans.

"Wait? You're sending Flea and Avry to rescue Estrid?"

"Do you have another idea? I'm open to suggestions," Ryne snapped.

Kerrick waited.

"Sorry. I don't like it, either, but I've no choice." Ryne lowered his voice. "I need Estrid. My army is small and we're scrambling to stay in this. Without her forces, it's just a matter of time until we're forced back over the Nine Mountains."

Not good. A stray thought struck Kerrick. Would he be able to cross the Nine Mountains? Forests grew between the ridges, but the peaks were bare. He might never see his home again. Refusing to dwell on those thoughts, Kerrick focused on the problem at hand—keeping Avry and Flea safe.

"What if I send a message to Noak asking for aid?" Kerrick asked.

"Noak? The leader of the northern tribes?"

"Well, technically, his sister, Rakel's, in charge, but he leads their warriors."

"Do you think he'll come?" Ryne asked.

"I've no idea if he will help. It wasn't too long ago he wished to slaughter our entire population, but Danny did save his people. We won't know unless we ask."

Ryne asked Kerrick to write a message. "I'll send someone

tonight." Then he sobered. "I can't count on him, so I'll need to go forward with the plan to rescue Estrid."

"When is the attack?" Kerrick asked.

"Two days from now."

It would take Kerrick four days to walk there. "Do you have any horses?"

"No. Big noisy creatures aren't good for guerrilla-warfare tactics."

Too bad Kerrick had sent Oya back to the northern tribes. He'd have to find another horse.

"I know you want to catch up with Avry and Flea. Then what?" Ryne asked.

"What do you mean?"

"With your forest magic, you're my best scout. You can get past enemy lines and I really need accurate information on where Cellina's forces are."

"I'd rather stay with Avry." If she wanted him. Kerrick worried she'd distance herself from him in order to avoid getting hurt again.

"I've two of my best squads guarding the infirmary. Once Estrid's rescued, Avry won't be in any more danger."

Kerrick just stared at his friend.

"She *shouldn't* be in danger, but... Yeah, we both know it'll find her." Ryne rubbed his hand along the stubble on his chin. "It's up to you. I won't order you to return. But think about this...." He paused as if debating what to tell Kerrick.

Kerrick braced for bad news. "Think about what?"

"Belen. No one has heard anything or seen him. But no one can get close enough to the enemy."

Ryne didn't disappoint. His words sucker punched Kerrick right in the gut, implying only Kerrick could discover where his best friend had been.

"Low blow, Ryne."

"I'm despicable, I know. And you shouldn't be surprised."

"I'm not."

"Will you think about it?"

"Yes. But Avry first."

"Of course."

"Anything else I need to know about?" Kerrick asked.

"I've heard rumors about a Skeleton King down in Ryazan Realm. He's gathered an army and is marching north."

"Bad news. We encountered him once when searching for Avry, and barely made it out alive."

"I sent a scout."

From Ryne's dour expression, Kerrick braced for more bad news. "And?"

"The scout returned with a package for me. The Skeleton King sent me a crown made from human bones and a note." He sighed. "He warned me that he was coming and he planned to conquer—his word, not mine—both Cellina's and my forces. And that when he is victorious over us all, I will crown him with this special crown."

"How much of a threat is he?"

"Pretty big for us. For Cellina, not so much. She has over two thousand living troops and close to a thousand dead ones. Plus a dead-ufa pack or three."

"Could that be another reason she's pulling out of Zabin? Clearing the way for the Skeleton King to come after us? Then with the sneak attack from the north, you'll be caught between them."

Ryne cursed. "Another reason why I need you, Kerrick. To find out how many troops the Skeleton King has. My scout learned nothing of value."

"I said I'd think about it."

Kerrick wrote a message to Noak and left soon after, heading south to Zabin. Traveling through the night, he avoided the various patrols, but he kept track of animals in the forest, seeking a loose horse. In the morning, Kerrick skirted small towns and farms, hoping to find someone willing to sell or rent him a mount.

By midafternoon he finally spotted two horses grazing in a large pasture near the woods. Summoning all his magical strength, Kerrick turned his skin and clothes to normal before leaving the forest. Each step forward required a concentrated effort. By pure determination, he reached the farmhouse.

He found the horses' owner and, if the man thought Kerrick's strained demeanor odd, he didn't seem to care once the two gold coins hit his palm.

"No saddle," Kerrick whispered to the farmer. "Just a bridle. Please bring him to the forest. I'll be waiting there."

Kerrick's legs shook as he hurried to return to the living green. As soon as he entered its domain, he collapsed.

Two seconds later, or so it felt, the man arrived with the horse in tow. "Hello?" he called, almost stepping on Kerrick. "Harper's all ready." He walked farther in.

Drawing on his final reserve of energy, Kerrick stood, changed to normal and caught up to the man, who jumped about a foot when Kerrick approached from behind.

"Thank you," Kerrick said, taking the reins.

The man nodded and then bolted back to his farm.

*He'll have an interesting story to tell his family.* When the man disappeared from sight, Kerrick mounted Harper. The dark brown horse instantly turned green, brown, orange, red, and yellow, exactly matching Kerrick and the rest of the forest. Handy.

Kerrick had a day and a half to reach the rendezvous spot. He spurred Harper into a gallop.

# CHAPTER 8

"You can't," Flea said after I explained what I needed to do to save Yuri's life.

I placed the syringe carefully on my pack to free my hands. "It makes the most sense."

"What if the serum doesn't work?" Flea dropped Yuri's hand and moved around to my side of the cot. "You can't die. We need you."

"We can travel to the Peace Lily before the third stage so you won't have to inject the serum in me."

"That is *if* the Peace Lily takes you. A big if." He crossed his arms. "No."

His posture was so like Kerrick's, I stifled a smile. "Flea, you of all people should know that *I* decide who I heal and who I won't."

"Yeah, well… You'll have to get through me first." He stepped between me and Yuri, who stared at us both as if we had lost our minds.

I waggled my fingers at him. "One touch, Flea, and you'll be down."

He waved his in the air, as well. "Me, too."

"Really? Did you learn something new when I was gone?"

"No, but I'm sure if I'm mad enough…" He dropped his hands in defeat. His heart wasn't on board with the threat.

But his boast gave me an idea. "You can touch me and see if the plague kills me for good or if I survive again. Then—"

"No. I'm not seeing when you're going to die, Avry. I can't." Flea hunched his shoulders as if I'd force him.

"That's okay. It wouldn't have changed my mind anyway. I'm going to heal him." I pushed Flea to the side and grabbed Yuri's arm.

My magic grew, pushing from my core and flowing toward Yuri where it died as if hitting a wall. I tried again and nothing happened. My healing magic refused to inundate Yuri's body and bring the sickness back into me.

"Did you cure him?" Flea asked, sounding peevish.

"No." I explained about the wall.

Flea glanced at Yuri. The young patient squeezed his eyes shut. Tears leaked from the corners and ran down his temples.

"The Peace Lily serum must still be in your blood, too," Flea said.

"Must be. Although I didn't think it would affect my healing abilities." So what had the Peace Lily wished for me to learn?

"Now what?" Flea asked.

"We'll try my original plan. If that's okay with you, Yuri?"

Without saying a word or even opening his eyes, he held out his arm. Flea returned to the other side of the cot and once again took Yuri's left hand in his. I picked up the syringe, found a vein and injected the serum into him.

"So cold, it burns," Yuri said.

Flea moved to get a blanket, but Yuri wouldn't let go.

I grasped Yuri's right hand. "It's going to hurt like nothing you've ever felt before. But don't despair, it will end."

Yuri peeked at me. "Now you tell me."

"Would it have changed your mind?" I asked.

"No."

Yuri's grip tightened and every muscle in his body tensed as the serum traveled throughout his body. It didn't take long for him to start screaming. He let go of our hands and curled into a tight ball, rocking and yelling.

I kept my fingers on his arm. My magic sensed the oily blackness of the plague fighting the cold whiteness of the serum.

Loren and Quain skidded into the doorway. They had their swords in hand. Odd wasn't far behind. They shouted questions at us.

"Go explain it to them," I said to Flea. "Wash your hands first."

"Will he be okay?" Flea asked.

"I've no idea. Come back when he's quiet."

"Okay." Flea shooed the monkeys and Odd into the hallway, then dunked his hands into the water bucket before scrubbing his skin.

"Up to the elbows," I instructed before returning my attention to Yuri.

His cries remained loud and strong. Having been in his position, I empathized with him. I'd never forget the raw agony. It had felt like acid dissolving my insides. The only thing I didn't know was how long it would take.

Each of his screams lasted for hours, or so it seemed. Helpless, I placed my hand on his shoulder to let him know I was there. Now I understood why Kerrick had attacked the Peace Lily when I'd been inside yelling myself hoarse. Right now I'd do anything to help alleviate Yuri's pain.

The volume and duration of his shrieks eventually dwindled. Then, in the space of a heartbeat, he died.

I gasped, frozen for a moment. Drawing in a deep breath,

I touched his forehead. No spark of magic. Nothing at all. I closed his eyes as the ever-present grief inside my heart expanded, washing over me.

It hadn't worked. Was that what the Peace Lily meant? Should I give up trying to use the Lily to save people? Were Flea and I the only possible survivors?

Yuri's eyes opened. Probably a reflex. But then he turned his head and his gaze met mine.

I stepped back. No life shone in his blue eyes. Pure terror gripped me. I'd created one of Tohon's dead.

Tohon's voice sounded in my mind. *Not one of* mine, *my dear. Yours. He's the first of Avry's dead.*

"Avry, stop yelling." Odd shook my shoulders.

I focused on him. His face was inches from mine. He seemed concerned. Did I have another nightmare? Yes, I remembered Tohon's sleek voice.

"What's wrong?" he asked me.

"I..."

"Oh, no," Flea said with his voice full of horror.

Odd turned. Flea stood next to Yuri, who had his dead gaze trained on me.

"Did she heal him?" Quain asked. He stood in the doorway with Loren.

"She..." Flea looked at me.

Oh, no was right. Not a nightmare, but I wished it was.

"Is he...?" I couldn't finish the question.

Flea's fingers curled into fists for a moment, then he steeled himself before touching Yuri's skin. He snatched his hand away as Yuri turned his head to look at Flea. "Yes."

I wilted, sagging against Odd. He grabbed me before I toppled.

"Will someone tell us what's going on?" Quain demanded.

Flea backed up. "He's dead. Like Tohon's dead soldiers."

Everyone stared at me with a variety of emotions. Horror dominated. Odd kept a firm grip on me. Otherwise I would have sunk to the ground. Yuri remained on his cot, staring at Flea.

"What do we do with him?" Quain asked. "Can we train him?"

"No," I said. "He shouldn't be. I'd never expected… My fault…"

Loren pulled his short dagger from his belt. "It's treated with Death Lily toxin. Should I?" he asked me.

"Yes. Please."

"Sorry, buddy," Loren said as he pricked Yuri's arm.

Yuri didn't flinch or react in anyway. We waited. There was always a slight delay before the toxin worked.

We kept waiting. Nothing happened. Yuri sat there not breathing, not speaking, not being, just there.

"Uh, now what?" Quain asked.

I had no idea. Why didn't the toxin work? Was it because Yuri had the plague, which was linked to Death Lily toxin?

"Decapitation," Loren said. "That's the only other thing that works."

"Maybe we should take him outside first," Quain said.

"No. I don't want anyone else to know about him." I shivered.

"We could do it after dark when everyone is asleep. Otherwise, you'll have a mess to clean up and explain." Loren wiped Yuri's blood off his blade.

"Can he walk?" Quain asked Flea.

"Why are you asking me?"

"He moved when you touched him. Don't you have an affinity with the dead?"

"No. I don't. Avry, did he die from the serum?"

I nodded.

"Avry's touch revived him. I'd think he'd follow *her*."

My touch. I remembered when I'd witnessed Tohon waking his dead. Although his had been dead before he'd injected the serum, he'd pressed his hand to their foreheads, and then, when they'd moved, he guided them by touch. After that, I didn't know how he'd trained them.

"We shouldn't kill him...er, again," Odd said.

"Why?" I pulled away from him, standing on my own wobbly legs.

"It's a chance to learn more about them."

"We know how to stop them. That's *all* we need to know," I said.

"Then why didn't the Death Lily toxin work?" Odd asked.

"I think it's because he had the plague."

"Think or know? Big difference."

"What are you suggesting?" Loren asked Odd.

Oh, no, not him, too. He used that same questioning technique Kerrick and Ryne'd been taught at boarding school.

"I'm suggesting we send a message to Prince Ryne and let him decide what to do."

Feeling stronger, I stepped toward Yuri. "No. His condition is *my* responsibility. I decide."

Odd grabbed my arm, turning me to face him. "I understand that. Do what you feel is right. But consider this. You created him. A healer. We always assumed Tohon used his life magic to revive the dead. What if it wasn't his life magic, but just magic in general? What if Sepp could add to the army of dead? Or one of Tohon's other magicians?"

A terrifying thought. I glanced at Yuri. A body empty of life. "You have a point. But how can we test your theory? I'm not going to kill—"

"Avry, we're at war. Fatalities are a regrettable aspect of it."

"Oh."

"No," Flea said. "I'm not doing it."

"Doing what?" Quain asked.

"Odd wants to test if *I* can revive the dead."

"You don't have to," I said.

Odd let go of my arm. "There's no one else."

"No way." Flea hugged his chest. "You can't force me."

I glared at Odd. "No one is going to force you, Flea. Besides, I don't have any more serum and the Peace Lily told me I'd only get one sack." And the lesson had been learned. Stop trying to use the Lily to revive the dead or it might just work.

"At least wait until you talk to Prince Ryne before you decide about Yuri. There's no need to rush. He can't do anything. He's not in any pain."

Odd made sense, but guilt and fear pushed me to fix my awful mistake right away. An illogical part of my mind thought if he had a proper burial, my guilt over killing him and turning him into an abomination would disappear. The logical part already acknowledged that I'd carry that guilt for the rest of my life. And then there was the fear. Had Tohon branded me like he'd claimed?

Unable to make a decision, I appealed to my guys. "What do you think?"

"Take him outside and finish this now," Flea said without hesitation.

"I'm inclined to agree with Odd on this," Loren said. "We should consult with Prince Ryne. He might have a different perspective. But, Avry." Loren met my gaze. "I'll support your decision either way."

Quain rubbed a hand over his head as if smoothing down imaginary hair. "Flea told us you couldn't heal Yuri even though you tried. I think we shouldn't tell Prince Ryne about the attempt or he'd be upset."

"Upset is putting it mildly," Loren muttered.

Quain ignored him. "Yuri was going to die regardless—"

"But I had no right—"

"Hush, I'm still talking. I think if it was me, and you turned me into the not dead, or whatever you call them, I'd want you to learn as much as you could from me in order to help our army."

"A rather long-winded way to say he agrees with Odd," Loren said.

I glanced at Flea. "Quain just had to talk it through." And he made another good point. While my heart agreed with Flea, the logical choice would be to wait. "Let's hear what Ryne has to say first."

Flea's face paled. I turned to him. "Remember, it's your magic. *You* decide if and when you'll use it. Not Ryne. Not me. Not anyone."

"Yeah, but Prince Ryne will talk circles around me, confusing me, and the next I'd know I'd be doing what he wants."

"Just follow your instincts." I reached out to touch his shoulder.

He jumped back in alarm. Stung, I stood with my hand hovering over empty space. I'd thought I had achieved the maximum amount of guilt a person could ever feel, but I was wrong.

We had a single day before we needed to leave to rendezvous with Captain Drisana. I informed Lieutenant Macon of the situation with Yuri, since those of us who knew were included in the rescue mission.

"He needs no care. He won't move. Just make sure no one enters this cavern."

Macon eyed Yuri with a queasy expression. Yuri remained on the cot.

The lieutenant gestured to Yuri. "You sure he won't move."

"Yes. I've sent a message to Prince Ryne. Once I hear from him, I'll decide what to do with Yuri."

"What if you don't return from the mission?"

Good question. "Then follow Prince Ryne's advice."

"And if he causes problems before then?"

"He shouldn't. But in that case, you can decapitate him."

Not happy about the situation, Macon grumbled, but agreed to assign a guard at the cavern's entrance.

I spent the rest of the day checking on my patients with Ginger. Flea avoided me, dashing away any time I even stepped in his direction. I would have laughed if it didn't hurt so much. The monkeys and Odd packed equipment and sharpened their swords, preparing for the mission. Gathering extra medical supplies, I put together an aid kit in case we had injuries.

We planned to leave an hour before dawn. Most of the team settled down next to the fire right after supper. Flea planted himself between Quain and Loren. They'd only had about four hours of sleep two nights ago. Me, too. But the thought of Tohon's sleek voice invading my dreams prevented me from lying down. He would gloat with glee, claiming Yuri was more proof that I carried his magic. Bad enough my own fears whispered that very same thing.

A few hours later, Ginger guided me to an empty cot. "Sleep. Or you'll be useless for the mission," she said, pressing down on my shoulders.

I perched on the edge, uncertain.

"Do you want a sleeping draft?" Her stiff-backed posture meant she wouldn't go away until I stretched out. She flicked her long brown braid over her shoulder, waiting for my answer.

Ginger reminded me of Loren—practical, intelligent, and stubborn when it suited her. Like now. Around forty years old, she didn't tolerate overly whiny patients, either.

"No, thanks."

"Then what are you waiting for? An order from the prince?"

I smiled for an instant. Should I tell her about how well I obeyed orders from Ryne?

Ginger pointed to the pillow.

"Okay, okay." I kicked off my boots and eased back onto the cot, resting my head on the pillow. Every muscle relaxed as a heaviness spread throughout my body. "Are you always this bossy?"

"Only when needed." She remained standing next to the cot. "Stop fighting it and close your eyes."

"Yes, sir." I managed to provoke a slight grin from Ginger before she faded. "All right, Tohon, your turn."

*"My turn for what, my dear?"*

*"Tell me things I don't want to hear. Your turn to gloat."*

*We walked through a forest, holding hands. I gazed at the greenery, flush with life. No autumn colors. Familiar clumps of trees and bushes passed and I realized we were in the silent-training area near Zabin.*

*"There's no need to gloat. You've finally accepted the truth. And see what you've learned already."*

*"That I'm capable of doing horrible things?"*

*"Don't be so hard on yourself, my dear. Experimenting and learning are essential. You already discovered quite a bit about the Lilys and how the toxin and serum work. You may even find a cure for the toxin and save lots of lives."*

*"Searching for a cure created the plague, Tohon."* As he was well aware, since he'd helped the healers with their research. *"I'm not going to be the cause of another one."*

*"How do you know another one hasn't already been started? You've even considered how strange it was for Ryne to get sick years after being exposed to the disease. And don't forget, I know all about Death Lily toxin. I've been experimenting with it for a long time."*

*Horror welled. "Did you produce a different strain?"*

*"Have you ever wondered why I helped the Healer's Guild?"*

*"You're dodging my question."*

*"Indulge me."*

*I mulled it over. "You had the time since your father picked your cousin to be his heir."*

*"Ouch. Keep thinking."*

*"Your magic makes all the lady healers swoon so I think you had your pick of evening companions."*

*He smirked. "The perks of being a life magician. But I was after more than a warm bed. Think devious thoughts, my dear."*

*In boarding school Tohon had wanted one thing: to be crowned king in his final year. Instead, Ryne had won the crown. But to Tohon, it was considerably more than a political exercise. He desired a kingdom more than anything. What would he do to gain it?*

*I stopped, shocked to my core, gaping at Tohon's serene expression. "You spread the plague. You murdered six million people."*

*"It's not murder, my dear. It's called biological warfare."*


"Avry, wake up." Odd sat on the edge of the cot. "You're yelling in your sleep."

"Sorry."

"Don't apologize to me. You're the one dreaming about Tohon."

Oh, great, I'd called Tohon's name. "I—"

"No need to explain. I understand. Tohon's the stuff of nightmares."

Sitting up, I said, "Is it time to go?"

"Soon. Cook made us a pot of oatmeal. Go and eat breakfast before we leave. Everything looks better with a full stomach." He patted his.

"Odd's philosophy on life?"

He smiled. "Is there any other?"

"Not worth listening to, I'm sure."

"Damn straight."

After consuming a bowl of steaming oatmeal, I gathered my pack and joined the monkeys, Flea, and the odd squad outside the cave. The coming dawn turned the eastern sky a charcoal gray. Odd signaled and, without a word, we headed northwest to the rendezvous point.

My thoughts returned to my dream. Had Tohon released the plague as a form of biological warfare, or was it just me thinking devious thoughts? The only reason Tohon's efforts to become king of all the realms had any chance of succeeding was because of the plague. Did it matter if he'd caused it or not? That knowledge couldn't change the past, and everyone already knew he was a monster. Why couldn't he try what Jael did and marry into the position? If the plague hadn't killed Estrid's son, Stanslov, it would have worked for Jael.

I returned to Tohon. Would he create a second form of the plague to use later? Kerrick had said one of Tohon's spies had attacked Ryne before he fell ill. The assassin had wrapped his hands around the prince's throat. And Yuri's encounter with the enemy had resulted in a gash on his neck. Did that mean the attackers were sick, too? They had killed the man who'd touched Ryne, but Yuri's opponent might still be alive. Doubtful I could find him, though.

Another devious thought struck. What if Sepp already knew that those who died from the plague were immune to the Death Lily toxin? What if he and Cellina had purposely released another form of the plague so they could create dead soldiers resistant to Ryne's best defense? Blow darts filled with toxin had been the most effective in neutralizing the dead soldiers who all wore neck protectors. A soldier had to be close to use the skull jab, which had less success.

My thoughts churned as we traveled through the forest in silent mode. No one spoke and, when we stopped for the night, we ate cold rations because it was too dangerous to light a fire. Odd set up a watch schedule.

Wrapped in my cloak, I curled up on the ground. Flea and the monkeys kept their distance from me as they'd done all day. I didn't blame them. If I'd seen one of them awaken the dead, I'd be keeping out of reach, too.

We arrived at the rendezvous point late the next afternoon. The location was a mile south of Estrid's manor house outside Zabin. A woman with short blond hair waited with two men. They wore civilian clothes, but their movements and body language pegged them as military.

"I'm Drisana from Ronel Realm. You must be Avry." The blonde woman held out her hand.

Hearing the correct realm, I shook her hand. "Yes, I'm Avry."

Drisana wouldn't let go. "Prove it."

"How?"

"Prince Ryne says you have a *powerful* handshake."

Oh. I sent a small bit of magic into her fingers, zapping them.

She clenched my hand harder, but otherwise her face showed no reaction. I increased the intensity.

The muscles along her jaw tightened. "Impressive." She released her grip.

I pulled away and gestured to my companions, introducing them.

She nodded. "Here's the plan. My team will lead an attack on the enemy bivouacking in the fields near the manor house. It will draw the soldiers from the house. At that time your team will breach the manor, find High Priestess Estrid and her staff, revive them, and leave."

Her tone suggested it would be easy.

"Where do we meet up after we rescue them?" Odd asked.

"Your team will head straight east. Another squad will be waiting to escort the survivors to Prince Ryne. My team will go north so don't wait for us," Drisana said. "I'm also assigning an additional squad to your team."

Odd nodded. "Good."

"What if we run into too many defenders inside the house?" Loren asked.

"Save whoever you can and get the hell out. The High Priestess is the priority."

"What time?" I asked.

"A few hours after midnight. Position your team near the manor. You'll know when we attack. Get in and get out as fast as possible. Understand?"

"Yes," Odd and I said in unison.

Odd glanced at me then turned to Drisana. "Captain, did Prince Ryne say who is going to lead our part of the mission?"

She gave him a tight smile. "If you have to ask, then it's not you, Sergeant."

Quain stifled a snicker.

"My instructions from the prince indicated Healer Avry would take point. You're familiar with the house. Correct?" she asked me.

"Yes. Has anyone confirmed that Estrid and her staff are still in the ballroom?"

"Our latest intel suggests they remain inside the house. As for their exact location… That's harder to determine."

And that would be a no. "All right, where's the other squad? Do they know how to go silent?"

"I believe Sergeant Saul's men had the training."

Odd and I grinned at each other.

"Where is he?" I asked.

"He said he'd meet you over by the rear entrance of the manor."

Perfect. "Thanks. Good luck."

"You, too."

"Let's go," I said to my team.

We headed northeast, angling around to stay within the forest and to avoid being seen by anyone near or inside the house. As we drew closer, a few off notes sounded nearby. I stopped the team.

"Come out, Saul," I called. "You're good, but not *that* good."

He stepped from behind a thick tree trunk. "I didn't want to startle you." Saul wore camouflaged fatigues. With his buzzed blond hair and blue eyes, he appeared to be Drisana's slightly older brother.

"Yeah, right," Odd teased.

Saul's gaze swept my companions. "Nice to see so many familiar faces."

"And we're back in familiar territory," I said.

"At least we're not trapped by the dead," Odd said.

"Yet," Flea added, meeting my gaze for the first time in days.

Lovely. I needed to have a little chat with Flea before the mission. Focusing on the matter at hand, I asked Saul, "Where's the rest of your squad?"

"A little farther north. I figured you'd remembered that back entrance."

Hard to forget. I'd used it to escape Tohon. "Any activity?"

"Nope. Been quiet all day."

I glanced at the darkening sky. "Let's go over the plan and get into position before it's full dark."

"What's there to plan?" Odd asked. "It's a straightforward mission."

"Uh-huh. And what happens when we reach the ballroom and no one is there?" I asked.

"We search the rest of the house."

"All of us together? Or do we split up and search different areas?"

"Oh."

"And what if we're attacked? Do we stay and fight or retreat?"

"Gee, Avry, you sound more like a general than a healer," Odd grumbled.

"I was a healer on the run for three years. I've learned the hard way to have plenty of backup plans."

"All right, you made your point. What are the contingency plans?" Odd asked.

I told him. He wasn't happy about a few of them, but since I was in charge, he couldn't do anything about it. Once the team understood, they moved to their positions to wait for the signal. I pulled Flea aside before he joined the monkeys.

He shook off my hand and stared at the ground.

"Flea, we need to talk."

No response, but he didn't turn away.

"You're going to need my energy to break the stasis trapping Estrid and the others."

His gaze snapped to mine. "What if I don't want to free them? No one asked me."

"Didn't Ryne discuss—"

"No, he just assumed I'd do it."

"Then why didn't you say something sooner?"

"'Cause I'm gonna do it. It's important. It's just… I don't want to use my powers. Look at what you did to Yuri with yours. It's horrible. I hate magic."

Flea had rotten timing. "I understand. I'm hating it, too,

right now. But let's just get through this mission, and we'll talk it through, okay?"

"There won't be anything to discuss. Once this mission is complete, I'm done using magic."

"It is your choice, Flea. Let's hope Sepp lied when he claimed he'd put Belen into a magical stasis."

"I'd wake Belen."

"Why?"

"He's my friend."

"Oh, so you'll help your friends but not the strangers who also need you?"

"Yes," Flea said with a belligerent tone.

"Hmm. Maybe I should do the same thing. I'd have more energy and not as many scars. Except…"

Flea refused to take the bait. He kept his sullen expression.

"Except, Poppa Bear would be disappointed in me, and I'd have a hard time sleeping at night, so I guess I'm stuck helping everyone." I shrugged. "Anyway, for this mission, you'll need me to share my energy with you. Will you be able to?"

"Yes. Is that all?"

I studied Flea, hoping this new attitude was just his way of dealing with his magic. Eventually, he'd accept it. Unless my mistake with Yuri had scared him away from using his magic for good. Yet another consequence of my actions.

"Yeah, we're done. For now," I said.

Perched on a low limb of a maple tree, I peered at the dark manor house. No lanterns glowed in any of the rooms facing our direction. A good sign. Bursts of laughter from the soldiers' camp floated on the chilly air. Other noises reached us as well, but none indicated distress. The moonlight cast shadows on the ground. At three-quarters full, it provided almost too much illumination for my comfort.

I traced the limb's bark with a finger. No magic hummed under my touch. Sadness filled me. How long should I wait and hope? Would I turn angry and bitter as years passed without any news of Kerrick? Or would I wall off my emotions? Actually, that last one sounded appealing. No grief, no guilt, no fear, and no worries. I hadn't been without at least one of them since the plague started six years ago. Of course, the wall would block joy, happiness, and love. Not like there was a lot of that going on right now, anyway. And the future... looked bleak to me.

A shout jolted me from my depressing thoughts. More yells and the rasp of metal followed. Clangs, curses, and thuds meant the other team had engaged the enemy.

We waited a little longer before my small team dashed across the open lawn. I reached the door first. Locked. Loren yanked out his lock picks, while Quain and Flea protected our backs.

"Damn, this has seven pins," Loren muttered.

"Do you need Quain's lightning juice?" I asked.

"No. This is almost... There." The tumbler turned. Loren pushed the door open and checked for guards before motioning the all clear.

Once we were inside, Odd and his squad crossed to the manor, and then Saul's men followed in the third wave. From this point on, we would use hand signals to communicate. Saul and his squad would keep our exit clear as we infiltrated the house. Odd's squad stayed with me, the monkeys, and Flea. We headed to the second-floor ballroom.

I took them up the back stairs. Cracking the door open, I listened. No sounds echoed off the marble-tiled floors. We eased into the hallway. No one had lit the sconces. Darkness lined the gaps under the doors. The area appeared deserted. And smelled of dust.

We reached the ballroom without trouble. The large double glass doors had been closed, but not locked. In the ballroom, moonlight streamed through the long windows like white gauzy curtains. Motionless bodies littered the ground.

Odd's squad moved in first in case of an ambush. He opened the doors, pushing them wide before they rushed in. They checked the other doors before signaling the all clear.

Women dressed in gowns and men wearing evening clothes lay in a haphazard pattern on the floor. Large crystal chandeliers hung from the ceiling, but otherwise the place was empty.

The monkeys and Flea fanned out to check the victims and search for Estrid. The High Priestess had worn a red silk gown with gold brocade when she had pledged loyalty to Tohon before Sepp had trapped her and her staff in magical stases. Flea would save her first.

Odd raised his hand, waving me over. He stood next to a woman in red.

Estrid? I moved closer.

The prone bodies surged to their feet.

# KERRICK

Even camouflaged by Kerrick's forest magic, Harper still remained a big noisy horse. While they traveled twice as fast as Kerrick could on foot, they attracted too much attention. A few patrols already tracked him and soon he'd be too close to Zabin to ride.

He stayed on horseback as long as he dared, releasing Harper late on the second day. Unfortunately, he still had to cover five miles and would miss the rendezvous time by hours. Kerrick hoped they planned to attack during the night or tomorrow morning as he headed south. As long as he caught up to Avry at some point, he'd be happy.

Dodging enemy patrols slowed his pace. And their numbers grew as he neared the city. He stopped for a rest and considered. Ryne had said Cellina pulled most of her forces to Vyg in order to lure him to Zabin and attack his flank. Did his scouts underestimate how many soldiers had remained?

With his new and improved senses, he felt whole companies moving through the forest. Way too many for Ryne's small forces to handle. Somehow Cellina had managed to trick the scout. Or the scout was one of Cellina's spies. He remained too far away to sense if any of Cellina's troops waited south of Zabin.

Ryne's comments repeated in his mind. *You're my best scout…
I really need accurate information.* If Kerrick hadn't been sick, he
would have sensed the extra soldiers and averted the major
fiasco that was poised to happen.

Despite the danger, Kerrick increased his pace to a run. He
had to warn the team in charge of creating the distraction. If
he stopped them, then Avry and her team wouldn't go into
the manor house, where Kerrick was sure another ambush
waited for them.

He arrived too late. The sounds of fighting reached him
before he neared the camp outside Zabin. And through his
connection to the living green, he discovered another trap
was poised to spring a few yards inside the forest. A wall of
soldiers lined up, creating a blockade, which would prevent
Captain Drisana's team from retreating to the north or east.

Kerrick concentrated on the string of soldiers and determined it hooked behind the manor house.

Not good. Avry's exit was obstructed, as well. He dug
his hands into the soil, strengthening his bond, seeking ir-
ritations to the south. Sure enough, another one of Cellina's
platoons lurked. Damn. The scout had to be a double agent.
How could someone miss the mass of humanity occupying
the woods around Zabin?

He pushed his awareness farther out. A group of ten intruders waited to the east. This group was well past the blockade
and probably one of Ryne's.

Kerrick considered. He needed to create an exit for the others. But how? Yanking his hands from the dirt, he jogged east.

It didn't take him long to find the squad. He crept closer.
The moonlight shone bright enough to observe them. They
wore the green fatigues that marked them as part of Estrid's
holy army. Nice to see not all of them had taken off once Estrid had been captured. Good news, except he didn't recog-

nize any of them. Quiet and watchful with weapons in hand, they appeared to be on alert.

Pulling magic, Kerrick transformed to normal. Not wishing to scare them, he backed up a few yards before crunching through the fallen leaves. He spread his hands wide so they didn't skewer him on sight.

With plenty of warning, the squad hid and then surrounded him as soon as he walked into their "trap." One man hung back. Kerrick spotted the sergeant strips on the man's sleeves.

"I'm on your side," Kerrick said. "Prince Ryne sent me." Not exactly true, but close enough. He explained about the blockade. "We need to clear a path for our soldiers."

The eight men and two women looked to their sergeant when Kerrick finished.

"You certainly know an awful lot about the mission," the sergeant said. "Who are you?"

"Prince Kerrick."

"Really? We heard he died fighting the northern tribes."

"You heard wrong. Look, Sergeant…"

"Vic."

"We don't have time for this."

"I'm not risking my squad. If that blockade is there like you said, a dozen of us aren't going to make a dent."

"We only need to clear one section," Kerrick said.

"And how do you propose we do that?" Vic asked. "As soon as we strike, the whole line will turn on us."

"I've a plan."

The sergeant laughed. "Good for you. Let us know how it works out."

Expecting resistance from the man, Kerrick encouraged the vines growing on a nearby tree to snake toward Vic's head. "There's a section of the wall that's not as closely connected to the others due to a dried-out creek that makes a deep dip in the terrain. My plan is to take out that section and replace Cellina's soldiers with yours."

"You're mad. One shout and we're done."

"Then I'll make sure they won't make a sound."

"You?"

"I'm a forest mage."

"Okay, I'll play along, *Prince* Kerrick. Just how—"

The vines looped around Vic's mouth and head, making an effective gag. When the man tried to use his weapon, the vines circled his upper body, trapping his arms. Half his squad rushed to help, but they were soon entangled, as well.

Before, Kerrick would have expanded all his energy to make those vines move. One perk of being a forest mage. However, now using his magic to look normal drained him.

A sword point pricked Kerrick's neck.

"Stop it now," a woman ordered.

Kerrick inclined his head. "I'm simply demonstrating my plan." The vines retreated, freeing the soldiers.

"Heck of a demonstration." Vic rubbed his cheeks.

"Will you come?" Kerrick asked.

"Yeah, what do you need us to do?"

"I'll trap the soldiers with the vines, but this time I'll also cut off their air supply, knocking them out. You drag them away and then take their place."

"Should we put on their uniforms?"

"No need. It's dark and they're similar enough. Plus we don't have the time. Ready?"

They sheathed their weapons and collected their packs. Kerrick led them back to the blockade.

Once they reached the dried creek bed, Kerrick whispered, "I'm going to disappear. You'll be able to see from here when the vines have done their job. I'll go warn Captain Drisana and send her your way."

Sergeant Vic nodded. Kerrick moved away and dropped his normal look. He edged closer to his targets—eight in all. Thick bushes and thorny briars grew along the creek's raised banks, creating a barrier between those in the dip and the others.

Kerrick knelt on the ground and visualized what he needed the vines to do. Concentrating, he directed the vines to drop down and quickly ensnare the soldiers all at once. While this action didn't require magical energy, his connection to the forest deepened and the task became a physical effort. Sweat soaked his shirt.

A few muffled grunts sounded as the vines captured the enemy, but none loud enough to raise an alarm. When the squad appeared to do their job, Kerrick staggered to his feet. He headed toward the fighting. Keeping to the edge of the forest, he crossed behind the POW camp and stopped.

The two armies fought in the training fields. They appeared to be evenly matched, but Drisana didn't know about the soldiers waiting just to the north. Kerrick scanned the fighters until he saw the familiar blond hair. He hadn't seen her since they trained together up in Ivdel Realm.

Kerrick gathered his magic. He pulled his dadao sword and stepped from the forest, heading straight for Drisana. Each stride drained him. Halfway there, one of Cellina's soldiers intercepted him.

Flashing his thick-bladed sword, Kerrick growled. The young man stared at the nasty-looking weapon and backed away. Kerrick kept moving even though each step cost him. The skirmish resembled…a skirmish. The enemy lacked a certain fierceness, as if the presence of the blockade meant they didn't have to try as hard. At least no dead soldiers fought among them.

He dodged a few other soldiers before joining Drisana. She

glanced at him briefly before continuing her fight. With Kerrick's help, they dispatched the man in no time.

"You look horrible. Did you come back from the dead just for me?" Drisana wiped the blood off her sword.

"I can't stay—" He ducked as a soldier swung his sword, aiming for Kerrick's throat.

Drisana engaged the man. "Go on."

"Don't go north. It's blocked."

She flicked a glance at him before returning her attention to the fight.

"Go east, find a dry creek bed and follow it. Tell your team."

"We have a team inside the manor." She feinted right and slipped her blade under the man's defenses, stabbing him in the stomach.

"I'll let them know." With his energy almost gone, he'd have to ask one of Sergeant Vic's squad.

"You can barely stand. Take Eva, she's fast and quiet." Drisana whistled and then shouted Eva's name.

A small, thin girl who looked to be twelve years old darted around fighters. She joined them in no time.

"Go with Prince Kerrick," Drisana ordered. "He'll fill you in."

"Yes, sir." Eva peered at him with a dubious expression.

He didn't blame her. "This way." Not bothering to see if she followed, he limped toward the forest.

When he entered the woods the strong pull to return eased. However, after a few feet, he sank to the ground. Turning to Eva, he said, "Don't let this scare you." He dropped his normal camouflage.

She appeared impressed by his transformation.

"I need you to deliver a message." Kerrick explained what

he wanted her to do. "Can you show Avry and her team the way out?"

"Yes, sir."

"Go east with them. You can rendezvous with Captain Drisana later."

Eva cocked her head. "What about you?"

"Don't worry about me."

She didn't look convinced.

"The forest will protect me."

"Nice."

He smiled. "Yes, it is. Now go, Drisana will be signaling a retreat soon."

"Yes, sir." She took off at a fast pace.

Kerrick worried she'd get caught. But after a few minutes he realized Drisana was right. Eva was quiet.

Completely exhausted, he lay back on the ground, hoping he'd done enough.

# CHAPTER 9

Drawing hidden weapons, the ambushers dressed in formal clothes attacked. Odd and his men reacted, pulling their swords and engaging them. Flea and the monkeys joined in. I counted the enemy. At least thirty, outnumbering us two to one. And all living.

"Don't use your daggers," I called over the din.

Everyone had coated their knives with Death Lily toxin just in case we encountered the dead. Their swords remained clean in case we engaged living soldiers. No one wished to use the toxin against a living person even if they were the enemy. That would be cruel.

One man lunged toward me. He thrust his sword at my stomach. I twisted. The blade sliced my skin. A line of pain registered distantly as I stepped in close. Unable to use his sword, he dropped it and, in one quick move, wrapped his hands around my neck.

I copied him, but when my fingers touched the back of his neck, I zapped him into unconsciousness.

"Avry, get over here," Odd yelled. He was backed into a corner with three soldiers advancing on him.

Weaving through the fighters, I snuck up on the men who had trapped Odd. I managed to zap two before being knocked to the ground. Two other ambushers picked me up under my arms and held tight. Unable to reach their skin, I kicked them without success. They dragged me toward the door. Icy fear flowed through me.

"Avry, duck," Quain cried.

I leaned forward. Air swept my neck. Then came the sickening sound of a blade cutting through flesh and bone. Warm blood soaked my back and arm. I remained hunched as Quain pulled back for another swing. More blood splattered on me. I wiped it from my face. Two headless bodies lay at my feet.

Quain helped me up.

"Company's coming," Loren called. "Time to retreat."

Only a few ambushers remained. We bolted from the ballroom. Pounding boots and shouts sounded behind us.

"What's the plan?" Odd puffed.

"Get to the stairs," I said.

Not bothering to check for enemies, we raced into the stairwell.

"Can we block the door?" I asked Odd.

He glanced behind. "No time."

We made it to the ground floor, where Saul and his men fought a couple dozen of Cellina's soldiers in the narrow hallway. These also were living and I wondered where the dead soldiers waited to ambush us.

"Oh, good, backup," Saul said, disarming his opponent.

"Except we brought more...uh...friends," Quain said. "How's the escape route?"

"Blocked," Saul said, engaging with another soldier.

"Stairwell," Loren shouted. "Keep them from coming out."

Odd's men moved to stop them. I stood in the middle, unable to help. All my knives had toxin on them.

"Avry," Loren called. He had disarmed a man and held him in a headlock.

I understood and darted in to zap the man into unconsciousness. After that, I zapped anyone my team trapped. We
had a nice surge of energy, pushing both sides back. But with
fatalities and injuries increasing and the large number of opponents, it would only be a matter of time. Fear pulsed in time
with my heart. I kept an eye on Flea. He held his own, fighting with a fierce determination. But for how long?

Should I surrender? I imagined Cellina would be quite
ecstatic to learn I'd been captured. And then I realized she
could threaten to harm Flea, the monkeys, and Odd if I didn't
heal Tohon.

No surrendering for me. This would have to be a fight to
my death. I refused to be put in that horrible position.

A ruckus behind the enemy's line caused a change in dy-
namics. The soldiers eased off their assault against us. It seemed
as if they were being attacked from the opposite direction.
Saul's squad took advantage of their distraction and increased
the pressure.

Then the stairwell group retreated.

"They're probably going to get reinforcements," Loren said.

"Then let's not linger," Quain said.

It didn't take long for us to dispatch the remaining soldiers.
The reason for our change in luck stood farther down the hallway. A group of caregivers from the infirmary held hollow
tubes up to their mouths.

My team hesitated, not sure what to make of this new de-
velopment. But I did. Christina, who had been my assistant
when I'd worked here, led the group, standing out in front.
She signaled and they all put their weapons down.

"It's okay." I pushed my way through. When I reached
Christina, I hugged her briefly. "I'm so glad you survived
the occupation!"

She gave me a tight smile that didn't reach her eyes. "You

taught me so much, they couldn't get rid of me. Although I'd rather have gone with you."

Ah, the reason for the stiffness. "I'm sorry. There was no time. Noelle had knocked Tohon out. We only had a few minutes." But I had a plan in place before that. Why hadn't I thought of taking Christina with us? Because all my focus had been on getting my sister to a Peace Lily before she died. Didn't work.

"Thanks for saving us," Odd said. He gestured to the fallen soldiers. "What did you use?"

"Darts filled with sleeping draft. We thought we should be prepared in case Cellina changed her mind about us."

"Good idea. Uh… Not that I'm ungrateful, but why did you help us?"

Christina met my gaze. "I heard Avry's name and came out to investigate." She shrugged. "If she is captured, things will go from bad to worse."

"Do you know if there are more soldiers coming?" Odd asked.

"No."

"Let's go before we find out." Saul signaled a retreat. "Back door, now!"

The odd squad led the way. A few of our team had to be helped.

"Come with us," I said to Christina. "All of you."

The caregivers exchanged surprised glances.

"But our patients…" Christina pressed her hands to her chest.

"Now or never, ladies," Saul said.

"We've set up an infirmary. You can work there if you want," I said.

"All right," Christina said. "I'm in."

A couple of the other caregivers joined us, but most stayed behind. We raced toward the exit. Christina kept pace with me.

"Why did you come back?" she asked.

"We came for Estrid."

"She's not here."

"Do you know where she is?" I asked.

"In the POW camp with the others."

I paused. "Is she…"

"Yes, she's still frozen."

Before I could process her comments, we reached the exit and stopped.

"What's going on?" Odd demanded, shoving people out of his way.

I followed Odd. Something blocked the door. Or rather someone.

A small girl stood with her arms crossed. "I've a message for Healer Avry."

"Who are you?" Odd asked.

"That's Eva, one of Captain Drisana's scouts," a man said. He stood near the front.

Odd jerked his thumb at me hovering behind him. "She's here. Now spit it out."

"You can't go straight east through the woods. There's a line of soldiers waiting for you. You need to follow the dry creek bed in order to get out. It's just north of here, then it turns east," Eva said.

"Is this from the captain?" Odd asked.

"No. The captain didn't know about the blockade. Prince Kerrick told her and then he sent me."

Did she just say… My heart stopped beating. I pushed Odd out of my way. "You've seen Kerrick?"

"Yes."

"Where?" I demanded.

"He's in the forest. He said the forest will protect him."

"We need to go, now," Saul said. "We'll figure this out later."

"All right. Go! Find the creek bed," I ordered.

They rushed out, heading north. When the girl moved to follow, I grabbed her arm. "Not yet. Show me where you last saw Kerrick."

"Now?" Eva glanced around. Shouts and a battle noises emanated from the northwest. "Captain Drisana is going to be retreating soon. And once that happens—"

"Those ambushers won't remain in place. Just tell me where he is. Please!"

She stared at me. "I'll take you. Come on."

We followed the others until we reached the forest, then the girl turned west, back toward the fighting and traveling just a few feet inside the woods. She moved with a quick confidence. But best of all, her passage was quiet.

I wished I could say the same about my heart. It thudded so loud, it drowned out the yells and clangs of metal nearby. Suppressing all hope, I focused on keeping close to Eva. It was quite possible she was mistaken about Kerrick. And to believe anything else at this time would be setting myself up for a crushing disappointment.

Eva paused. I searched the surrounding area for any soldiers. The high fence of the POW camp showed through the thinning trees. Dark forms raced along the outside of it. Drisana must have signaled the retreat.

"He was here," Eva said. "Then he turned the same color as the forest."

Only Kerrick could camouflage himself like that. Despite my best efforts, hope surged. "He probably left. This is a dangerous spot."

"No, he was sick or something. He was lying on the ground."

Oh, no. I touched a nearby bush, seeking the tingle of his magic. Nothing. Don't panic. Kerrick might be unconscious and in need of my help. He couldn't have gone far. Remembering how I found him before, I drew in a deep breath. Damp earth, the scent of fallen leaves, and smoke from the fires burning in the soldiers' camp all laced the air. No spring sunshine.

I considered. If he was injured, he'd go farther into the forest. Crawling on my hands and knees, I searched the ground, exploring with my hands.

"Uh, Healer Avry…" Eva said.

"Go. Before you're—"

"Are you insane?" Loren asked. Quain and Flea stood next to him. The fierce expressions on their faces meant they'd carry me from the woods if they had to.

"If Kerrick's here, he's safer than you. Come on!" Loren grabbed my elbow, hauling me to my feet.

"No." I yanked my arm from his grasp and stumbled back. An invisible hand wrapped around my ankle.

"Avry?" asked a bush.

I squealed with pure joy and crouched down, finding Kerrick. Arms snaked around my back as he pulled me close. The rest of the world disappeared as I clung to him, breathing in his scent, feeling his chest move. Bliss.

"Avry," he sighed.

"Where did she go?" Flea asked.

"Flea's here?" Kerrick released me, but I stayed next to him as he moved into a sitting position.

His magic buzzed through me and his camouflage disappeared. The monkeys and Flea beamed at him.

Kerrick frowned. "Get out of here before the blockade—"

The unmistakable ruckus of an army on the move exploded around us.

"Too late," Eva said. She balanced on the balls of her feet as if ready to bolt.

Kerrick pushed up the sleeves of his arms. "Grab on, gentlemen." He grasped my hand with his. "Eva, you, too."

The others huddled around him, touching his arms. Kerrick's magic stopped and we all blended in with the forest. Strange.

"Cool," Quain said.

"Quiet," Kerrick whispered. "They're coming."

With Kerrick in the middle, we drew in close together, making our group as small as possible for six people. No one moved.

Soon, soldiers passed us. A few quite close, and one man headed directly toward us. We braced for impact, but he stumbled, tripping on a vine and missing us by inches. In fact, many of the soldiers who ventured too close to us had problems with that pesky vine.

As we sat there for over an hour, I learned a few things. Kerrick didn't use his magic on that vine or our camouflage, which was the opposite of how it worked in the past. And after the fight in the manor house, we were in serious need of a bath. Except Eva, who smelled like roses and kept unnaturally still the entire time.

A million questions for Kerrick bubbled up my throat, but I held them for later. When we escaped this situation, he'd have some serious explaining to do. Funny, I hadn't thought *if* we escaped. Guess my outlook was rather optimistic. Hard not to be when I held Kerrick's hand.

After another hour or so, Kerrick said, "Most of them have moved east. We can sneak north."

We stood and stretched, unkinking stiff muscles. The blood

had dried on my clothes. Kerrick had let go of my hand. He no longer blended in with the forest, but lines of strain etched his gaunt face. Thinner and paler than I'd ever seen him, Kerrick wiped a hand over the stubble on his chin.

I laced my fingers in his, feeling his magic again. Sharing my energy with him, I beamed at him. He flashed me a smile in response.

What a night. All that work and we didn't rescue Estrid. I glanced at the POW camp. So close.

Flea noticed the direction of my gaze. "How much time do we have until they come back?" he asked Kerrick.

"The woods are crowded with patrols. Any one of them could return. Why?" he asked.

"Estrid's in the POW camp. We could get her out before—"

"Too risky," I interrupted. "I'm sure the camp is well guarded."

Flea grinned. "It is, but we left a back door."

"Oh, yeah," Quain said. "Prince Ryne said it might come in handy someday."

"Back door?" I asked.

"An escape route," Loren explained. "When we hid inside during Tohon's encirclement, we used a hidden exit to come and go without being seen."

"How long would it take?" Kerrick asked.

"Not long to get inside the fence, but the complex has five or six buildings."

Kerrick considered. "We have two hours until dawn. You have one hour to find Estrid, and then you have to return regardless."

"Are you coming?" Loren asked.

"No, I'll stay here and ensure no one sets up an ambush," Kerrick said.

Eva offered to stay with Kerrick. "Probably safer with you guys than trying to rendezvous with the captain right now."

Quain huffed. "You don't know us very well."

I hesitated. The desire to remain with Kerrick warred with the need to rescue Estrid. Duty won.

"Don't go anywhere," I ordered Kerrick, stabbing a finger at the ground.

"I won't," he said, but a haunted look clouded his eyes.

"Promise?"

"Oh, yes." He leaned in and kissed me.

I wrapped my arms around his neck, deepening the kiss.

"Uh…Avry, time's running out," Loren said.

Breaking away, I gazed at Kerrick. "I'll be back."

He smiled. "You'd better."

I joined the others.

"Our door leads right into the training ring. So we'll check the converted stables first, then the smaller buildings," Loren instructed. "We're only saving Estrid. Most of the guards should be by the front entrance, but the first sign of unfriendlies, we retreat. Understood?"

Nodding, I found it interesting how Loren had stepped up to take the lead on this mission. He went first, followed by Quain, Flea, and finally me. We crept to the complex. Built of large barn doors tied to thick posts, the solid fence loomed over us. Keeping to the fence's shadow, we traveled a few yards to the west.

When Loren signaled a halt, Quain pulled a thin metal pick from his pocket. He ran the edge of the pick along small cracks in the wood. Then he hooked the pick into a divot and pulled a three-foot-high panel away from the fence. Ah, the back door.

"Clever," I whispered to Flea.

"Remember when the POWs escaped and Prince Ryne's men helped fix the fence?" Flea asked.

"They added this then?"

"Yup."

Wow. Ryne had really been thinking ahead.

Loren shushed us and climbed through the opening. Quain gestured for Flea and me to go next. He entered last, closing the door behind him. We stepped on the soft dirt of the training ring. No longer used for horses, this area had been the exercise yard for the POWs when Estrid had been in charge. The roof overhead blocked most of the moonlight.

After pausing to let our eyes adjust to the darkness, Loren continued. To me, the guys resembled darker blobs against the blackness. I wondered how we would find Estrid without light.

Before entering into the main stable area, Loren dug in the loose dirt off to the left. A faint metallic jingle sounded. Then he reached up along the wall and this time a clang rang out. Quain passed me, joining Loren. He muttered and cursed under his breath. Eventually a small yellow glow filled a bull's-eye lantern. Loren slid the shutter until only a thin beam of light pierced the darkness.

They'd left a back door and an escape kit. Handy. We crept into what had once been stables. Now the stalls all had metal bars and thick locks. As Loren swept the light over one empty cell after another, I considered. Why would Cellina bother to lock up people who couldn't move? Who needed no care?

I caught up to Loren. "She's not here. Is there a storage shed inside the complex?"

He glanced at Quain and Flea.

"There's that hay barn," Flea said. "There wasn't anything inside it except a couple straw bales."

"Show us," Loren said.

Flea took point and we stayed close behind him. He slipped

from the stables. Loren closed the lantern, hiding the light. We scanned the area for any guards before crossing the open space between buildings. A creepy sensation raised the hairs on my arms as I imagined hidden gazes watching us.

Leading us to the smaller barn, Flea paused outside the entrance. Was another ambush waiting for us? He pulled on the door. The hinges squeaked. We hunched over as if under attack.

"Sissies," Quain said as if he hadn't flinched, as well. He entered first.

We filed in around him.

Loren moved the lantern's slide, letting the light out. "Bingo."

Prone forms lay on the bales and were piled on the floor. They appeared to have been tossed without care. They all wore yellow POW jumpsuits. We spread out, searching the bodies for Estrid. Except Flea. He stood near the door, almost pressing against it. His arms were wrapped around his stomach and he had a panicked look on his pale face.

"Found her," Loren said.

Estrid had been placed on a stack of bales near the back.

Loren waved Flea over. "Come on, Flea, we're running out of time."

"I..." Flea swallowed. "Can you bring her over here?"

"Why?" Loren asked.

"He's going to be sick if he gets too close," I said, moving to join Loren. "Quain, we need your muscles."

Stepping on a few of the others, the three of us managed to carry Estrid to Flea. With a queasy grimace, Flea crouched next to her. He touched her forehead then spun to heave, spilling the contents of his stomach in a wet plop. I placed my hand on the back of his sweaty neck, sending him energy. After a few moments, he stopped.

"What—" Estrid started.

"We'll explain everything later," Loren said. He helped her to stand.

"Who—"

I turned so she could see my face.

"Oh, Avry." She glanced around. "My staff?"

"No time," Loren said. "Let's go."

With Estrid in the middle, we retraced our steps back to the stables and out the back door. Estrid tsked over the hidden exit, but otherwise remained quiet. Impressive. My anxiety increased as we entered the forest. Would Kerrick still be here?

We returned to the location we'd left Kerrick and Eva. Sounds of moving soldiers filled the forest around us, but that wasn't why I panicked. Kerrick had disappeared again.

"Now what?" Quain asked.

Loren scanned the forest. "North?"

"You asking or telling," Quain said to Loren.

"Kerrick said north," I said before they could launch into an argument. "We go north." And hope we'd find Kerrick and Eva on the way.

This time, I took point, moving slowly to compensate for Estrid's noisy inexperience. Dawn's rays helped with our progress, but the sunlight reflected off of Estrid's bright yellow jumpsuit. I worried the garish color would make her visible for miles. Digging into my pack, I removed my cloak and gave it to Estrid. The gray color didn't clash as much against the browns, reds and yellows of the forest. That thought led right to Kerrick as all my thoughts had since we rescued Estrid. Had his eyes changed color with the season? Where was he?

After a few hours of dodging patrols, Loren asked, "Where are we going?"

Good question. If we turned to the northeast, we could reach Ryne's headquarters. If we went east, we could rendezvous with the others and return to the infirmary. But without Kerrick's forest magic, I'd no idea how many of Cellina's troops were between us and either destination.

"I'm open to suggestions," I said to Loren.

He glanced at Flea. "I think we should find a safe spot to rest."

A good idea, except I didn't know where we would be safe. I considered my options. A cave? Perfect if we could find one. The trees? I gazed into the canopy. No low limbs and the coverage would be thin. A cluster of Lilys? They would keep any sane person away. I pulled off my pack and found the Lily map.

"Where are we?" I asked.

"North of Zabin," Quain said.

"Really, Quain? Do you think that's helpful?" I snapped, then regretted my irritation. "Sorry. Any idea how far north?"

"Six miles," Eva said, surprising us all.

Just like his namesake, Flea jumped a foot.

"Where's Kerrick?" I asked.

"He should be here soon."

"Why didn't you wait for us?"

Eva frowned at my harsh tone. "A patrol came through and we had to move. Since then we've been clearing a path for you."

"And you couldn't tell us this?" I demanded.

She put her hands on her hips. "We didn't have time to come back and tell you what you should have figured out on your own." Eva gestured to the surrounding forest. "Why else would there only be a few patrols around?"

I bit back my reply. With all my other worries, I hadn't thought about the ease of our travel.

"I'm sorry, Avry," Kerrick said into the silence. "I know I promised to stay, but we had the opportunity to lead the enemy on a merry chase, enticing them farther away from you." Lines of exhaustion marked his face. He all but swayed on his feet.

My anger dissipated. "We need to find a safe place to rest. Any ideas?"

Kerrick smiled. "There's a cave nearby."

I groaned. "I had a feeling you'd say that."

Nearby to Kerrick didn't match my definition of nearby. We hiked four miles to the northeast. I held his hand and shared my energy with him. His magic vibrated up my arm with a pleasant tingle. He squeezed my fingers in gratitude, which alarmed me. Normally, he'd have shaken off my efforts, claiming he didn't wish to sap my strength.

He must have depleted his energy luring the enemy patrols away. Guilt over my earlier anger surfaced. Even though he had a legitimate reason, I still felt...bereft.

We reached the cave system by midafternoon. Kerrick and Eva collected firewood while we gathered stones to build a fire pit. Flea supervised. He'd refused my offer to help him during the trip and had plopped onto the ground as soon as we arrived. Estrid sat next to him. She huddled under my cloak. I studied her expression for a moment. She hadn't said anything all day and I worried she might be in shock.

After we arranged the pit to Loren's liking, Eva entered carrying an armload of kindling. "There's another pile of thicker logs just outside." Eva dropped the thin branches into the pit.

"Hey!" Loren pulled them out. "You can't just dump them there."

"Why not?" she asked, confused.

"He has a whole *system*," Quain explained. "Each branch must be in its proper place to construct a pyramid, which is the optimal configuration for wood-burning perfection."

"I don't hear you complaining when you're warming your fat a—" Loren glanced at Eva "—rear end."

"It's not fat, it's all muscle," Quain said.

As they argued, I retrieved the bigger pile, noting another one had been stacked next to it. I scanned the woods, searching for Kerrick.

Eva joined me and scooped it up. "Are they always like that?" she asked.

"Yes. Another friend of ours nicknamed them the monkeys."

"Fitting." She returned to the cave.

I waited, but Kerrick must have gone for another armload of wood. Inside, flames stretched toward the ceiling, merrily consuming Loren's pyramid. Quain joked with Flea and it almost seemed like old times. Kerrick was no longer missing and we just needed to find our lost Poppa Bear.

Eva ducked back outside while I placed my load of wood onto the growing pile next to Loren.

She brought in another stack. "Prince Kerrick said he'd take first watch."

"Oh, no. He has lots of explaining to do," I said.

"So do you," Estrid said.

Glad she appeared to be snapping out of her funk, I didn't look forward to filling her in on the events of the last two months. "After we eat," I promised before dashing outside.

Another pile of wood had arrived, but Kerrick wasn't in sight. I waited for a few moments. Unable to keep still, I strode into the forest. The desire to yell for him climbed up my throat. Instead, I stomped through the fallen leaves, crunching them under my boots and not caring that I made noise.

"Avry, settle down," Kerrick said. He leaned against a tree trunk a few feet away.

"What's going on?"

"Someone has to keep watch."

"Uh-huh. What's going on?"

He sank to the ground and rested his forehead on his knees. Alarmed, I knelt next to him. Touching his arm, I said, "It can't be that bad. You're alive! Whatever else is going on we can deal with it. What happened to you?"

Kerrick lifted his head. Leaning back on the trunk, he pulled me close, wrapping his arm around me. I snuggled in, pressing my cheek against his chest, almost content to listen to him breathe. Did it matter what happened? He was here with me.

After a few heartbeats, he said, "I promised you I wouldn't die from the Death Lily toxin. Do you remember?"

"Of course. I've thought of nothing else since that night. It's what kept me going when everyone said you'd died."

"Your faith is what kept me alive."

Warmth spread through my chest, but I waited, sensing there was more.

"But it came with a price."

# KERRICK

Avry pulled away from him. It was what he'd feared all along. Ever since they'd reunited, he wondered how they could be together when he couldn't leave the forest, when he had to use magic to appear normal. Misery settled in his chest.

"How bad?" she asked.

He explained everything to her, from getting sick to waking in the forest and all the limitations he'd discovered so far. She remained quiet the entire time, and he knew she'd eventually put the pieces together. "And here I am, trapped out here while you and the guys are joking around inside. We'll never have a normal life."

She laughed. Shocked, he stared at her as she struggled to control the fit of giggles.

"Sorry," she puffed. "But what made you think we'd ever have a *normal* life before?"

His guts twisted. "Well…after the war…I was hoping for… you know…marriage…"

Her sea-green eyes softened. "And it will be lovely. However, I'm a healer and you're a prince—our lives will never be normal."

"Not now that I'm stuck in the forest."

"That's a minor problem. We can live in an elaborate tree

house or plant trees all around the castle in Alga. If Tohon can build a garden on his roof, we can make it work."

"I can't travel to Alga."

"Who says? I can still share my energy with you and there are woods between the ridges."

His dark mood lifted. "You know, you're making it hard for me to sulk."

"Good." She leaned in and kissed him.

Desire shot right through him. At least that hadn't changed. He deepened the kiss and drew her closer.

She broke away far too soon. "I have to explain a few things to Estrid first and see that the guys are settled. I don't want them disturbing us later." Her gaze burned with promise.

Kerrick didn't want to wait. "They won't disturb us now. Even they can figure that out."

"Should we tell the monkeys and Flea about you?"

"Yes, they need to know. But not Estrid or Eva."

"Agreed." She chewed on her lower lip. "Let me try something before I go." Avry took his hand in both of hers.

Her magic spread through him with a soothing warmth. He resisted soaking it in and reenergizing.

"You're not sick, just exhausted. Hmm… I sense the connection you have to the living green. Oh." She released his hand.

"What?"

"I think if your link to the living green was broken…" Avry paused.

Kerrick braced for bad news. He'd memorized her every expression, her every mannerism. The way her long graceful fingers worried the sleeve of her tunic said more than her words.

"It's just a guess, but that bond is keeping you alive," she said.

No surprise. "Break it and I die."

"Perhaps. This is…unprecedented. I'm sure we'll figure it out."

"Yeah, add it on the list right after defeat Cellina's army," he grumbled.

"Remember when the Peace Lily saved me?" Avry took his hand again.

A strange change in subject, but he trusted her. "Of course." It had been the best moment of Kerrick's entire life.

"And I wondered why it saved me and how. Do you recall what you said?"

"I said I didn't know nor care. That I considered it a gift."

Avry pressed his palm against her cheek. "This is exactly the same thing. I consider it a gift."

He caressed her smooth skin with his thumb. "I also remember how we celebrated." Heat built deep within Kerrick. He slid his hand to her neck, pulling her against him.

She gazed up at him. "We were alone then."

"We're alone now. No one within…" He concentrated, letting his senses extend throughout the forest. "A couple miles."

"Did the living green tell you that?" she asked.

"No. I'm part of the forest, I just…know." It was hard to explain.

"You told me before it has a voice."

"It does, but with this…" Kerrick gestured to the surrounding forest. "It doesn't need to say anything."

"What does it sound like?"

"It's neither male nor female. I hear it in my head. Why?"

"The Lilys speak to me the same way, and I wondered if perhaps it was the living green instead." Her gaze grew distant. "No, it's another consciousness. Otherwise the Death Lily would have known where you were." Her forehead crinkled. "That means there are three living beings that can communicate. I wonder if there are more."

He loved watching her puzzle out a problem. "I thought you said the Peace Lilys didn't talk to you."

Pain creased her face. "Twice now. Once after Noelle died."

"Sorry, I've forgotten."

Avry shook her head. "So much had happened while you were in the north, and again in the last month."

"When was the second time?"

A mix of emotions flashed before Avry said, "I've done a horrible thing, Kerrick."

He wrapped his arms around her. "Impossible."

"But you don't—"

"Have you refused to heal someone in need?"

"No, but—"

"Have you put your well-being ahead of another?"

"No, but I—"

"Have you ignored a plea for help?"

"Kerrick—"

"Have you harmed a small furry animal?"

"Now you're being—"

"Have you slept with another man?"

"Kerrick!"

Her face reddened in what he hoped was outrage and not guilt. "What? I'm thinking of horrible things. That's one."

Avry straightened, breaking his hold. "Well, here's another one. Have you animated the dead?"

He searched her expression. No humor sparked in her eyes. He thought back to their conversation. They'd been talking about Peace Lilys. "Animated like Flea?"

"No, like one of Tohon's. Are you going to add that to the horrible list?"

Torn between being impressed by her ability and wishing to comfort her, Kerrick chose his words carefully. "Tohon's, yes, but not yours."

"Why not? The result is the same."

"But the intention isn't. Your intent was to save a person's life."

She seemed surprised. "How did you know?"

"Because it's *you*. You will do everything you can to save a life."

"But—"

"Tell me I'm wrong."

Avry tried. Explaining what led up to the "horrible thing," she never mentioned anything he'd consider even bad. Her actions were logical, practical and kind—Avry to a tee.

"…and now Flea is freaked out and avoiding me." She hunched down as if guilt pressed on her shoulders.

"He's young. He doesn't understand. Unless you're planning on creating a whole army of them…?"

She gave him a flat stare.

"I didn't think so. Concentrate on the positive. This is an opportunity for us to learn more about Tohon's creations. Does Ryne know?"

"Probably."

"He'll know what to do with…Yuri. In the meantime, don't let this affect you. There was no way you could have predicted that would have happened. Unless you can see into the future…?"

Another sour look, but he suspected her heart wasn't in it.

"Too bad, because that would come in handy right now."

"Like who will win this war?" she asked.

"I'm thinking more of the immediate future. I would ask my beautiful prophetess if I will get lucky tonight." He stroked her arm and twined his fingers with hers, drawing her toward him.

"I know the answer to that." A sly smile tugged on her full lips.

"Do tell."

She leaned closer and whispered in his ear, "Not tonight."

Kerrick pouted.

Avry slid her arms around him. "Your prophetess says you're getting lucky *now*. Estrid can wait." She nuzzled his neck with her nose, pressing her body against his.

Heat flushed through him. He shifted to lie back onto the ground, taking Avry with him. Now side by side, Kerrick kissed her deeply. His hands slipped under her tunic, seeking skin as he proceeded to make her prediction come true.

# CHAPTER 10

Snuggled next to Kerrick, I allowed my worries and fears to disappear. All that mattered was he'd survived the Death Lily toxin. We'd overcome his limitations. And if not, then I'd live with him in the forest. Better than living without him.

I stretched and pushed up on my right elbow. We'd both fallen into an exhausted sleep soon after our reunion. The sun hung low in the sky, which meant we'd slept through the afternoon.

My body still tingled pleasantly. I would have enjoyed the view of his muscular chest, but he blended in with the ground. So did I. As long as I touched him, my skin matched the forest's colors.

My stomach growled, reminding me I hadn't eaten since… I'd no idea. And Kerrick's recovery had taken a toll on him. His hip bones stuck out.

Kerrick mumbled when I untangled my legs and broke skin contact to search for my clothes. They hadn't gone far. Our lovemaking had been slow and intense, unlike our last reunion, which had been fast and passionate. I dressed and had to sweep my hands over the ground to find him again.

He snagged my wrist and yanked me close. "Don't go."

"Estrid's waiting and I'll bring food if there's any left. Loren's making his road stew."

He grumbled, but released my arm and once again turning invisible.

I hesitated. "You won't—"

"I'll stay right here unless an enemy patrol comes through," Kerrick said. "Then I'll lead them away from the cave and double back."

His words were sincere, yet the knot in my chest refused to loosen. "We should leave after full dark. It'll be safer. We need to catch up to my team and deliver Estrid to Ryne. Do you have any idea where he is?"

"No, but I can find him with my tree mojo."

I smiled over Quain's term for Kerrick's magic. As I strode away, my worries and fears returned, including the new one—that Kerrick wouldn't be there when I returned. Especially since I could only feel his magic when he used it to look normal. I paused and turned around.

Kerrick appeared. He shooed me away. "I'm already missing you."

The monkeys, Eva, and Flea slept, but Estrid stared at the fire. Loren's stew pot rested on a few glowing embers and my mouth watered. Estrid watched me as I filled a bowl with the steaming goodness.

I sat next to the High Priestess. "Did they fill you in?" I asked her between bites, pitching my voice low so I didn't wake the others.

She turned her gaze to me. "Yes, except they wouldn't tell me why Prince Ryne would risk so much to rescue me. Will you?"

"I think you should hear it from him."

"What if we're captured?" Her voice cracked with fear and echoed loudly against the stone walls.

I agreed, that thought was unpalatable. "Then we'll have other things to worry about."

She blanched and the wrinkles on her face deepened. At that moment, she appeared to be in her early sixties—ten years older than her true age.

"Even though we're in enemy territory, we have Kerrick and should be able to avoid a run-in with unfriendlies," I said so she wouldn't panic.

"If he's not too exhausted from doing *guard duty* all afternoon." Quain smirked.

I ignored him. All but Flea had roused at Estrid's cry. I checked on him. No sweat on his brow, or other symptoms of a fever. No mumbling or agitation. He appeared to be in a deep sleep. I searched my memories. When he had awoken Quain from the stasis, he'd gotten sick to his stomach, but hadn't acted tired.

I debated touching him. He'd refused my help earlier, but if he was this worn-out, we couldn't leave tonight as planned. Plus I was responsible for him. Placing my fingers on the back of his hand, I sought signs of an illness, and, finding none, I shared my energy with him. I pulled away before he could drain me dry.

As he woke, I straightened.

He stared at me with confusion for a moment, then asked, "Is it time to go?"

"Soon. How do you feel?"

Flea sat up. "Better. Hungry. Is there any stew left?"

Glad he didn't flinch because of my proximity, I said, "Just save a bowl for Kerrick."

"He must be starved. I'll go relieve him," Quain said.

"He won't come in," I said.

"Why not?"

Aware that everyone's attention was focused on me, I did

a little creative explaining. "He's keeping track of the enemy patrols with his tree mojo, and if he comes inside, he might lose them." I smoothed my tunic. "I told him I'd bring him a bowl."

Loren said, "Once Flea's done stuffing his face, I'll take it out."

"Hey," Flea protested around a mouthful.

"In the meantime, we should prepare to go," Loren said.

Since I hadn't unpacked, I waited by the fire as they rolled up their bedrolls and Flea finished his stew. When Loren was ready, he brought the pot out for Kerrick.

The events over the past day repeated in my mind. I hoped the rest of my team had escaped the blockade.

"Did Odd get out?" I asked Quain.

He shrugged. "Don't know. Once we realized you weren't following us, we changed direction to find you." He glanced at Estrid. "We were mad that you'd run off, but, considering the outcome…"

But at what price? We'd lost a number of soldiers in the battle to escape the manor house.

Loren returned. "Time to go."

We doused the fire and filed out. The moon was a bit brighter, and the air had turned quite crisp. Eva and the guys had donned their cloaks and Estrid wore mine. I wrapped my blanket around my shoulders. Memories tugged. Not the first time nor, I was sure, the last that I'd used my blanket as a cloak. Knowing I'd warm up once we were underway, I ignored the chilly breeze.

Kerrick scouted ahead as we hiked northeast at a cautious pace. Estrid's bumbling seemed overly loud and I thought we'd be marked for sure. No one talked. Throughout the night, off notes and crunchings of others sounded closer than I'd liked. A few times, Kerrick stopped us and we hunkered down until the danger passed. At those times, my heart pumped hard as if I'd just sprinted uphill.

By dawn, we twitched at every unexpected noise. Kerrick found another cave for us to hide in.

"Lots of patrols around," he said at the entrance. "No fire this time."

"What's the watch schedule?" Quain asked.

"I'll stay in the forest. No one's going to get close without my knowledge," Kerrick said.

Quain looked at Loren.

"Sounds good," Loren said, ducking inside. I followed and set up my bedroll for Estrid to use. Then I joined Kerrick outside. "Did you tell Loren what happened to you?"

"Not all of it, but he trusts me." Strain shone on his face.

"Kerrick, relax."

He held out his hand. I laced my fingers in his. He dropped his normal camo and I turned foresty.

"You did more than scout, didn't you?" I asked.

"Cellina's army is determined to find us."

Not good. "Us in particular, or the members of Ryne's attack teams?"

"I don't know, but they're being very methodical."

"Then you need to rest." I tugged him down to his bedroll, spooning in next to him.

He smoothed my hair off my neck, then draped his arm around my waist, pulling me tight against him. "I'd hoped to consult my prophetess on my future." His voice sounded husky and his fingers slid under my tunic.

"Can you sense other people in the forest while you're sleeping?" I asked.

"No, but the living green sends me a…pulse, a warning of danger if anyone comes near me."

"Did it do that before?"

"No. What does this have to do with my future?" Kerrick's hand moved lower.

I grabbed his hand, trapping it on my stomach. "The prophetess says you will sleep now because it's vital."

Kerrick made a small huff of disappointment.

"You're guaranteed to get lucky when we're safe. Better?"

"Oh, yes." He kissed my neck and nibbled on my ear.

"Behave or I'll sleep in the cave."

He chuckled. "An empty threat. Besides, we're safe right now."

And I'd learned over the past year that there was no guarantee we'd have a later. I released his hand and turned to face him.

"But what about the prophetess?" he asked.

"She changed her mind."


With hiding in the daylight and traveling at night, it took us four more days to loop wide around Zabin. According to Kerrick, Odd and the others had headed south toward the infirmary. I'd worried Cellina's troops would find the new location, but the enemy patrols didn't swoop that low. So far.

"What about Ryne?" I asked Kerrick during a rest stop.

"I'm not sure where he is. He might be hunkered down in the mines."

"Might be?" That didn't sound encouraging.

"Ryne's too smart to get caught. He'll figure out what's going on and meet us at the infirmary."

"Why the infirmary?"

"Because it's safe for now. And he knows that's where you'll go."

True. I was anxious to get back to attend to any injuries that might have occurred during the skirmishes. Also, Estrid concerned me. She hardly ate and kept quiet most of the time.

Similar to Eva, but while being subdued seemed more Eva's natural personality, it wasn't Estrid's. Perhaps she just needed time to adjust to the new reality.

After two more days of travel, we arrived at the infirmary. One of Lieutenant Macon's men must have signaled our approach because Odd stormed from the entrance before we reached it. Glad he survived, my good mood faded when he headed straight for me.

"Where the hell have you been?" he demanded.

"Hi, Odd, nice to see you, too," I said.

"Cut the crap. You didn't follow any of the contingency plans, you endangered your friends, you—"

Kerrick materialized from the forest, or at least that was what it looked like, and stood next to me. He wore his flat, unreadable expression. But Odd didn't back down. He eyed Kerrick with open hostility. Two inches taller than Kerrick, Odd possessed the lean, hard muscles of a longtime soldier. So did Kerrick, but he had been exhausting himself every night keeping us safe.

Odd returned his attention to me. "I see you found him."

"And the High Priestess," I said.

He gazed past my shoulder and gasped. "Thank the creator!" He hustled to her and escorted her into the infirmary, all the while fawning over her.

I guess I shouldn't have been surprised. After all, he'd been recruited into her army and had fought for her as she conquered Casis and Pomyt Realms. Odd's reaction to her arrival was an example of why Ryne needed her help.

Flea swept his bangs to the side. "Humph. The creator had nothing to do with her rescue."

"Yeah, he should have cried, thank the Flea!" Quain said.

"Ooh, I like. We should use it all the time," Loren added.

They tried out variations of it as they headed inside with Flea trotting behind them.

"Guess I'll stay here until I receive new orders," Eva said, following the monkeys.

I turned to Kerrick. "I—"

"Go check on your patients. I'm going to find a soft spot and sleep for a week."

"I don't think the monkeys or Flea will let you. They've been good about not pestering us for answers, but I'm sure once they've eaten and are rested, they'll be bugging you."

"That's fine. By then, I'll be lonely." He smiled.

"I wouldn't be so certain of that." I leered.

"Does my prophetess have good news?"

"I'll have to consult my crystal ball."

"Then make haste, my love. I await your prophecy." He grabbed my hand and kissed the back.

Despite the warm tingle that shot up my arm, I said, "I'm not falling for your princely moves."

"Darn. That move should have melted you with desire and caused you to give in to my princely charms." Humor sparked in his eyes.

"Then that settles it."

"Settles what?"

"I'm not a princess."

"Thank the Flea!"

I yanked my hand from his. "Don't start. Now go get some sleep." I shooed him before I entered the cave. Just past the threshold, I paused and glanced back.

He remained standing in the same spot, watching me. I might not be a princess, but he understood what I needed.

Inside the cave, Odd had found Estrid a comfortable chair and a change of clothes. Instead of the yellow POW jumpsuit, she wore a red skirt and white tunic. Impressed by his fast acquisitions in a place where we all wore fatigues, I watched the ruckus around the High Priestess. Color had returned to Estrid's cheeks, she spoke with animation and she'd attracted a number of soldiers. She was back in her element. A good sign.

An idea occurred to me. Would Estrid be willing to release Melina from the monastery if I asked her? We did save Estrid's life and I also saved her granddaughter's life. It would be an easy way to keep my promise to Mom. It couldn't hurt to ask. But not now. I'd wait until later. Avoiding the crowd around the fire, I headed for my patients. Christina sat next to a man, talking to him, but she shot to her feet as soon as she noticed me.

"I'm so glad you escaped," we said at almost the same time and then laughed.

"I see you didn't hesitate to help out," I said.

"And I see you put my information to good use." She gestured to Estrid.

"Yes, thanks for that. Now I owe you two."

Christina smiled, showing straight white teeth, which complemented her olive skin and dark hair. "I'll remember that the next couple times I'm sick."

"Deal." Glancing around, I counted cots. Four more patients than when I'd left. Not bad. "Do you know where Ginger is?"

"She's resting. We're sharing her duties."

"Great. Can you walk me through the patients?"

"Sure."

We stopped at each patient and Christina explained the person's injury or illness. Most had minor ailments that the caregivers had already treated. One woman didn't rouse when we stopped by her cot. A large gash marked her forehead.

"Private Tori hasn't woken since she arrived yesterday, but she swallows the broth we feed her."

I rested my fingertips on her neck, feeling her pulse and allowing my magic to flow into her, seeking the sickness. At first it found nothing, but a blackness pumped through her heart and tainted all her organs.

"She's either been poisoned or she ate Hogs Breath berries," I said.

"Is she going to die?" Christina asked with alarm.

"Depends. If it's the berries, then she'll recover on her own, but if it's poison then I need to heal her before it gets worse."

"You're too fatigued."

I agreed. Plus I'd shared my energy with Kerrick every night. I considered.

"Can you bring that lantern closer?" I asked Christina.

She hefted it and I checked Tori's mouth. If she had eaten the pink berries, the seeds might still be stuck in her teeth or the juice might have stained her tongue. Nothing. Perhaps the broth washed them away.

"Have you examined her skin?" I asked.

"Not too closely. We made sure she didn't have any broken bones or other injuries."

"Help me remove her shirt."

We stripped her from the waist up, exposing purplish-red bite marks on her upper arms, breasts and shoulders. She hadn't been bitten hard enough to break the skin, which was why Christina had missed it.

Christina covered her mouth. Her eyes wide. "Do you think she's been…"

"I hope not."

Rolling her over, we removed her pants and undergarments. More bite marks lined her legs and hips, but after a quick check, it didn't appear that she'd been raped. Thank the Flea! But she had been poisoned. An ugly puncture wound on her thigh oozed pus and blood.

"What's this?" Christina pointed to a black mark in the middle of Tori's back.

It was a tattoo of a skull wearing a crown of bones. Horror welled as I guessed the significance. The Skeleton King. He must have captured Private Tori.

I explained my suspicions to Christina. "I have to heal her so she can tell us what happened." My magic surged through her, cleaning the poison from her body and drawing the power into me.

Christina grabbed my elbow, steadying me. "You should lie down."

"No. Take me outside." I hated to bother Kerrick, but if my strength failed, I'd need his energy.

I leaned on Christina. A few inches shorter than me, her left shoulder fit right under my arm. As we passed the fire, Odd sprang to his feet. He supported my other side. The world spun.

"What's wrong?" he asked.

Christina answered, but her words faded into a buzzing noise. Black-and-white spots swarmed around me like flies. My legs refused to hold my weight. Then fresh air roused me for a moment.

Odd's voice cleared. "…doesn't make sense, it's warmer inside… Oh."

The sweet smell of spring sunshine engulfed me. I sank into it.

"…message for me," Ryne said. "Private Tori remembers being tortured by the Skeleton King. He grilled her on our defenses and locations and when she refused to answer, he'd bite and lick her, claiming he was tasting her. An effective method. She eventually told him all she knows." He sounded defeated.

"Did she learn anything about his forces?" Kerrick asked.

"They blindfolded her, so she doesn't remember much about where she was or details about his troops. Her patrol had been assigned to sweep down near the border with Tobory and Sectven Realms. I didn't expect them to encounter any trouble. The Skeleton King is much closer than my estimate."

Another problem to deal with. I wondered if I kept my eyes closed, maybe all our problems would go away. I ached from head to toe. Cocooned in softness and warmth, I considered giving into the desire to return to sleep.

"Once Avry's recovered, I can scout for you and find out exactly where the Skeleton King's been hiding," Kerrick said.

Oh, no. He wasn't going anywhere. My eyes wouldn't open so I reached out through the blankets, blindly seeking Kerrick.

"Avry? Can you hear me?" he asked, clasping my hand. His magic tingled along my skin.

My throat refused to work. I nodded instead.

"You've absorbed a very potent poison. It will take some time for all your senses to return."

I longed to ask how long, but all I managed was a squeak.

Kerrick's voice deepened with emotion. "You've been sick for three days. You struggled just as bad as when you healed Belen."

Belen's injuries had almost killed me. If Kerrick hadn't stayed with me either time… I squeezed his hand in gratitude.

"Flea helped. He shared energy with you when I depleted mine."

Oh, Kerrick. "You…" The word hissed from my tight throat. Better than a squeak.

Kerrick smoothed my hair away from my forehead. "Don't lecture me unless you want me to return the favor."

A blurry orange blob smeared the blackness. It pulsed, growing brighter. Firelight? Guess my eyes were open after all.

"Ryne's here," Kerrick said. "He arrived this morning."

"Hello, Avry. Good to see you...er...recovering," Ryne said.

I peered in the direction of his voice. A fuzzy man-size bush sat next to the fire. More darkness hovered beyond him. Nighttime or the limit of my blurry vision?

"We'll discuss the poisoning and the plague victim when you're able," Ryne said. "However you *must* stop healing these fatal cases," he commanded.

He could flat out order me to stop, but it wouldn't matter.

"This isn't the time—" Kerrick started.

"It's the perfect time. She can't argue with me."

Kerrick laughed. "Like that will make a difference. Avry will heal who she wants regardless of your desires. I thought you'd figured that out by now."

The furry edges sharpened. Ryne's features came into focus. He gazed at me with a desperate intensity. Deep lines of exhaustion marked his face. Mud spattered his pants. I'd never seen him so...disheveled.

"I know. But she has to realize that she is *vital* to our success. We're so close to understanding the Peace Lilys, and Yuri—"

I pushed to a sitting position. "What about Yuri?" My throat burned with the effort to speak.

"He's an..."

"Careful," Kerrick warned.

"An opportunity to learn more about our enemy. Avry, you need to think about the bigger picture. Without the Death Lily toxin, we're done."

He'd said the same thing about Estrid. And Danny could harvest... No. The young healer was safe on the other side of the Nine Mountains. I glanced at Kerrick. He peered at me in concern. Although I'd argue I was the one who should be concerned. Gaunt and haggard, Kerrick's face showed the strain of giving me his energy. And I didn't doubt he'd do it again if I healed another near-fatal patient.

"Okay," I said, sinking back down into my cocoon of warmth.

"Okay, what?" Ryne asked.

"I'll think about it."

"But—"

"Go away, Ryne." I waved my free hand. "We'll talk later." Then I yanked Kerrick closer and lifted the blanket.

He slid in next to me along with a pocket of cold air. I shivered. He wrapped me in his arms and dropped his magic. I snuggled in close, resting my head on his shoulder. A slight rustle sounded as Ryne left.

Kerrick huffed with amusement. "Ryne obeys your orders better than you do his. Maybe you should be in charge."

"I'm not ruthless enough."

"True. And I, for one, am glad. He is right, though. For purely selfish reasons, I agree that you need to be more selective about who you heal."

I growled.

"Easy. I didn't say you should listen to him. You know I'll support you regardless. And so will Flea."

My nurturing instinct flared. "Don't push him. He needs guidance, not orders."

"I can be subtle."

I pulled away to look at him. "You? Subtle?"

"Yes."

"You're about as subtle as Estrid hiking through the woods."

"Hey." But his protest lacked heat as he struggled to keep his eyes open.

I reached up and closed his eyes and stroked his rough cheek. "Sleep." And for once, he listened without arguing. Progress.

★ ★ ★

"With the Skeleton King creeping in from the south, should we relocate the infirmary?" I asked Ryne between big bites of stew.

We sat around Kerrick's fire a full day after I'd woken from the poison. Kerrick and I had slept almost twenty hours straight. After bathing and changing clothes, we both had been starved. Ryne, the monkeys, and Flea had brought out supper, joining us.

"Not at this time," Ryne said.

"Why not?" Kerrick frowned at him. His wet hair glistened in the firelight and he'd shaved. But it would take more than one day of sleep to erase the dark smudges under his eyes.

"If we have to engage the Skeleton King's forces, the infirmary should be close to the action."

A cold knot settled in my chest. I hadn't thought about that.

"And then there's the concern about the plague," Ryne added.

"Concern? That should scare the crap out of us," Loren said. "If Cellina can start spreading the plague again, we're screwed."

"I don't believe it's the same plague," I said.

All five men stared at me in horror.

"Actually, that might be some good news."

No response.

"And the rest of his squad mates didn't sicken even though they carried him for a few miles. Is that also good news?" Loren asked.

Good question. I dug into my memories. My mentor, Tara, had taught me the various pathways that a sickness could enter a body—through the nose, the skin, blood, saliva, and during intercourse. In Yuri's case, blood was the most likely pathway. He had that gash on his upper right arm.

"Ryne, when that spy grabbed you, did he cut your skin?" I asked.

His fingers stroked his neck as he mulled over my question. "His fingernail scratched my throat, but I can't remember if he drew blood or not."

"It might have been a dart or tiny needle. Did you find anything like that?"

"No, but it's not like we searched. It happened so quickly and, once he was dead, we thought the danger was gone."

"How much of this is pure speculation?" Loren asked.

"Most of it," I admitted. "Yuri and Ryne could have avoided being exposed to the original plague. Except…" I met Ryne's gaze.

"My sister was one of the first to sicken and I stayed with her until the bitter end." Ryne frowned, remembering.

"And don't forget Avry's speculations have saved our asses a few times," Quain said.

"If Avry's right, this new plague is more accurate," Ryne said. "Instead of wiping out thousands of people, it'll just kill those infected. Looking at it from a military perspective, it's better because it won't kill your own soldiers as long as you're careful."

His comment reminded me of Tohon's claim of using biological warfare during one of my nightmares. Not that I could rely on a dream, but it triggered another revelation.

"Ryne survived the original plague," I blurted.

"Old news, Avry," Quain teased.

"And so did Kerrick, Belen, Cellina, Stanslov, and Jael. Don't you think it's a heck of a coincidence that they all survived?"

Kerrick leaned forward. "And I've met a few others from our class who lived through it while searching for Avry."

"Tohon never stopped wanting to be king," I said. "But it

would be a hollow victory if his old classmates weren't alive to pledge loyalty to him." And it explained his rage over Jael's escape.

"Are you saying he protected us somehow?" Ryne asked.

"Perhaps."

"But that means he had to know about the plague before…" Ryne gasped. "He caused the plague."

"Not without help," I added. "The Healer's Guild was experimenting with dangerous material and are also to blame. He could have predicted the inevitable and done nothing to stop it."

"Just as bad," Quain muttered.

"Or, knowing Tohon, he helped it along." Kerrick jabbed the fire with a stick. "How did he protect us? After school, we all went our separate ways."

That I couldn't answer.

"The reunion," Ryne said. "Remember a year after we graduated, we all returned for the crowning of the next year's king. Tohon was there."

"But why kill Stanslov after he protected him?" I asked, poking holes into my own theory.

"Putting a knife through someone's heart is more personal than them dying far away unseen," Ryne said. "He hated Stanslov."

"And infecting you later?"

"I turned into a real threat once I crossed the Nine Mountains with my elite squads."

"Even if you're right, how does this help us now?" Quain asked.

Ryne answered. "We know Cellina has tapped into Tohon's research and isn't afraid to use it."

"Still not helping."

"It aids me in understanding her, but how about the fact

our enemy now has another weapon at their disposal? This new plague. Don't get cut during battle and you should be fine. How's that? Better."

Quain flopped back onto the ground. "No."

I agreed.

"What about the Skeleton King's poison?" Loren asked. "Is that another weapon?"

"Of course. And we know he won't hesitate to use torture."

The rest of us stared at the fire. All probably contemplating a grim future.

"Do you have any *good* news?" Flea asked, speaking up for the first time. He sat on the opposite side of the fire.

"We haven't encountered any dead squads in a few weeks. Either we've neutralized the bulk of them, or Cellina has pulled them back into Vyg Realm." Ryne tapped a finger on his lips. "It's a nice reprieve. As for Cellina and the Skeleton King, we'll just have to outsmart them."

"Good thing we now have Estrid and her army," I added, hoping to brighten the mood further.

Ryne and the monkeys exchanged a significant glance.

Uh-oh. "What aren't you telling me?"

Ryne ran a hand over his face and suddenly he looked twenty years older. He hunched over as if all his responsibilities pressed down on his shoulders. They probably did, considering he was twenty-seven and the fate of our world rested with him.

"Come on, Ryne. Fess up," I prodded.

"Estrid decided to gather all her forces and acolytes and return home to Ozero Realm."

# KERRICK

The news about the Skeleton King had been bad enough, but now Kerrick felt as though the ground had just dropped out from under him. Without Estrid's forces… No, he wouldn't go there. It was too horrible to contemplate.

Avry's face lost all color. "You're joking, right?"

"I wish," Ryne said. "Estrid's terrified and plans to seal her borders tight, not letting anyone in or out."

"That strategy won't work if Cellina's army reaches Ozero Realm," Kerrick said.

Ryne shook his head. "I tried every conceivable argument and used every ounce of reason and logic I possess to convince her to stay and fight."

"Does anyone else think she's an ungrateful bitch?" Quain asked.

Loren raised his hand. "Me."

"I wasted a perfectly good dinner for her," Flea said only half joking.

"What about her army?" Kerrick asked Ryne, hoping for a bit of good news.

"She sent orders out to her soldiers to return to Ozero immediately and I've sent word out that all are welcome to stay."

"Did you say pretty please? I'm not above begging," Quain said.

"Any takers?" Kerrick regretted the question as Ryne's expression darkened.

"No."

"Not even the odd squad?" Avry's voice broke.

Kerrick glanced at her. Odd had been the grunt who'd charged from the infirmary all concerned and protective when they'd arrived. A twinge of jealousy touched his heart. Did she care for him? Were they more than friends? Her pale face revealed a hurt betrayal.

"It's tough for Odd right now," Ryne said. "Estrid's still here and he'd pledged to fight for her, as did all of her forces. However, I'm thinking once she leaves, we'll have a few… defectors."

"Wait. Estrid's still here?" Avry asked.

"Yes, she's organizing her retreat."

"In *my* infirmary?" Color returned to her cheeks in an instant.

Kerrick exchanged a look with the monkeys. All were glad Avry's ire wasn't aimed at them for once.

"Just settle down." Ryne put his hands out as if placating a skittish horse.

Wrong move. Kerrick suppressed a grin.

Avry shot to her feet.

Ryne stood, as well. "We have to be diplomatic about this. Estrid might have a change of heart and return. She *is* the High Priestess. We don't want to ruin our relationship with her."

"Burning bridges and all that, eh, Ryne?" Loren asked.

"Exactly."

"Isn't Estrid burning a bridge by leaving?" Flea asked.

"Oh, yeah, a huge conflagration," Quain quipped. "But she has all the bridge builders on her side, while we're left with a burned mess."

"Exactly," Loren said.

Avry's entire body stiffened with that stubborn determination Kerrick knew so well. He'd feel sorry for Ryne, but the man had brought this on himself. And truthfully, if Ryne was going to meekly let Estrid walk away, he deserved it.

"I'm going to talk to her," Avry declared. "The High Priestess owes me one." She glanced at Kerrick.

"I'll be here. Go burn some bridges."

She nodded and strode toward the cave. Ryne shot Kerrick a sour look before hurrying after her. Wide grins spread on the monkeys' faces.

"This is too good to miss," Quain said, following Ryne.

"I'd better make sure Quain behaves." Loren jogged to catch up.

Kerrick glanced at Flea. "You can go, too. I don't mind."

"Nah. Who wants to listen to a bunch of people arguing? Avry isn't going to change the High Priestess's mind. I've seen that look before."

He studied Flea. The young man had pulled his knees to his chest. Flea drew in the dirt with a finger.

"What look?"

"The death stare."

Not what Kerrick had been expecting. He delayed his response by adding another log to the fire. "I'm not familiar with that term."

"She's seen her death. Looked it right in the face. Had that moment of knowing she'll die."

"But she was frozen in the stasis. Sepp calls it a fake death."

Flea shrugged. "A person's life doesn't need to be in danger. It's the realization of not *if* you'll die, but *when* and *how*. The inevitability of it. It leaves a nasty taste in your mouth."

"That's true for everyone."

"Yeah, but we ignore it. For her, it's right there, staring at her."

Kerrick wasn't sure if Flea was right or not. But there was no denying Estrid was terrified. "You said you've seen the death stare before. Where?"

"Every time I gaze in a mirror."

Oh, no. "Flea, you're—"

"Don't. You can't see it. You're not a death magician."

He resisted the urge to argue with Flea. Avry had said to be subtle so he tried another approach. "Do I have it?"

Surprised, Flea glanced up and met his gaze for a moment before returning to his earthy sketches. "No."

"Why not? I've been on the edge of death a couple times. I've had a taste of the darkness. My connection to this world is as thin as a blade of grass."

"Even though it's true, you don't believe it deep down. You have too many reasons to live."

True. Avry topped his list. "And you don't?"

Flea shrugged. He used the heel of his boot to smooth the dirt, erasing his doodles.

"I can name a few."

"Yeah, well... Everything's different now," Flea said.

"Because of the magic?"

"Yeah. It ruined *everything.*" Flea pounded his fist on the ground. Puffs of dirt floated up on either side.

Kerrick considered his words with care. "Yeah, it's a real bummer that Quain's still around to annoy us, and—"

"Don't lecture me, Kerrick! Bad enough Avry stares at me with...pity and disappointment." Flea scooped up a handful of dirt and flung it into the fire.

"She doesn't—"

"Come on. We both know she does. She is all about sacrificing herself for others. My behavior's been... Well, not even to the lowest of her standards. Sure, I rescued Quain and Estrid, but now I can't... Death is all around me. I can't turn it off."

Flea's confession alarmed him, but he kept his face neutral. "Are you saying that when you look at me you see my death?"

"No, but if I touch you then I might."

Might. Interesting word choice. "How about when you evaluate Avry's patients?"

"Yeah, I see it. I didn't tell her, 'cause I was hoping I'd learn how to control it. To keep from going that...deep. But each time, it comes quicker. And now it's a flash. I get everything from current situation until death in one rush."

That explained his refusal to use his magic. "Then why did you say you might see my death?"

"I can't see Avry's, so I'm guessing her magic blocks mine."

And Kerrick wasn't about to suggest he try with him. Kerrick had no desire to frighten Flea or to learn about his ultimate end. Instead, he said, "I don't remember Sepp ever saying he could foresee a healthy person's death. But Sepp managed to fool me over his loyalty, so he could have been keeping other secrets as well."

"You think Sepp wants an apprentice?" Flea asked darkly.

"I don't think he'd be a good mentor. Avry might be able—"

"No."

Kerrick studied Flea. Something had happened between them. He remembered Avry saying Flea had been avoiding her since she'd reanimated Yuri. Which might explain why he hadn't told her about the flash.

"Avry didn't intend for Yuri—"

"I know. But it happened. Just like the plague. Healers mucking about with things they shouldn't be, giving Tohon the means to kill millions. Yes, magic saved you and Avry and Quain and me, but it's done far more damage."

It was hard to argue with the logic. Plus Flea's tight fists meant he wouldn't be receptive to any opposing views at the moment.

"Okay," Kerrick said.

Flea peered at him in suspicion. "Okay, what?"

"I understand and support your decision not to use magic."

Openmouthed, Flea gaped at him. Kerrick fought to keep a smile from his face.

Recovering, Flea asked, "What's the catch?"

Ah, he'd been hanging out with the monkeys too long. "Ryne has this book about magicians. I'd like you to read about death magicians." He held up a hand, stopping Flea's protest. "Just read, not practice or try anything. Just read. That's all. Can you do that for me?"

Flea grumbled, but agreed.

Kerrick changed the subject, asking about Flea's training. "Has Loren shown you the Gahagan attack yet? It's one of my favorites."

They discussed sword fighting. Kerrick noted how Flea had relaxed, acting a little bit more like his old self. But he had a long way to go.

Loud voices interrupted their conversation. Avry and Ryne arguing. Kerrick and Flea exchanged a look.

"I don't know why Ryne bothers," Kerrick said. "She won't listen to him."

The argument stopped when Avry strode into the clearing. Flushed and pissed off, she struggled to regain her composure. Ryne followed, appearing equally riled.

Not wanting to add to the tension, Kerrick waited.

Flea had no such qualms and said, "Estrid's still leaving."

No one corrected him. Flea had been right.

"And so are we," Avry said.

# CHAPTER 11

"You are not," Ryne said.

"Unless you plan to hold us against our will, we're leaving tonight," I said.

Ryne's red face turned crimson, which I didn't think was possible.

But before the prince exploded, Kerrick stood and stepped between us. "What's going on?"

"Estrid refused to stay, so we need to beat her back to Ozero," I said.

"Why?"

"Once she seals the borders, we won't get another chance to rescue Melina. I promised Mom I'd make sure she was safe."

Kerrick turned to face me. "Melina's in Ozero?"

I told him about her run-in with Estrid's purity priestess. "They sent her to the monastery in Chinska Mare. And Estrid won't release her."

"Ah."

"You can't go," Ryne said. "We have far greater problems to deal with. The Skeleton King, Cellina's invading army, dead soldiers, and diminishing resources all outweigh the rescue of one girl."

"And how am I going to make a difference with all that?" I demanded.

He stared at me as if I'd just lost my mind. "Aside from healing my soldiers, you harvest the Death Lily toxin."

"Except I've gotten all the sacks around here, and you said the dead patrols hadn't crossed the border with Vyg." Plus I wasn't going to consign Melina to living the rest of her life in a monastery. "All I need are a couple horses and we'll be back in two weeks. And I can harvest more toxin sacks for you."

"How do you plan to rescue her?" Ryne asked.

"I'll figure it out on the way."

"I've been there. The place is a fortress. You'll never get in."

I kept my cool...barely. "Tohon's castle is a fortress, yet we managed to rescue *you*."

"Avry, think about it." Ryne reined in his temper. "That was a different situation. You were invited inside his castle. You had help. Kerrick can't even leave the forest and Chinska Mare is a big city. You'll need two weeks just to map the layout."

"Then it might take us a little longer. It doesn't matter, Ryne. We're going regardless."

"You keep saying 'we,' yet you haven't consulted with anyone about this suicide mission."

Good point.

"She doesn't need to," Kerrick said.

"I'm in," Flea added.

"We're packed," Loren said. He entered the clearing with Quain. Both had their knapsacks over their shoulders.

Warmth and gratitude spread through my heart.

Ryne studied us. "If you leave, it will be considered a desertion. If you survive, don't bother coming back or I'll have you arrested on sight." The cold, hard tone of his voice indicated he meant it. Without another word, he left.

Uh-oh. I glanced at my guys. Would they stay?

"Is that considered burning a bridge?" Flea asked into the silence.

"Oh, yes," Loren said.

"I'd like to see him try to arrest me," Quain said.

"You don't—" I tried.

"Nonsense," Kerrick interrupted. "Let's get packed before Ryne can order everyone not to help us. Flea, gather your things. Loren, grab some travel rations. Quain, fresh water. Avry, medical supplies and your pack. Meet back here in ten minutes."

The men rushed to obey as Kerrick assembled his travel pack.

I lingered until he noticed me still standing there. "Thanks."

"Anytime. Now git! You have nine minutes."

"Yes, sir!" My smile lasted until I reached the cave. Estrid held court in her corner of the infirmary. The shortsighted, ungrateful, selfish woman had refused to listen to reason. As the creator's chosen representative, she ensured I wouldn't be joining her religion ever.

I skirted the crowd of people, keeping an eye out for Ryne. He wasn't in any of the common areas. Rifling through the medical-supply cabinet, I only took a few items, making sure there was plenty left for the patients. A line of containers gave me an idea and I swiped one. Most of my personal things were with Kerrick, but I stuffed the rest in with the supplies.

When I finished, I turned and almost ran into Christina. She stood in my path with her arms crossed.

"Where are you going?" she asked.

"On another rescue mission. I'll be back."

"Were you planning on telling me?"

No, and another lump of guilt landed on the proverbial pile I carried. "Time's tight and I'd figured Ryne would fill you in. But I realize now that it would be wrong to leave without talking to you. Sorry."

A brief smile touched her lips. "So what's going on?"

I detailed the mission. Mindful of the minutes ticking away, the words tumbled from my mouth in a fast rush.

"That's going to be almost impossible. That place is a fortress."

Ryne had said the same thing. "How do you know?"

"I grew up in Chinska Mare," Christina said.

Without stopping to consider, I said, "Come with us."

She crinkled her nose. "I…can't…. Too many bad…memories. However…" She searched for a piece of parchment, then grabbed a stylus and sketched. "There's an abandoned aqueduct that is underneath the city. Now, it doesn't go under the monastery, but there is an entrance nearby." Christina marked an X on her sketch. "If you somehow manage to rescue your friend and reach this entrance, follow the water. It should lead you out on the south side of the city."

"Should?"

"It's been years, and there's always the chance one of the tunnels has collapsed or been blocked off. A river of water used to flow under the city, but the High Priestess wanted to control the water, so she diverted it to an enclosed pipeline only her people can access." Christina handed me the paper. "And watch for smugglers—they use the tunnels to get into the city."

"This is wonderful. Thank you."

"Don't thank me yet. Getting into and out of the monastery is the real challenge. The guards don't take kindly to strangers and have orders to kill on sight."

Lovely.

"I'm surprised Prince Ryne approved this mission," she said.

Unable to lie to her, I said, "Uh. He didn't. We're going without his permission." I braced for her reaction.

"He's left you high and dry before. I'd say that's fair. Good luck."

"Thanks." I rolled up the parchment and added it to my stash.

As I wove through the patients' cots, I spotted Odd standing near Estrid. I should probably say goodbye, but his betrayal still hurt. How could he leave when he knew what we faced? I almost tripped over my own feet as I realized I was about to do the very same thing. But I planned to return despite Ryne's threat. Did that count for extra…morality points? Ah, hell, who was I kidding. I was just as bad as him. And, no, I didn't wish to say goodbye to Odd.

Shouldering my pack, I hurried out before Kerrick sent the monkeys to fetch me.

No surprise, they all waited near the entrance.

"What took so long?" Kerrick asked.

"I'll tell you on the way. Let's go before Ryne changes his mind and arrests us now."

Setting a quick pace, Kerrick led us east through the dark forest. He kept his normal appearance so we could see him. A small bit of moonlight lightened the darkness, but not enough to discern smaller obstacles like vines, rocks, and exposed roots. We stayed close behind Kerrick, trusting him to find a safe path.

As we traveled, I filled them in on Christina's aqueduct. "She wouldn't come along. She mentioned having too many bad memories there."

"I don't blame her," Loren said. "Chinska Mare is the main center of Estrid's religion. It might have changed, but before the plague, the streets were filled with acolytes seeking people not following their commandments. They raided houses looking for alcohol, musical instruments, or other banned items and dragged the poor person or even whole families in for punishment. They were big on punishment. I think the acolytes were paid by the body."

"Sounds like a great place. Can't wait," Quain grumbled.

"It's good she stayed behind. Christina hasn't had the silent training," Loren said.

"Estrid didn't either and we managed," Quain said.

"Yeah, but it took us three times as long to get anywhere."

"Are we going to find horses?" I asked Kerrick.

"I'd rather not," he said.

"But we need to stay well ahead of Estrid. Ideally we should be long gone before she arrives."

No reply.

I tried again. "We'll only use them to cross Pomyt Realm. There shouldn't be any danger along the way. And once we reach the border, we can stable them for when we return."

"All right, I'll see what I can find," he said. But he didn't sound happy.

We continued on in silence. The plan was to travel all night, stop for a brief rest at dawn, then continue on until nightfall. By then we should be far enough away from Ryne's forces to switch to daytime hours.

A respectable plan, except recovering from the poison had taken more out of me than I'd thought. My steps slowed and drawing breath became difficult. Kerrick and Flea also seemed to struggle. They had given me a considerable amount of their energy, although neither of them would admit to being tired. I concentrated on Melina, seeking strength from her plight. It worked for another hour, but then I had to stop or fall flat on my face.

Kerrick turned around. "What's wrong?"

"I—"

"Can you find us a safe place to rest?" Quain asked. "I need my beauty sleep."

Loren opened his mouth, probably to tease Quain, but he closed it after a moment.

Kerrick nodded. "There's a cave—"

"No caves," I said. "We stick together."

He gave me a tired grin. "All right."

We trudged through the forest for an eternity before Kerrick stopped.

"This is a nice high spot. We should be safe here and if the forest alerts me to any danger, we'll have time to prepare. How much beauty sleep do you need, Quain?"

Quain pretended to fluff invisible hair. "A few hours should do it, don't you think, Avry?"

"Dawn will wake us and that should be enough." I hoped.

Kerrick wouldn't risk a fire so we set up our bedrolls in a circle. I shared mine with Kerrick. He slid in behind me and covered us with his blanket. With his arm around my waist, warmth soon engulfed me.

"Does anyone else miss the old days?" Quain asked into the sleepy silence.

"Old days as in before the plague or before we found Prince Ryne?" Loren asked.

"Missing the time preplague is a given. I meant before Prince Ryne."

"I miss the simplicity of those days," Loren said. "We had one mission."

"I miss Kerrick and Avry arguing," Quain said with a laugh. "It's too boring with them being all lovey-dovey."

"Give it time," Loren added.

"Hey," I said.

"You know it's true." Loren settled on his pillow.

Kerrick agreed and I elbowed him in the ribs. Chuckling, he said, "Although I like it better when she's fighting with Ryne."

"Well, I *don't* miss being chased by mercenaries," I said. Tohon had set a bounty on healers and once word had spread that I was with Kerrick and his men, they'd come after us in force.

"And I don't miss all those awkward meals with Avry glaring at Kerrick," Quain said.

"He deserved every one of them," I said, remembering.

"Not all," Kerrick protested.

"Yes, all."

"No. You were just too stubborn to understand—"

"Told you," Loren said, gloating.

I clamped down on my reply. No sense arguing about past events even half-kiddingly. He lived and breathed right next to me. All else were mere annoyances of the past.

Silence descended as the others fell asleep, or so I thought.

"I miss Belen," Flea said.

Quain and Loren were quick to agree.

My insides turned cold and Kerrick's arm tightened around me. "We do, too," I whispered.

"Since we're not welcome to return to Prince Ryne's army, we should search for Belen after we rescue Melina," Flea said.

Not a bad idea. "I'm in."

"I'm all for it." Kerrick pushed up on his elbow. "But before we go rushing off, we need to have an idea which direction to search. With Melina, we know exactly where she is. If Belen's been taken by Cellina, he could be anywhere in Vyg, Sogra, or Lyady Realms. That's a lot of ground to cover and it's all in enemy territory."

"But we haven't heard a word. Not even a hint of where he might be," Loren said.

"Tohon claimed to have turned him into one of his dead soldiers, but Sepp said he froze Belen in a stasis. Neither can be trusted to tell the truth," I said.

"After Melina, we concentrate on Belen. Agreed?" Flea asked.

It was unanimous. Kerrick settled back. He pulled me in tighter.

"It's fitting we make sure Melina's safe first. Remember how upset Belen was when she went missing?" Loren asked.

"Good thing he didn't find those kidnappers, or he'd have ripped their arms off." Quain made a tearing sound.

"They deserved to have their arms ripped off," I said. The men had quite a profitable operation. They'd kidnap older teens and sell them to men looking for wives. One of those activities that had benefited from the loss of almost all law enforcement due to the plague.

"The ladies we rescued wanted to cut off another body part," Kerrick said. He still sounded horrified by the idea.

"Oh, yeah," I said. "Too bad Mengels's town watch had re-formed or I'd have given them my sharpest knife."

The monkeys groaned in sympathy. Men.

"Uh, Avry. Can you heal…uh…you know…man pain or would a patient need a male healer?" Quain asked.

Suppressing a fit of giggles, I imagined his face was bright red, even the top of his bald head.

Loren laughed. "What's the matter, Quain? Did your last encounter give you a case of the clap? I didn't know cows carried that disease."

A yell followed a grunt and then the unmistakable sounds of two men wrestling accompanied a cloud of dirt.

"That's enough, you two," Kerrick said in his no-nonsense voice.

They stopped, both panting from the exertion.

"Quain, you really need to ignore Loren's comments," I said. "He's just doing it to get a reaction from you."

"And he falls for it every time," Loren said.

"Easy," Kerrick said to Quain.

"If he stops, we'll lose hours of entertainment," Loren added.

Quain didn't twitch, but his glower promised Loren future pain. Loren kept his amused expression, unfazed by his friend's demeanor.

"Enough. Everyone needs to get some sleep. I want to cover at least twenty miles tomorrow."

Ugh. The monkeys fixed their bedrolls and settled down.

My thoughts returned to Quain's question. "I've never had to deal with any…man pain before, but if I do, I'll let you know how it goes."

"Thanks," Quain deadpanned.

Once again everyone quieted down. I was about to drift off to sleep when Flea said, "I miss being Flea."

"You're still Flea. Nothing's ever gonna change that," Quain said.


Dawn arrived far too soon. Groggy and achy, I balked at leaving the toasty warmth of Kerrick's arms. The air had cooled overnight and a light frost coated the ground.

We ate jerky for breakfast and packed up, continuing east. Kerrick set a brisk pace. Gazing at the surrounding landscape, I searched my memories. When I'd traveled to Galee to become Tara's apprentice, I'd cut through Pomyt Realm. While Grzebien was the largest city in Pomyt, the realm had many smaller settlements tucked around farm fields and wooded areas. That was true for all the realms. Most had only two or three large cities.

Which meant we shouldn't have to go too far out of the way to remain in the forest until we reached Ozero. Now all we needed were some horses. Except Kerrick avoided all the small towns and farms we passed.

I understood his reluctance to ride the noisy animals, but time was critical. After we bypassed a farm with horses grazing in a pasture, I reached for his shoulder, or rather where I thought his shoulder should be, since he'd gone woodsy as soon as we had set off this morning. I touched nothing but air at first. Then he took my hand and my skin turned the colors of the forest.

"Hey," Quain said right behind me. "Give a guy some warning before you just disappear, will ya?"

Flea stood next to him, but Loren stayed back in the rear-guard position.

"Sorry," I said, but stared at Kerrick. When we both blended in, I had no trouble seeing him clearly. At those times, he was all mine.

"Something wrong?" he asked in a low voice.

"Yes, why did you pass that farm? They had horses, lots of them."

"We're not ready for horses."

"We or you?"

"We. Trust me on this." He squeezed my hand.

"All right."

He let go and vanished once again.

"Welcome back," Quain said to me. "Remember those times we wished Kerrick would disappear?"

"I can still hear you, you know," Kerrick said.

"Is that so? I'd thought maybe you had vines growing out of your ears or something. Since you're now…a weed of the forest?"

Kerrick the weed. My laughter bubbled up my throat, unstoppable. The boys joined in.

"Go ahead and laugh," Kerrick said. "We'll see who's laughing when you all need to hide and I'm suddenly a rare plant, unable to be found."

"Empty threat, weed boy," Quain said.

"Oh, I think you know me better than that. I hope you look good in white, Quain. I've heard the Ozero priests make all their initiates wear white."

"Really? I heard they don't let them wear any clothes for the first two years," Loren added.

"Wouldn't they get cold?" Quain asked, sounding worried.

More laughter, but this time Kerrick joined in. Quain's face turned red.

"Don't listen to them," I said. "Ever. You can trust me or Flea."

"I've heard they tattooed the creator's name on your…er… man part," Flea said.

Loren high-fived the young man.

"Don't encourage him." I swatted Loren's shoulder. But we all knew it was too late. Flea had been monkeyfied.

We resumed our trek. I tried not to count all the horse opportunities passing us by. Stopping for a quick meal, we pressed on until the sun dipped low.

Kerrick reappeared. He pointed to a narrow trail. "Keep on this path. It'll lead you to a clump of Lilys, which will make an excellent camp for tonight. I'm going to do a little exploring. I'll meet you there." He met my gaze. The promise to return shone in his eyes.

Even though I'd rather go with him, I stayed with the others as we followed his directions. The scent of vanilla filled the air around the Lilys. While they waited, I walked up to the cluster of six. Five Peace Lilys and one Death Lily. It hissed, parted its petals and dropped two toxin sacks onto my open palms. Ryne might arrest us on sight, but he wouldn't refuse more toxin. I thanked the plant, tucking the sacks into my pack.

The monkeys and Flea kept well away from the Death Lily.

I ignored the Peace Lilys. After the debacle with Yuri, I never wanted to interact with another Peace Lily again.

Waiting for Kerrick was difficult, but I had to admit his choice of campsite was ideal. No one would dare approach a clump of Lilys.

Loren and Quain debated about setting a small fire. Tired of cold food, Quain hoped for at least a mug of hot tea.

"Just wait until Kerrick returns," I said, setting up my bed-roll. "There must be a reason he wanted to explore." Like rounding us up a couple of horses, I hoped.

However when Kerrick arrived a few hours later, he was alone. And his serious demeanor said more than words.

"No fire. Pack your stuff, we're leaving," Kerrick ordered.

We assembled our gear.

"What aren't you telling us?" I asked as we hustled through the forest.

"I'll explain when we get there."

Intrigued, I kept the rest of my questions to myself.

After a couple miles, he stopped and gestured to a rocky slope, covered with vegetation. "There's a cave entrance hidden behind those vines. I want—"

"No caves," I snapped.

"Just hear me out. We're being followed by a couple of groups of soldiers. I don't know if they're just returning to Ozero as per Estrid's orders, or if they are searching for us in particular. Just to be safe, I want you to stay out of sight, and that cave's the best thing around right now."

"And what about you?" I asked.

"I'm going to get closer to the groups and try to learn their intentions."

My unhappy heart wished to protest. Wished to tag along. But my practical side knew I'd be a hindrance.

Quain and Loren swept the vines aside. A damp puff of rotten leaves and bat guano wafted out. Wonderful.

"Stay here until I return," Kerrick said.

"Uh, no offense, but what do we do if you don't?" Quain asked.

"If I'm not back by morning, go on without me. Ozero is a straight shot east."

Loren shook his head. "You know we won't. Just tell us which direction the squads are and save us all some time."

I nodded in encouragement.

"Fine. One's almost straight west, the other is southwest about two miles south of the first, but I don't expect trouble."

"Yet that's the problem with trouble," I said. "It has no manners at all and arrives unexpected most of the time."

# KERRICK

He waited as Avry and the others entered the cave. She lingered behind. Before ducking inside, she turned and met his gaze. Kerrick had kept his normal appearance, expecting this. Every time they parted, he understood her need to reassure herself that he'd return.

Even after she disappeared into the darkness and beyond the reach of his magic, Kerrick remained in place for a few more moments just in case she peeked out. Satisfied that all was well for now, Kerrick headed west, dropping his visage. Turning normal no longer drained him as much. He suspected he'd either regained some of his strength or pulling the power had turned into a reflex.

Interesting how they'd fallen back on old habits. And keeping Avry and his gentlemen safe in the forest remained his job. He dreaded the time when he'd have to stay behind while they continued into Chinska Mare.

Kerrick picked up his pace, hoping to catch the squads settling down for the evening. That was when they'd be the most chatty.

Voices drifted through the trees as he neared the west group. The forest had already counted eleven irritants. Eleven living things that didn't belong in its borders. Kerrick used his magic to determine the intruders were a mix of men and women soldiers. Getting close was ridiculously easy for him. They'd posted a couple guards, but he was just about invisible. Still, there was no need to be in the center of activity. Kerrick leaned against a nearby tree and listened to the various conversations.

"Did you see Ron's gash? Nasty with green oozing out."

"Quit your jawing and fetch me more firewood."

"You two have the third watch. Don't fall asleep again or I'll wake you with the pointy end of my sword."

"If it doesn't rain, we'll be home in eighteen days. I haven't been home in two years. I hope my girl hasn't found someone else."

Kerrick focused on the men talking about home.

"Two years? She's probably married with a babe or two by now. I made sure and married my Sarah before leaving."

"I didn't think it would take this long or I would have," the first man said.

"It sounds like we'll be home for good. No more of this sneaking through the woods, poking at the enemy. It'll be nice and simple just protecting our borders."

Kerrick watched as the squad set up their camp with practiced ease, joking with each other as they completed their tasks. Kerrick had heard and seen enough. This squad wasn't a threat.

He headed south toward the second group. Smaller, with seven male intruders, the squad hiked through the woods at a cautious pace. Quiet, too. Kerrick wondered if Avry had trained these men.

Memories of teaching her how to move with the sounds of the forest came unbidden. He'd enjoyed those lessons. Probably more than her, as she'd hated him then. And then the game of hide-and-seek… Kerrick grinned at how she had sniffed him out. Avry might have learned a lifesaving skill, but he'd learned again not to underestimate her. She was one smart cookie.

Kerrick followed the squad until they stopped for the night. Using his magic, he concentrated on the men and cursed under his breath. He recognized one of them. Kerrick eased closer. They kept their conversation to a minimum, lit a small fire, and posted more guards than the other.

The weak firelight reflected off their strained faces and they froze at any animal rustle or natural forest noise. Kerrick put the few clues together. They weren't supposed to be here, and he suspected the leader had given his men a choice and four members had decided to remain behind. Kerrick stretched his senses along the roots of the forest, seeking another squad that might have been sent after them. Nothing.

He could stand here and guess all night, or he could ask. Pulling power, Kerrick uncamouflaged. Testing their abilities, he scuffed the dirt as he walked and rattled a few leaves.

Four of the seven men had their swords out and faced in the right direction, including Sergeant Odd. Impressive.

The sergeant relaxed when he recognized Kerrick. "At ease."

His men sheathed their weapons, but stayed alert.

"Running home to hide under your High Priestess's robes?" Kerrick asked, baiting him.

"My home is in a small town near Koo in Ryazan Realm," Odd said.

"Well, then, you'll want to make a right at the next tree and head straight south."

"Cute, but I'm not planning on going home until I see this through."

Kerrick waited.

"I'm not going to explain myself to you. What do you want?"

"Confirmation."

"Of what?"

"That you're not a threat."

Odd grinned, but there was nothing humorous about it. "To who? Because the answer changes depending on the person."

Nice. "To Avry."

"Do you mean the woman you left in the middle of the night without so much as a word? The woman you tortured by disappearing for over a month?"

Kerrick refused to be provoked. He had started this, and Odd's comments revealed quite a bit. Keeping what Avry called his flat stare in place, Kerrick said nothing.

"If you're referring to her, *she* has nothing to fear from us."

"And her companions?"

"We've no problems with the monkeys or Flea."

"Good. And since you're no threat to me, I'll be—"

"So the mighty Prince Kerrick can fight off seven men now? Did you disappear to a secret training camp?"

"Avry understands what happened and that's *all* I care about. I do like the secret-training idea, but you can go ahead and assume whatever you wish. However, there's one thing that's indisputable."

"And what's that?"

"You can't fight with a tree in your lap, or vines wrapped around your legs." He nodded to Odd. "Until the next time." Then he dropped the normal camo just in case they doubted his abilities.

No reaction from Odd, but a couple of his men started. Kerrick backed away, thinking if he hurried, he could return in time to get a few hours of sleep before dawn. With Avry wrapped in his arms and tucked in close, sleeping had been his favorite part of the day.

"Kerrick, wait," Odd called.

He paused.

"We came to help Avry on her mission."

Kerrick rematerialized. "Help how?"

"Some of my guys grew up in Chinska Mare. Plus as soldiers in the High Priestess's army, we blend in better."

"Until the High Priestess learns of your treason."

"Which is why I hope the plan has us well away before that unfortunate time."

There was no sense letting Odd know they hadn't discussed strategy yet, so Kerrick mulled over Odd's offer. Could they trust him? What if Odd was working undercover for Estrid and planned to sabotage their mission? Odd's comments about Avry clearly indicated where Odd's loyalties belonged...with Avry. Better than with Estrid.

"All right, get your things packed. We might as well travel together."

When they finished, Kerrick led them toward the cave. He'd just about exhausted all his energy, so he trained his attention only on the immediate area. Big mistake. By the time they reached the cave, it was empty.

# CHAPTER 12

The off notes woke me from a light sleep. Quain stood a few feet away. His sword reflected the weak moonlight. More faint rustles sounded. Not Kerrick. Even if he was angry at us, he would be soundless. Unless something was wrong.

"Should I wake the others?" I whispered.

"We're awake," Flea said.

"What do you think, Quain, five or six?" Loren asked in a low voice.

"Maybe more. They're good."

Fear chased away all sleep fuzziness. I pushed my blankets aside and stood. "Let's move closer to the Death Lily."

"And be breakfast? No thanks," Quain said.

"It won't eat you if you're with me." I palmed two throwing knives.

We backed toward the Death Lily. The intruders would have to pass the Peace Lilys to get to us, but hopefully they'd balk at the sight of the Lilys. We had returned to our original campsite after the fumes from the bat guano had overwhelmed Flea.

"Flea and Quain, you take the left side. Avry and I'll get the right." Loren gripped his sword as he stared at the patch of forest where the slight noises emanated.

I considered who'd attack us in the middle of the night. Cellina, Jael, Estrid, Ryne—we certainly didn't lack for enemies.

The off notes stopped and Kerrick materialized on the far side. I relaxed until he focused on me. Exhaustion and anger creased his face. Was that why he'd sounded like a whole squad of soldiers?

"Why didn't you stay in the cave?" Kerrick asked in his flat tone.

"The place stank of bat sh—" Quain started.

"Flea fainted," I interrupted. "It was unhealthy to be in there."

Kerrick's shoulders drooped. I hurried over to share my energy. But before I reached him, he turned and called, "All clear."

A group of people entered the clearing. Surprised, I stopped until I recognized Odd. I glanced at Kerrick. "What's going on?"

"They came to help you."

All my fear and uncertainty fled and I rushed over to Odd, hugging him. "Oh, Odd, I'm so sorry."

His arms paused halfway around me. "Sorry about what?"

"For thinking bad thoughts about you."

He squeezed me tight. "Ah. Well, I had a hard time deciding between the High Priestess and Prince Ryne. But when I found out what you were up to, it was easy to decide."

"Thank you."

He pulled away, smiling at me. "Anytime. So what's the plan?"

"Um."

His smile faded. "You do have a plan, right?"

"I'm working on it. First we need to find some horses."

"What about getting into the monastery?"

"I have an idea, but…" I met Kerrick's gaze.

A hard expression gripped Kerrick's face. "I'm not going to like it. But let's face it, I'm not going to like *anything* that puts you in danger, but that can't stop you. We all knew this would be a dangerous mission."

I stepped over to Kerrick, lacing my fingers in his. "Are we ready for horses now?"

"Yes."

"Do I really have to wear this thing?" Quain asked in outrage. He held an acolyte's robe at arm's length. "I thought I'd be on the escort team."

"You don't have a uniform, and none of ours will fit you," Odd said with an amazing amount of patience, considering it was the fifth time he'd repeated it.

"That's what you get for being so fat, Quain," Loren said. He pulled an identical red robe over his head.

Quain fisted his hand and bulged an impressive bicep. "Oh, yeah, do you want to see what this *fat* can do?"

"That's enough, boys," I said, donning my—what do I call it?—not-a-virgin robe? It matched the monkeys' except for the color. Mine resembled dark brown mud and I wore it over my black travel clothes. Thick and heavy, it'd be hot as hell in the summer. "Ooh, pockets! Lots of pockets to hide stuff in."

"As long as they don't search you," Odd said, killing the mood.

That was one of our big what-ifs. We had a number of those this-will-work-if parts of our plan. No plan was perfect… right?

We'd gotten horses to travel to within a couple miles of Chinska Mare. It had taken us six days, half the time as if we had walked.

In order to get past the city guards, we needed a cover story.

My idea would not only get us into the city, but into the monastery, as well. Quain and Loren would impersonate priests returning from Sectven Realm with an impure, unmarried girl—me as Irina—in tow. They'd deliver me to the monastery and hopefully be allowed to stay and pray.

Odd and his squad would be escorting us since they just had happened to run into us on their way back to Ozero. Claiming they were obeying the High Priestess's orders to return to relieve a few of the guards on duty at the monastery, Odd and his squad would become part of the security team while Flea and Ives would remain in the city to explore the aqueducts and map an escape route.

As one of the men who had lived and worked in Chinska Mare before the war, Ives was familiar with the day-to-day routines. He'd been the one to steal the robes from one of the creator's houses of worship. Since we'd been in Ozero, there appeared to be a worship house in every town.

My job would be to find Melina as quickly as possible while the others figured a way out of the monastery. It sounded simple…right?

As we changed and practiced our stories, Kerrick fed and watered the horses. He'd find a stable for them once we left. He'd been unusually quiet ever since Odd and his men had joined us. While we were gone, he'd planned to find that southern aqueduct exit and meet us there. Once we reached that point, he'd be in charge of getting us out of Ozero without encountering any trouble. And he'd help us lose any pursuers.

We had all the angles covered…right?

"We'll leave two hours before the shift change," Ives said. "That will get us there right at the end of the day shift. At that time, those guys won't care who they let in. They'll be more interested in when their replacements arrive than any-thing else."

We finished going over the plan. I handed Odd the con-tainer I'd swiped from the infirmary and explained how it worked. With about an hour left before we needed to leave, I packed my bag and then headed toward the horses. Kerrick had found six hardy Tobory horses so we could double up. Yet only five stood.... Oh. It popped into sight along with Kerrick. He cleared a stone from the horse's hoof.

I smiled. "For someone who doesn't like horses, you sure know a lot about them."

"It's not a matter of like or dislike," Kerrick said. "They're useful at times and must be cared for. And since I've noth-ing else to do..." He checked the horse's other hooves before moving to the next one—the large chestnut-colored stallion shifted his weight obligingly.

Ah. The reason for his...moping? I'd been so busy planning Melina's rescue, I hadn't had much time to spend with him. We shared a mount and a bedroll, but hadn't had any privacy.

When he finished with the stallion, I blocked him from checking another. I wrapped my arms around his neck. His magic buzzed along my skin. "That can wait. I've something else for you to do."

He met my gaze as he pulled me closer. The tingling sen-sation intensified, going deeper.

"I understand that staying behind is hard," I said. "I've been on the waiting and wondering side of things too many times to count. All I can do is promise to be as careful as possible. Knowing you're here is plenty of incentive for me to hurry back."

"If you don't, I'll come get you." A stubborn resolve flashed in his eyes. "I might be trapped in the forest, but I'm not with-out *other* resources."

"I believe you. After all, you're skilled at a variety of activities." I raked my fingers through his hair. It had grown just past his shoulders—the longest I'd seen it.

"A few," he admitted in a husky voice.

The heat from his body reached me through two layers of clothes. Or was that from my own internal fire? "Don't be so modest. I'd bet you could find us a nice secluded little—"

Kerrick picked me up. His magic disappeared, but my body still hummed as we turned the colors of the forest. I hooked my legs around his waist. He kissed me as he carried me to... I'd no idea. All without missing a step.

When he laid me down, we broke apart for a moment. "Impressive." I panted even though I hadn't done any of the work.

"I'm just getting started. Next step, getting rid of all these annoying layers." Impatient, he tugged on the brown robe.

"Yours, too," I said, pulling on his short cape.

Soon we had a pile of clothing next to us. I shivered in the cool air. But I wasn't cold for long. Kerrick warmed me up until a bonfire raced through my body.

A few heartbeats later...or so it seemed, time ran out. With great reluctance, Kerrick and I untangled and dressed.

Before we headed back to the others, he drew me close. "Do I need to lecture you?"

"No, I already promised to be careful."

"Get in and get out. Don't dally."

"Dally? Seriously?"

His expression darkened. "Avry."

"All right. No dallying and no more lecturing."

Kerrick pulled an orange leaf from my hair. "Sorry. It's... difficult for me to remain behind. You have my heart, my soul, my life. I'm an empty shell without you."

Emotions lodged in my throat. I squeezed him tight.

"You're never alone, Kerrick. You and I are linked. Inside you is all of me. And I'll be there forever."

He tipped my head back and kissed me with such passion that I forgot about the mission and all the world's problems in that moment of utter bliss.

"Hey, lovebirds," Quain called. "Stop raking the leaves. It's time to go."

I broke off the kiss. "Raking the leaves? Is this one of those guy euphemisms?"

Kerrick sighed. "No that's a Quain-ism. He has many of them."

"Don't tell me."

We returned to the campsite hand in hand. The others had shouldered their packs and waited for me.

"I'll be at that southern exit," Kerrick promised, whispering in my ear.

"I'll see you there."

Kerrick and I shared one more kiss before he pulled power and we appeared normal.

Odd frowned at us. "We need to leave now or we'll miss the shift change."

I squeezed Kerrick's hand before letting go. Picking up my knapsack, I slung it over my back. "I'm ready."

The monkeys and Flea said goodbye to Kerrick. I tapped my chest over my heart in a silent goodbye to him. He smiled.

Setting the pace, Odd walked in front with Flea next to him. I stayed between Quain and Loren, and the rest of the odd squad followed behind. After a few steps, I glanced back. Kerrick stood in the same spot, watching us. His hand rested on the center of his heart.

Unable to stop the silly grin from spreading over my face, I faced forward. Who'd have thought Kerrick had a sentimental side? Not me.

"Uh, Avry, or rather, Irina. You're supposed to be contrite and repentant," Quain said.

"I will be once we get closer."

"As long as we're not surprised by a patrol. Without weed boy, we don't— Ow!" An acorn clipped Quain's forehead, leaving a red mark.

"You were saying?" I asked.

"Forget it." Quain rubbed his temple and glared into the woods.

We continued on in silence. Before we reached the city's gates, I tucked a few essential items into the various pockets of my robe and clothes underneath. They'd probably confiscate my pack and search it.

A two-story-high cerulean-blue marble wall surrounded the city of Chinska Mare. Thin white veins snaked through the smooth marble. According to Ives, the city had two gates, one on the west side and the other on the east.

A line of people and wagons waited to enter the city. Odd led us to the end of the queue. A few of those waiting nearby turned and stared at us. I gazed at the worn cobblestones as if dejected. We shuffled forward until it was our turn to state our business.

Odd started to explain, but the guard waved us through with an impatient gesture, just like Ives had predicted. Ives and the men who knew the city the best moved up to the point position and led us through the narrow unmarked streets.

The rows of buildings leaned against each other. Skinny houses mixed with businesses in a haphazard way. Factories sprawled in all directions as if plopped there from high above. I imagined old buildings squashed underneath them. The odor of rotting garbage dominated. A plume of gray smoke engulfed us. We choked on the acrid fumes that burned our eyes.

The citizens hustled by, avoiding eye contact. Red-robed

acolytes patrolled the streets. They peered at us with suspicion, but no one approached. It took me more than a few moments to figure out what was off about the tight and cramped city. Even though it was a large city filled with people and industry, it was quiet. No one laughed, talked, yelled, or said much of anything. Even their footsteps were muted, as if they wore rubber-soled shoes and boots. Creepy.

After an hour, I'd lost track of the turns we'd taken. The sunlight faded and the lamplighter crews lit the city's lamps. Even they went about their work with hardly a word. After a few more hours of navigating the dark streets, Ives stopped us and warned the monastery was around the corner.

We checked our disguises one more time, and I adjusted my hidden contraband. Turning the corner, we all stopped and stared. Made of pure white marble, the building stretched for blocks in either direction. No windows marked the walls that stretched upward in multiple tiers. Each tier was smaller than the one below like layers on a giant wedding cake. Halfway up the eight-story structure, towers soared above the monastery, resembling candles. And this was just what we could see in the semidarkness.

This humongous structure made a fortress look tiny in comparison.

I stared at the monastery as my heart did flips in my chest. I'd be lucky to get out, let alone find Melina. Our plan seemed too simple for this monstrosity. Plus we only had a week at most before Estrid and the bulk of her army returned. Kerrick had sensed her in the forest along with many others just before we crossed Ozero's border.

After I lectured Flea on staying out of trouble and made him promise to be careful, Flea and Ives said goodbye and slipped away. I met Odd's questioning gaze.

"It's not too late to back out," Odd said.

"No. We'll stick to the plan. Make sure you don't lose that container."

He gave me a tight smile. "Yes, sir."

"Ready, boys?" I asked the monkeys, holding out my elbows.

Quain grabbed my right arm. "Kicking and screaming?"

Loren latched onto the other. "Dragging your feet? Perhaps dead weight?"

"I'm going to go for the full-out, desperate struggle," I said.

"Ah, a little bit of everything." Loren's tone held approval.

"Nice." Quain tightened his grip.

As I fought with all my strength but not my magic, they hauled me up to the single entrance. Two lamps burned brightly within a few feet of us. Iron hinges connected the oversize oak doors to the marble walls. A huge oval door knocker was the only thing on this side. No knob. No keyhole. Not even a peephole.

Odd used the door knocker. A heavy clap reverberated through the oak. After a few moments, Odd knocked again. My skin prickled with the feeling of being watched. I glanced up and spotted a couple guards peering over the edge of the roof of the first tier.

They didn't say anything, but soon the door creaked open. A priest stood in the threshold. I increased my struggles to break free.

He frowned at the monkeys. "Subdue her."

Quain pulled both my arms behind my back. Loren backhanded me across the cheek. He faked the amount of force so it was a glancing blow. I pretended to be hit harder, spinning to the side and collapsing to my knees with a cry of pain— just like we had practiced.

When Loren hauled me to my feet, I hung my head. Cradling my cheek with my hand, I acted as if cowed.

"Better," the priest said. "Who are your traveling companions?"

Loren explained.

The priest nodded. "We've heard the good news about the High Priestess's return. Come inside, Brothers."

We entered a long hallway. When the door thudded shut behind us, the sound hit me harder than Loren's blow. My mouth went dry and I swallowed a knot of fear. It took me a moment for my eyes to adjust to the dim candlelight. The priest led us to another set of doors. These had thick iron bars and two guards on the other side waiting.

"They are servants of the creator," the priest said to the guards.

I wondered if it was a password. The guards unlocked the doors and we passed through the first of many such barriers. Narrow corridors cut between them. It reminded me of a maze. After each well-guarded double door made of bars or steel or thick wood, we turned left or right. Other plain doors marked the walls, but we didn't stop. We crossed six such barriers. Odd barely concealed his panic.

After the seventh set, we stopped at a chamber where two priestesses worked behind massive desks piled with folders. An open door on the other side revealed a dark corridor.

"Another penitent for you to process, Sisters," the priest said.

The woman on the left rose and disappeared down the hallway. The other continued with her work.

"There is no escape," the priest said to me. "You are here to beg for forgiveness from the creator. Behave or suffer the consequences. There is no forgiveness from us. Only the creator can grant that."

Lovely. The priestess returned with four guards. Satisfied,

the priest led my companions away. Odd glanced back. He kept his expression neutral, but his gaze showed his fear.

"Sit," the priestess ordered, gesturing to a wooden chair in front of her desk.

The four guards stared at me. What would happen if I refused? They were armed with long sticks made from a reed. Bamboo maybe? No cutting edge, but I'd bet they'd sting when slapped against skin. No sense causing trouble. Not yet. I sat.

Tucking a strand of brown hair behind her ear, she pulled a sheet of parchment and asked me my name.

"Sergeant Irina of Gubkin Realm."

"Wrong answer," she said, snapping her fingers.

Fire raced across my back. The force of the blow sent me to the floor, gasping in pain. Two guards yanked me back into the chair. I hunched over until the burning eased.

"Your name is Penitent Two-Five-Nine-Seven." She nodded at the man behind me.

He grabbed my left arm, pulled my sleeve up and slapped a metal cuff around my wrist. It clicked into place, pinching my skin. He released me and I examined the inch-wide metal. The numbers two, five, nine, and seven had been etched on it. Were there 2596 other penitents incarcerated here? I shuddered at the thought.

"What's your name?" she asked again.

"Penitent Two-Five-Nine-Seven."

"Good. I hope this means you're a fast learner. It will save you a lot of pain and punishment." She leaned forward. "The rules are simple. Obey and pray for forgiveness." The priestess stood. "Follow me."

I hurried after her, and the four guards stayed close behind me. She escorted me to a washroom. With the threat of the armed men right outside the door and under her watchful eye, I removed my clothes and the layers of grime. When I finished, she handed me a clean brown robe and undergarments. She wouldn't let me put on my travel clothes or boots. So much for my hidden contraband.

Barefoot, I followed her through a maze of corridors, chambers and a half dozen locked doors. She finally stopped at a double-barred door guarded by four men.

"This is your sleeping quarters. Tower number ten. After supper, all penitents report back to their towers for the night. There are bunks on every level. Find an empty one. Prayers start at dawn."

She left me with the door guards. They wrote my number down on a list, opened the doors, pushed me inside, and relocked the heavy metal doors.

Locked in a tower. I almost giggled at the thought.

I stepped deeper into the dark room. Bunk beds four high had been stacked around the circular room. The light from the guard station reflected off a dozen pair of eyes. The occupants of the beds stared at me. Was Melina here? Doubtful.

"Uh…hello," I tried.

One woman slipped from a lowest bunk and approached me. She put a finger to her lips. "It's lights out," she whispered then pointed to the guards. "There's an empty bunk on level five. We'll talk tomorrow after supper." She hurried back to her bed.

I climbed a thin corkscrew stairway, counting levels. Lanterns had been set into barred alcoves in the walls of the stairwell. They illuminated the steps while still being unreachable. Which meant I couldn't use fire as a diversion.

No one on level five said a word or even moved when I entered. I found an empty bunk and lay down on the hard wood. No mattress, blanket, or pillow on mine or any of the other beds. Guess penitents didn't deserve comforts.

I didn't sleep that night. The guards tromped up the tower at various times, checking on us. They counted, too, making sure we were all there.

As the night wore on, a queasy lump swirled in my stomach. I'd been optimistic in our chances for success. Overly optimistic.

Morning arrived. Not in the usual way with the slow brightening of the light, but with the gruff voices of the guards, yelling at us to get our lazy asses out of bed. We filed out of the tower and down a corridor. None of the penitents spoke a word. Remembering what the woman had said last night about talking after supper, I kept silent.

We entered a dining room already half full of women. After going through the chow line to collect my breakfast—an unappetizing bowl of mush—I found an empty seat. My stomach almost revolted at the pulpy smell as I tried a mouthful. A gritty cold paste coated my tongue and tasted like a wad of wet parchment. Yuck. I pushed the bowl away.

The others at my table watched me in amusement as they shoveled the mush into their mouths. I scanned the faces of those around me, searching for Melina. The ages of the women ranged from sixteen to fifty years old. Some met my gaze, while others quickly looked away. And a few kept their attention fixed on their bowls of mush.

All wore the brown robes and most had dark stains down by their knees. Their long hair had either been braided, pulled back into a bun, or hung loose. No one had short hair. And no Melina, either. Did we eat in shifts? Or were there more dining rooms? Based on the size of this place, I guessed it had plenty of room for everyone to eat at one time.

Guards patrolled around the edges of the tables with their reed sticks in hand. I followed the others' example and didn't make eye contact with them, but I kept track of their locations. So it wasn't unexpected when one man stopped next to me. However, the sharp line of pain across my shoulders surprised a yelp from me.

"Eat," he said, pointing to my bowl with his weapon.

"I'm not—" Another sting landed on my upper arm.

"Eat."

I pulled the bowl toward me and took a bite. The disgusting texture hadn't improved.

"More." He remained by my side until I choked the rest down.

After we finished, we lined up to use the privy before heading to the prayer room. I paused at the threshold, amazed by the immense square room. Penitents streamed in from multiple entrances and formed long rows facing the same direction. Well over two thousand people. Pushed from behind, I followed the woman in front of me until a guard yanked me from the line.

"New penitents stand in the front until they learn how to pray." He escorted me to the front row.

I stood next to a young woman who flinched any time one of the guards came close to her. Nothing was between us and the stone wall. I'd expected an altar or a religious artifact.

Once the shuffling noise of bare feet on stone stopped, a priestess arrived in a silky robe that flowed around her as she moved. She reached the front and gazed at us.

"You are filthy sinners who do not deserve the creator's forgiveness. Get on your knees and beg for it," she ordered.

Everyone knelt. The collective thump echoed off the walls. I quickly complied, joining them.

The priestess spread her arms wide and raised them. "Look upon the creator's glory and pray for forgiveness."

The skittish girl next to me craned her neck back and stared up. So did the others. I copied them. Far above, the sunlight struck a beautiful square stained-glass window. The intricate design showed a progression of pictures, and I guessed it must be the story of the creator. The monastery's boxy tiers framed the window. Each upper tier smaller than the one below it. Like being inside a wedding cake.

Believing there would be more orders, I glanced back at the front. The priestess had disappeared and a guard stood in her place.

He strode over to me. "Keep your gaze heavenward while you pray. This will be your only warning." He touched the reed hanging from his belt.

I returned to contemplating the stained glass window. It had enough detail to keep my interest for a while. However, my neck soon protested the strain caused by the angle. I bent my head to rub out the kink. Big mistake.

Thwack. The reed cut across my cheek and brought tears to my eyes. The guard raised his arm, pointing up. I gazed at the window again. It didn't take long for the muscles in my neck to cramp and I had to decide between that pain and being whipped by his reed. Enduring as long as possible, I tried to keep still, but as the day continued without any new orders I had to relieve the strain from time to time, earning another slap with each infraction.

Eventually my legs trembled from kneeling for so long. My lower back ached as if I'd been shoveling stones. And my skin burned with multiple welts.

The angle of sunlight changed at a snail's pace. Sounds of others getting slapped broke the silence from time to time. The ladies in the front row fared the worst. As the new sinners, we hadn't built up the endurance to stay in one position for hours.

When the sunlight faded and the colored glass turned black, the priestess returned and allowed us to stand.

Relieved, I straightened. My legs cramped and at first refused to hold my weight. The other penitents in the front row also staggered to their feet. Fresh blood stained many of their robes at knee level, including mine.

We returned to the dining room, ate another bowl of wet parchment, lined up for the privy, and were ordered to our towers. All the while I searched for Melina. And because I hadn't been paying attention, I'd no idea which way to go to find my tower.

Asking a guard resulted in yet another welt. I had to suppress the desire to zap him and take his reed.

Another penitent took pity on me and gestured for me to follow her. After we'd all been accounted for and the tower doors locked, we were allowed to speak until lights out. Everyone but me and the woman who had spoken to me the night before retreated to the upper levels.

She introduced herself as Fydelia and I told her my name. One of my many concerns disappeared. I'd worried everyone called each other by their number and since I didn't know Melina's it'd be impossible to find her.

"Let's go up a few levels and have a chat." Fydelia glanced at the guards.

We climbed up to level three. The others already on that level stared at me with curious expressions, but seemed content to let Fydelia do all the talking. I guessed her age to be around forty.

"Whatcha think of your first day?" Fydelia asked.

"It was horrible," I said, rubbing the back of my neck. It throbbed.

"You'll get used to it or…"

"Or what?"

"Or go insane. Some do."

My thoughts reeled over the whole getting used to it or going insane bit. "Is that—"

"Yep. Every single day is the exact same routine. If we didn't have these few hours to talk, we'd all be insane."

"Who says we're not?" one woman called.

A few laughed.

"Yeah, well, we help each other out here. There's no fighting among ourselves and we don't form gangs. We're not going to make anyone's life harder than it already is. I'll show you some exercises to ease the cramps, but first tell us what's going on? We haven't had any news in months."

I filled them in. They listened intently, leaning forward to hear every word.

"The High Priestess is returning?" Fydelia asked.

"As we speak."

"Damn." Fydelia exchanged a glance with another woman before returning her attention to me. "The war's going badly, isn't it?"

"Yep."

Her forehead creased and she asked me a few more questions about Estrid's retreat. At one point a low whistle sounded and everyone dispersed. Fydelia pulled me to sit next to her on a bunk. Soon after two guards arrived to check on us.

When they left Fydelia said, "They do random checks and if they see us grouped together or doing our exercises, they come more frequently. And if it seems we're too friendly, they'll break us up and assign us to different towers just in case we're planning something." She huffed.

"Exercises?" I asked, hoping to prompt her in that direction. My legs ached and even though I healed faster, I still felt pain.

Fydelia gave me a hard look. "If you're thinking to rat us out to curry favor from the guards, think again. They'll punish you just as hard as us and then you'll be branded a traitor. If you think it's bad now…having over two thousand penitents pissed at you is a hell you don't want to experience."

"I won't say a word."

She studied my expression for a few seconds. Then she led me up to the sixth level of the tower. Women stretched their muscles in a variety of ways. Fydelia showed me how to relieve the cramps in my neck, lower back, and thighs.

"It's not a miracle cure," she said. "It is just a matter of building up your endurance and stamina. It'll get worse before your body adjusts. After that each day will be a little bit better. And once you get through the physical trials, we'll help you with the mental."

"Mental?"

"Once the pain in your body no longer occupies your thoughts, it's a long day staring at that window."

"Oh."

I repeated the exercises Fydelia had demonstrated. From time to time a thump sounded from the level above. More exercises, or something more?

Hard to believe, but the next day was worse than the first. My neck cramped as soon as I tilted my head back. And all my aches and pains flared anew. Keeping still proved almost impossible. A guard stayed by my side the entire day.

When the day's prayers finished, my legs refused to unbend. Fydelia appeared by my side and helped me to my feet. On our way to the dining room, I not only searched for Melina, but for Odd or the members of his odd squad. I needed a sign that our crazy scheme might work. Otherwise, I'd go insane. Too bad I didn't recognize any of the guards.

Later Fydelia joined me as I stretched in the tower.

"Hang in there, Irina. A few more days and then it'll be better," she said.

A few more? Not a pleasant prospect. "What happens if I refuse? Will the guards just whack me all day?"

"No. They'll take you down to the crypt, and…" Fydelia wrapped her arms around her chest.

"Kill you?" I asked in a whisper.

"I wish. The crypt is a place of punishment. Refusing to pray will get you two days down there. The bigger the sin, the longer the stay."

"Do I want to know—"

"No. Trust me."

I debated pressing her for details. My imagination tended to run rampant. With those dire thoughts swirling around my head, I about jumped out of my skin when a thud sounded from the level above us.

"More exercises?" I asked Fydelia.

She pressed her lips together, considering my question. "When you're ready, I'll show you."

"You mean when you trust me?"

She smiled. "There's that. And I'd like to know who you're looking for."

Busted. No sense waiting any longer, I had planned to ask her soon. "Melina from Mengels in Sectven Realm. Do you know her?"

"Depends."

"I'm a friend."

"So? It's not like you'll have a chance to chat and catch up."

True. "I'd like to know she's okay… Well, as okay as you can be in here. And, I've a message from her mother." Which wasn't exactly true, but Melina would be glad to know her mother worried about her.

Fydelia stared at me for a moment then she fiddled with the

frayed hem on her robe. "She had a rough start and ended up in the crypt. But like most of us, after one trip down there, she learned her lesson and hasn't given the guards a reason to take her back. Melina's surviving."

Better than being insane. Another worry off my shoulders. "Do you know which tower she's in?"

"No."

Now it was my turn to study Fydelia. She'd answered too quickly. "Are you trying to protect me? Keep me out of trouble?"

She huffed in amusement. "You're a sharp one, aren't you? Of course I'm trying to help you. I told you that before." Fydelia pulled a thread from the hem, wrapping it around her finger. "I've been here longer than most. I've seen a few penitents disobey the rules over and over. Their stays in the crypt stretch longer and longer until they never return."

The lump that had been my supper rolled over, threatening to push bile up my throat. Fear and uncertainty churned inside me. I'd panic, except I trusted my guys. The vision of Odd's expression flashed before me and I repeated the words to myself. I. Trusted. My. Guys.

"What's the message for Melina?" Fydelia asked.

"Why? She's in another tower. You can't talk to her, either."

Again Fydelia hesitated.

"What else are you keeping from me?" I asked.

"I'm not telling you everything for a reason. When you're taken to the crypt, the guards ask you questions. Lots of questions. They sense we're not as obedient as we act. Weaker penitents will blab and we'll all suffer."

Ah. "And you don't know if I'm the type to blab."

"Right."

I mulled over what I'd learned so far. They had some type

of silent communication system in place. "All right. Can you please tell Melina that I have a message for her?"

"And just how are you going to deliver this message?"

"I figured she'd arrange that. It's obvious you trust her."

"How do you know that?" Fydelia demanded.

"You didn't ask me how *you'd* get my message to *her,* which means she didn't blab to the guards."

Fydelia tapped a finger on her temple. "Too sharp, Irina. That will get you into a whole heap of trouble."

Funny, I already thought I was in a whole heap of trouble.

Over the next two horrible days, I spotted Odd and another man on his squad among the guards, bringing me a bit of mental relief. I kept track of the times when the shift changed. No Quain or Loren, but I hadn't seen any priests. No Melina, either. I worried Fydelia hadn't delivered my message in order to save me and Melina from getting into trouble.

Day four in hell, Odd caught my attention while we filed in for prayers. He gestured, using the signals we'd developed for the times silence was needed during a patrol. Too bad I'd forgotten most of them. I shook my head.

After the torture of staring at the stained glass window, I shuffled to the dining room. Halfway there, Odd yanked me out of line. The others didn't miss a step as they kept moving.

"Did I hear you talk, Penitent?" he demanded.

"No, sir."

He struck me on the arm. It sounded painful, but didn't even sting.

"Who gave you permission to speak?"

This time I kept my mouth shut.

"That's better. Next time I hear a sound from you or your friend, I'll take you *both* down to the crypt. Understand?" He gave me a significant look.

I nodded. Odd wanted me and Melina to get into trouble together. Perhaps he'd worked out an escape route from the crypt.

*When,* I mouthed.

"Before prayers," he whispered then pushed me back into line, disrupting the flow.

Cheered by the thought of getting out of here, I ate without gagging at the taste of the food. Now I needed to convince Fydelia to deliver that message to Melina. And if she wouldn't, I'd try another tactic.

However, in the slight confusion of visiting the privy before reporting to our towers, Melina found me.

She grabbed my hand and pulled me aside. No guards lurked in this section of the corridor, but it wouldn't last.

"What are you doing here?" she whispered. No time for niceties.

"I came to rescue you. Again." I couldn't resist adding that.

Incredulous, she gaped at me.

"Get taken to the crypts before prayers tomorrow. Trust me, we have it all worked out." I hoped.

"Rescue me?" she asked.

"Of course."

"No."

Now it was my turn to gape. "You want to stay here?"

"No, but I can't leave them, Avry. You've seen what goes on in here. We have to rescue *them all.*"

# KERRICK

For the third time since he'd known Avry, he watched her walk away, heading right into danger. Each time, he'd felt powerless and sick to his stomach despite the very good reasons for him to stay behind. Or, in the case of her going undercover in Estrid's holy army, for them to split up. Ignoring the logic for a moment, Kerrick wished he could go all caveman on her. Drag her to a safe location, order her to not leave his sight, and protect her.

Of course, she'd fight and he'd only get two steps before she'd zap him. And if he'd been attracted to meek women, he'd have married that beautiful mouse his mother had tried to push on him ten years ago. Not for him. And those qualities he loved about Avry—smart, independent, selfless, and stubborn—were what drove her to risk her life for others.

Kerrick had followed Avry and the others until they'd reached Chinska Mare. Then he stood at the edge of the forest as they waited in line to enter the city. After they passed through the gate, he returned to the horses.

Once they rescued Melina, they wouldn't need the horses. Better to elude pursuers without the noisy creatures. Yet... Kerrick studied the big russet male. Despite his size, the stallion walked with a light graceful step. And he hadn't spooked. Not once.

The horse eyed him with intelligence. Or was that Kerrick's imagination? Still, Kerrick wondered if he could train the horse to move silently through the forest. Once he found the aqueduct's southern exit, he wouldn't have much else to do. And a quiet horse would be quite handy.

"What do you say, boy? You up for a challenge?" Kerrick asked, stroking the horse's neck.

The horse snorted and pawed the ground. Kerrick decided that was horse for yes. He also thought the horse needed a name. Huxley was the first name that popped into his head. Hux had been the stable master for Kerrick's father and had taught Kerrick how to ride and care for horses. He'd also been one of the first to die of the plague.

"How about Hux? Do you like that name?" he asked.

Another snort and paw. Kerrick was two for two.

After he checked on the other horses, Kerrick led them to a nearby stable and sold them. The effort to leave the forest to handle the sale exhausted him, and he slept until late the next morning.

He mounted Hux, then headed southwest at a walk. Slacking the reins, Kerrick let the horse choose the path while he listened to the sounds created by Hux's hooves on the forest floor. A rustle of leaves, a crack of a twig and a scrape as he brushed a hoof over a fallen branch. Not bad. Most people made more noise than that.

Kerrick spurred him into a trot. At this pace, the horse chose his steps with more care, creating less noise. The canter was all drumming hooves and loud crashing. Not good.

Keeping Hux did have one benefit. He'd reached the south side of the city by late afternoon. Although the trees near the city's southern wall had been chopped down and the vines pulled from the marble, the rest of the forest had been allowed to grow right up to it. He guessed the exit would be covered with greenery.

The forest sensed the wall as a rocky barrier thwarting its efforts to expand. Kerrick stretched his awareness, but didn't feel any holes or gaps. Guess he'd have to find it the old-fashioned way.

He urged Hux to go east, paralleling the wall. When they reached a small muddy stream, Kerrick entered it and turned the horse left. Splashing in the water, Hux raised his head as if startled, but he didn't balk. A few steps later, Kerrick smelled a foul odor. Probably what upset Hux. It wasn't mud that turned the water brown, but sewage and offal.

However, the stench meant they'd found the exit. And sure enough, the stream led right into the wall. Bushes and saplings covered most of the round hole, but the middle above the water remained clear.

Kerrick dismounted and examined the duct. Boot prints both coming and going marked the mud near the water. The bushes had been pruned back just enough to let a man pass without brushing against them. Someone had used this exit quite recently. Probably to go inside the city, since Kerrick didn't sense anyone nearby.

The vegetation reached inside the duct so Kerrick led Hux away and tied him to a tree. Then he made a torch and returned. Cringing at the smell, he entered and explored the tunnel, hunching over so he didn't hit his head.

The greenery stopped when the light from the opening faded into blackness. The pull from the forest increased with each step, but he pushed as deep as possible. He found a wagon, which confirmed his suspicions.

Smugglers were using this passage to bring in black-market goods. No surprise, considering all forms of entertainment were illegal in Chinska Mare. Kerrick imagined the smugglers earned a large profit due to the danger.

He retreated to where he'd left Hux, mulling over his discovery. The smugglers wouldn't be happy that their secret entrance was known. The empty wagon meant no one was inside the city at the moment, or else they'd have taken the wagon to deliver the goods. Not much Kerrick could do at this point. He'd keep alert for intruders and hope the smugglers didn't return anytime soon.

To pass the time, Kerrick trained Hux. Or rather, he tried. His father's stable master had worked with their horses, but Kerrick hadn't been interested in that trade. Kerrick used positive reinforcement and repetition, hoping for the best.

On the third day of his vigil, the forest pulsed with unease. Irritants had intruded, leaving the main path and heading this way. Kerrick counted five. Three men and two women. He led Hux farther away, then sought a strategic position to watch them.

Crashing through the underbrush, one of the men cursed. "I'm bringing my machete next time," he growled.

"Good idea, Jack, and why don't you invite a priest along, too. Save us all some time," another man groused.

"Shut up, Sylas," Jack said.

The smugglers each carried a barrel probably full of alcohol. Short swords hung from their belts and each had a dagger tucked on the opposite side. They aimed for the tunnel.

"Ugh. It stinks," one of the women said. "I thought the ducts were no longer in use."

"They ain't, princess. This is just runoff from the streets," Jack said.

"Smells like profit to me," the third man said, chuckling.

Kerrick thought fast. He needed to keep the entrance clear. And, although Avry and the guys could handle five armed opponents, the smugglers might ambush them in the dark tunnels. Casualties were not an option.

He had to stop them now.

# CHAPTER 13

"All? As in all 2095 of them?" I asked Melina.

"Yes."

"That's impossible." I didn't even know if the two of us would make it out, let alone thousands.

"Then I'm not leaving." She dashed away.

Stunned I stood there until a guard noticed and reminded me with two strikes of his reed that I needed to report to my tower. The sting from his weapon barely registered as I hurried back. Now what?

Could everyone escape? They vastly outnumbered the guards, but all the guards inside here only had keys to the towers. We couldn't get far without the rest of the keys. And the guards on the other side wouldn't open them for us. Unless Odd could steal all the keys?

I trudged up to the sixth level. Stretching my legs, back, and neck muscles, I concentrated on the problem. I understood why Melina wanted to rescue them all—my stomach soured at the idea of leaving them behind—but…

Fydelia joined me. "Did you talk to Melina?"

"Yeah, thanks."

"Didn't go as you expected, did it?"

I met her gaze. And she accused me of being too smart for my own good. No sense lying to her. "No."

She nodded.

Taking a chance, I asked, "Has anyone ever escaped?"

If she was surprised by the change in topic, she didn't show it. "Nope."

"Has anyone tried?"

"Yep."

"And?"

"The guards can't be seduced or bribed or tricked—it's been tried dozens of times. And the last time there was a riot, guards from the outer perimeters flooded the prayer room brandishing swords. It wasn't pretty."

"Were you here?"

"It was right before I arrived, so I got an up-close look at the consequences." She shuddered.

So much for overpowering the guards. "Has anyone been forgiven and released?" I asked.

"Nope."

No surprise. A thud sounded from above.

Fydelia gnawed on her lower lip. "If we had weapons, it'd be a different story." She gave me a pointed look.

Many of these women had been soldiers in Estrid's holy army. If they kept their skills sharp... Another muted thump. "You're still training, aren't you?"

"Yep."

"*All* of you?"

"Yep."

"Just in case?"

"We've been here a long time. And you never know when the opportunity will arise. And I'm thinking you're that opportunity, Irina."

Gee, no pressure. "I don't—"

"Weapons and opportunity, Irina. We'll do the rest." She left.

If only it were that easy. I spent the rest of the night mulling it over. Aside from the wood from the bunk beds, we had no other materials to make weapons. The metal spoons we used during meals could be of use. Except the guards would notice if a couple thousand spoons went missing.

Eventually, I drifted to sleep.

*"My, my, what a pickle you're in, my dear," Tohon said. He lounged next to me on a huge canopy bed, wearing only his black silk pajama pants. "Trying to save the world, again?"*

*"I thought I banished you," I grumbled.*

*"You thought wrong." He patted the space next to him, inviting me closer.*

*"Not even in your dreams, Tohon."*

*He tsked. "Nasty. Kerrick's influence, no doubt. That man really needs to die. He's been…so close." Tohon sighed. "At least he's not here to disturb us, my dear."*

*I ignored him.*

*He laughed. "And you left poor Ryne to deal with all the nasties to save one girl."*

*"We're going to rescue them all," I shot back.*

*"Now who's being overconfident?" He linked his hands together and rested them on his chest. "You might as well just stay here, my dear. It'll be safer."*

*Unable to resist, I asked, "Why?"*

*"The Skeleton King wants to taste you, Cellina wants to tear you apart, and Ryne wants to chain you to the infirmary. Here they just want you to pray."*

*"I don't believe in the creator."*

*"Then pray to me, my dear."*

When I woke the next morning, no brilliant ideas had struck me while I slept. However, if desperate, I could point

Melina out to Odd and have him take her to the crypt on a trumped-up infraction. *If* I could find her. But that plan felt wrong. Maybe Odd would have an idea.

I lingered behind at breakfast, letting the others file out. Odd signaled me and this one I knew. *All set?*

I shook my head. He scowled.

When the room emptied, he fisted the collar of my robe and pushed me against the wall. "What's going on?" His voice hissed in my ear.

"Change of plans."

"Time's short. *She's* close."

Only one she— Estrid. I told him what I hoped to do. "We can't leave them."

"You. Are. Insane."

"They've been training. We just need weapons."

"You need to reconnect with reality. It's impossible."

"Use the sleeping powder I gave you on the guards." I knew that container I swiped would come in handy.

"It won't take them all out."

"Better than none. We have to try."

He groaned. "When?"

"After supper before we're locked up for the night."

"Give me a couple days."

"Do we have a couple days?"

"It'll be tight. I'll signal you at breakfast when we're set. Make sure the women are ready."

"I will."

As I knelt and stared at the stained-glass ceiling, I planned how we'd incapacitate the tower guards. An all-out riot wouldn't work—too noisy. Better to have small units striking at the same time. Half-forgotten memories of conversations between Ryne and his officers flared to life. Ryne had

stressed the three key elements in a successful attack were surprise, speed, and intensity.

A familiar female voice startled me from my planning.
Oh, no. I snuck a quick glance in the direction of the commanding tone. Jael. She walked with two priests. What was
she doing here?

"Yes, I'm very excited the High Priestess is returning," Jael
said not sounding excited at all. "And I want to make sure all
is well for my mother-in-law's arrival."

Murmurs of assurance from the priests. The desire to hide
pulsed in my chest, but I remained in position to keep from
attracting attention.

"Are all the penitents healthy?" Jael asked.

"Yes, General," one of the priests said.

General, eh? With Estrid and her officers trapped and then
frozen in stasis, I'd bet no message of Jael's deceit had been
sent to Chinska Mare. So this was where Jael's been hiding.
Smart, very smart. But now that Estrid was returning... What
did that mean for Jael?

"Are they fed and bathed regularly?" Jael asked.

"Yes, General."

"And this is where they pray all day?"

"From sunup to sundown."

"I want to see their sleeping quarters, and then I'll take a
look at your schedules and the books."

"Of course, General. Right this way."

Their footsteps faded and I bit my lip. Jael's presence complicated things. Big-time. Her powers could ruin all my plans.
Or could it? She had told me she could only affect a dozen
people at a time with her air magic. She would increase the
danger, but we couldn't stop now.

For the first time since I'd been in the monastery, the day

flew by. After we returned to our towers, I explained every-thing to Fydelia. Her smile grew as I talked.

"No guarantee that this is going to work," I said. "And now we have General Jael to worry about."

"We'll make it work," she said. "I already have teams in each tower."

"You do?"

"I told you, we've been training for a long time. And we'll keep the attacks quiet."

"You won't have weapons until Sergeant Odd shows up with his men."

"Not a problem. All the tower guards have are their reeds. I just could never figure out how to get past the next barrier without weapons."

"I want to be a part of tower ten's strike team," I said.

She studied me. "Do you know hand-to-hand combat?"

"I have the hand-to-hand thing down. Don't worry, I can hold my own."

Fydelia didn't appear to be convinced. I told her about my powers.

And for the first time since I'd known her, Fydelia looked rattled. "You're that healer who helped Melina?"

"Yep."

"You came to rescue her again?"

"Yep."

"Are you crazy?"

"Apparently. But I promised her mother," I fessed up. "Melina wouldn't cooperate with my original plan, and she had an excellent reason. We can't leave all of you."

"Thank the creator."

"Are you sure you want to do that? After all, the creator is the reason you're in here. Plus you might want to wait to see how all this ends up first."

"Have faith."

I laughed. We continued to discuss the details. "How will you let the other towers know when to attack?" I asked.

"During prayers." She grinned. "We're packed in so close that there's lots of communication going on then. The guards can't watch all of us at the same time. Give me your hand."

Curious I held out my right hand. She turned it so my palm faced up. Then she traced a pattern on my palm with her finger nail. "We signal hand to hand. I can do this without looking."

"What did it mean?"

"It's time."

After lights out, I lay on the hard wood of my bunk, marveling at the turn in events. If we rescued them all, that would be a big blow to Estrid. But I kept a tight grip on my emotions. Too many unknowns, and too many things had to go right, which Tohon gleefully pointed out in my dreams every night.

I'd relax later when we rendezvoused with Kerrick. Perhaps we'd celebrate with a private party—just the two of us in a cozy hollow. My body warmed at the thought. I missed him.

Cold, harsh reality intruded in the morning. Roused by the guards, we filed out, ate breakfast, visited the privy, and knelt for prayers. Neither Odd nor any of his men was among the guards. Unease swirled. I spent the day listing all the things that could go wrong—a very long list.

The next morning, I spotted one of Odd's men with the guards. He ignored me, which meant I'd have to endure yet another day on my knees, staring at the ceiling. I searched my memories, recalling just how many locked doors we'd crossed on our way in. My gaze drifted to the levels framing the window. Remembering the monastery had resembled a wedding cake, I guessed each frame was a floor. I counted eight floors. The towers had seven levels, which fit with what I'd seen. The top of the towers didn't reach the highest tier.

Interesting. There were also eight sets of doors on the way to freedom. That meant we were on the ground floor and in the dead center of the square building.

When we returned to our towers, I realized Fydelia had been right. After seven days on my knees, I didn't feel quite so stiff and sore and I had healing powers. How long would it have taken my body to adjust without my magic? My opinion of these women increased.

On my eighth day of penitence, Odd signaled me during breakfast. Thank the Flea! At this point, I craved action. Any action other than staring at a window. Now I understood why some women had gone insane.

I caught Fydelia's attention and raised my eyebrows. She kept her face neutral, but a spark flared behind her eyes. Game on.

*Last time, last time, last time.* I chanted the words in my mind to keep from screaming out loud. Reviewing the attack plan only lasted so long—it was imprinted in my brain at this point. I sneaked a few glances at the guards, earning a couple of whacks. Of the forty-eight inside the center area, only Odd and two of his men were on our side. That left forty-five.

I scanned for Jael, as well. She hadn't returned since I'd last seen her, but she had to be up to something. After an eternity, the sun set. Needing my strength, I shoveled the wet paste into my mouth. At this point, even Quain's squirrel soup would taste divine. Not that I'd tell him.

I joined the line heading to our tower with Fydelia and the ladies who had been chosen to carry out the attack. With my heart climbing up my throat, I followed the team.

The four guards of tower ten checked off penitents as the women showed them their bracelets. "…number four-three-seven. Number two-nine-one. Number six-zero-four. Number one-five-nine-five. Number— Oof!"

Fydelia and her team didn't hesitate, striking so fast the men didn't have time to grab their weapons. The team pounced and immobilized the men all in utter silence as I darted in and touched the napes of the guards' necks, zapping them to ensure they'd stay knocked out for a few hours.

"Quick, drag them inside," Fydelia ordered in a low voice. "Strip them. Joelle and Suzanne, change clothes, now."

I raced around to the other towers, knocking out any guards that were still conscious and helped to subdue those who resisted. All the guards were locked inside the towers and stripped. Volunteers donned their uniforms.

Finding Melina in tower four, I gestured to her. "Stay close to me until I say so. Understand?"

With a gleam in her eyes, she nodded. "Thanks."

"Save it for later."

Odd helped at tower three. "The others?" he asked.

"So far, so good." I zapped the man he had in a head lock. "Oh, and keep an eye out for Jael."

"Jael's here?"

"She was." I explained about her visit as we headed for tower one.

Odd cursed an impressive and creative string of expletives. At tower one, the women had cornered Odd's man. Blood dripped from a gash on his forehead.

"He's with us," I said, examining the cut. "Not deep, you'll live."

He glanced at the women surrounding us. A variety of fierce and determined expressions glared at him. "Are you sure?" he asked.

"Have you hit any of them since working here?"

"Of course not."

"Then you're good. Come on, you're needed up front."

The three men stood in front of the first set of locked doors. Fanned out behind them were nine women disguised as guards. Together they represented the first shift change of the evening. Hopefully the men on the other side wouldn't look too close. The other two thousand plus penitents waited out of sight. They didn't make a sound.

Odd knocked on the door at the appropriate time. The panel slid back. Melina grabbed my hand.

"Yeah?" a voice asked.

"The princesses are secure," Odd said.

Oh, please.

"Who thought of that code?" the guy grumbled, but he unlocked the door.

When it swung open, Odd stepped forward. "Brother Quain thought we should be nicer to the ladies."

"These aren't ladies, they're—"

Odd grabbed him by the throat. "Careful what you say."

The women surged forward. The replacement guards had been waiting in the narrow hallway just behind the guy dangling from Odd's fist. A cry rippled through them. While they didn't have swords, they had their reeds and had a little more notice than their colleagues inside. However, a few swayed on their feet, staring sleepily at the strangely quiet ruckus around them. Odd must have laced their supper with my powder.

Instructing Melina to keep out of the way of the fighting, I entered the fray to zap a guard or two. During one foray, a guard hooked his arm around my neck.

"Stop, or I'll kill her," he cried.

No one listened to him. I touched his hand, sending waves of pain into his body. He yelped and sank to his knees, bringing me down with him. Unable to reach the sweet spot, I called for help. Melina and four women pried him off of me and held him so I could knock him out.

By that time, the others had been neutralized. I touched the remaining guards.

"Weapons?" Fydelia asked.

"We stashed a half dozen in the break room down the hall, but there are more once we get past the next barrier," Odd said.

All good. And no sign of Jael.

Fydelia and her group followed Odd. I glanced behind at the lines of women. A few panted from the effort, a few sported cuts and bruises, and a few grinned with vicious delight while the rest appeared nervous. No one said a word. All those days praying in silence had been the perfect training.

Now armed, Fydelia signaled us to follow her and Odd. We crept along the hallway until we reached another set of locked double doors. Fydelia swept her hand out and the women behind me and Melina formed one line, pressing against the left wall.

Taking up positions to either side of the doors, Odd, Fydelia, and the five ladies with the swords waited. And waited. And waited.

I kept expecting the women to murmur with impatience and questions. Maybe because I had to bite my lip to keep from asking Odd what the heck we were—

The rasp of metal and a loud clang sounded. The doors opened and three priests entered with two guards right behind them.

"I assure you, Brothers. We've been holding penitents for fifty years. No one has ever escaped," the priest in the middle said.

Odd and Fydelia jumped them, disarmed the guards, and

pinned the priests to the wall with swords pointed at their chests.

"You were saying, Brother Keidan?" Quain asked, holding his hands up.

"I..." Brother Keidan stared at Fydelia in utter shock.

"Well, there's a miracle," Quain said. "First time Brother Wind Bag has been speechless."

"Avry, are you going to introduce us to your friends?" Loren asked.

Fydelia glanced at me. "Avry?"

"I'll explain later. Those two are part of my rescue team." I introduced them to her.

The women let the monkeys free.

Loren reached under his robe and pulled out a set of my throwing knives bundled together. "Thought you might want these." He tossed it.

I caught it in midair. "Ah, Loren, you really know how to spoil a girl."

"I aim to please."

"Real touching," Odd said drily. "But we need to stay focused. And we'll need Keidan's robe."

"Strip," Fydelia ordered, poking the priest with her sword's tip, drawing blood.

He scrambled to comply.

Odd hooked a thumb at the guards. "Avry, could you?"

I zapped them, and after Keidan stripped, I knocked him out, too. Odd handed the red robe to his man that hadn't gotten cut. He donned it.

"You said there were more weapons?" Fydelia asked.

"Right this way." Odd led.

We all followed him into the next hallway. Two barriers down, six more to go. They collected another dozen swords and with the three "priests" in the front, they tricked another set of doors open. A fight ensued, but I waited to use my knives. After subduing the guards, we picked up more swords. And my pack. The monkeys had stashed it with the weapons.

"It was in the crypt," Loren said, gesturing. "We just managed to get it here after you pulled your little surprise on us."

"You're the best." I blew him a kiss.

"Hey, what about me?" Quain asked.

"You're second best, as always," Loren said.

Quain drew breath to argue.

"Not the time for this, gentlemen," Odd said.

Managing to get past two more barriers, we ran into bigger trouble at the sixth set of locked doors. We no longer had the element of surprise. No one answered our knocks. Shouts and screams echoed as guards arrived from other entrances, pinning us in.

A handful of armed women rushed to get between the guards and the unarmed penitents, forming two lines of defense on both sides of us. From here on out, we'd have to keep these lines so the others behind us could escape without harm. Quain yanked his lock picks from his pocket and knelt by the door.

Just as he popped the lock, it burst open, knocking him back. The guards who pushed through spotted the red robes and paused for a moment in confusion. It was all Odd and Fydelia needed. They pounced. More defenders waited on the other side of the doors and, even though a few of them moved as if drugged, it was a struggle to fight our way into the next hallway.

The number of guards increased as we broke through the seventh barrier. But the women would not be stopped. Determined, driven, and fierce, they filled the narrow space, sweeping away the opposition like raging flood waters.

Keeping Melina close, I stayed right behind Odd and the

monkeys. The last set of doors led to the outside. And blocking our path to freedom were a dozen priests. Alert and prepared for battle with a long swords in each hand, they waited for us.

I wiped sweat from my face. Tired from using my powers, I blinked at the final obstacle, calculating our odds. I tucked Melina behind me. At least Jael wasn't among them.

"Oh, hell, no," Fydelia said. "They're not stopping us." She raised her bloody sword into the air. "For the girls!"

Repeated and shouted over and over, the cry rippled along the women. Time to get out of the way. I flattened my body against the wall, pushing Melina with my arm to do the same.

The women surged forward, intent on their targets. Steel clanged on steel, guttural growls mixed with higher-pitched shouts as they engaged in a fierce battle. No chance for me to dash and zap. This melee was primal. A desperate fight for survival. And their sheer numbers gave the women the advantage.

Odd and the monkeys stood in the thick of things. I gripped Melina's hand, unable to tear my gaze away as an ache grew in my chest. Stabbed and sliced, women either stumbled back or collapsed in a heap. Others dragged them from harm then took their place.

Palming one of my knives, I aimed with care. Unexpected in the midst of the fight, my blade pierced a shoulder. The wounded priest lost his momentum and Quain pressed his advantage. With one quick strike, he buried his sword into his opponent's stomach.

A queasy slush coated my throat. While I hadn't made the killing blow, my actions had resulted in the man's death. As a healer, it violated my purpose in life. As a penitent, it was a necessary evil.

Keeping the image of two thousand women on their knees in my mind, I aimed again. Odd and the monkeys battled their way to the doors with an impressive amount of skill. While

Quain worked on the locks, the others protected him. I threw my remaining knives, helping them.

It seemed Quain moved in slow motion. Unable to just stand there any longer, I joined those assisting the casualties. Melina followed. More than a dozen had been injured. Blood splattered their robes, matted their hair, and dripped from cuts. I checked each one. A couple had already died. And a few would soon—their injuries fatal. And one young lady teetered on the borderline. The slight woman had been stabbed in the ribs and had a punctured lung. I could assume her injuries. But should I?

I glanced at Melina. She ripped strips of cloth from the bottom of her robe, making bandages. Mom would be proud.

A loud bang then a crack sounded. The fighters flinched, but when the fresh air swept in, erasing the odors of sweat and blood, it recharged the penitents. They doubled their efforts and the remaining warriors fell.

"Quick, this way," Loren ordered.

They streamed out into the dark street with Quain in the lead. For each wounded lady, two friends supported her. Careful of her ribs, I pulled the borderline patient over my shoulder. Small and thin, she weighed almost nothing.

By the time I reached the street, Flea and Ives had joined Quain. The women pooled around them, drawing unwanted attention. I caught up to them.

"What are you waiting for?" I demanded.

"We're trying to figure out another route through the tunnels," Ives said. "With this many people, the one we lit will draw too much attention."

"Stick with your original route. Staying hidden is no longer a priority."

"We should make sure they all escape," Quain said.

"They need to follow the lanterns. We set them this afternoon," Flea said.

"Ives and Flea, take point," I ordered. "Keep Melina with you. Odd, you and the monkeys stay with Fydelia and her team to ensure we assist as many women as possible."

Melina protested, but I cut her off. "Go with Flea. I'll catch up."

"What about…?" She gestured to the injured girl.

"I've got her. Now go."

They took off at a run and the women followed. I moved slower. But I encouraged those streaming past me to keep going. Turning left, we traveled through an alley for a couple blocks before entering the underground aqueducts. I gagged on the rotten smell. The splashing sound of hundreds of pairs of bare feet in the cold wet muck echoed throughout the stone tunnel. The noise alone would call every guard and priest down on us. The lanterns were spaced far enough apart to create little pockets of darkness, but close enough that those pockets only happened in straightaways.

Eventually, I was the last in line. Or so I thought. Footsteps splashed behind me, and I turned to ask for help as the girl had grown too heavy for me. And just when I'd thought we'd avoided Jael, there she stood, wearing a penitent's robe and holding a sword. Her fury pressed on me like a wet blanket. Or was that her magic? This wasn't going to end well.

"Side tunnel, now," Jael ordered, indicating a left branch.

I headed into the tunnel, walking until the light dimmed.

"Keep going," Jael said.

I pushed deeper into the darkness until ordered to stop.

"Put the girl down."

Setting the girl on the ground, I knelt next to her. Her breath rasped in painful gulps. There was just enough light to see fresh blood had soaked her robe.

I turned to Jael. "I need to heal her."

"No you don't." Jael stepped closer. "You need to stop interfering, to stop ruining all my plans. To just stop!"

"How did I—"

"These women were mine. *I* planned to rescue them and use them for my new army and you...you..." She sputtered with rage. "You. Need. To. Stop."

I braced for Jael to suck my breath from my lungs or use the air to smash me against the stone walls. But she ran straight at me. I jerked in surprise right before the blade of her sword pierced my chest just below my right breast.

Pain exploded as my ribs broke. Air whooshed from my right lung. After she yanked the blade out, I collapsed to my knees, sucking in air laced with tiny needles. Fire burned around my heart. I keeled over on my left side.

Jael leaned over me. "That should stop you."

And this time, I agreed with her.

# KERRICK

Kerrick had to keep the smugglers from entering the aqueducts. Concentrating, he encouraged the bushes to thicken around the five smugglers' legs, impeding their forward motion so the vines had time to wind around their ankles. Because it was the middle of autumn, he needed to use his magic to spur the sluggish vegetation.

"What the…" Jack swore.

"The vines!" Princess dropped her barrel and yanked her sword out.

Kerrick increased his efforts, hoping to trap them before they could cut the vines.

"Just calm down," Sylas said.

But his companions ignored him. Dumping the barrels, they thrashed and swung their swords.

"Death Lily," the third man cried out. "Has to be—"

"Not possible," Sylas said.

"You lying sack of— Eep." A vine twisted around the other lady's sword arm.

They fought and struggled, but the vines soon ensnared them. While they accused and blamed each other for their predicament, Kerrick leaned against a tree, panting from the exertion.

What now?

He listed his options. One—keep them immobilized until Avry arrived. It'd work for a day, maybe two, but after that it would be cruel.

Two—the forest could transport them away from the entrance and then release them. But what would stop them from returning with more armed men and cutting a path? Nothing.

Three—scare them away. How? Every citizen of Ozero Realm was terrified of the priests and acolytes. Perhaps he could... No. If they'd been caught by priests they'd be arrested, not warned off. What about a rival gang? He huffed in amusement. A gang of two—him and Hux—real scary. And yet... Something snagged in his mind. A ghost of the forest. That wouldn't quite work. But when combined with Quain's weed boy...

A silly idea popped in his head. He almost dismissed it, but, upon deeper inspection, it might just work if he could pull it off with a straight face. If the monkeys ever found out, he'd never hear the end of it. Best to ensure they didn't find out.

Kerrick mounted Huxley. The contact transformed the horse's hide into the colors of the forest. Signaling Hux into a quiet walk, he headed back to the trapped smugglers. Before they reached them, Kerrick stopped Hux and invited the vines to spiral up Hux's legs. The horse cocked his ear back and turned his head to peer at Kerrick with his left eye, questioning.

Kerrick patted him on the neck. "It's okay," he whispered.

The easygoing horse seemed satisfied and stood still while the vines wrapped around them both. Weed Boy, the ghost of the forest was ready to make a grand entrance.

Moving at a slow pace to accommodate the vines, Kerrick and Hux stepped into view. The smugglers' bickering ceased the moment they noticed him.

With a booming voice, Kerrick asked, "Who dares enter *my* forest?"

They stared at him for a moment. He hoped they saw a giant leaf creature.

"Uh," Jack said. "This isn't your—"

"Silence!" Kerrick raised his arm.

The vines holding Jack gagged him, muffling his cries of distress.

"Anyone else care to correct me?" Kerrick asked.

The rest remained quiet.

"Good. You must leave *my* forest and never return. Or..." Kerrick urged the vines to tighten around the captives, making it hard for them to breathe. When he was certain they'd gotten the point, he eased the pressure. "Understand?"

They nodded. Even Jack.

"Good. Now be gone!" He swept his arm dramatically— the monkeys would be giggling by now.

The vines dragged the smugglers along the forest floor. Kerrick and Hux followed. When they reached the main path, Kerrick had the vines release the smugglers.

They staggered to their feet and, without a backward glance, bolted down the path. Kerrick wondered if they'd warn their cohorts away, or if he'd have to deal with more intruders before Avry and the others arrived. He resigned himself to the fact that weed boy might be needed again.

He waited until the dust of the smugglers' passage had settled, then allowed the vines to drop from him and Hux. The horse snorted as if commenting about the strange antics of humans. Kerrick didn't disagree with him.

They returned to the campsite. Kerrick dismounted, landing on weak legs. While his connection to the living green remained a part of him, he struggled to manipulate the foliage. Unlike in early autumn, he now needed to draw power in order to use the forest. And each day it was a little bit harder.

Kerrick stretched out on his bedroll. Exhaustion pressed on him. Using his magic shouldn't be this draining. It had depleted his energy before he sickened, but now it required double the effort. Why? He'd no idea. Too tired to puzzle out the logic, Kerrick rolled onto his side and fell asleep.

The next morning, Kerrick kept his vigil and stayed alert for potential problems while continuing to train Huxley. Each day he stayed busy to avoid sinking into dire speculation over why Avry hadn't arrived yet.

By the eighth day, Kerrick had to admit something had gone wrong at the monastery. He'd promised to rescue Avry if she'd gotten caught. Now all he needed to figure out was how.

The main problem was his inability to leave the forest for long. But what if he took the forest with him? How? Would the vines stretch into the aqueducts? Probably, but not all the way into the city. What if he carried bushes with him? He'd need his hands. And Hux wouldn't fit in the tunnel.

Remembering the wagon, Kerrick fetched it. He wove vines together and made small sheets. Then he dug up two bushes and, careful to pack the dirt around their roots, he wrapped the root ball in the sheet and tied it tight.

With the bushes in the wagon, Kerrick entered the aqueduct. He pulled the wagon behind him with one hand and held a torch with his other. Passing the end of the greenery, Kerrick felt the familiar pressure return. Damn. Kerrick used his magic to continue on. Soon after, he struggled to move forward until he reached the end of his invisible tether. The light from his torch illuminated numbers and letters that had been painted on the walls. An intersection was just a few feet away.

Bitterness pulsed as he debated his next move. If he depleted his strength now, he'd be useless. Kerrick needed a better idea. Retreating to the forest and Hux, he rested and mulled over the problem.

By the time he'd regained his energy, the sun had set. Not that it mattered in the dark tunnels, but he also hadn't formulated a plan.

Kerrick huddled next to a small fire. Maybe he'd been rash to scare the smugglers off. He could have paid them to go into the city... And what? Find Flea and Ives? They were supposed to report back to him if something went wrong inside the monastery. Their absence meant they, too, encountered trouble. The smugglers wouldn't break into the monastery for all the gold in his pocket; everyone in Ozero Realm was terrified of the priests.

Even though he had the entire forest at his command, he couldn't do a damn thing to save Avry. Not without help. And who would help him? Not Ryne. Noak? If the tribesmen did travel south with his warriors to aid Ryne, perhaps Kerrick could intercept them. But when should Kerrick abandon his vigil? Tomorrow morning? No. The sooner the better.

Energized, Kerrick hopped to his feet and packed up his meager supplies. He spread the burning logs out and went to fetch water to douse the flames. As he scooped up dirty water, a faint rumble reached him. It emanated from the aqueduct. He approached the entrance and leaned in to listen.

The sound grew louder. Water rushing? Kerrick wondered if it was a good idea to be standing at this spot. Curiosity kept him in place. More splashing followed, and a drumming that echoed off the stone walls. When a voice cried out over the din, Kerrick yanked his sword free. A glow from a torch lit the interior and he backed up.

Friend or foe? He'd find out soon. Retreating to a better position, Kerrick waited.

From the amount of noise, Kerrick guessed at least a company of soldiers was racing toward the exit. It couldn't be Avry and the others, they wouldn't produce that much—

Flea and Ives burst from the aqueduct. Kerrick's relief didn't last long as more people streamed out. Were they being chased?

He pulled power, turning normal and intercepted Flea who stumbled through the underbrush with Melina right behind him. She carried a torch.

"What's—" he tried.

"We have them all." Flea gestured to the others wildly.

People continued to pour out. Some carrying torches, others swords. All wearing robes and no shoes. All women.

"All? As in *all* the girls in the monastery?"

"Yes, over two thousand. We must keep moving."

Kerrick heard the number, but he didn't quite comprehend it until the forest protested the trampling of the bushes and vines by so many feet. He didn't recognize anyone else.

"Which way?" Flea demanded.

Sneaking through the forest was no longer an option. They needed to get to Pomyt Realm fast. Kerrick pointed. "Head straight. When you reach the path, turn right and follow it."

"Are you coming?"

"Where's Avry?"

Flea gestured behind him. "Back there somewhere."

The tightness around his heart eased. "I'll catch up. I want to make sure everyone gets out."

Flea nodded and, calling for the others to follow him, he ran. The women formed a single line. Many glanced at him as they passed. They regarded him with a variety of expressions, mostly curious, but the ones clutching swords shot him hostile glares as if he'd dare to attack them. No one said a word. Strange and smart.

The women continued to race by. Kerrick scanned the faces,

searching for Avry. An amazing number of people gushed from the tunnel. And he fully expected priests to be close on their heels.

After the main surge finished, the slower escapees—the wounded and those supporting them—trickled out. Avry should be with this group. Instead, Odd and his men assisted them.

Kerrick didn't hesitate. He approached Odd. A woman covered in blood and gripping an equally bloody sword stopped and stepped close to Odd as if to protect him. Kerrick ignored her. "Where's Avry?" he asked Odd.

Surprised, Odd glanced around. "Didn't she come out?"

"No."

"She should have."

Kerrick stifled the desire to strangle the man. "That doesn't help."

Odd exchanged a look with the woman. "I thought she was ahead of us."

"She was carrying Palma," the woman said.

"Palma was injured, right?" Kerrick asked even though he knew the answer.

"Yes, badly. She—"

Odd cursed. "She stopped to heal her."

"But I didn't see anyone. I made sure we were the last and I extinguished the lanterns," the woman said.

"Avry probably ducked down a side tunnel so no one would stop to help and risk getting caught," Kerrick said. "Is anyone chasing you?"

"No one from the monastery—the women were thorough, but I'm sure the priests will organize a posse to come after us," Odd said. He cursed again. "Fydelia, you catch up with your ladies. Kerrick and I will go back and find Avry before they do."

If Odd had stabbed him in the stomach, it would have felt better than knowing Avry was in trouble nearby and he couldn't help her.

"I can't." Kerrick forced the words out.

He watched Odd enter the tunnels. The sergeant carried a torch and Kerrick's life. If something happened to Avry... He stopped his dire thoughts. Instead, he prepared to intercept the priests and guards from the monastery.

Kerrick expected dozens to chase after the women. What he didn't expect was Jael exiting the aqueducts holding a bloody sword.

Shocked, he observed her. Jael wore a penitent robe. Surely she hadn't been incarcerated, too. What was her game? Her beautiful face was creased into a scowl as she scanned the woods. The trail left by the women was clear. At least she was alone. For now.

Kerrick had to intercept her. But he wasn't sure how to do it. Her air magic was much stronger than his forest magic. Perhaps he could ensnare her in vines and knock her unconscious. Then what? She'd be impossible to incarcerate or rendered harmless.

"Kerrick, I know you're here. Show yourself," Jael called.

He pulled power and turned normal, hoping to distract her from the vines creeping toward her legs.

"Wow, you look terrible," she said.

"Right back at you, Jael. Brown isn't your color."

"I agree. Red is much more suited to me." She held up her bloody sword. "Isn't it pretty?"

He recognized the smug gleam in her eyes. Fear for Avry pumped through him.

Jael jabbed the weapon forward in a mock attack. "And shoving this into Avry's heart was a thing of beauty."

His world spun, but fury trumped pain. Kerrick stepped closer to her.

"I'm going to savor that look of astonishment on her face for a long time," Jael said. "She thought I'd use my magic, but the vibration as the blade scraped bone tingled all the way up my arm." Jael held her hand up, stopping Kerrick's advance with a wall of air. "Not that I'm averse to using my magic."

The vines wrapped around her legs. She tsked. "You know better than that."

The wall of air changed direction. Instead of pressing on him, it pulled away, taking his breath with it. He doubled his efforts, urging the vines to move faster. If he could just get to her before he passed out... Kerrick struggled to draw a breath. Dizzy and lightheaded, Kerrick sank to his knees. Desperate for air, he dug his fingers into the dirt and wrenched every last bit of his magic to him, hoping to block Jael's attack.

But an odd thing happened. Roots erupted from the ground and burrowed into his legs, hands, and arms, twisting around Kerrick.

Jael laughed. "How perfect. The forest agrees with me."

Sharp pain pierced him as the roots bit into his skin. *What the hell?* His vision turned to snow. Soon he'd get another taste of the darkness, and he feared he wouldn't find the light again.

On the edge of blacking out, Kerrick fought to stay conscious and won. *Huh?* Energy infused him, but no air filled his lungs. Not wasting time to figure it out, he focused on Jael.

The vines had continued to circle her, but she remained calm, watching him with keen interest. Only when the vines encircled her neck did she fight. Too late. Soon trapped, she stared at him in horror.

"How?" she squeaked.

Without air, Kerrick couldn't talk. Rooted to the ground, he couldn't move. But his connection to the living green strengthened and, with a thought, he commanded the vines to tighten around her throat.

Jael's magic finally released Kerrick as she thrashed. Air rushed into his lungs and he pulled in a few deep breaths. The roots retreated underground. Pain flared anew. Blood ran down his hands.

Kerrick stood and moved closer to Jael. "Enjoying the taste of your own medicine? It's rather awful being denied the simple act of breathing, isn't it?"

No response. Terror, panic, and fear flashed on her reddening face. He hesitated a moment—was there another way? He spotted the sword lying next to her. It was coated with Avry's blood. She didn't deserve mercy.

"Goodbye, Jael. I'm afraid there's no chance of us ever getting back together."

# CHAPTER 14

I struggled to sip air. The effort ringed my chest with sharp daggers of pain. The light in the distance faded as the tunnel spun. Lightheaded, dizzy, and nauseous, I drifted into and out of consciousness. The water soaked into my robe. Or was it sweat?

Heat burned my skin followed by uncontrollable shivers. The motion was pure torture. Why couldn't I just pass out? Or die? I really didn't care which one at this moment. Although Kerrick would be upset and Loren and Quain and Flea and…

Odd? My name. He called my name. Torch light flickered. Or were they spots in my vision? I didn't have breath to talk. Instead, I slapped the water with my hand. Or was it blood?

Then he was there, shining a much-too-bright light. I squeezed my eyes shut. His hands slid under me, but I squealed with pain when he tried to lift me and he stopped. Part of my brain noted that my right lung must be healing in order for me to have enough air to make that pathetic sound.

Odd asked, "What can I do?"

"Save the…" I gestured to the girl next to me.

"Sorry, Avry. She's dead. What else can I do?"

"Wait."

"For what?"

I opened my eyes and met his gaze.

"Oh." He sat back on his heels. "That's unacceptable." Odd took my hand.

He wasn't a magician, so he didn't have any power to share, but his presence soothed me. I closed my eyes.

"Do you know about Kerrick's...er...problem?" he asked.

"Yes."

"I'm sorry for giving the guy a hard time about disappearing. That's rough. He should be here instead of me. I can't help you. Well, except to ramble on, trying to keep you awake. Avry, are you still with me?"

"Yes."

"Good. 'Cause if you die, Kerrick's going to kill me. Probably strangle me with some vines. Or have a tree fall on top of me. Or feed me to a Death Lily."

I shook my head.

"Easy for you to say. You didn't see his face when he couldn't come in here with me. Too bad that he's missing out on this...unique smell, and I hear soaking in sewer water is great for the skin. My butt's going to be baby soft."

Despite the burning pain, I smiled at Odd's well-meaning prattle.

A vibration rippled the water. I squeezed Odd's hand, shushing him. The distant sound of boots clattered on the stone. Odd extinguished the lantern.

"Company," Odd whispered, letting go of my hand.

I opened my eyes. Blackness pressed on me. As the drumming grew louder a faint light filled the tunnels. Odd stood in front of me. He held his sword, but the tip of the blade pointed down.

"This way," a voice called.

"Keep up," another said.

The light brightened, filling the main tunnel and leaking into ours. Would they spot us?

Odd pressed against the wall. "Don't move."

That wouldn't be a problem. The brightness and sound increased in small jumps. Each time I blinked, it seemed they'd hopped closer. A few minutes ago I wouldn't have cared if I was discovered, but I still struggled to breathe. The searing pain was a good sign. And of course, I didn't want Odd caught.

When the torches came into view, I flinched. Two priests held them close to the ground, illuminating the obvious tracks of two thousand plus people. Hopefully, they wouldn't notice the few heading in this direction.

The priests paused, sweeping the torches back and forth. I longed to stifle my rasping. With his dark uniform, Odd blended in. And the filthy muck coated my exposed skin and stained my brown robe black. Perhaps they'd view me as a lump of discarded garbage. It matched how I felt.

After a lifetime, they moved on. They streamed past the entrance to our tunnel. Not as many as I'd expected. Had they sent others aboveground? Would they rally their troops to get between the women and the border?

"Avry? Still with me?" Odd whispered.

"Yes."

"Can I pick you up? We really need to get out of here."

"Jael," I said.

"General Jael? What about her?"

"She's here."

Odd cursed. "All the more reason to leave."

"Let me try." Since there was nothing wrong with my legs, I tucked them under me, then pushed with my arms to straighten. Every inch of my chest flared with such pain, I gasped.

Odd reached under my arms and lifted me to my feet. I

yowled. My world spun and my legs refused to hold me up. If Odd hadn't kept his grip, I would have toppled.

"Guess I can't carry you over my shoulder," Odd said.

"No. Give me…a minute."

"Hell, Avry, you're gonna need a few days. Sorry about this." He adjusted his grip, sweeping me into his arms like a baby.

Pain pulsed to my extremities and back again. Noise and sensations faded to a buzz and I might have blacked out. Hard to tell when inside a pitch-dark tunnel.

"Can you see?" I asked Odd once I regained my senses.

"No."

"Then how—"

"Hush, I'm counting steps."

Oh. A rubbing sound accompanied a slight vibration along his left arm. His shoulder must be in contact with the wall. Smart.

After a while, I dozed in his arms. When he stopped to rest, I was jolted awake.

"Still with me?" he asked.

"Yes." I drew half a gulp of air. "And I think I'm past the danger."

Odd squeezed me to his chest. "Thank the creator."

I yelped. "Still in lots of pain, though."

"Oh, sorry." He relaxed his arms.

"I can try to walk."

"No."

"Worried about those vines?" I teased.

"No," Odd said in a flat tone.

I longed to see his expression. After a few more minutes, Odd lurched to his feet and continued. He navigated with confidence. Impressive, considering he hated tunnels.

Fresh air laced with the scent of living green roused me. Odd slowed, probably thinking the same thing as me. Where was Jael? And what did Kerrick do when the priests had exited the duct? I hoped he'd stayed hidden, avoiding them both. But he might have attacked them in order to protect the escaping women.

My pain forgotten, I worried about Kerrick. "Careful."

Odd crept to the edge and peeked out, then grunted in either admiration or in disbelief. He stepped clear. The weak rays of dawn shone on the priests all trapped in vines. They struggled and shouted to no avail.

"Your boyfriend's been busy," Odd muttered. "Probably exhausted himself."

Kerrick appeared beside us. Joy shone on his face. "I've plenty of energy left," he said, despite the skin clinging to his gaunt and pale face. He held out his arms.

Odd hesitated before handing me over. Kerrick's magic swept over me like a healing balm. He squeezed me tight as I snuggled against him, his scent a welcome break from the reek of sewage.

"Thank you," Kerrick said to Odd in a strangely formal tone.

Odd nodded. "I'd better catch up with my squad. We might encounter trouble before we reach the border."

"Watch out for Jael," I said to Odd.

"She won't bother you," Kerrick said in his flat tone. "But troops are moving to intercept the women as we speak."

"How soon?"

"Two days."

They'd be only halfway to the border with Pomyt. Not good. Unless… "What if they go south to Tobory Realm? It's shorter and unexpected."

"Lots of Death Lilys down there," Odd said.

We both stared at him.

"Will you be able to catch up by then?" Odd asked me.

Already feeling stronger, I glanced at Kerrick.

"We'll meet you at the border."

"See you there." Odd turned to go.

"Odd, wait." Kerrick set me down.

The leaves under me pulsed with his magic, keeping our connection. Kerrick dug in a pocket and produced a lumpy orange berry about the size of a gold coin.

He handed it to Odd. "Tell the women to collect and eat these. They're edible and will give them energy. Stay away from all the other berries, most are poisonous."

Odd tucked it into his pocket. "Got it." Then he took off.

Kerrick knelt next to me. He pulled a clump of wet hair off my face.

"Why won't Jael bother Odd?" I asked. "Did you—"

"Yes."

"Why?"

"She said she killed you. And no jail cell could hold her. She was just too dangerous to keep alive. At least now she's being useful for a change."

I waited.

"As fertilizer for the forest," he said.

"Is there a chance she'll come back like you did?"

"No."

I searched my feelings. No sadness or guilt, and relief dominated. Ryne might be mad at us, but we'd neutralized a threat.

"You just had to rescue them all, didn't you?" Kerrick asked, but his tone remained soft.

"Wasn't my idea." I told him about Melina. "Besides, it was the right thing to do."

"It's going to be a challenge getting that many women to freedom. Plus they'll need clothing, shoes, and more than berries to eat."

I smiled. "I'm sure you're up to it."

"Well, first things first." He picked me up. "You lost weight." He scowled.

"The food was awful. I'm going to write a letter of complaint."

His scowl eased. "After you're healed." He turned.

"Where are we going?"

"To a safer location."

"What about the priests?"

"They can hang out here for another day and give the women a head start."

He carried me to a small campsite and laid me on his bedroll, then wrapped me in his blanket. Lighting a fire, Kerrick stared into the flames for a moment. The bright glow highlighted his exhaustion.

"How bad is it?" he asked.

With the energy he'd already shared, I no longer gasped for breath. My left lung functioned normally, but the right was still punctured. And my ribs... Pretty bad. "I don't want you to deplete your strength—"

"That's not what I asked."

"On my own, I'd need a week to heal."

Kerrick stretched out next to me, pulling me close. "Good thing you're not alone."

His magic soaked into me. The pain eased and I relaxed, falling asleep in his arms.

The snuffling of a large creature woke me. Darkness surrounded us. The fire had died. I drew in a deep breath. My right lung no longer wheezed, but my ribs protested the motion with tweaks of pain. Better than the fire that had stabbed deep with every movement.

A soft whinny sounded close by. Confused, I scanned the surroundings as my eyes adjusted to the dim moonlight. A black horse-shaped shadow pawed at the ground near Kerrick, who didn't wake at the slight noise. The stubborn man had poured every ounce of strength into helping me.

Disentangling myself, I stood and returned to my normal coloring. The horse didn't shy away. I recognized him as the large russet male Kerrick and I had ridden on the way to Chinska Mare. Had he followed Kerrick? A couple feed bags sat by the fire ring. Kerrick must have kept him.

"What's the matter, boy? Are you hungry?"

The horse bobbed his head. Taking that as a yes, I opened a feed bag and held it while the horse munched. When it was empty, I dropped it next to the others and noticed my pack. I stared at it in amazement. How did it get here? Had I carried it with me despite my injuries?

I sorted through the contents. My boots, travel clothes, and a few other necessities like soap remained inside. The desire to bathe pulsed through me with a sudden intensity. Stiff with dried blood, mud, and sewage, my tattered robe resembled a discarded rag. My skin itched and muck caked my hair.

Reluctant to wake Kerrick, I turned to the horse. He seemed intelligent and hadn't run off despite the ruckus. "Water?" I asked.

The horse glanced at Kerrick, then walked away. Slinging my pack over my shoulder, I followed him, hoping he wasn't heading to the aqueduct. Moving almost without sound, he led me to a clean spring. He dipped his head and drank. I waited until he'd finished before ripping off my clothes and wading into the cold, waist-deep water.

An ugly red gash marked where Jael's sword had punctured me. Deep purple-and-red bruises spread out from the injury. Careful of my ribs, I sat down and dunked my head, then scrubbed every inch of my body twice. I considered a third rinse, but my teeth chattered and my hands were numb.

I climbed from the pool. The horse watched me as I squeezed the water from my hair then shook off as much as I could.

"Thanks," I said to the horse.

"Humph."

Was that… No. "Kerrick?"

He appeared next to the horse, looking drained. "Imagine how I felt when I woke up and discovered my horse had stolen my girl."

I laughed. "I'm sorry, Kerrick, but it was love at first sight."

"I can understand that. I'm loving what I'm seeing right now." He leered.

Oh. I grabbed my travel clothes from my pack. Before I could put them on, he closed the distance between us.

"Not so fast." Kerrick kissed me.

I warmed immediately, wrapping my arms around him. But a familiar foul odor intruded and his stiff shirt scratched my skin. I broke away. He'd gotten dirty carrying me.

"What?" he asked.

"You stink."

He glanced down. "It's my only shirt."

I dug through my pack, producing his other shirt. "No it isn't."

"Ah. I wondered where that had gotten to."

"I was keeping it safe for you."

"Mighty nice of you." He cocked his head to the side. "How about a deal? I'll get washed up if you join me?"

Tempting, very tempting. "Do we have time? We have to meet the others."

Kerrick glanced at the horse. "Hux is fast, but with two of us… Ah, hell." He kicked off his boots and pulled off his soiled shirt and pants.

"Hux? You named the horse?"

"Yeah. Avry, meet Huxley."

Huxley snorted and moved closer.

"Hello." I scratched him behind the ears. "What happened to your reluctance to having a big noisy creature around?"

Kerrick grabbed my soap and plopped into the pool. "I've been training Hux how to be quiet."

Huxley nudged me with his nose, pushing me closer to Kerrick. Then he headed deeper into the forest.

"Hux thinks we have some extra time," Kerrick said, laughing. "We're not going to get another chance for a while." He splashed me. "Come on in, the water's—"

"Cold." I shivered, but joined him.

"No worries, my love. I'll warm you up in no time."

One of the things I loved about Kerrick—he kept his promises.

I had to admit, Hux's ability to move through the forest with hardly a sound was impressive. Even with two people on his back, he galloped as if we weighed nothing. However, every jolt reminded me of my broken ribs. We'd been on the road for a day and, according to Kerrick, we'd traveled at an angle, which was how we'd arrived at the border a few hours before the women.

"They have to keep to the paths," he explained. "The briars would rip their legs to shreds."

About to ask why Hux didn't have any trouble, I realized the answer. Kerrick's forest magic. He made full use of his power as we waited for the women. Leaving me next to a bonfire, he took Hux hunting and returned with two stags. I helped him butcher the animals and threaded thin ribbons of meat onto twigs to cook.

When the women arrived, they were grateful for the fire and the food. They took turns standing close to the flames, warming up. Everyone looked worn out, including Kerrick. He'd eaten and then disappeared.

Flea, Ives, Odd, and the monkeys found a spot to plop. I joined them.

"Any problems?" I asked.

"Just the usual," Loren said. "Cold nights, hungry women, blisters, and lots of whining from Quain."

No response from Quain. He leaned his head back on a tree trunk with his eyes closed.

"Estrid's troops?" I asked.

"Our change in direction gave us a little more time," Odd said. "But they're about half a day behind us, and finding us won't be a problem. We've left a gigantic trail."

"Where's Kerrick?" Flea asked.

"Resting, I hope. He's beyond exhausted," I said.

Flea met my gaze. "Do you think I could..."

"You don't look any better, Flea."

"Yeah, well, it's a different kind of...tired."

True. Expending magical energy was unlike using physical energy, but there was a hard limit to both. "You can try, but don't go overboard like Kerrick does."

Flea stood and scanned the trees. "Where..."

"Just look for Huxley...the horse. He stays close to Kerrick."

No one commented—more proof they'd all sapped their strength.

"Now what?" Odd asked.

Loren gestured to the clumps of women. "Once we cross the border and find the ladies some decent clothes, they should break up into smaller groups and disperse to the other realms."

"Will Estrid's troops chase them over the border?" I asked.

"Depends on how pissed she is," Odd said. "Technically she's not allowed, but since the plague..."

All bets were off.

I gazed at the quiet women. They resembled a brown carpet spread along the forest floor. Fydelia moved among them, talking and checking on their cuts and bruises. Melina stayed with the wounded, whom I'd been neglecting. Grunting in pain, I stood, intent on helping.

Fydelia noticed me and came over. "Avry, I want to thank you for—"

I held up my hand. "Still not out of the woods yet."

She smiled at the pun. "We won't go back without a fight."

"We're thinking you'll need to separate into small groups of five or six at some point," Loren said. "You can all disperse back to your lives."

"Oh, no," Fydelia said. "We won't be doing that. We're trained soldiers. Avry told us about Prince Ryne and his efforts. We plan to fight for him."

Shocked, I gazed at her. "All of you?"

"At least ninety percent. A few are older, and the years in the monastery affected others." She tapped her temple.

"That's generous," Loren said.

"It's logical. What's the point in going home? If Cellina's army wins, or that Skeleton King, we all suffer the consequences. Better to not let that happen."

"I wish Estrid believed that," I said.

Quain had opened his eyes while Fydelia talked. His brow wrinkled as he pursed his lips. "Do you think Prince Ryne would welcome us back now?"

"Oh, yes. With open arms," Loren said.

"Do we *want* to go back?" he asked.

"It's not a matter of desire. It's like Fydelia said, logic. He needs us, and he's going to be very happy to have twenty-three hundred more soldiers," I said.

"Maybe he won't argue with you anymore," Quain said.

"I doubt it," Kerrick said.

He and Flea joined us. The dark smudges under Kerrick's eyes were lighter and he moved with his usual grace. Flea must have successfully shared his energy. Flea's bangs covered his eyes. I studied him, seeking signs of fatigue. He hunched his shoulders and plopped next to Quain.

"Why?" Quain asked Kerrick.

"They have different views. He'll do what needs to be done for us to win the war, even if that means sacrificing squads. Avry's more focused on the individual."

"If that was true, we'd be sitting here with just Melina," Loren said.

"We set out to save Melina because of Avry. She had no idea this would happen," Kerrick said.

"I don't care why you came," Fydelia said. "I'm just happy you did. We owe our freedom to Avry."

"No. You owe it to yourselves. If you hadn't kept training, you'd still be inside the monastery," I said.

"Yes, yes. You're all wonderful," Odd said. "However, we do have a company of soldiers on our tail and probably should get moving."

The monkeys and Flea looked at Kerrick.

"One hundred and sixty-two soldiers."

"Find us more swords and we'll take care of them," Fydelia said with confidence.

"Best to outsmart them for now," Kerrick said.

I recognized the glint in his eyes. "You have a plan?"

"Yes. I'll hide your tracks and plant a false one for the soldiers to follow."

"That's a big job," Odd said. "Think you can pull it off?" Kerrick didn't answer.

"If Kerrick says he can, then he can," Loren said.

Quain smiled. "Yeah, he's king of the weeds now."

Instead of throwing an acorn at Quain, Kerrick's expression turned queasy. I suspected there was something he hadn't told us.

The guards stationed outside the infirmary blocked our way. They pointed their swords at me, Kerrick, and the monkeys. The bulk of the women stayed behind with the others and Huxley. Kerrick's trick with the tracks had worked long enough to give us a nice lead. And once we'd crossed through Tobory and into Pomyt, Estrid's soldiers abandoned the chase. With stops for provisions and sleep, the trip to the infirmary had taken us a total of twenty days.

"We've orders from Prince Ryne to arrest you on sight," a sergeant said.

Quain laughed. "You can try."

"Easy," Kerrick said.

"Where is Prince Ryne?" I asked.

The sergeant puffed out his chest in indignation. "You are traitors. We will not divulge his location to you."

"Uh-huh. Did he return to HQ?" I asked.

But the sergeant would not be deterred. He yanked out a pair of manacles and his squad followed suit.

"How many of those do you have with you?" Quain asked.

"Enough for all of you."

"Are you sure?" Quain whistled.

The bushes rustled and a hundred armed women surrounded us.

"You want to answer that question again?" Quain smirked.

"Two thousand, three hundred and forty-six," Ryne repeated in disbelief.

Haggard, thin, and haunted, Ryne appeared to have had

a rough time of it since we'd left over a month ago. Guilt for leaving tweaked in my chest until I remembered our argument.

"Are we still traitors, Ryne?" I asked.

"Careful how you answer," Kerrick warned him.

We sat around a campfire outside the infirmary with the monkeys and Flea. Fydelia remained in the infirmary with Odd. Ryne had just arrived. He rode in on the horse that had carried the soldier with the message that we'd returned. It took a total of six days, and we'd all rested in the meantime. Although Kerrick still moved as if a deep weariness had soaked into his bones. I worried he was getting sick, but he was quick to wave off my concerns as soon as I'd voiced them.

I'd also checked on the patients and found they'd been well taken care of in my absence. But what had upset me the most were the four cases of the new plague. Ginger and Christina had isolated them, and had been careful to wash their hands after treating them. However, I wouldn't let my caregivers risk getting sick now that I'd returned. I couldn't heal them, but I could ease their suffering with various herbs. Although seeing them had been a painful reminder of my horrible mistake.

Yuri had accompanied Ryne to HQ. It made sense for him to be there, but an uneasiness drifted in my chest. I still felt he was my responsibility.

Without any clouds to obscure the stars, the night air had cooled fast and there would be frost on the ground by morning. The official start to winter was nine days away.

"Yeah. Don't piss us off, or we'll take our girls and go," Quain said to Ryne.

Kerrick shot him a look, but Quain kept his smug expression.

"No, you're not traitors," Ryne said. "I regretted my harsh words after you left. However, I still believe your decision to go was unfounded and reckless."

"Even after we've given you two thousand, three hundred and forty-six reasons that it was well worth the effort?" I asked.

"Are you telling me you knew this would happen?" Ryne challenged.

"No. And I'll admit there were times…" I shuddered at the memory of kneeling for hours "…that I agreed with you."

"And I should learn to trust your instincts. Shall we call a truce?" Ryne asked.

"Agreed." I shook his hand.

"Aww, nuts. Avry, you should have gloated some more," Quain said.

We all ignored him. Flea poked at the fire with a stick. Bright sparks spiraled up into the air. He'd been extraquiet ever since we returned from Chinska Mare.

"How's the war going?" Kerrick asked Ryne.

"Aside from a few skirmishes along the border, it's not."

"Isn't that a good thing?" Loren asked.

"You would think so, but Cellina's up to something big. Our scouts who returned from Vyg have reported seeing fewer living soldiers than there should be, and more activity from the squads of dead soldiers, which is the opposite of how it's been these past few months. She also pulled her troops from Zabin. Which makes me wonder where her soldiers are going."

"Any ideas?" Kerrick asked.

"Nope."

They exchanged a significant glance. My heart squeezed as I realized Kerrick would offer to scout for Ryne. Maybe not tonight, but soon. And while I understood the need, I already missed and worried about him.

"Any word about Belen?" I asked.

"Nothing, sorry. But lots of reports on the Skeleton King," Ryne said.

Now it was Quain and Loren's turn to exchange a look. This one was full of horror.

"We ran into him when we were searching for a healer," Loren said.

"That's one sick bastard," Quain said.

"His army is on the move. And he sent me another message." Ryne rubbed a hand over his face.

Oh, no. "Another bitten and tattooed soldier?"

"Worse. He sent me a box of bones with a letter. The bones belonged to two of my scouts that had gone missing. He taunted me, saying to stop with the sweeps and scouts, to bring my army to Sectven Realm because his troops were hungry for a fight."

"Wait, I thought he was down in Ryazan Realm?" I asked.

"Not anymore. He's invaded half of Sectven Realm."

I leaped to my feet. "Sectven! Mom lives there. And we just rescued Melina."

# KERRICK

Kerrick understood Avry's concern. He felt it, too. Mom meant a great deal to him. And from the worried expressions on Flea's and the monkeys' faces, they cared for her, as well.

He grasped Avry's hand before she could rush off to organize a rescue party. Pulling, Kerrick tried to get her to sit back down next to him.

She resisted. "We need to warn Mom."

Ryne opened his mouth to respond, but Kerrick shot him a let-me-handle-this look.

"It's *Mom,* Avry," Kerrick said. "She has her sources of information. She probably knows more about the situation than we do right now. In fact, I wouldn't be surprised if she hasn't already cleared out of her inn and has traveled somewhere safe."

"Nowhere is safe. Plus she wouldn't leave without knowing what happened to Melina."

Ah, hell. Avry had a point. He considered their options and found a solution that would appease both Avry and Ryne.

"I'll go," he said. "I'll take Hux and be there in three days. If Mom's still there, I'll tell her about Melina and escort her here." Kerrick glanced at Ryne. "I'll also gather better information about where this Skeleton King is and how big his forces are."

Avry rounded on him. "Didn't you just hear Ryne? He sent the *bones* of the last two scouts in a *box*."

"Those scouts weren't forest mages," he said. "You know I'll be careful."

"What if he already invaded Mengels?" Loren asked.

"Then I won't go near the city. Mom's inn is at the edge, but if it looks like it's been commandeered, I'll keep away."

Except Ryne, no one seemed overly pleased with his plan, but despite Avry's outburst, no one else argued. It made sense. Ryne kept his face neutral, but Kerrick had known him long enough to recognize the subtle change in his demeanor. Between the addition of two thousand plus soldiers and Kerrick scouting for him again, renewed hope flared in Ryne's eyes.

Avry returned to her place next to him. She leaned on him and he wrapped his arm around her shoulders, tucking her close. The warm scent of vanilla filled his nose.

She sighed. "I'd go with you, but I'd just slow you down. Besides…" Avry glanced at Ryne. "I'm needed here."

Again, Ryne impressed Kerrick by not showing his approval over Avry's good sense. Or commenting on it. Instead, he stood. "I need to talk to Fydelia and determine how to best integrate her women into our forces. Kerrick, let me know if you need anything for your mission. Do you know when you're leaving?"

Avry stiffened. They both knew he should head out right away.

"In an hour or so," he hedged.

Ryne nodded and returned to the infirmary. The monkeys lumbered to their feet, stretched, and yawned with jaw-popping exaggeration.

"We're beat," Loren said.

"Yeah, dog tired," Quain agreed. "Time for bed. Come on, Flea."

"I'll catch up with you in a minute," Flea said.

They peered at him, but then ambled off.

Once they were gone, Flea shoved his stick deep into the fire and met Kerrick's questioning gaze. "I'm going with you."

Avry drew a breath, but he squeezed her shoulder, warning her to keep quiet.

"Why should I take you?" he asked.

"I can help you when you can't leave the forest. Like purchasing feed for Hux and blending in with the street rats to find out information. That's how I survived before I met you, remember?" Flea inclined his head toward Avry. "And I'm not useful here. Besides, all these soldiers think I'm just a kid—even the caregivers. You *never* treated me that way."

Kerrick sensed there were more reasons, but he refrained from asking. Avry had said to be subtle with him. While it would be harder to scout with Flea along, he thought the young man had presented a valid argument. Plus Kerrick had a bad feeling he might need Flea's energy. Every day it was harder to keep the relentless fatigue at bay.

"All right. Go pack and be back here in one hour."

Flea jumped to his feet. "Yes, sir." He dashed toward the infirmary.

Bracing for Avry's anger, Kerrick waited. The silence extended and he worried he'd upset her.

Instead, she relaxed against him, snuggling in closer. "At first I thought it was a horrible and reckless idea to take Flea, but—and I can't believe I'm saying this—he needs this. It'll be good for him. And you'll protect him."

She had such confidence in him, but Kerrick remembered failing Flea. He'd died under Kerrick's care before. Only dumb luck had saved him. A Peace Lily and not a Death Lily had accepted Flea's body, preserving it until Avry returned to awaken him.

"It wasn't your fault," Avry said, reading his mind. "Jael—"

"Was after me."

"No, she was after *us. All* of us. She didn't want Ryne healed and knew it would take all of us together to rescue him." Avry pulled away and gazed up at him. "I think Flea will be good for you, too. I won't have to worry about you as much."

Interesting. "Why not?"

"You'll be extracareful. And he'll keep you from doing something dangerous or stupid."

He widened his eyes in mock horror. "Me? Do something dangerous? No way."

She laughed. The sound flowed through him like a warm brandy, igniting a fire in his heart.

"I noticed you didn't protest the stupid part," she teased.

"Ah, my love, I'm guilty on that one."

"Well, I can't think of any examples right now."

He wrapped his arms around her, pulling her toward him. "I have one example of my stupidity."

"Do tell."

"I should have told Flea to come back in *two* hours."

Huxley arrived at the same time as Flea. Kerrick marveled over the horse's ability to sense when Kerrick needed him. After giving Avry another kiss goodbye, he slung his pack over his shoulder and mounted Hux. Flea hopped up behind him.

He spurred Hux into a gallop, heading southwest toward Mengels. Just as he'd predicted, it took them three days to reach the outskirts of town. They hadn't encountered any of Cellina's patrols, but he sensed a few squads for the Skeleton King's army. They also didn't see any citizens once they crossed the border and entered Sectven Realm. Not a good sign.

And his connection with the living green tugged at him, pulling him down even though he remained in the forest. He had noticed it before when it had dug its roots into him to save his life. He'd hoped it would dissipate after he rested. But it seemed more pronounced. Was it just another quirk of his bond with the living green, or something more dire?

Could he be transforming into more a part of the forest? One with roots? Not a pleasant thought. Kerrick sighed. Not much he could do about it. Instead, he focused on the task at hand.

From their vantage point in the woods to the east, Mengels appeared to be a ghost town.

"It's almost winter. Maybe they're all inside," Flea said in a hopeful tone.

Kerrick just looked at Flea.

"Yeah, well. It's better than them all being captured or killed by the Skeleton King."

Pointing to the buildings, Kerrick said, "There are no signs of a fight. The windows are intact. No burned buildings. No scuffs in the dirt. No bloodstains. There's another explanation."

"And that is?"

"You tell me."

Flea huffed, but gazed at the town. One of the larger towns in Sectven, it had survived the brutal plague years almost intact, a rarity in the Fifteen Realms. Kerrick believed it was the cool heads of Mom and other town officials who had kept the population calm, plus the dedication of the surviving town watch who'd stayed at their posts even when friends and family died around them.

"There's no smoke coming out of the chimneys," Flea said. "And there are no wheel tracks in the mud from yesterday's rain. No sign of wagons or horses, either. They've left town."

"Very good. How long ago?"

Flea drew in a deep breath. "There's a slight odor from the chamber-pot dumps and no fresh horse droppings—just a few dusty-looking piles. A week, maybe two?"

"Which one?"

"I don't know."

"Think about the past few days, Flea."

He dipped his head, letting the bangs cover his eyes. "If they'd left within a week, we'd have seen them because the only safe place is east to Tobory Realm or northeast to Pomyt Realm. So two weeks."

"I concur. You'd make a good scout."

Flea stood a little straighter. His swiped the hair from his face, exposing a glimmer of humor in his eyes. "And trade in the luxurious life of a death magician? No, thank you."

"You've been hanging out with the monkeys too long."

"I consider them my mentors."

"No, no, no. I can think of a better mentor for you."

Suddenly wary, Flea crossed his arms over his chest. "Who? Avry?"

"Oh, no. She'd smother you. I had someone else in mind." Kerrick waited to see if Flea'd take the bait.

"Who?"

"My Great-Aunt Yasmin. She'd set you straight in no time."

Flea gaped at him. "Isn't she, like, a hundred years old?"

"She's ninety, no, ninety-one by now. But don't let her age fool you. Grown men are terrified of her."

"Uh-huh," Flea said, catching on to the joke. "Nice one, *Kerry*."

Surprised and impressed that Flea knew Great-Aunt Yasmin's nickname for him, he said, "Touché. Who told you?"

"Belen. He told me to never use it or you'd pound me. You won't, will you?"

Kerrick laughed. "Back before the plague, I would have. Now I think it's very foolish to fight over something as silly as a nickname."

"The stakes are a lot higher now," Flea agreed.

"Yes, and we should get back to the task at hand." Kerrick sniffed the air. "I think there are a few citizens still in town."

"How can you tell?"

"From the smell. After two weeks, the dumps wouldn't be pungent and there's a faint tang of lime which means someone is making sure the smell isn't worse. Come on." Kerrick retreated deeper into the forest.

"Where are we going?"

"The Lamp Post Inn is on the western side of town."

"Do you think Mom's still there?" Flea hurried after him.

"If she's not, I'm sure she left a message for Melina."

Hux waited for them. They mounted and Kerrick urged Huxley into a gallop. The sun hung low in the sky and he didn't want to lose the light.

Taking Huxley almost to the edge of the forest, Kerrick stopped the horse when he spotted the red wood of Mom's inn through the bare trees. He and Flea inched closer and studied the inn. The shutters were closed and no smoke curled above the roof. No lights gleamed under the door or through the slats. All seemed quiet.

He signaled Flea. Since the forest almost grew to the inn, it didn't tug as hard on Kerrick as they crept toward the back door. It was locked. Flea grasped his sword's hilt and kept an eye out while Kerrick popped the lock. They entered the common area. Dust coated the bar, tabletops, and Mom's teapot collection. No tablecloths or silverware in sight and only a pile of ashes remained in the hearth.

Kerrick checked the kitchen while Flea searched the guest rooms upstairs. The oven was cold. No dirty dishes had been stacked in the sink. Food hadn't been abandoned. Which meant they hadn't left in a hurry.

Returning to the common area, he joined Flea.

"The rooms are empty," Flea reported. "Beds are stripped and the lanterns are cold and without oil."

"Thoughts?"

"They're gone. But they had enough time to pack."

"I'd agree with you except for one thing."

"And that is?" Flea asked.

"Mom's teapot collection on the mantel. No way she'd leave without it."

"Maybe that's the message for Melina."

"Excellent point. Check inside them."

Flea stood on the hearth and lifted the lid on each pot.

"Be careful up there, dearie. Them's my favorite pots," Mom said.

Kerrick spun. She stood behind him. Her white hair had been pulled up into a tidy bun and she wore a clean white apron over her full-length skirt.

"Where did you come from?" he asked.

An impish gleam lit her face. "Good evening to you, too, Mr. Kerrick."

"Sorry, Mom." He pecked her cheek. "Good to see you well."

"And you and your young pup are a welcome sight. Have you got news for me?"

"Yes." He told her about Melina's rescue.

When he finished, she groped for a chair and sank into it.

Worried, Kerrick knelt next to her. "Melina's fine. She's helping in the infirmary near Grzebien."

She shooed him away. "Don't fuss over me. You've taken such a weight off my shoulders, my legs didn't know how to handle it."

"I can't take all the credit. Avry is the one who insisted."

"She's a miracle that girl. She promised..." Tears spilled from Mom's eyes. She dabbed at them with a corner of her apron. "She kept her promise."

"That's Avry. She's true to her word."

Mom drew in a deep breath and glanced around the inn. "Now I can leave."

"To catch up with the others?" Flea asked. He remained on the hearth, leaning against the bricks.

"Oh, heavens, no. I'll go help Melina and Avry. I'm sure those soldiers don't know how to cook a decent meal." She bustled to her feet. "Let me grab my bag of cooking pots and utensils."

"Uh, Mom?" Kerrick asked, stopping her. "Where is the rest of the town?"

"Scattered. As soon as the Skeleton King crossed into Sect-ven Realm, they started the evacuations."

"Yet you stayed."

"Of course, dearie. I wasn't going to leave until I heard from Melina. Besides, Mr. Belen still needed care."

# CHAPTER 15

After Kerrick and Flea left, I kept busy to keep from worrying about them so much. Ginger and Christina handled the few incoming injured soldiers, consulting with me on the serious cases. I concentrated on caring for the new plague victims. As I changed linens and emptied bedpans for the four men, I puzzled over a possible cure.

Between the Healer's Guild healers and my own knowledge of the nature of the disease, there was little left to discover. But still… A niggling sensation deep in my heart just wouldn't quit. It reminded me of one of those wooden building sets my brother Criss used to assemble. Knowing he had all the pieces, he'd get so frustrated when he couldn't get them all to fit. To make matters worse, our brother Allyn would sweep in half-distracted, glance at the incomplete structure and scattered pieces and point to the part Criss had been searching hours for.

Our father had claimed Criss just needed to take a break and look at the project from a different angle. Perhaps I should apply that logic to the problem of curing the plague. I considered. Digging deep into memories, I recalled the conversation I'd had about the plague with Ryne and Kerrick before we'd rushed off to save Melina.

We'd discussed Tohon's involvement. He'd either created

the plague or helped spread it. But that hadn't been what had snagged my interest. The notion that Tohon had protected his classmates had been the real surprise. One I hadn't followed up on due to Estrid's defection.

Maybe I shouldn't focus on the victims, but on the survivors. How had Tohon protected them from the plague? And why did one-third of the population also survive? Did he protect them, too? Hard to rule a kingdom without subjects. But even harder to protect three million people.

Perhaps it was something they ate or drank? That might explain Tohon's classmates, but not the others. No family had survived intact. It stood to reason that a family would all eat the same food. Unless it was something with an unusual taste or odd flavor that most people didn't like.

The tanglefish from the Ronel Sea was considered a delicacy, but most people couldn't get past the horrible smell to eat it. And most of those who loved the slimy stuff lived along the coast. Tastes in food were regional and the plague had spread evenly throughout the Fifteen Realms.

I needed to talk to Ryne about what they ate and drank at their boarding-school reunion before I dismissed that hypothesis. Keeping with that line of thought, I considered perfumes and colognes. Distilled from flowers and plants, those were also very subjective—with some loving a certain scent while others were repelled by it. Perhaps Tohon had sprayed his classmates. Again this hypothesis wouldn't go anywhere until I talked to Ryne. Good thing he hadn't left for HQ yet.

Ryne had commandeered a corner of the infirmary. He'd been organizing Fydelia's lady warriors—Odd's nickname for them—into smaller units based on their skills, and explaining his military strategies to them. The monkeys and Odd taught them how to go silent in the forest.

I waited until Ryne was alone before approaching him

around midafternoon. It was four days after Kerrick and Flea had left—two more days until they returned. Ryne hunched over a map that had been spread over a table. Red arrows and Xs marked the parchment. His posture reminded me of my brother Criss. Perhaps he needed to take a break and look at it from another angle, as well.

"Do you have a minute?" I asked.

He glanced up. "Sure." Gesturing to a nearby stool, he tossed his stylus onto the table and sat down.

Ryne no longer looked so haunted. But the dark circles under his eyes hadn't disappeared. I suspected he'd need a month's worth of sleep to recover fully.

I explained my theory. "Can you tell me everything you did during that reunion, including what you ate and drank?"

He stared at me a moment. "That was…ages ago. Another lifetime. I can't even remember what I ate this morning."

"Start with anything unusual, especially when Tohon was around. What struck you as odd."

Ryne leaned back in his chair. "Tohon was civil to me. Considering how livid he'd been when the headmaster had announced the king for our class, I was surprised at his change in attitude. Tohon hadn't been one to forgive and forget. But then I'd assumed he'd matured in the past year."

"Did he prick you or scratch you by accident? Or invite you to share a meal with him?"

"No, he didn't touch me." Ryne gave me a sardonic smile. "I was smart enough to keep out of his reach. Once we'd learned of his life magic, we all avoided his touch. As for meals, we attended a few banquets together, but so did all the returning alumni."

"Did he give you anything? Cologne? Candy? Wine?" I asked.

"Not that I can recall."

"Did you eat something you've never had before? A delicacy or rare dish?"

Ryne shook his head. "Sorry, Avry. Nothing stands out."

Too bad. Guess I'd have to wait and ask Kerrick when he returned. I stood. "If you do remember something later—"

"I will let you know. It'll probably be in the middle of the night. My thoughts churn rather chaotically when I'm trying to sleep and odd ideas or forgotten memories pop out without warning, waking me."

My healer instincts kicked in. "I could give you a very mild sleeping draft that would ease the chaotic thoughts while still allowing you to be roused if needed."

"Oh, no. Those ideas are the best. I wouldn't want to stop them."

"All right. Feel free to wake me if a memory about the reunion pops."

"Will do. Oh, and that reminds me. How are your nightmares? Are you still dreaming of Tohon?"

"Yes. But only when I'm not with Kerrick." They'd started again a few days after he left.

"Sorry to hear that."

"Me, too." I stepped away, but paused as a soldier arrived. He'd drawn his sword and he kept glancing at the cave's entrance. Alarm shot through me. The soldier appeared to be terrified.

"My lord, you have a…visitor." The man swallowed.

"Who is it?" Ryne asked.

"I…we…don't know. He said—"

A commotion at the cave's entrance interrupted the man. Sunlight was blocked as a knot of guards rushed after a huge man, who seemed to pay them no mind even though they were well armed and shouted for him to halt. He strode toward Ryne.

I moved closer to Ryne, who stood as the giant neared. Or at least he gave the impression of being massive. Perhaps it was his thick muscular arms and broad shoulders, or the wide curved sword hanging from his blue sash. White fur boots matched his white pants and sleeveless tunic. In this weather? It was almost winter.

He stopped a few feet short of Ryne. The guards fanned out around him, but they kept their distance. The giant gazed at Ryne with ice-blue eyes and it seemed as if the air in the cave cooled by ten degrees.

"I've come," the man said.

Ryne smiled. "So you have. Welcome, Noak of the Sokna tribe. I'm honored and very glad to see you."

Ah. Kerrick's northern friend. Everyone relaxed slightly.

Extending his hand, Ryne said, "I'm Prince Ryne of Ivdel Realm."

Noak shook it, then turned his icy gaze on me.

"And this is Healer Avry of Kazan Realm." Ryne gestured.

"Healer? Magic Man said all healers die." Noak's cold tone cranked the tension back up.

I glanced at Ryne. He nodded.

"I did die, but I was revived," I said.

Noak stepped close to me. He held his hand out. Not for a handshake, but with his palm up as if he wanted me to place my hand in his. Remembering what Kerrick had said about Noak's Winter Curse, I hesitated. Then I spotted the monkeys and Odd inching their way through the guards and felt safer. I reached out.

He grasped my fingers. Ice zinged through my arm. I shuddered.

"You are linked to Magic Man." His hard expression turned contemplative.

"I… We…" I glanced at Ryne for help. Noak still clasped my hand.

"Prince Kerrick's out on a mission, but will be returning soon," Ryne said.

A pulse of coldness tore through me, leaving me gasping for breath.

Noak scowled, but released his grip. "You request help. Who needs killing?" he asked Ryne.

Ryne didn't miss a beat. "Let's not rush ahead. I need to know how many soldiers are with you, and what your fighting style and strengths are before I can devise a plan of attack. Is your army nearby? I'm surprised my scouts haven't reported them to me." He frowned at Odd, who shrugged.

"My warriors are where Magic Man said to come."

"And why didn't you remain at HQ with your warriors? I left instructions with my second in command," Ryne said.

"Little Brother wished to be here." Noak strode to the cave's entrance and shouted for Little Brother.

Ryne and I exchanged a look. Kerrick had only mentioned that Noak had a sister and father. Curious. We waited.

After a few minutes, a thin figure half Noak's size joined him. But he dashed past the large tribesman and headed straight for me. I glimpsed his face before he almost knocked me over as he wrapped his arms around me with rib-crushing strength.

"Danny!" Heedless of my ribs, I hugged him tight.

He squeezed harder and I gasped, "Can't breathe."

Danny let go and pulled back. "Sorry, but I didn't quite believe Kerrick when he said you were alive until I saw you."

"If you knew about Avry, why didn't you tell Noak?" Ryne asked.

"'Cause I gave my word to Kerrick not to tell anyone. Is he here?"

Danny bounced on the balls of his feet as he glanced around, but he spotted the monkeys and they pounced on him. They ruffled his shaggy black hair and slapped him on the back. The boy had grown a foot since I'd last seen him over seven months ago.

Ryne dismissed the guards, ordering them to return to their positions. He invited Noak to join him to discuss strategy. Understanding the hint, the monkeys led Danny over to the main fire to catch up on the news. I trailed after, noticing that Noak kept an eye on his little brother and on me. When my gaze met his, a chill raced up my spine.

Danny recounted his adventures with the tribe. Most of the stories we'd heard from Kerrick, but it was fun hearing Danny's side of the story. We ate our supper as we listened.

"...I got this funny, twisty feeling in my guts and I knew I needed to touch Kerrick, but he stopped me and told me to wait. We experimented later and—" Danny pulled up the sleeve on his right arm and pointed to a tiny scar near his elbow "—that's my first scar. It's Kerrick's."

We exclaimed over the faint line. Encouraged, Danny continued his tale. "...and after Kerrick left, I stayed and helped them. They were real sick."

"Were?" I asked.

A huge smile spread on Danny's face. "I healed them, Avry! I figured it out with your journal and with Rakel's help, we cured them."

"That's wonderful. What ailed them?"

"They'd been eating cloovit leaves and slowly poisoning themselves."

"Why would they eat cloovit?" Quain asked. "Everyone knows—"

"They don't. It resembled a rare plant that grows in the Vilde Lander. One that is considered a delicacy."

"How did you figure it out?" I asked.

Danny launched into a story about how he tried to treat the symptoms by finding herbs that might work. "Then I'm walking through the town and there's this lady with an armful of cloovit leaves. I felt like a lightning bolt had just struck me. Then I felt like an idiot for not thinking of it before."

"Don't let that upset you, Danny," Loren said. "Quain feels like that all the time. Ow!"

Quain clocked Loren.

"I see those two haven't changed," Danny said, showing he'd grown in more ways than his height.

"I think they have a disease and are stuck in adolescence," I said. "Do not look to them as role models."

Danny grinned and glanced over at Noak.

Interesting. The gesture reminded me of another question I had for the boy. "Little Brother?"

"I'm tribe now." He told them about healing Rakel, Noak's sister, and challenging the tribe's leader. "And that really put the pressure on us to find a cure. If the tribespeople kept dying, we would have had to fight Noak and his dad, Canute." Danny hooked a thumb at Noak. "He's a teddy bear compared to his father."

"Kerrick didn't know this, did he?" I asked.

"No way. The details of Canute's abdication weren't public knowledge. I didn't tell him 'cause I knew Kerrick wanted to get back to you. He'd have never left me if he'd known."

"I'm glad it worked out," I said. "Plus you gained a valuable experience."

"That I did, but I've lots to learn. That's one of the reasons I'm here. I also wanted to help with the wounded."

"You were safer in Alga," Loren said.

Danny gave him a mulish look.

Loren laughed. "Does his expression remind you of any-one, Quain?"

"I thought that stubbornness was learned at healer school, but it must be instinctive," Quain said.

Danny chuckled. "Whenever I was being difficult, Kerrick said I reminded him of Avry."

"Hey," I protested, but it lacked heat. After all, we knew just how difficult I could be.

"Where's Kerrick?" Danny asked.

We filled him in on our adventures.

"...and Kerrick should be back in two days," I said.

"Good, I've lots to tell him."

"So you intend to stay here?" Loren asked.

"As long as it's okay with Avry." Danny widened his eyes in a pretty-please, puppy-dog, I'm-so-cute-how-can-you-say-no look.

"It's all right with me." Another chill brushed my spine. Noak was staring at me again. "Will it be okay with Big Brother?" I inclined my head in Noak's direction.

"Yep. Don't let him scare you." Danny gestured to the sur-roundings. "This is all strange to him. The tribespeople are used to flat, open land where you can see for miles. They're uncomfortable in the woods and they almost panicked cross-ing the Nine Mountains." He chuckled. "We had to travel at night so they couldn't see down."

I smiled at his confidence. "You'd make a good ambassa-dor."

He ducked his head. "Well...I spent a lot of time with them. I am a bit worried how the warriors will do fighting beside Prince Ryne's army. It was only a few months ago they hated us and wished to slaughter us all."

"Lovely," Quain said with a queasy squint.

"That's an excellent point, Danny. Why did he come to help us?" I asked. "His tribe was safe and healthy in Alga."

"I convinced them that if we didn't stop Tohon and his army of the dead, our tribe wouldn't be safe for long. I also think Noak and the warriors were bored. Their two tribes had to play nice in order to survive and, although Noak won't admit it, he likes Kerrick."

"Nice job, Danny. With the addition of Noak's warriors and the monastery women, Prince Ryne's army is going to be quite dangerous."

"If the enemy ever attacks us," Loren muttered.

"We shouldn't wait. Going on the offensive is not a bad thing," Odd said, speaking up for the first time since Danny had arrived. "Look what happened to the High Priestess's army. We waited and waited and waited for Tohon to engage us in battle, giving him plenty of time to set his trap. Plus Prince Ryne said the dead were on the move again."

"And Tohon has to know the tribesmen are here," Danny said. "The warriors didn't bother to hide their presence and they sounded like a herd of lost cows in the woods."

That was the second time Danny mentioned Tohon. I opened my mouth to inform him about Tohon's frozen state, but another thought popped. "Did they scare the farmers and villagers? It must have been mass panic."

Danny straightened. "No. Once we crossed the Nine Mountains, we didn't see a soul."

Odd cursed.

"Wait, it makes sense," Loren said. "Cellina tried that back-door sneak and probably scared everyone away."

"That was closer to Zabin. Maybe she's trying the same move again, but this time going farther to the north," I said.

Loren rubbed a hand over his short hair. "That's pretty far.

It'll take a long time and they'd be cut off from their main army and supplies."

"With Prince Ryne only harrying patrols and small platoons along Vyg's border, they've had plenty of time to travel circles around us," Odd grumbled.

I stood. "Once he's done talking to Noak, I'll tell Ryne and let him figure it out. He may already be aware of the situation." I swept a hand out, indicating the rows of cots. "Danny, do you want to check patients with me?"

He shot to his feet. "Of course!"

Quain groaned. "I don't think I can handle another healer." He poked a finger at Danny. "Just don't be all nurturing and smother us with concern. We get enough of that with Avry."

"Don't worry, Quain. If you do something stupid, I'll let you suffer. Pain is an excellent teacher, and even *you* can be trained to avoid acting dumb in the future."

"Nice!" Loren high-fived Danny.

As Danny and I walked over to the patients, I asked, "Where did you learn that?"

"Noak. They're not big on coddling their people. If a tribesman could heal on his own, Noak believed he should and that I should save my energy for a more injured patient."

That sounded familiar. I glanced at Ryne and Noak. They appeared to be deep in discussion, but Noak caught me staring. An icy finger slid down my spine. That was the third time that had happened. Was it my imagination? Or was it his ice magic? A strange uneasiness swirled inside me as if Noak could read my thoughts and emotions. What had he meant that I was bound to Kerrick?

Too many questions without answers. And the thought of asking Noak… Not palatable. I returned my focus to Danny.

After I introduced him to my staff, they stared at him in wonder.

"Another healer? Why, that's wonderful!" Ginger said.

"You'll be such a big help, especially when Avry decides to dash off on some crazy mission again," Christina teased.

I showed Danny where we kept the supplies and explained how we decided on the type of care—magic or medicine or both. We stopped at the first patient, Private Caleb.

"Tell me what you find," I said to Danny.

Danny touched the young man's hand. "His left wrist is broken and he has a stab wound on his upper right thigh."

Suddenly lightheaded, I grabbed the edge of a cot to keep from toppling. Yes, I'd known he had healing powers, but just like Danny had said before, I didn't truly believe until now. Relief bubbled up from deep inside me and I felt lighter. No longer was I the only healer in the Fifteen Realms; the pressure eased just enough for me to draw a breath without that tight band of worry constricting me.

Not that the worry would ever leave me. Danny was only thirteen years old and I would make sure we didn't heap lots of pressure and responsibility on his thin shoulders like Flea. Understanding hit me hard, and I groped for the cot's edge again.

Poor Flea. He'd been grappling with this new power, trying to understand it and there I was, pressuring him to experiment to use a magic he didn't even understand. No wonder he'd refused. I'd been such an idiot.

"Avry, are you all right?" Danny asked.

I straightened. "Yes, fine. Let's continue."

Danny touched each patient, accurately reporting illnesses, fractures, and injuries. Then I led him to the cavern with the plague victims.

He stopped at the entrance. "They've been poisoned with Death Lily toxin."

"Why do you think that?" I asked.

"They reek of anise, are covered with sweat, and remind me of the kids at King Tohon's. The ones who didn't live."

Tohon had injected Death Lily toxin into young children, hoping a few would survive and become healers.

"Go ahead and touch one. See if you get anything different."

Reluctance dragged at his feet.

"They're not contagious to healers," I assured him.

Biting his lip, Danny pressed two fingertips to the closest man's temple. "Oh. It's not the toxin. But it's similar. He's going to die. Can I heal him?"

"No!" I batted his hand away. "He has a form of the plague. If you take his sickness, then you'll die."

Horror welled in his eyes. "The plague's back?"

I explained about the new strain. "I think something protected the survivors of the first plague, but they are vulnerable to this one. And I believe this one has to be injected into the body to work."

"And why am I safe?" Danny asked.

"As a healer, you're immune to Death Lily toxin, which is at the heart of this plague." But as I said those words, I wondered if they were true. After all, I had died after I'd assumed the plague from Ryne. There must be something else that protected them from contracting the disease. If I could figure it out, I could cure the plague.

Danny yawned. I told him to wash his hands and go find a place to sleep. "Loren and Quain have their bedrolls set up in the small cavern to the left of the cave's entrance if you want to join them."

"But the patients—"

"Are fine for now. Don't worry. I won't hesitate to wake you if you're needed."

Unhappy, but all out of arguments, Danny scrubbed and

then left. I checked on each of the men and made them as comfortable as possible for the evening. My bedroll had been set up near the cavern's entrance so I'd be close by if needed by my caregivers or the patients.

I considered the problem of the plague as I washed my hands. The water felt colder than normal, causing my finger bones to ache. The sensation crept up my arms. I hugged them to my chest and turned to face the reason for the iciness.

Noak stood a few feet away. Shivers threatened to break out, but I clamped down on my emotions. There was no need to fear this man.

I shooed him out of the cavern, explaining about the danger. When we reached a safe distance, I stopped. "Do you need something?"

"Your hand," he said, holding out his own.

"Oh." Not sure how I could refuse without insulting him, I placed my right hand in his, bracing for the blast of ice. He didn't disappoint. I stiffened as the now-familiar wave of frigid cold raced through me.

Noak's grip tightened. "There's another."

"Another what?"

"Bond. Deep inside, but there." Noak thumped his chest.

"Bond?"

"You are linked to Magic Man and this other."

Fear melted the ice. "Who?"

"Another man of magic. Stronger than Magic Man, but his link to you is weaker for now."

Tohon? But he was encased in a stasis. Or so we believed. "How do I break that link?"

"This other must die."

# KERRICK

A teapot crashed to the hearth, shattering into pieces—just like Kerrick's thoughts.

"Belen's here?" he asked Mom.

Mom frowned at the destroyed teapot. Small shards littered the bricks around Flea's feet. "No. He left a few days ago."

Flea jumped down. "Where did he go?"

"South to spy on that nasty Skeleton King." Mom tsked. "I told him to wait until he was fully healed, but the big oaf had it in his thick head to go investigate."

Now Kerrick needed to sit down. He sank into a chair. "Wait. Belen's injured?"

She glanced at Kerrick and then Flea. "My goodness, didn't you get my message?" Mom clasped her hands together. "No wonder you're in such a state."

"Can you start at the beginning, please?" Kerrick asked.

"Of course, dearie. Mr. Belen arrived at my door about a week after midsummer's day. The poor man's head was cracked open. He had dozens of cuts, bruises, and a handful of stab wounds. His right arm had been broken in two places and his left ankle was shredded. Something had chewed right through his leather boot." She shook her head. "Those injuries should have killed him. But there he stood, swaying on his feet, dripping blood on my clean floors and insisting all he needed was a piece of pie and a good night's sleep."

Kerrick smiled. "That's Belen."

"We managed to get him into a bed before he collapsed. He slept for so long, I'd feared he'd never wake up."

"How long?" Flea asked.

"Two months! I sent a message to Avry right after he'd arrived."

"Zabin was under attack then," Flea said.

"I heard the news later, and figured it was the reason Avry didn't come. But I'd hoped the note made it to her."

Kerrick considered. The message was probably intercepted by Tohon's army, which would explain why Tohon lied to Avry about Belen getting captured. He'd known Belen's situation and location.

"When he woke, I'd expected him to not remember a thing," Mom said. "A blow like that should have scrambled his brain. But that thick skull of his saved him. Once he found out how long he'd been asleep, he'd wanted to charge right off." She smoothed her apron with a quick flick of her hands as if still affronted by Belen's lack of good judgment. "Of course, his leg muscles couldn't hold his weight and he'd had nothing to eat but broth and bits of soggy bread for months. Took my bartender and two of my regulars to get him back into bed."

"I'd bet Belen fussed about that," Flea said, grinning.

"Oh, yes. Mr. Belen wasn't the best patient. He kept insisting he needed to get back, but between the dizziness, headaches, and weakness, I wouldn't let him go. And he listened to me until that horrible Skeleton King invaded Jaxton."

"Was he better by then?" Kerrick asked.

"Much. But I'd hoped he'd be back to full strength before he left." Mom fisted her apron. "I'm worried he'll run into trouble."

Kerrick rushed to assure her. "Belen can be impulsive, but he's smart and a good scout." As long as he kept his distance from the Skeleton King, he should be fine...unless he ran into one of Cellina's patrols, or priests from Estrid's army. "What happened to the priests that were staying here?"

"Ran off as soon as they heard about the High Priestess's surrender to King Tohon."

"Where did they go?" Flea asked.

"Don't know. Don't care. I was just happy to see the backs of their robes."

"Have you heard anything about Cellina's army?" Kerrick asked.

"Who?"

Interesting. The news about Tohon's status hadn't reached her. Perhaps Cellina was keeping it quiet. Kerrick filled Mom in on the news.

"Goodness, such a to-do. Poor Prince Ryne is stuck in the middle and surrounded by enemies."

Her comment sounded a warning inside his head. "Why do you say that?"

"Because the High Priestess is to the east, and this Cellina is to the west, and the nasty Skeleton King is south."

"More like southwest," Flea said.

"South," Mom insisted. "He's taken the city of Dina in Tobory Realm, too."

Shocked, he stared at Mom. Ryne's information was dangerously out of date. No wonder he'd been so anxious to have Kerrick scouting for him.

Kerrick stood. "Flea, take Mom and Huxley and return to Grzebien. I'll—"

They both protested.

"I'm going with you," Flea said.

"No need to babysit me," Mom said. "I can take care of

myself. Have been for days. You boys go and find Mr. Belen, then we'll all travel together."

Kerrick calculated. Jaxton was three days away on horseback, which would add six days at the minimum to this trip. "Avry—"

"Is going to be so ecstatic to see Belen, she'll forget to be mad at you for being late," Flea said.

True, but he hated to worry her again. Perhaps he could send a message. "Is anyone else in town?" he asked Mom.

"A few diehards that refuse to leave. Not what you're looking for, dearie." She shooed him. "Go. The sooner you leave, the faster you'll return."

Three days later, Kerrick and Flea neared the outskirts of Jaxton. During the trip, they'd spotted a few groups of refugees, heading west at a fast pace, but no one else. And no sign of Belen. Using his connection to the forest, Kerrick searched as far as his senses could stretch, which was only about two miles now, less than half as far as he could before this…lethargy. Frustration gripped him.

Within the distant he scanned, Belen was not in the woods. That meant one thing. He was in Jaxton, either hiding or as a prisoner of the Skeleton King.

They waited until nightfall. Kerrick planned to follow the glows from the campfires of the Skeleton King's army to locate them. He didn't expect the loud chanting and drumbeats that started at full dark. He instructed Flea to leave with Huxley at the first sign of trouble.

"Yeah, like that will happen," Flea said.

"Could you at least pretend you'll follow my orders?"

"I could."

Kerrick waited.

"Oh, okay. I'll run away like a bunny with a hound on his tail." He saluted with two fingers.

"A simple 'yes, sir' would suffice."

"But not be near as entertaining."

Shaking his head, Kerrick planned to limit Flea's time hanging out with the monkeys.

Kerrick circled to the east of town. Bright orange light pulsed near the edge of the forest. At first he thought it was a huge bonfire, but then he recognized the building—the apartment house. Where he'd first seen Avry. Flames engulfed the structure as smoke billowed into the sky.

Figures danced around the fire, pounding on drums. They wore white armor and elaborate headdresses made of...human skulls? Kerrick squinted, but the horrific image only clarified. And the white armor—bones.

Revulsion, deep and primal, bubbled up his throat, tasting bitter and feeling like ash in his mouth. The plague had killed millions in a short period of time. Unburied dead bodies had been one of the unfortunate ramifications of that time. But it was despicable to use their bones for armor.

Kerrick scanned the crowd, watching the dancers. No one stood out or appeared to be the Skeleton King. No Belen, either. Slipping south, he spotted a number of smaller campfires. The town's square was filled with milling soldiers and an array of tents. It seemed odd that the army hadn't occupied the buildings. And where were the townspeople? The best way to survive an invasion was to play host and hope the army would leave soon.

He continued south. Kerrick counted soldiers, estimating their numbers. He also noted their weapons—swords, knives, clubs, pikes—all fashioned with, he guessed, bone handles and hilts. From this distance, he couldn't be certain.

Looping around to the west, he realized the soldiers didn't

act like they'd just conquered a town. No celebrating, laughing, drinking, or debauchery. Unless there were more men inside the buildings? But besides the chanting and drumbeats, the rest of the town remained quiet. Still no Belen.

He stopped behind the jailhouse. It was the best place to keep the captured townspeople and, perhaps, Belen, as well. Leaning against a tree, Kerrick waited and watched. Near the building was a large fire pit. No flames crackled. Instead, bright red coals glowed, pumping out heat. Spits of meat sizzled over the coals. A man turned them, one at a time. Enough meat to feed a substantial army. From what he'd seen so far, he estimated the army to be about two thousand strong.

After a couple hours, the Skeleton King approached the jailhouse. No doubt the man was the infamous king. His armor covered him from head to toe and resembled a skeleton. His helmet had been constructed from a skull. And a crown carved from bone sat atop his head.

The Skeleton King pulled open the door and shouted. His words were garbled at this distance. Kerrick crept closer.

"…need our offering. The moon's at its zenith," the Skeleton King said, stepping back as guards wrestled with two screaming men, dragging them over to a broad wooden table near the cook fire.

Horror welled. Kerrick recognized the design. He started forward, grabbing his sword's hilt, but stopped. What could he do? He'd use all his strength just to reach the man. After that, getting caught and killed along with them would be the only outcome.

The guards strapped the first prisoner to the table. The Skeleton King spread his arms wide, tipped his head back, and howled at the moon. When he finished, his soldiers howled an echo. Then the king brandished a knife and in one quick motion, sliced the prisoner's throat. The man who had been turning the spits rushed to collect the gushing blood in a bowl.

Kerrick clamped down on a cry as anguish and impotent rage flowed through him. His grief intensified when the second prisoner joined the first. The howling repeated and another bowl was filled with blood.

The Skeleton King took both bowls and strode toward the large bonfire. After a few minutes the drumbeat changed its cadence. The rest of the soldiers followed the Skeleton King. But not the cook. He remained behind, tending the spits.

Before Kerrick could decide on his next move, the wind shifted. The strong stench of burned flesh sent him to his knees, gagging and retching.

They wouldn't...

They couldn't...

The cook grabbed a meat cleaver. Without the slightest hesitation, he butchered the victims on the table.

They did.

# CHAPTER 16

I stared at Noak, trying to gather my wits. He'd just informed me that I was bonded to Tohon and in order to break the bond, Tohon must die. I'd love to oblige him, but Tohon was safely behind enemy lines.

"What will happen if he doesn't die?" I asked.

"Without Magic Man here, the other's bond grows stronger. He will destroy your link with Magic Man."

Not good. Terrifying actually. But it would explain why I didn't have the Tohon nightmares when I was with Kerrick.

"He must die before link with Magic Man gone," Noak said.

"Even if I knew where he was—"

"You know." Noak tapped me on the chest. "Answer is here."

Lovely. "But I can't reach him. He's well protected."

"Then you are lost." Noak released my hand.

"What does that mean?"

"Once a bond is forged, it is unbreakable."

Yikes. "What does this bond do?"

"You linked by magic. You can use his power and he can use yours if you equal. Unequal, the stronger one will take the weaker's magic and use it all for himself."

Noak studied my expression. "Yes. That one is stronger than you and Magic Man." He nodded and walked away.

I expected to warm up once the tribesman left, but this time the cold persisted, soaking deep into my bones. Even knowing I'd get no sleep tonight, I lay down on my bedroll. I pulled the blanket up to my chin. Shivers raced along my skin as I imagined Tohon's smug smile.

After tossing and turning for what seemed like hours, I jerked the blanket off and checked on my patients. Only one required another dose of pain medicine. The rest slept. I organized supplies, rolled bandages, and kept busy until dawn.

Christina took one look at me and ordered me to bed.

"But I'm—" I tried.

"Exhausted and will be of no use to anybody until you get some sleep." She crossed her arms. "Do I need to ask Sergeant Odd to escort you to your bedroll?"

About to give in, I paused. "Why Odd and not Loren or Quain?"

"You listen to him. Unlike the monkeys. Now go." She pointed.

All out of arguments, I shuffled to my bedroll. Before going to sleep, I checked on the plague patients. A convulsion shook Private Jannes. He had reached stage three and only had two more days left to live. Two of the most hellish days in his life. I'd experienced what he now faced and knew dying would be a relief. I mixed a draught of pain and sleep powders for him, hoping to ease his final hours.

After Jannes gulped the medicine down, I eyed the sleep powder. If I drank a weak dose, would it keep Tohon away? Or would it prevent me from waking up and escaping Tohon?

And then an idea popped into my head. Noak had said I knew where to find Tohon in my heart. What if that worked for other information? Would Tohon know what Cellina's been up to? Would he tell me? Only one way to find out. Ugh.

Unhappy with the prospect of encouraging Tohon in my dreams but unable to pass up the opportunity to learn more, I slid under my blanket. After that, I don't remember even resting my head on the pillow.

*"So now you believe me, my dear." Tohon poured a cup of tea and handed it to me. "I've been telling you for months. But it appears the ice giant from the wildlands has more credibility than me." He huffed as if affronted then settled across the table. Tohon peered at me over the rim of his steaming cup. His deep blue eyes held a predatory glint.*

*Glad for the table between us, I sipped my tea. The sunlight reflected off the squares of colored glass embedded in the table's clear glass top. We sat in Tohon's forever garden. Constructed on the roof of his castle in Sogra Realm, the rectangular glass room contained a variety of leafy trees, lush bushes, hanging vines, and even pools of water. The humid air held the thick scent of living green mixed with the sweet aroma of flowers. Minus Tohon, it was a perfect place.*

*I glanced at the beauty surrounding us. "Will all this die when it turns cold?" The first day of winter was four days away.*

*He raised an eyebrow. "Why would you think that?"*

*"Because you're..."*

*"Trapped in a stasis?"*

*"Yes."*

*"It's different for me. I'm a life magician, so while my body is frozen, my mind and my magic remain active. Otherwise we wouldn't be talking." He gestured with his free hand. "These trees will continue to thrive as long as I live."*

*I considered. "But don't you need to be nearby?"*

*He smiled his killer smile, flashing white teeth. "I am, my dear. This is where Cellina has dumped me. I'm not complaining. It is my favorite spot."*

*Yet he used the word* dumped. *Interesting. However, he gave me an excellent opening.* "Do you talk to Cellina in her dreams, as well?"

"No. She lacks magical power, so I cannot connect to her."

*Ah.* "How about Sepp? Do you communicate with him?"

*Tohon drank his tea, but he kept his gaze on me. His brow furrowed as if the beverage was too bitter.* "No."

"Why—"

"Aren't you full of questions tonight. Next you'll be asking me about Cellina's attack plans."

"Since you mentioned it…"

*He set the teacup down. It clanged on the saucer.* "All I know about her plans, I've learned from you. And I'm guessing from your half-empty infirmary that she hasn't engaged Ryne's pathetic army in quite some time."

"We think she's setting a trap like you did with the dead soldiers." *I shuddered at the memory of the ring of buried soldiers that had surrounded Estrid's army.*

"Not without Ulany."

*Ah, yes, Ryne had killed her.*

*Tohon's anger pulsed.* "He shot her with a dart filled with the Death Lily toxin you *sent* him."

*Oh.*

"At least she died right away and didn't linger in agony like some do."

"You mean like my sister." *My turn to snap.*

"I didn't want to hurt her, but you made me so mad that day."

"So it's my fault she died?"

*He gazed at me with a quizzical squint.* "Of course."

*While I agreed that I held some of the blame and felt guilty about her death, the fact that Tohon failed to see that his actions also played a part in her death just proved, once again, that he lacked basic human compassion and a conscience.*

"*I don't regret my actions. Your dead soldiers had to be stopped,*" I said. "*What I do regret is missing your heart with my sword.*"

"My *sword*. You used *my* sword." Tohon growled.

I laughed. "*Ouch.*"

Tohon stood. I clutched my chair arms. He couldn't hurt me in my own dream. Could he?

"*If I were you,*" Tohon said, "*I'd be worried about what Cellina's up to. We stayed up many late nights discussing strategy. She's smart and devious. Who do you think came up with the idea to bury my dead soldiers?*" Tohon smirked. "*It's not so funny now. Is it?*"

I jerked awake. Disoriented, I stared at the ceiling. Torchlight flickered on stone. Had I slept all day? Hard to tell inside a cave. Private Jannes groaned in pain. Clambering to my feet, I checked on him. White blisters marked his skin and a few bled where he'd scratched at them. I dug into my pack and retrieved the gloves Belen had given me. Sadness gripped my heart for a moment, but another cry from Jannes spurred me into action. I slipped the gloves onto the private's hands, then cleaned and coated the blisters with a salve.

When I finished, I glanced up and met Sergeant Phelix's gaze. He had pushed up on his right elbow. Sweat stained his nightshirt.

"That'll be me soon. Won't it?" he asked.

I wanted to lie to him. "Yes."

"Ah, hell." He sank back down and hooked his arm over his eyes.

I stood there unable to speak. There were no words of comfort to offer. My healing powers were useless. Nothing would stop the inevitable. Instead, I held Phelix's hand until he fell asleep.

After I cared for the others, I searched for Ryne. It appeared as if he hadn't moved from the corner. Noak sat with him and I hesitated, unwilling to interrupt them. Scared of the ice giant? Who, me?

Ryne noticed me and gestured for me to join them.

"What's up?" he asked.

I glanced at Noak. No icy chill raced over my skin. A first. Was it a good sign or bad? Ryne misinterpreted my silence and asked Noak to give us a few minutes.

Noak nodded and headed toward the main fire. Danny sat with the monkeys and a number of other soldiers. They held bowls of stew, and Quain demonstrated an attack move with his spoon. Laughter echoed until Noak arrived. Then quiet descended in a heartbeat.

"No one is quite sure what to make of him," Ryne said.

"The logical part of our minds knows he's here to help us, but, let's face it, he's the monster under the bed."

Ryne laughed. "That he is!"

I stared at Noak's broad back. If he was the monster under the bed, who was Cellina? The ghoul in the closet? The jack-in-the-box?

"What's wrong?" Ryne asked.

"Do you know what Cellina's planning?"

"No."

"How about theories? Is there something you're not telling me?"

Ryne tapped his finger on the table. "What brought this up? Another dream?"

It irked me that he'd guessed right. "That and experience, Ryne. You've a tendency to keep information from me and disappear. I'd just like a little warning this time."

"I've a *theory* about Cellina's plan and I think she's sending her troops farther north to loop in behind us. I'm going to send half my troops to intercept her. You should be safe here."

"Should?"

"We're at war. My theories are just that—theories. I can only control the actions of my army."

"She's not going to catch you by surprise?"

"I hope not. That's why you saved me. Right?" He grinned.

"So you could save us."

"That's the plan."

"And you're not going to use me as bait?"

"Avry, I won't knowingly use you as bait. I promise."

"Knowingly?"

"We're at war. Things change in a heartbeat." He glanced over to the fire. "I'm leaving for HQ tomorrow, taking Noak and the lady warriors with me. They'll be part of that northern force. Lieutenant Macon and his men plus the odd squad, Loren, and Quain will stay with you, guarding the infirmary. I suspect Danny will want to remain, as well. And…" He peered at me as if trying to read my mood. "When Kerrick and Flea return, I'd like them both to join me at HQ. Their help is vital."

I clamped down on my instinctive reply of no way. Instead, I said, "Flea has refused to use his power."

"I know. But he's had enough time to adjust. He can't keep avoiding it. His powers can make a difference in the outcome of this fight."

"I'll relay your message." And let them decide.

"Thank you."

I nodded and then joined the others at the fire. My stomach growled as soon as I smelled the stew. Ladling a bowlful, I listened as Quain asked Noak questions about the wildlands. Danny answered a couple. He talked with confidence about the tribespeople as if he'd been born one of them. I hid a smile. The boy had been in a horrible situation and he'd managed to turn it around, creating allies from enemies. Perhaps Flea would also come to terms with his unique situation. One could hope.

★ ★ ★

After Ryne and the others left, we settled into a routine. Quain groused about babysitting duty, but the others seemed happy with the arrangement. And Odd planned to take his squad out on patrols, sweeping the surrounding area in wider and wider loops in case the enemy attempted to sneak up on us.

As we neared the first day of winter, my worry increased. First, Kerrick and Flea hadn't returned as expected. Granted they were only two days late, but my imagination kicked in and created terrible reasons for the delay. Second, more victims of the plague arrived at the infirmary. And not just a handful, but a steady stream of sick patients.

The small cavern I'd been using to keep them quarantined overflowed. I commandeered two more caverns. By the first morning of winter, I counted a total of twenty-four. Jannes had died.

By the end of the day, I had thirty. Danny helped me. We grouped them by their stages. Those experiencing stage one stayed together while those in the throes of stage two filled another. Stage three remained in their original location; moving them would cause them too much pain.

After helping to carry a woman into the stage-two area, Danny paused and looked at me with a slightly horrified grimace. "King Tohon did the same thing with the kids he injected the toxin into." He gestured. "Divided us by how sick we were."

"It makes sense for the caregivers and I think it's a kindness," I said.

"Yeah. They're scared enough. Seeing your friends die and knowing that's your fate…" He shuddered. "It would be cruel. At least when they reach that stage, they're too sick to be aware of their surroundings."

The voice of experience. Tohon had taken Danny's childhood, and I wished I could send Danny to Alga Realm where he'd be safe and wouldn't have to deal with the horrors of war. Where he could be a kid. And while I was wishing, I'd send Flea along, too.

A soldier sat up suddenly and flung his blanket to the ground. He yanked his sweat-stained shirt off and fanned his face. I poured him a glass of cool water and added a pinch of fever powder before hurrying over to him.

Catching sight of his back, I stopped. A black mark stained his skin. Dirt? I moved closer. When I reached his bedside, the mark was horrifyingly clear—a two-inch-long tattoo of a skeleton wearing a crown of bones.

Clamping down on my growing panic, I kept my voice even as I asked, "Danny, can you fetch Odd?"

"Sure." Danny rushed away.

"Wash your hands first," I yelled after him.

He returned and scrubbed.

"What happened to you before you got sick?" I handed the sergeant the drink.

He swept a hand out. "You mean before my whole squad started puking?"

"Yes, Sergeant…"

"Gylon." He gulped the drink then wiped his mouth with the back of his hand. "Nothing happened. We were out on patrol and didn't encounter the enemy."

"Did you see anyone?"

"We helped that guy out, remember, Sarge?" another man lying nearby asked.

"Oh, yeah. The man's wagon wheel had broken and we helped fix it. No biggie," Gylon said.

"Are you sure we fixed it?" A private pushed up on her elbow. "I don't recall that."

"That's 'cause you took rear guard, Tyra, watching our backs," yet another soldier added.

She frowned. "And I thought I saw...something before getting stung by a bee."

A few of the others piped up. "I was stung."

"Me, too."

"Must have disturbed a nest."

"Stung? Are you sure?" I asked Tyra.

Tyra pointed to her neck. I examined the area. A tiny red puncture marked her skin. Not a bee sting, but evidence that she'd been hit by a dart. I checked the others. All had puncture wounds. The squad had been ambushed and didn't even know it.

"Where were you?" I asked.

"South," Sergeant Gylon said. "Prince Ryne wanted us to sweep the area to ensure no one tried to get in behind Grzebien."

My panic boiled up my throat. "How far?"

"Two days, but with everyone so sick, it took us twice as long to get here."

The Skeleton King had been two days south of us four days ago. Bad, very bad.

Even worse, he had a powerful weapon. The new plague.

# KERRICK

On his knees, Kerrick leaned against the back of the jail-house. He held the hem of his shirt over his nose and mouth, taking deep breaths. The image of the cook butchering two men seared into his mind while the acid from his stomach burned up his throat. His body shook as he fought the desire to retch. The Skeleton King and his army ate their victims. Horror mixed with revulsion, and he lost the battle and dry heaved over the grass.

More howling pierced the air, along with a set of rapid drumbeats. The bonfire sizzled and Kerrick wondered if the two bowls of blood the king had collected from the victims had been tossed into the flames. Kerrick sank back onto his heels and covered his mouth again, blocking the foul odor of burned flesh.

When he'd regained his composure, he peered around the corner of the building. He eyed the spits of meat over the coals. How many people had they killed? Was Belen one of them? *Not going there.*

He locked his emotions away. At this point, second-guessing would be a waste of time. Kerrick reviewed the facts. The victims had been taken from the jailhouse, so there must be more locked inside. And he had to rescue them. Tonight.

He crept around the side, searching for the window they'd used to rescue Avry a little over a year ago. Almost at ground level, it had been boarded up, which meant the iron bars hadn't been replaced. *First thing to go right all night.*

Now the hard part. Should he wait until the army settled down for the night or do it now while they were preoccupied? The prison cells had been built belowground. The prisoners would need help climbing out the window. Kerrick scanned the area. Ivy grew on the pasture fence and jailhouse walls. Another chant started. Would the Skeleton King return for more victims? He couldn't bear for anyone else to die.

A plan formed. Kerrick pressed his palm to the ground. He concentrated on Flea and Huxley. They remained where he'd left them. Closing his eyes, Kerrick envisioned his location and his need, hoping one or both of them would pick up on his silent message.

Huxley pawed the ground and then started in Kerrick's direction. Soon after, Flea followed. Good.

While he waited for them, Kerrick worked on the boards, prying them loose with his dagger every time the chanting and howling grew loud enough to cover the noise. He'd gotten a couple free when he sensed Huxley nearby. They had reached the edge of the forest behind the jailhouse. Kerrick joined them, turning back to normal.

"This is beyond creepy," Flea said when he appeared. "What's with the noise, the awful smell, and that howling?" he asked in an urgent whisper.

"Later. First we need to rescue—"

"Belen? Is he in there?" Flea pointed to the jailhouse.

"I hope. Do you remember how we rescued Avry last year?"

"Yes, but Loren—"

"I've a substitute for your leg holders."

Flea glanced at Huxley. "Won't he be too noticeable?"

"He's staying here. Don't worry. I've a plan."

"And the distraction?"

"With all that noise, I'm hoping we don't need one."

"Lots of hoping going on here, Kerrick."

"We've had flimsier plans."

Flea grinned. "True. Lead on before they stop."

They returned to the window and finished pulling off the boards, exposing the stumps of the bars that had been left when they'd used Quain's lightning juice to cut through them. Kerrick then concentrated on the ivy growing on the fence, encouraging it to weave into a ladder and elongate. It resisted, but he pushed through its reluctance. The effort sapped him and he needed a boost of energy from Flea. Once he recovered, Kerrick dropped the ivy ladder into the cell and then wiggled through the tight opening.

"Stay here," he instructed Flea. "The prisoners can climb up the ladder. You need to help them out and direct them to Huxley."

"Okay."

Kerrick descended. At the bottom he stood for a moment, letting his eyes adjust to the semidarkness. Even with the ivy hanging next to him, he felt the strong tug from the forest and combined with the energy he needed to maintain a normal appearance, he had to be careful not to drain all his strength.

Now accustomed to the dim light, he glanced around. No surprise this cell was empty. But men and women stared at him from its neighbors.

"Who—"

He put a finger to his lips. "I'm here to help you escape." Kerrick kept his voice low. "It's very important that you keep quiet and follow my instructions. All right?"

They nodded. Kerrick pulled out his lock picks and went to work. He unlocked the closest cell and showed them the ladder. While they took turns, he unlocked the other cells and searched for Belen. Three to five people shared each cell. No Belen. Grief and frustration mixed into a tight ball in the pit of his stomach.

He asked the others about Belen. "He's a big guy, black hair, looks like a bear," Kerrick whispered.

Most didn't answer, but one woman said, "He's down below. He fought the guards and gave them such a hard time, they locked him in the pit. Poor guy hasn't had any food or water in days."

After all the cells had been opened, Kerrick found the hatch to the pit. It'd been bolted to the floor and secured with a thick lock that shone—brand-new. He cursed under his breath. Inserting his tension wrench and diamond pick, Kerrick wished for Quain's lightning juice. This wouldn't be easy. He worked on the lock until his fingers cramped. His energy dipped.

"They're all out," Flea said. "Fifteen total."

Kerrick strode to the window. "Lead them to Mom's."

"But—"

"Go."

But instead of obeying him, Flea climbed through the window and dropped down beside him. "How can I help?"

"You can't." Biting down on his anger, Kerrick turned and resumed his efforts to pop the complex lock. Sweat soaked his shirt and stung his eyes. His fingers slipped on the pick and he clamped down on a growl of frustration.

Flea tapped him on the shoulder. "Company."

The clang of a door echoed. Flea gripped the hilt of his sword, but Kerrick stopped him.

"A dagger's better for an ambush." Kerrick stood and drew his blade. He motioned for Flea to stand to the right of the main door, while he stepped to the left. He'd been wrong. Flea could help.

They waited. The jailhouse had two sets of heavy double doors from the processing area to the cells. Metal screeched as the second set was unlocked. A beam of lantern light sliced the darkness, then grew wider as the doors swung open.

Kerrick didn't hesitate. "Now!" he shouted then grabbed the closest guard and spun him, ramming his head into the wall. The man crumpled in a heap.

He turned. Flea struggled with two men. Kerrick pulled one off the boy and slit the guard's throat. Two more guards rushed into the fray, armed with swords and prepared for a fight. Kerrick discovered that bone armor was quite effective against his dagger. And their sharp rapiers snaked in past his defenses, finding flesh.

Kerrick drew his dadao sword. Even though he didn't have much room to swing, he hoped the thick curved blade would intimidate them. Aside from a brief pause, it failed to impress them.

They pressed their advantage and Kerrick retreated. Soon his back hit bars. He was trapped and near the end of his energy. Flea made a strangled cry. Kerrick dropped his normal camouflage and increased his attacks, hoping to slip past them. Besides a grunt of surprise, the two men kept lunging with their thinner weapons. Fighting in tight quarters against two, Kerrick knew it was just a matter of time.

Another cry sounded and then the guard on the right jerked and toppled. His partner turned and Flea touched the man's face. He froze and fell back.

Flea clutched his stomach, looking queasy.

Kerrick sheathed his sword and put a hand on Flea's shoulder. "Keep it together, Flea. There might be more."

Flea drew in a deep breath and straightened.

"Good. Watch for reinforcements." He checked the guards' pockets, searching for keys, and found a ring of them. Sorting through them, he isolated a large silver one that shone as if new. Kerrick returned to the pit's lock and opened it.

Excited, he threw the bolt and opened the hatch. Two giant hands reached up and wrapped around his neck, yanking him into the blackness.

# CHAPTER 17

Danny returned with Odd on his heels. I intercepted Odd at the door.

"What's wrong?" Odd asked.

I explained.

His face paled. "Are you sure?"

I showed him Gylon's tattoo. The sergeant cursed after learning of his new decoration, but hadn't put all the pieces together yet. The Skeleton King's troops had ambushed Gylon's squad and infected them with the new plague.

"How close?" Odd asked.

"Two days south, but that was four days ago."

Now it was Odd's turn to curse. He bolted from the cavern to send a messenger to Ryne. Would it reach him in time?

Sergeant Gylon wanted to go with him. "I'm feeling better," he protested when I refused to let him leave.

"That's because of the fever powder. Rest now, you'll need your strength for later." Covering him with his blanket, I tucked him in. "Is your entire squad here? All ten?"

"Yeah." Grief filled his eyes as he realized their fates matched his own.

I squeezed his hand. His squad was still in shock over getting the bad news that they had, at most, six days to live. Once the reality sunk in, it was going to be rough. Their reactions would run the gamut from denial, anger, and grief to pleading, bargaining, and bribing me to save their lives. Some would hit all the emotions, others only a few and one or two would not say a word, keeping it all bottled inside. I suspected Sergeant Gylon would remain stoic to help his squad.

Checking on the others, I asked them to show me their backs. Everyone had a Skeleton King tattoo.

"What does it mean?" Private Tyra asked.

The other members of their squad peered at me. It meant the Skeleton King might be right outside the infirmary, and he was the one infecting our soldiers with the new plague.

Instead of upsetting the squad further, I said, "It's a taunt from the enemy." Then I settled them for the night, dispensing fever powder.

When I finished, I scrubbed my hands and found Odd arguing with Lieutenant Macon.

"...should confirm their position before sending Prince Ryne a message," Odd said.

"It's been four days, they could be at our doorstep, I'll need the extra manpower if they attack," Macon said.

"Then we'll do a short sweep," Odd said. "Avry, what do you think? Did Gylon's squad have any more information?"

"Send a message to Ryne right away. Tell him that the Skeleton King has access to the plague virus and his troops are south of the infirmary," I said.

"How far?" Odd asked me.

"We can't waste the time finding out. He needs to know they're there. Last time I talked to him he was getting reports that the Skeleton King had invaded Sectven."

"All right." Odd rushed off to send a message.

"Do you think he'll attack us?" Macon asked.

Answering Macon's question, I said, "Yes."

"What about a short sweep?" Odd asked me, returning.

"No."

"Why not? We need more information."

"Because they're armed with darts filled with the new plague and have been busy using them. Do you want to join the others who are dying in the infirmary?"

"No." Odd scratched his chin. "How did the Skeleton King get the plague virus?"

"From Tohon, but I've no idea if he stole it or if Cellina gave it to him. If she did, it means they've teamed up." A horrible prospect.

"Why team up? With the ability to spread the plague to her enemies, she could infect the Skeleton King's entire army."

"Perhaps she's too squeamish to engage in biological warfare. Maybe they worked out a treaty. Does it matter? He has it and it's an effective way to win a war."

"But it's risky. Even though you said this new strain has to be injected, what's to stop us from…" he gestured to the patients "…collecting their blood or spit or whatever and using it to infect his army?"

I stared at him in amazement.

He held out his hands as if in surrender. "What did I say?"

"Odd. You. Are. A. Genius!" I hugged him and kissed him on the cheek.

"I am?"

"Yes. Danny," I yelled. "Grab a couple syringes and come with me."

"Okay." Danny rushed over to the supplies.

"What did I say?" Odd repeated.

"I'll explain later."

I hurried to the stage-three patients with Danny right behind me.

"What's going on?" he asked.

"They're suffering from the new plague. The one that has to be injected."

"Yeah, we know that."

"It's the same one Prince Ryne had."

"So?"

I stopped just inside the cavern. "So I survived the new plague."

"Didn't the Peace Lily save you?"

"After I died."

"Uh, Avry, dying is the opposite of surviving."

I waved his comment away. "Technically it was the combination of the serum and Kerrick's magic touch that brought me back."

"Still not following you," Danny said.

"I might have built up a resistance to the plague. Like after you get the stuttering cough once, you never get it again? The Healer's Guild had been doing research on the reasons for that before the plague."

"Oh, yeah, you mentioned it in your journal. Do you think this is the same?"

"It might be. I'd assumed the reason I couldn't heal Yuri of the plague was because of the Peace Lily serum in me, but what if it was something else? Isn't it at least worth a try?"

"I guess. What do we have to do?"

"Help me draw my blood," I said, gesturing to the syringes in his hand.

"Oh."

Together we managed to get one vial full of my blood. I strode over to Sergeant Phelix, my sickest patient. I'd ask him for his permission, but he only had hours to live and was incoherent.

"But what if your blood kills him? Don't you still have Peace Lily serum in you?" Danny asked.

"As long as we don't touch him, he won't become like Yuri." I pushed Phelix's sleeve up past his elbow, found the vein and injected my blood into him.

After a few moments, Danny asked, "How long until we know if it worked or not?"

"If he lives until tomorrow, we'll know it worked."

"I really hope he lives."

"Me, too." I checked on the others. They should last long enough for the results of my experiment. "Go to sleep, Danny, I'll wake you if anything happens."

He nodded, washed his hands, and left.

I kept vigil, sitting next to Phelix. My thoughts turned to the Skeleton King. Despite what I'd said earlier, it did matter how he'd gotten the plague. If he teamed up with Cellina, could Ryne's army stop them? Between the sheer number of enemy attackers and the plague, we didn't stand a chance.

My dire thoughts caused my temples to pound. I rested my aching head on the edge of Phelix's cot. My stomach grumbled, complaining that I'd forgotten to eat. I'd been so excited about the possible cure—please work! If I believed in the creator, I'd be praying for success. Instead, I dozed.

*"Do you really think this one is going to work?"* Tohon asked. *"The last experiment you tried didn't go well for you, did it?"*

*We sat at the glass table in his forever garden again, drinking tea as if we were old friends.*

*"We're more than friends, my dear. Our connection runs deep."* He leered.

*Ignoring his comment, I said, "If Phelix dies, I'm not going to touch him and create another dead soldier."*

*"Whyever not? He's more useful that way. He can't help anyone while rotting in the ground. You're wasting resources."*

*"Practical and horrific. Hard to believe you're still single."*

"Cute. But I'm sure your Prince Ryne considered the very same thing before his sudden windfall of personnel."

I'd like to argue with Tohon, but Ryne had brought Yuri to HQ and said Flea's help was vital. I swirled the tea in my cup. The brown liquid spun, forming a dip in the center.

"What? No snarky reply? My, my, something must be bothering you, my dear. Perhaps I can help."

I almost laughed. Almost. Many uncomplimentary words described Tohon, but the man was intelligent. "Maybe you can. Would Cellina make an alliance with the Skeleton King?"

"It depends on what he offers her. She has plenty of soldiers, but it is harder to fight on two fronts. Better to join forces until the bigger threat is taken care of. I'd use him until he no longer served my purposes."

"You'd break a treaty?"

"Of course. I don't want to share power, my dear."

But would Cellina be that ruthless? This was the same woman who couldn't kill Kerrick. She risked her life lying to Tohon so he'd believe Kerrick was dead. I didn't know her that well, but from our encounters, the whole biological warfare and teaming up with the Skeleton King didn't seem like Cellina's style. If she wasn't the one making alliances and spreading the plague, then who else had access to Tohon's research and supplies? Sepp!

Except he worked for Cellina. Or did he? He was a powerful death magician with an ego to match. Perhaps he called the shots. That fit better with the plague attacks.

"It's a pleasure to watch you puzzle things out, my dear."

"But it doesn't help our current situation."

"I disagree. Knowing your enemy is very important. And I'm surprised your Prince Ryne hasn't figured it out yet. Unless he has…."

Once again, Tohon took the cheap shot, dredging my subconscious to bring forth all my fears.

"You should trust your instincts, Avry. Except the one to sacrifice *your life for another. That one you should ignore. But for all the others, there's a reason you have those fears. Call it experience, observation, or just a gut feeling—you shouldn't discount them."*

Advice from a psychotic megalomaniac. Wonderful.

*"An* intelligent *psychotic megalomaniac. Big difference."*

*"Stop reading my mind."*

*"You do know how ridiculous that is? I'm in your mind and you're in mine. You can do it, too, you just choose not to."*

*"I'm not brave enough to taste your special kind of darkness."*

*"What you see is what you get, my dear."* He stretched his arms wide. *"Aside from underestimating you, I've no regrets and no guilt. All I've done has been with the purest intentions to unite the Fifteen Realms. I didn't create the plague, just capitalized on its existence."*

It was pointless to argue with him. Instead, I tested his I'm-an-open-book claim. *"Tell me what happened to Belen. Is he one of the dead soldiers?"*

*"Ah, Belen. I intercepted a message about him."*

*"And?"* Concentrating on his thoughts, I sought the truth.

*"And he—"*

"Avry, wake up," Danny said. "Sergeant Phelix is still alive!"

Jolted from my dream, I sat up. So close. Another minute and I'd have found out what happened to Belen.

"Avry? Hello?" Danny waved his hands in front of my face. "Sergeant Phelix?"

"Sorry." I turned my attention to Phelix, pressing my fingers to his throat. A faint pulse throbbed. But more important, my magic sensed his symptoms had lessened.

My sleep fog disappeared in a snap as I realized what it meant. I hopped to my feet and grabbed Danny's arms.

We jumped up and down like fools, shouting, "It worked! It worked! It worked!" at the top of our lungs.

"What worked?" Loren asked. He stood in the entrance

with Quain and Odd. Swords drawn, half-dressed and bare-foot, the three appeared to have been roused from their beds.

"We found a cure for the plague," I cried.

"*You* found a cure," Danny said. "I just helped."

"I couldn't have done it without Odd." I grinned at him.

"Me? What did I do?" he asked.

I explained about how Odd's comment sparked the idea to use my blood as I picked up the clean syringe. Danny helped me fill it with my blood and I injected it into another patient.

When I finished my explanation, all three of them had huge silly smiles.

"Danny, can you get me two more syringes? I'll finish with the stage-three patients and then move on to stage two."

After I'd injected the remaining patients, I gave the syringes to Danny. "Ask Ginger to sterilize them, please. And bring me more."

"Will do." He snapped a salute and shot out the door.

"This calls for a celebration," Quain said. "I've some whiskey I've been saving."

"With breakfast?" Loren asked.

"*As* breakfast. This stuff's so good, you don't want to ruin it with anything else."

"How about later? After I heal…" The room spun. I reached for the wall and missed.

Odd grabbed my elbow, steadying me. "When's the last time you ate?" he asked.

"Uh…"

"That's what I thought. Blood loss and no food is a dangerous combination."

"Uh…"

He tsked. "And the injustice of it is that you would yell at us for not taking care of ourselves, yet you can abuse your body without anyone giving you grief."

"Technically, you're giving her grief right now," Quain said.

"But it doesn't work. She won't listen to me."

"Don't feel bad, she doesn't listen to *anyone*," Loren said.

"Hey! I'm standing right here."

"No, you're swaying." Odd tightened his grip. "Come on. Food first, then sleep, and then you can go back to work." He guided me from the cavern.

"Good luck with that," Quain muttered.

Our happy party settled around the fire. A few of my caregivers checked patients, but otherwise the main area was empty at this early hour. Odd insisted on fetching me a bowl of oatmeal and a handful of apple slices. It didn't take me long to devour them. The others wished to spread the news of the cure, but I asked them to wait. It might not work for everyone and Phelix might have a relapse. Despite my initial excitement, there were too many unknowns at this time. Plus I didn't need the news to reach our enemies.

"If you wanted to keep it a secret, maybe you shouldn't have screamed 'it worked' at the top of your lungs," Quain teased.

I ducked my head. "I couldn't help it. Besides, only you three woke up."

"Others did as well, but they rolled over and went back to sleep," Loren said. "We knew it was you and…"

"And it's always better to check than be sorry," Quain added. "'It worked' could be code for the dead are invading."

"Wow, that's…really random, Quain. Aside from you, who would ever put those two things together?" Loren asked.

"Shut up, Loren." He threw a spoonful of oatmeal at his friend.

"You're asking for it now, pup." Loren aimed at Quain with a full spoon.

"That's enough, boys," I said, pushing Loren's arm down.

"Thank you for coming to check on me. And now, if you'll excuse me, I need to return to my patients."

They watched as I clambered to my feet. Weak-kneed but steady, I searched for Danny. He helped Ginger clean the syringes.

"Amazing, Avry, simply amazing," Ginger gushed.

I put a finger to my lips. "Keep it under wraps for now. Just in case."

"Of course. But we have to tell Christina!"

"Of course."

Danny collected a handful of syringes and followed me to the stage-three cavern.

Sergeant Phelix gave me a weak grin.

"I hope you don't mind, but I tried a new medicine on you," I said to him.

"I don't mind at all. I feel so much better." He pushed up on his elbow. Hope brightened his face. "Will it...?"

"It might save your life."

He clasped my arm. "But you said—"

"I did, but that was before yesterday. Today's a whole new day. And the best thing you can do is rest and regain your strength. Are you hungry?"

"Yes." He said the word as if amazed by the answer.

"Good. I'll get you breakfast after I check on the others."

As I moved away, Danny whispered, "I thought you were waiting to make sure the cure worked before saying anything."

"Positive thoughts equals positive healing. The mind plays an important role, and if a patient is convinced he's going to die, it counteracts his recovery."

The other three appeared to be improving. Relief made me giddy and lightheaded—either that or the blood loss. I stifled a giggle. After asking one of the caregivers to bring Phelix a tray, I moved on to the stage-two cavern. Breakfast had just been served and those who could stomach the food ate, while the others had placed their bowls on the ground.

I glanced around with dismay. With twenty patients, it was the biggest group. And I'd need a lot of blood. This group also had more time to live. I decided to inject them with half a syringe of blood each and, if it didn't work, I'd give them another half.

Instead of drawing my blood in plain sight, I led Danny to an empty cavern where he helped me. Soon my arms resembled pin cushions. The cave spun and my hands shook.

"It's okay, Avry," Danny said. "I'll inject the blood. I need to learn anyway."

I kept a hand on his shoulder as we headed back. "Ask them permission first," I said, puffing. "And start with Gylon. If he agrees, then his squad will, too." Although I couldn't imagine anyone *not* agreeing.

Danny approached the sergeant. He held up the syringe, its bright red contents unmistakable. "This might save your life. May I inject it?"

Gylon looked at me and then back at Danny. "Hell, yes, son."

I instructed Danny on the proper way to insert the needle and push down the plunger. "Only halfway. Save the other half for the next person. But make sure to wipe the metal tip with alcohol between patients."

Within three patients, he had a rhythm. No one refused the chance to live.

After a while, my legs threatened to give out. I sat next to Gylon, watching Danny.

"What changed?" Gylon asked. "Yesterday you said there was nothing you could do. Today it's 'this might save your life.'"

"I had an epiphany."

"And the 'might'?"

"I don't want to oversell it. It's very promising, but…"

"Nothing worse than false hope."

"Exactly."

When Danny finished, he escorted me to my bedroll. I collapsed onto it and managed to say, "Wake me if the half dose doesn't work."

"They have a few days, Avry. No need to suck yourself dry." Danny pulled the blanket over me.

I murmured a thanks and passed out. The best thing about the depth of my exhaustion—Tohon didn't invade my dreams.

However, shouts of alarm and pounding boots intruded way too soon.

Odd barked out orders nearby. "Don't let her leave the cave. Understand?"

"Yes," Danny said.

Flinging off my blanket, I stood, then plopped back down as a wave of dizziness flowed up my body. "What's going on?" I called out.

"We're under attack," Danny said, stepping into the cavern with a grim expression.

"Who?"

"I don't know."

"I must go help." I crawled over to my pack, gathering my knives.

"That's what Sergeant Odd said you'd do. Avry, you're the only one who can cure the plague. If you die…"

"But if they get inside, I might die anyway. At least, I can—"

"You're weak and not thinking clearly."

I bristled. "And you're thirteen years old."

"And I'm acting smarter than you. You can't just rush off into a situation when you have no idea what's going on. I did that once and it caused Kerrick a lot of trouble. You're needed here. We should prepare for casualties."

Damn. He was right. I staggered to my feet, but still tucked a few knives in my belt just in case. "All right. Food first, or else I'll be useless."

Danny smiled. "That was easy. I thought I'd have to sit on you."

"Then I'd just zap you."

"Zap? What's that?" he asked.

"Something you should know and this is the perfect time." I explained to him how to use his healing powers to defend himself as I grabbed a handful of bread and cheese. "When you heal, your power flows out to the injured, but when you want to hurt someone, you push out the power and zap him. Think of sparks from a fire or lightning striking—a burst of energy. Try it." I held out my arm.

Danny grabbed it and zapped.

"Ow!"

"Sorry."

"Don't apologize. You'll learn how much force to use with practice. But it'll do for now. And if you zap at this spot…" I touched the back of his neck between two vertebra. "You'll knock a person unconscious. But it has to be right on that spot or it won't work. It'll still hurt the person, but everyone has different pain tolerances." I swept my hair to the side so he could find the location. "That's it. I'd let you practice, but…"

We both glanced at the cave's entrance. Two soldiers stood at the mouth. They held their swords ready, but the clangs of metal and shouts didn't draw them from their position.

Worried for my friends, I asked, "Did the monkeys go out, too?"

"Yeah, everyone except the caregivers. Sergeant Gylon wanted to join them, but I threatened to tie him to his cot."

"You've got good instincts, Danny. If we are invaded, don't let anyone know you're a healer. Okay?"

"Okay. What about you?"

I laughed. "It's far too late for that. I'm infamous."

He scrunched up his nose. "Shouldn't that be famous?"

"Depends on who you're talking to."

I finished eating and we helped Ginger and Christina lay out extra bandages and thread for sutures. Every loud clash sent my heart into my mouth. When we'd run out of tasks, I checked on the plague patients.

Gylon's squad no longer lay in their cots. They sat together, talking animatedly. As soon as they noticed me, they insisted I allow them to fight.

"No. You are to stay here," I said.

"Why not?" Gylon asked. "We feel great."

"You might still be contagious, and I don't want you getting our soldiers sick."

"Oh."

A scuffle sounded from the main cavern. "However, if the enemy attacks you here." I pointed down. "Feel free to defend yourselves."

"Yes, sir!" Gylon and his squad rushed to arm themselves.

I hurried out, arriving in time to see the two guards at the entrance drop their swords and backpedal into the cave.

Oh, no. I palmed one of my knives, but wilted when Odd, Loren, and Quain arrived with their hands on their heads. Bloody, bruised, and pissed off, they led a stream of soldiers who fanned out as soon as they entered, with their swords at the ready. Cellina's? Or the Skeleton King's?

Once my friends reached the center, they turned. Holding my breath, I waited. It was the enemy's move. Sure enough, a soldier strode into the cave as if she owned the place.

She put her hands on her hips and surveyed the area with

a cocky smirk on her face. The smirk spread when the traitor met my gaze.

"No hello for your old friend?" she asked me. "Don't be
rude, Baby Face."

"Go to hell, Wynn."

# KERRICK

Strong fingers cut off Kerrick's air, rendering him unable to speak. He tapped on the arms holding him in the air. *Come on, you big oaf! Remember the signals!*

"Belen," Flea said in a loud whisper. "Stop, you're choking Kerrick."

"Flea?" Belen rasped, confused. His grip relaxed a bit, then he tightened it again. "Hell. You almost fooled me, you filthy cannibal. Now back away or your man dies."

"It's me. Flea. A Peace Lily and Avry saved me. And if you kill Kerrick, Avry's gonna kill *me* and then *you* even if you are Poppa Bear."

Belen tossed him aside. Kerrick landed hard and remained on the ground, gasping for breath as Belen scrambled from the pit.

"Flea! You're alive," Belen cried.

Kerrick didn't need to see them to know Belen had Flea wrapped in one of his famous bear hugs. Having felt the same thing about the boy, he understood Belen's reaction.

"Not if you keep making so much noise," Flea said in a muffled voice.

Lumbering to his feet, Kerrick rubbed his throat. "Hey," he croaked.

A big shadow loomed over the opening. "Sorry, Kerrick." Belen reached down.

Kerrick clasped his friend's hand and Belen pulled him up with ease.

Then Belen wrapped an arm around his shoulders. "Thanks."

"What's taking so long?" The Skeleton King appeared at the entrance, then stopped as he noticed the prone forms.

"It's an escape," Belen said, tackling the king.

They hit the floor with the sound of bones crunching and a grunt of pain. The Skeleton King's helmet and crown flew off. Kerrick rushed up to help Belen, but halted. Belen had knocked the king unconscious.

Kerrick picked up the king's crown. It was similar to the one he sent Ryne. Although not quite as big.

Belen took the crown from Kerrick. "This filthy cannibal needs to die."

"Yes, he does."

"Do it," Flea said.

Belen swung the heavy crown and brought it down on the Skeleton King's head, crushing it. Blood and brains squirted out from the crumpled skull. Flea threw up.

"That takes care of the Skeleton King," Kerrick said, thinking Ryne should be pleased.

"Not quite," Belen said. "This is just one of his princelings. Sadistic bastard, though. Good riddance."

Oh, no. Kerrick put his hand to the wall as a sudden wave of pure exhaustion washed through him.

"One of...?" Flea's voice squeaked. "How many are there?"

"At least five that I know of. Damn things have invaded the south and are spreading."

"Do you know where the Skeleton King is?" Kerrick asked.

"No. He's been lying low. Probably worried about assassins."

Voices shouted from the processing area. Reinforcements.

"Time to go," Kerrick said.

The three of them raced to the window. Kerrick locked the cell as Flea and then Belen climbed out.

As he grabbed the ivy, Kerrick heard a ruckus outside the jailhouse. When he reached the window, he saw Belen tossing guards like they were rag dolls. Climbing out, he yanked the ivy from the jail and concentrated on sending it to twine around the guards' feet. A temporary measure. He spotted more guards running their way.

"To the woods," Kerrick ordered.

They jumped the fence and bolted for the forest. The fifteen people they'd rescued huddled around Huxley. The horse snorted at Kerrick.

"Lead us to a good spot, Hux." Near the end of his strength, Kerrick mounted to keep from tripping over his own feet. He said to the others, "Form a single line and follow the horse, *exactly*. Step where he steps." He tossed his sword to Belen. "Take rear guard."

Belen raised his bushy eyebrows at the dadao but helped organize the townspeople. Even though Kerrick didn't need light to travel in the forest, there was just enough moonlight to see the shape of the trees and other obstacles in their path. Plus most of the leaves had fallen, allowing more illumination to reach the ground. However, the blanket of leaves on the forest floor presented another problem.

Sounding like a herd of cattle, the group jogged through the woods with Hux taking point. Kerrick's magic alerted him when the guards entered the forest. He lost count after fifty. Too many by far. He urged Hux faster. They wouldn't outrun their pursuers, but they might outsmart them.

The forest covered the signs of their passage, and after an hour, Hux slowed. Hux had found a small clearing next to a rocky outcrop. Perfect.

Kerrick gathered everyone around. "The guards are closing in. I need you to touch Huxley with your hand or be in skin contact with someone who is touching him. My magic will camouflage us all through the horse. Some of you can sit on the rocks or the ground. If you break contact at any time, you'll be seen. Hopefully, the guards will give up the search, but we'll stay hidden and make no noise as long as it takes. Understand?"

Nods and a few "yes, sirs" sounded. Kerrick moved Huxley next to the outcrop and waited for everyone to settle into a comfortable position. A few sat on the rocks, holding hands and making a human chain. Flea and Belen stood near Hux's head.

"This is new," Belen said in a low voice.

Flea huffed. "You haven't seen nothin'. It'll take us hours to fill you in on all the *new*."

Kerrick hushed them. "Everyone ready? Operation Disappear starts now." He rested his hand on Huxley's neck.

"Operation Disappear?" Flea chuckled. "Now who's been hanging around the monkeys too long?"

"Quiet." But Kerrick couldn't help smiling despite the dangerous circumstances. They'd found Belen!

He'd lost a great deal of weight and was pale. Except where a thick scar crossed from the back of his head to his right temple, his black hair had grown long and bushy, matching his beard.

It didn't take long for the noise of the Skeleton King's soldiers to reach them. Kerrick tensed. Black figures moved through the woods, heading in their direction. A few cursed and a couple stumbled. Kerrick connected with the living green. Sluggish, it resisted his efforts to thicken the under-brush surrounding the clearing. Using the ivy for the rescue had almost depleted Kerrick's resources. Kerrick saved the little bit of strength he had left instead.

The sky lightened, diluting the blackness above. Not good. The rising sun might expose them by casting their shadows on the ground. He watched as the soldiers drew closer. Kerrick urged them on. It would be a race against the sun.

Five of them entered the clearing, while the others contin-ued past. Two aimed straight for them. Kerrick pulled magic. He focused it at a tree root growing underground. The root surfaced above the dirt, high enough to trip them and knock them off course. Then he used his magic to shake the trees to the left of the outcrop, drawing them away.

He sagged forward, lying over Huxley when they took the bait. Flea touched his wrist and energy flowed into him. Kerrick squeezed the boy's shoulder in thanks. It still amazed him that Flea, Avry, and he could share magical energy be-tween them. After a minute, he pulled Flea's hand away. No sense draining Flea when his magic might be needed. This wasn't over.

"Stay quiet," he whispered to the others. "They'll be back."

The sun rose. Kerrick frowned at their long black shadows stretching across the clearing. Nothing he could do but wait. And wait. And wait.

The shadows shortened as the sun climbed higher in the sky. He kept tabs on the soldiers. They had fanned out and covered a wide swath of forest. Too wide for Kerrick and the others to sneak past.

By midday the soldiers had given up and retraced their steps. Once again a few wandered too close and Kerrick dis-tracted them.

Kerrick dropped the camouflage when the soldiers were a

couple miles away. Everyone groaned and stretched stiff muscles. He slid off the saddle and Huxley shook off the hands, then trotted in circles. After he fed Huxley, Kerrick collapsed onto the ground.

"We shouldn't linger long," he said to Belen, who had plopped down beside him.

Belen agreed. "Those filthy cannibals are like an infestation. They're quick and strip everything down to the bone."

"Will one of his followers take the princeling's place?" Flea asked, joining them.

"I don't know. I've been out of it for a while." Belen rubbed the scar on his head.

"And instead of listening to Mom, you decided to take on the Skeleton King's army all by yourself," Flea said.

"I just went to scout and gather information for Prince Ryne. But I saw them…" Horror reflected in his eyes. "And, well, I couldn't just stand there and watch them butcher those people." He grinned. "Did a fair bit of damage, too."

Kerrick debated if he should explain to Belen how he shouldn't have charged into the fray without first considering the consequences, but it was Belen and no matter how logical his argument, Belen wouldn't listen. He'd just smile and say it turned out fine in the end. Except one of these days, it wouldn't.

"What's the plan?" Flea asked.

"We'll take them to Mengels. They can gather supplies and head for safety and we'll head home," Kerrick said.

"Home?" Belen asked.

"Back to the infirmary where Avry and the others are," Flea said.

"Is everyone—"

"Quain and Loren are as annoying as ever."

"I actually missed those guys," Belen said with amazement.

"Don't tell them. They can be insufferably smug," Flea said.

"I know *that*. What don't I know? How did Avry and a Peace Lily bring you back to life?" Belen asked.

Flea glanced at Kerrick.

Despite his bone-deep fatigue, Kerrick lumbered to his feet. "Fill him in along the way. We need to get some distance between us and the cannibals."

Kerrick organized the rescued townspeople into a single line again. He mounted Hux and the group headed northeast toward Mengels. Flea joined Belen in the rear position, explaining everything that had happened since Belen had gone missing.

Even though he tried to keep a brisk pace, eighteen people on foot took six days to travel back to Mengels. Which meant Kerrick and Flea were now nine days late and hadn't even left Mengels yet.

Of course, Mom insisted on feeding the refugees a hot meal and giving them a good night's sleep before she'd leave.

"They've had a terrible time. It's the least I can do," she said, waving off Kerrick's objections.

Another delay. At this rate they'd be sixteen days late, arriving a week after the first day of winter. He hoped Avry would forgive him for worrying her once she saw Belen.

Instead of spending the extra time brooding over the wait, he searched for a horse strong enough to carry Belen and Mom. Perhaps he needed two horses. Since everyone had evacuated Mengels, Kerrick spurred Huxley out of town, then let the horse decide which direction to go.

After a few hours, Huxley found a small farm northwest of town. The farmer and his young family had packed a wagon, tying on crates and furniture. Two horses had been harnessed to it with two waiting nearby. And a few more grazed in a pasture behind the farmhouse.

Kerrick called a greeting so he didn't alarm them. Even so, the man grabbed a shovel and stepped between Kerrick and his three small children.

"Easy, sir, I'm just looking to buy a couple horses. Do you have any for sale?" Kerrick asked.

The man tightened his grip.

Pulling his money pouch from his belt, Kerrick spilled a few gold coins into his palm. "I can pay you."

Now the man relaxed. "You lookin' to evacuate?"

"Yes."

He nodded. "You should have left days ago."

"I could say the same to you."

The man grinned, exposing large crooked teeth. "True. But my babe was too sick to travel." He hooked a thumb at his wife. She held an infant. "You hear any news?"

Kerrick told him what he knew. The wife's strained expression eased.

"We've a few days, then. Good. How many horses are you lookin' for?"

"Two."

It didn't take long to negotiate a price, and soon Kerrick headed back to the Lamp Post Inn with a barrel-chested black horse and a cream-colored mare.

After another day, they finally set out for the infirmary early in the morning. Belen rode the cream-colored horse. She'd taken an instant liking to him and wouldn't let Mom mount her. It would have been funny except Kerrick had been too impatient to appreciate the irony.

Flea and Mom rode the big black, which Flea had named Coffee. He'd also named Belen's horse Tea, claiming the horse's color reminded him of tea mixed with milk.

"Avry's favorite drink," Flea said as if that ended all discussion, which it did.

Huxley carried Mom's sacks of cookware, food, and the teapots that she'd insisted on bringing along. Kerrick could never say no to Mom. Hux jingled when he trotted, but with Coffee and Tea pounding behind them, moving quietly was no longer an option.

Again the woods were empty of travelers. They encountered no one the first day and through the living green no intruders disturbed the forest's peace within a few miles of them. But by midday on the second day, it was a different story. A sense of unease grew in Kerrick's heart.

After a couple hours, Kerrick stopped Huxley and dismounted. He placed his palm on the ground, seeking the disruption. Just at the edge of his awareness, he encountered a big problem.

Soldiers. Lots of soldiers, filling the woods south and east of them. Filling the space between him and Avry.

# CHAPTER 18

"Go to hell? Is that all you can come up with?" Wynn asked me, amused. "I betrayed you and killed your boyfriend. I'd expected something...nastier."

She believed Kerrick had died, interesting. I wondered what other misinformation she had. She'd kept her black hair buzzed short and the scar along her cheek had faded to a light pink.

"Unlike you," I said, "I have scruples."

"Too bad your *scruples* couldn't protect you." She gestured to the monkeys and Odd standing in the center of the infirmary. "Apparently, neither could they. But don't be too hard on them, they were outnumbered thirty to one."

"Where are the others?" I asked.

She sucked a breath in between her teeth. "Beyond your help, Baby Face."

I glanced at Loren. "Lieutenant Macon?"

"We're all that's left," Loren said with a mixture of anger and sorrow.

"See? I'm not all bad. I know they're your friends." Wynn's expression remained smug.

Remembering my dream with Tohon, I guessed she'd planned to use them to guarantee my cooperation.

"What do you want, Wynn? You know I won't agree to heal Tohon."

She drew her knife and advanced on Odd. He stood his ground and glared at her with such intensity that if he were a fire mage, she'd be a pile of ashes by now.

Wynn pressed the tip to his throat. "Not even if I threaten his life?"

"No," I said.

"How about the monkeys?" she asked, sweeping an arm out.

"No."

"What about someone younger? Like that young fellow standing next to you?"

Danny had followed me into the main cavern. Oh, no.

"I wouldn't let her," Danny said, crossing his arms. "Tohon would kill thousands more than you."

Wynn chuckled. "No love for the king, eh?"

"Not from anyone in here," Danny said.

"Probably a good thing. Love is dangerous." Wynn stepped away from Odd. "People do crazy, idiotic things for love. Take my sister, Cellina, for example. All her time and energy went into finding a healer for Tohon, despite the fact that Sepp and I liked Tohon right where he was."

Not what I'd expected her to say.

"Surprised, Baby Face?"

"A little."

"Well, you know what surprised me? That Cellina found herself a healer."

Her words sliced right through me. Another healer? Mixed emotions—happy there was another, and terrified that Cellina had reached him or her first. "Who?"

"She tracked down that little girl who escaped with you."

It would have hurt less if she'd stabbed me with her blade. "Zila? But she's—"

Wynn pointed to Danny. "Younger than him, I know. But according to Tohon's research notes, he hypothesized that the people injected with the Death Lily toxin will develop healing powers years earlier than those who are pricked by the Lily due to the amount of toxin that is injected. And he was right."

Danny clutched my arm. Horrible scenarios played in my mind. Poor Zila. "Is she… Is Tohon…" I couldn't say the words out loud. If I did, they might come true.

"Now wait. You're jumping ahead of the story. Cellina failed to inform us of the little healer when she tricked Sepp and me. She agreed that the Fifteen Realms was better off without Tohon and we should allow him to die. Sepp touched Tohon and we retreated to give Cellina some privacy." Wynn laughed, but the harsh sound lacked humor. "Imagine our surprise when Tohon comes striding out."

"And Zila?" I asked.

"Don't know. Don't care. Sepp and I took off before Tohon could kill us."

My mind swirled with all the information Wynn had dumped on me. Grief for Zila jumbled with the horror of Tohon's recovery. "If Tohon's alive, then why are you here?"

Wynn drew her sword. "Since you've caused so much trouble, killing you would make a lot of people happy." She advanced.

"No," Danny said, stepping in front of me.

The monkeys and Odd joined him.

"You'll have to get through us, first," Quain said.

"Aww, that's so sweet." Wynn snapped her fingers.

Her soldiers rushed in and subdued the four of them. Danny lasted the longest, as he zapped anyone who touched him. Atta boy. But they quickly caught on and trapped his hands behind his back.

Wynn approached me. "You asked me what I wanted, why I was here. Right?"

"Yes."

She stopped two feet in front of me. "I'm here to recruit you. We want you to finish what you started and kill that bastard."

I stared at Wynn. She wanted me to kill Tohon. "Why can't you?"

"We can't get near him."

Now I laughed. "What makes you think I can get close enough? I almost killed him before. He'd never let me near him again."

"Remember what I said about love? People do crazy idiotic things. He's in love with you. He'll welcome you back and keep you by his side."

Probably in chains. "Which means Cellina will want my head."

"There's that. No plan is perfect."

I sorted through the logic and nothing convinced me I had any chance of repeating my attack on Tohon. Only Noak's comment about us being bonded kept me from dismissing the idea out of hand.

"No. I'm not doing it," I said.

"Did you think you had a choice? I'm sorry, but you don't. You are coming with us no matter what. We can drag you out of here or you can cooperate."

I wilted. "And you'll leave them alive?"

"Sure. Why not."

"Can I fetch my pack first?" I asked.

"All right."

"And I need Danny for a moment. I need to show him how to care for a very sick patient in my absence."

"Hagar, Keelin, go with them," Wynn ordered.

"That wouldn't be wise. The patient has the plague."

She crinkled her nose then turned to the man holding Danny. "Let the boy go. If you're not back in five minutes, Baby Face, I'll start slitting throats."

"Danny, grab a few medical supplies, please," I said.

He rubbed his wrists, but headed over to the infirmary. Many of the caregivers had remained at their posts. He picked up a few syringes and we retreated to the stage-one cavern. Of course, they wanted to know what was going on.

"Just stay here for now," I said. Then to Danny, "There's six patients, so let's fill three syringes," I instructed.

"What if more come in?" he asked as he pricked me with the needle.

"When these guys are fully recovered from the plague, their blood will also carry the cure. You can use their blood to heal new cases."

"Oh, that's good." He filled the next two.

"Inject that into them while I go pack my stuff."

"You're not really going with her, are you?"

"Do you have another idea?"

Danny scowled. "Not right now."

"Let me know if you come up with a plan." I hurried to the next cavern.

Sergeant Gylon ambushed me with a series of questions ending with, "What should we do?"

"Wait until I leave with the enemy. If they renege on their promise not to hurt those in the main cavern, then I need you, your squad, and all the others to stop them. There are six more soldiers in the stage-one area and four in the stage-three area, although I don't know how much they can help."

"Why don't we attack them now and keep you here?"

"There are too many of them and they have Sergeant Odd, Loren, and Quain literally by the throat."

Gylon followed me to where I'd set up my bedroll near the entrance to the stage-three cavern.

"We'll send a rescue party after you," he said.

"Thanks, but you'll still be outnumbered. Better to wait until Prince Ryne arrives." I packed my things.

The sergeant talked to the four patients. Happiness swelled inside me for a moment as I marveled at the healthy color in their cheeks and seeing two of them sit up and grab their swords a mere day after they'd been on the edge of dying.

"Remember, lie low until I leave," I said. Then I joined Danny. "Stay here."

"But—"

"That's an order."

"All right." But he didn't sound happy about it.

I hugged him. "If Kerrick returns, tell him…"

"I will. That is, if he hangs around long enough to listen to me."

"Make sure he waits for Prince Ryne. Even he can't counter so many on his own."

"I'll try."

I returned to the main cavern.

"Where's the boy?" Wynn asked.

"Back with the plague patients. We isolated them."

"All right." Wynn made a sweeping gesture toward the cave's entrance. "After you, Baby Face."

I met Loren's, Quain's, and Odd's gazes. Their anger, frustration, and grief was clear on all their faces. Not much I could do, I turned and left the cave. Wynn followed, but before she joined me outside, she called back to her men.

I caught two words—*clean up*—but it was enough to fill me with rage. Rounding on her, I said, "You promised."

"I changed my mind."

"Then so can I." I lunged, wrapping my hands around her throat and zapping her with my magic.

Two soldiers grabbed my shoulders and dragged me off her. As I struggled, something sharp jabbed into my arm. I glanced down. A dart stuck into my bicep. The plague?

Wynn smoothed her shirt down. "It's Death Lily toxin."

Strange choice. "But I'm immune."

"I know it won't kill you, but it will make you more co-operative."

Oh. As the toxin spread throughout my body, my mind disconnected and floated above my head like a cloud of smoke. If I'd been inside a Death Lily, I would have joined with the being's consciousness, sharing thoughts. Instead, I remained intangible and unable to control my own body; however, my thoughts stayed clear—a small mercy.

One of Wynn's men grabbed my wrists and tugged gloves onto my hands. He then tied them behind my back, effectively preventing me from any skin contact, which would have allowed me to flow into his mind and read his thoughts. Putting a hand on my shoulder, he guided me forward. My body obeyed and I walked beside him.

Wynn kept pace next to me. "Wow, it's as if someone blew out your inner flame, Baby Face. Nothing left but an empty lantern. And I had to kill everyone. I can't afford to leave any witnesses behind, and I'm sure that stubborn ox Odd was already planning a rescue party. Not that I couldn't handle him and a few soldiers, but this is far easier. Besides, we don't take prisoners."

She'd used *we* again. Was she referring to her and Sepp? And why tell me all this? Perhaps she felt guilty over Odd's murder. She had truly cared for him at one point. I hoped Sergeant Gylon and the others had saved my friends. And while I was glad Kerrick and Flea hadn't been caught in Wynn's trap, worry for them churned deep in my heart. Where were they? Had the Skeleton King captured them?

Mulling over all she'd told me, I avoided agonizing over my friends and Kerrick. I considered the possibility that Tohon was still encased in a magical stasis and this was an elaborate trick. For what purpose, I'd no idea.

Plenty of other questions circled my mind as we traveled that night. Why would Wynn come in and bother making that big speech if she planned to capture me and kill everyone else regardless? Wynn had the manpower. Perhaps she wished to gloat first. Too bad I had no control over my voice and couldn't ask her.

The sun rose to our left. The direction surprised me. I'd assumed we headed northwest to Tohon's castle in Sogra Realm. But the location of the sunrise meant we had journeyed south instead.

After a few hours, the toxin wore off and my mind reconnected with my body. I'd planned to hide that fact, but I stumbled and fell forward, striking my head on the ground. Pain stabbed above my right eye. My arm muscles complained about the tight bindings that dug into my wrists and my legs ached with fatigue.

Who knew being disembodied had its perks?

"We'll rest here," Wynn said. She crouched down next to me. "We can do this one of two ways, Baby Face."

"Go on, I'm all aquiver."

"Cute." She stood and kicked me in the stomach.

All my other pains disappeared in a hurry as fire blazed inside my guts. I curled into a ball, enduring the wave of agony.

When I'd recovered, Wynn returned to her position. "Are you paying attention?"

"Yes."

"What, no sarcastic reply? I'd hoped to crack a few ribs this time."

I wisely kept my mouth shut.

"All right, here's the deal," she said. "You give me your word not to run off or harm me or my soldiers, and I'll untie your hands and won't drug you with Death Lily toxin."

"No deal, Wynn. I can't trust you." Plus I planned to bolt at the first opportunity.

She shrugged. "Suit yourself. And just so you know, I'm not feeding you."

Oh, joy. I struggled into a sitting position. Wynn's squad passed around chunks of bread and cheese and drank from their canteens. Thanks to her kick, I wasn't hungry at all. But then my stomach grumbled. So much for denial.

"Where are we going?" I asked.

She pressed her lips together as if debating what she should tell me. "To meet up with reinforcements near the border."

"Of Tobory Realm?"

"Yes."

I put a few clues together. Tipping my head in the direction of her soldiers, I said, "Are they defectors from Tohon's army?"

"Some are."

"And the rest?"

Wynn refused to answer.

"What happens if I kill Tohon? Who will take charge of his troops?" I asked.

Wynn ignored my question.

I answered instead. "Let's see. Cellina? No. She had her chance to step up and didn't take it. You?" Cocking my head, I studied her.

She glared at me.

"No, not you. You're a backstabbing traitor. No one will

follow you. Uh…present company excluded, I guess. Perhaps they're here only because Tohon is scarier than you."

A few of the soldiers behind Wynn suppressed smiles. Ah, I'd hit close to the target.

"Careful, Baby Face. I hear cracked ribs are very painful even for healers."

"All that's left is Sepp. I always thought he had a superiority complex." I considered. "Sepp's not smart enough." And then all the little clues clicked together. The "we" she'd referred to wasn't just her and Sepp. "You joined the Skeleton King's army and you brought him a present, didn't you?"

"Shut up."

"That's how the Skeleton King got the new plague virus. You turned a dangerous man into a deadly force. You do know he'll just chew you up and spit you out, right?"

"I said shut up." Wynn aimed her boot at my head.

Pain exploded and I spun into darkness.

# KERRICK

Hundreds of bodies intruded, irritating the living green. Kerrick dug his fingers into the soil, seeking one particular life force among them. Avry didn't cause the same nuisance as the others, but since he'd been saved by the forest, he could sense her cool vanilla presence.

Except this time. She'd been there, to the east of him, then…poof, gone. It also appeared that the bulk of the soldiers headed south, away from Grzebien.

Instead of resting for the night, they had raced to the infirmary, Kerrick stopping only to check the location of the army and to care for the horses. He wiped the dirt off his hands.

"You don't think…" Belen shook his head as if unable to voice his fears.

"It's a guessing game at this point," Flea said. "Better to just get there and worry later."

Belen studied the boy. "I haven't been around, so how'd you get so smart without me?"

"I've been learning from the best." Flea flashed his lopsided grin.

"And he is…?" Belen prompted.

"Quain. That man's a fountain of wisdom."

Belen's deep laugh rumbled right through Kerrick. He soaked it in, relishing the moment.

"A fountain!" Belen sputtered. "Oh, he's a fountain all right. A fountain of bull—"

"Mr. Belen, mind your language around the young man," Mom admonished.

"Sorry, Mom." But he sounded far from contrite. Instead, he frowned at Kerrick. "Don't you know better than to let Flea spend unsupervised time with the monkeys?"

"He'd pulled his own disappearing act," Flea said.

"Oh, right, that forest thing." Belen ran his fingers over his scar. He gestured to Flea and Kerrick. "Between us and Avry, we could form a special squad. The Presumed Dead unit."

At another time and place—like when they were all relaxing around a campfire safe and warm—that comment would have been funny. Not now. Not when he'd no idea what had happened to Avry, if anything.

"And we've all had a taste of death," Flea said in a quiet voice. "On both sides. We've been the griever and the grieve-ee."

"*Grieve-ee?* Is that even a word?" Belen asked.

"Yes."

"So sayeth the death magician?" Belen teased.

"Yes."

Belen chuckled. "We'll have no more presumed dead. We confirm with our very own eyes from now on. Otherwise, we assume the best. Got it?"

"The death magician agree-eth."

Kerrick tried being optimistic. Avry could have just gone into a cave. Despite her aversion to them, she was smart enough to realize they made a safe place to overnight in. Taking Flea's advice to act now, worry later, Kerrick checked Hux's saddle, ensuring the girth straps hadn't loosened. "Let's go."

They mounted and continued, closing in on the infirmary just as he'd estimated, sixteen days after leaving. He slowed the horses. Soldiers patrolled around the entrance, doing wide sweeps. Once he confirmed they were friendlies, Kerrick approached the closest.

The man relaxed as he recognized Kerrick.

"What's going on?" Kerrick asked the guard.

"Too much for me to explain, sir. Sergeant Odd's in charge, he'll fill you in."

"Where's Healer Avry?" he demanded.

Shaking his head, the man waved him off. Kerrick debated between grabbing the man and forcing him to talk, or... Hell. He spurred Huxley toward the cave's entrance.

Flea jumped down from Coffee. "I'll fetch them."

Kerrick helped Mom dismount. "Go on inside, Mom, I'm sure there's a warm fire and food."

"Oh, no, dearie. Not until I hear what happened to Avry."

Belen removed the tack from Tea, then moved on to Coffee's. Flea returned with Odd, Loren, and Quain. No Avry. Her absence was a red-hot poker right through his heart. The monkeys tackled Belen, whooping and teasing him.

Kerrick endured the moment of levity as he braced for the bad news. Odd waited, studying him with a hostile expression. *Odd's going to blame me.*

When the monkeys settled, Odd asked him, "What took you so long?"

In no mood to defend his actions, Kerrick ignored the question. "Where's Avry?"

Odd crossed his arms. "She's alive. The traitor Wynn took her south with a large company of soldiers as backup. They want her to assassinate Tohon."

So many things jumped out at Kerrick. First, Avry was alive, the best news. But... "Tohon?"

"Back in the king business, according to the traitor. Whether or not you can believe her…" Odd shrugged.

"Why didn't you chase after them?" Flea asked.

"They had approximately one hundred and fifty soldiers, Flea. We have twenty." Odd looked at Kerrick. Accusation blazed in his gaze. "We would have had more, except they got the drop on us and killed my men, Lieutenant Macon, and all of his squad."

Ah. "And if I'd been here, they wouldn't have died? I'd have made a difference against one hundred and fifty soldiers?"

"We would have had more warning."

"You did have warning," Loren said. "Remember, Sergeant Gylon encountered the enemy two days south of us. We sent a message to Prince Ryne."

"But we'd assumed it was just a patrol. Kerrick would have been able to determine how many soldiers."

"And then what would we have done?" Kerrick asked. "Ryne's main forces are too far north."

"We could have evacuated."

True. But would they have caught up to them in the end? Kerrick refrained from mentioning that. Instead, he asked Odd to explain everything from the beginning. "But first tell me how they cured Tohon."

Odd reported the events as if talking to a superior officer—concise and emotionless. Kerrick wished he could say he listened to Odd with the same detachment. His emotions twisted into a tight knot over Zila's capture and the unknown fate of his brother and Great-Aunt Yasmin.

"…we sent another messenger to Prince Ryne and have been waiting for instructions from the prince," Odd concluded.

"Danny?" Kerrick asked.

"Inside. I wouldn't let him come out until I knew it was safe."

Another bit of good news.

"When are we going after Avry?" Quain asked.

"We?" Kerrick gave him his flat stare.

"Yes, we," Belen said. "We're stronger together than apart."

"And with your tree mojo, we can slip in, grab Avry, and sneak out with no one the wiser." Quain dipped his hand as if sliding it under a door.

Loren grinned, looking years younger. "We need to rescue our healer. Just like old times."

An enthusiastic chorus of agreement sounded. Kerrick knew it would be a waste of energy to argue. Nor was it the time to tell them his suspicions about his waning tree mojo. Every day it grew harder to access his connection to the living green.

"All right, get a good night's sleep, gentlemen, we leave at dawn."

The monkeys pulled Belen with them inside the cave. Flea helped remove Mom's bundles from Hux's saddle. He carried them into the infirmary.

Mom patted Kerrick on the arm. "Be careful, dearie. That King Tohon's a nasty man."

"Hopefully, we'll free her before we encounter Tohon."

"If you do see him, take that big old sword of yours and chop his head right off!" Mom grabbed her bag of teapots and headed for the cave.

Odd watched her go with his mouth open. "Did she just…?"

"Yes. You don't mess with Mom."

"Anything else I should know?"

"Let her take over the cooking. You won't regret it."

Just then a high-pitched squeal sliced through the night. Melina tore from the cave and tackled her mother. They went down with a clatter of teapots and Kerrick hoped for Mom's sake the pots survived the fall. Sounds of the happy reunion reached Kerrick and he drank them in, wishing Avry was here to see this.

Melina and her mother clambered to their feet and, with tears streaking their faces and their arms around each other's shoulders, they went inside.

Kerrick committed the scene to memory so he could recount it in detail to Avry when he rescued her.

"What about if Prince Ryne arrives with reinforcements and wants to go after Wynn?" Odd asked.

"Good question. Give me a minute." Kerrick crouched down and laid his hand on the ground, seeking irritants to the north and east. Nothing. He sought signs of soldiers to the west. Still nothing. But his range remained limited to a couple miles.

He straightened. "When did you send the message?"

"We sent one right after Gylon's squad arrived. That was... six days ago. And the second was dispatched four days ago immediately after the attack."

"On horseback?"

"Of course. Why?"

Kerrick calculated. Ryne should have gotten both messages by now. And according to Odd, except for Melina, the lady warriors had left with Ryne, but they were on foot, so they wouldn't have gone too far and could have been diverted back to the infirmary. Or at least be within Kerrick's circle of perception. Or would they? His circle shrank every day.

"Odd, you're on your own for now. There's no backup within two miles. Unless they're farther away."

"Any enemy coming our way?" he asked.

"No. Wynn's force is heading toward the border."

"Should I send another message?"

"No. Keep all your soldiers close."

"All right." Odd nodded and walked into the cave.

Kerrick cared for the horses, watering and feeding them. Running his hand over their legs seeking hot spots, he hoped they'd be rested by the morning. He built a small fire and determined the best direction for them to travel in the morning, mapping the quickest route in his mind.

Worry for Avry swirled in his thoughts. Kerrick tried not to dwell on her predicament and instead wondered what outrageous stories Belen and the others were reciting by the fire inside the cave. Muted chuckles floated from the entrance, along with a delicious-smelling stew. Mom worked fast.

As the air cooled, he inched closer to the flames. Even with the pop and sizzle of the burning wood, it was too quiet. Too... Kerrick longed to join the others, but he needed to conserve his strength for tomorrow. A weakness had soaked into his bones.

"Kerrick?" a familiar voice called.

Danny stood nearby, holding a bowl and peering at the campfire. Kerrick pulled magic and turned normal. A big grin spread on the boy's face as he raced over to him. He gave Kerrick a one-armed hug.

"I would have come out sooner, but I had to finish my rounds," Danny said.

"Finish your rounds? My, don't you sound all official," Kerrick teased.

The boy puffed up his chest. "I'm useful." Then he sobered. "I'm sorry about Avry. We—"

"Do *not* apologize. Nothing you could have done."

"I know. It's just..." Danny growled with frustration. "She'd just made a major breakthrough and now..."

"What breakthrough?"

"Didn't Odd tell you?"

"No." And he'd like to throttle the man, but he hid his annoyance.

"She cured the new plague!"

Kerrick's shock lasted mere seconds. If anyone was going to figure it out, it'd be Avry. *That's my girl.* He gestured for Danny to sit beside him. "Tell me."

Danny plopped down and thrust the bowl into his hands. "Forgot. This is from...Mom." His lips twisted over the name as if he'd never said the word before.

Poor kid probably hadn't. Kerrick rummaged in his pack for a spoon.

"It's the best stew I've ever had. You should have seen Judd's face. She took over the cooking without a word. He was angry until she turned his boring stew into this."

Kerrick scooped up a mouthful. The venison melted on his tongue. Ah, yes, he'd missed Mom's cooking. Before the next bite, he prompted Danny. "The cure?"

As Kerrick ate, Danny told him how Avry followed the logic. "Can you believe that? All from Odd's comment? I didn't think it'd work!"

He smiled at the boy's enthusiasm, remembering when Flea had been that full of energy and life. Although, Flea's outlook had improved and Kerrick hoped Flea'd continue to make progress.

After Danny left, Kerrick lay by the fire mulling over all the information he'd learned today. They had a number of assets—Death Lily toxin to counteract the dead soldiers, Noak and Fydelia's warriors, Flea's magic, and now a cure for the plague. But where was Ryne's army? Had Ryne truly fallen for Cellina's distraction at the Healer's Guild? And was Zila dead, or had she survived Tohon's chest wound? They'd have to wait until Tohon was defeated...again. Otherwise, they'd—

Kerrick shot up. Zila had been in Alga. Cellina had to have crossed the Nine Mountains to kidnap her. Easy to do since only a few Algan patrols guarded the passes. Plus the fighting had been contained to Pomyt and Vyg Realms so the threat level was low. Would Tohon send troops across the Nine Mountains to travel east and then cross back over the Milligreen Pass? A long journey, but that would drop them in right behind Ryne's army. And with the Skeleton King creeping up from the south, Ryne would be caught between both forces. A perfect strategy.

He'd warn Ryne, but they needed every man here to protect the patients. The prince might have already come to the same conclusions based on the last message Odd had sent. Perhaps that was why Ryne hadn't dispatched anyone south to protect the infirmary.

Too many questions without answers circled. Kerrick would tell Odd his suspicions in the morning. Avry remained his priority.

"And just when you think it can't get any worse..." Odd rubbed a hand over his face. "We're sitting ducks here. We're going to evacuate. I've been scouting for another location."

Impressed, Kerrick agreed. "East?"

"I'd rather not say just in case..." Odd gestured.

"He's too polite to say in case we're captured," Quain said.

Odd ignored Quain. "I'm sure you'll find us regardless of the direction. Good luck." He shook Kerrick's hand and retreated into the cave.

"Considering he wanted to murder you yesterday, I'd say that was progress," Loren said.

"I'm feeling all warm and fuzzy inside." Quain hugged himself.

"Are the saddlebags packed?" Kerrick asked.

Flea cinched one of Coffee's tight. "Just about. How are we doubling up?"

"You and me on Hux, the monkeys on Coffee and Belen on Tea. After we rescue Avry, you can ride with Belen."

"Good to hear you have more confidence than Odd," Belen said.

"Of course he does! He's Weed Boy, ghost of the forest," Quain said.

Belen sighed. Flea chuckled. Kerrick just shook his head. It would be an interesting trip.

He mounted Hux. "All right, gentlemen, here's the plan. Wynn has a five-day head start, but they're on foot. We're going to cover as much ground as the horses will let us. They'll set the pace."

"And when we get there?" Loren asked.

"I'll figure that out then."

"Just like old times," Quain said. "Lead on, weed boy."

"…it's the only way," Quain said.

"And we don't have time to make anything else work," Loren agreed.

After three days of hard riding and little sleep, Kerrick wasn't in the mood for the monkeys' antics. But that didn't mean they didn't have a valid point.

They'd caught up to Wynn's battalion at the Tobory border near sunset on the third day. Her soldiers had made camp and appeared to be waiting for a larger army—most likely the Skeleton King and his soldiers, traveling north from Dina—to join them. Kerrick had figured out that Wynn and Sepp must have joined forces with him. Why else would she travel south? Plus it explained how the Skeleton King had gotten the new plague virus.

When the king's forces merged with Wynn's in two days' time, the chances of rescuing Avry plummeted to zero. Kerrick had only felt a few flashes of Avry's presence in the forest.

Not enough to pinpoint her location among Wynn's soldiers and their tents.

"You need *all* of us to search for her," Belen said.

"All right. Let me find a patrol to ambush." Kerrick placed his palm on the ground. The living green was harder to reach with each passing day of winter.

Quain rubbed his hands together. "Now we're talking."

"Pee-ew. Man, that's rank. Just my luck to get the uniform of the guy who hasn't bathed in weeks," Quain grumbled under his breath as he tugged at the sleeves of his stolen shirt.

Kerrick and the others had climbed into the lower tree branches and had, according to the monkeys, jackknifed a small patrol. They'd donned the patrol's uniforms.

"Don't call attention to yourselves," Kerrick said. "Just take a look around and report back here in two hours. Even if you find Avry. Understand?"

Nods and one "yes, sir."

"All right, go."

They scattered, each taking a different section of the camp. Kerrick waited until they'd moved into position before leaving. A large cluster of tents near the southern edge of the encampment was his target. With extra guards and the most activity, it appeared to be an obvious location for a prisoner. Of course, it could also be a decoy or a trap. Which was why Kerrick chose it. He could get close without being seen at all.

Lantern light glowed inside the biggest tent. Shadows moved along the fabric as soldiers entered and exited. He crept to the back side and listened to the various voices.

"...never know what hit them."

"I can't wait to go home..."

"...enough of this getting-into-position crap, I'm ready for action."

"…she's stubborn, that's for sure."

"But she'll be too weak to…"

Hearing the word *stubborn,* Kerrick lifted the tent's fabric, peering underneath. A half dozen soldiers sat around a crude wooden table, playing cards and drinking. No sign of Avry. Not letting disappointment slow him down, he moved on to the next tent. And then the third, fourth, and fifth. Nothing.

When time ran out, Kerrick returned to the rendezvous point. Frustrated and sick to his stomach, he hoped one of the others had found her.

The monkeys returned first and just by their expressions, he knew they'd struck out, too. Belen arrived next. His massive shoulders drooped and he shook his head.

After a few tense minutes, Flea joined them. His pale face held tragic news.

"No," Kerrick whispered, meeting Flea's gaze.

"I saw her with my own eyes, lying there…" Flea blinked back tears.

"But—"

"Her eyes were open. Even in the dim light, I knew."

"You can't—"

"I can, Kerrick. I'm a death magician. I know."

"No. We've been wrong before. Show me." And when Flea hesitated, he ordered, "Show me right now."

Flea led them to a small unremarkable tent among a group of them. No guard stood at the entrance and not much activity surrounded the area. Kerrick told the others to wait in the woods. Not caring if anyone heard him, Kerrick headed straight to the tent and flung open the flaps.

Moonlight illuminated Avry's prone form. She stared at the ceiling with dead eyes. Agony sliced through him. Flea was right.

# CHAPTER 19

The expression on Kerrick's face as he stared at me matched Flea's. In his mind, a lifeless body combined with unseeing eyes equaled dead girl. But I was far from dead—just disconnected from my body due to the Death Lily toxin. Although thrilled that nothing had happened to him during his mission to Mom's, I willed him closer.

Come on, Kerrick! You of all people should know better.

He stepped toward me. Too slow. Come on! My frustration built as he took his sweet time to kneel beside me. Kerrick reached to close my eyes.

The instant he touched my skin, I flowed into him. *I'm not dead,* I said in his mind.

He jerked back, breaking contact. I popped out, returning to an intangible cloud above my head.

Come on, figure it out. I urged. Time wasn't a luxury.

The deep lines of grief around his eyes eased as realization sparked. Kerrick cupped my cheek. "Avry?"

*Yes. Get out of here. It's a trap!*

*Not without you.* He scooped me into his arms and stood. My body blended in with the surroundings, matching him. But we'd lost our skin contact and I hovered again. Not good.

The tent flaps snapped, boots shuffled on the dirt and a

bright lantern light flooded the room, casting our shadows onto the ground and the back wall of the tent. Kerrick turned to face the four soldiers who had entered.

"Now," a voice ordered.

Two soldiers heaved a thick rope net over us. Kerrick staggered with the extra weight and before he could recover, the men rushed him, knocking us to the ground. The struggle lasted mere minutes. Useless and a dead weight, my body hindered Kerrick's movements just as effectively as the net. They took his sword and then all four men sat on him, pinning him down. Just what I had hoped to avoid.

"All clear," the same voice called.

The tent flaps parted and Wynn strode in with two more soldiers. "Let's see who we caught in our Baby Face trap." She peered at the net in confusion.

"They're camouflaged," a soldier said.

"Baby Face, have you learned a new trick?" Wynn asked, even though she knew I couldn't answer. "No. That's not a healing power, but a... Kerrick! You lived. Come on and show yourself."

I waited for him to use his forest magic, imagining the place filling with vines, but nothing happened. Instead, Kerrick dropped the camouflage. Did he have a plan?

"I can't believe it," Wynn said, moving closer. "You survived the toxin. Are you a healer now?"

Kerrick refused to answer her.

She pulled a dart from her pocket and held it up. "This is Avry's next dose, but I'm more than willing to try an experiment. If you're a healer, you'll live, if not..." Wynn shrugged.

"I'm not a healer," Kerrick said in a strained voice.

"Then how did you live?"

"Avry sucked all the toxin out."

"I'm not sure I believe that. Let's try anyway." Wynn bent down to prick Kerrick.

I screamed without sound.

"Wynn, stop," Sepp said as he entered the tent.

"But don't you—"

"Yes, I want him dead, but the Skeleton King wants to do the honors. Seems he caused some trouble in Mengels. I'm to freeze him until we rendezvous with our king." Sepp's voice sneered over those last words.

Not much love there. Interesting.

Wynn stepped away from Kerrick.

While everyone's attention had been focused on Sepp and Wynn, Kerrick had tugged at my shirt, exposing my back. He touched my skin and we connected.

*Did I hear that right? Are Sepp and Wynn working for the Skeleton King?* Kerrick asked.

*Yes.*

*That's just great.* His tone implied otherwise.

*Why aren't you using your magic?* I asked.

*It's winter. Too cold.*

*What does—*

*How much longer will you be…detached?*

*No idea. Sorry.*

*No, Avry, I'm sorry for not getting back—*

*Hush. You came to rescue me.*

*Some rescue.*

Sepp approached.

*Love you with all my heart, Avry.*

*And I love you, but don't you dare give up or I'll be mad at you!*

*Who said anything about giving up?* "Even with the Skeleton King's help, you'll never outsmart Tohon, Sepp," Kerrick said.

"I've no idea what you're talking about. I'm following orders."

"The Skeleton King has probably already worked out a deal with Tohon. And I'm sure it involves turning you, Wynn, and Avry over to him."

"Your scare tactics won't work." Sepp gestured. "Separate them. The king doesn't want her frozen."

The guards stood, yanked the net off Kerrick and tossed me aside. They yanked him to his feet and held him tight.

"When I give the signal, release him," Sepp instructed the guards. "Otherwise, you'll be frozen, too."

And then the best sound in the world cut through the tension. Ripping fabric followed by widening gaps of moonlight. The tent filled with people and a flurry of action.

Familiar voices shouted and barked orders.

Quain, "Don't let the bastard touch you."

Kerrick, "Use the net!"

Loren, "I'll take the two on the left."

Flea, "Hold him still."

Quain, "Finish this. Reinforcements are coming."

And the most wonderful voice of all, Belen, "He's mine. You take care of the short guy."

Loren, "Watch out!"

Kerrick, "Flea, don't—"

Wynn, "That's quite enough."

Everyone stopped and turned. Wynn held Flea in front of her like a shield. She held the dart filled with Death Lily toxin close to his neck. "No one moves or I'll kill him," Wynn said.

Did Kerrick remember the toxin couldn't hurt Flea?

Kerrick said. "Go ahead."

Yes! But everyone else yelled, "No!"

Kerrick recovered his weapon and tightened his grip on the hilt. Flea put his hand on Wynn's arm.

Wynn's brow creased. "You're willing to sacrifice this boy?"

"I'm not a boy," Flea said. "I'm a death magician who is about to neutralize you." He froze her in a magical stasis.

Flea had learned how to use his power. Yay Flea!

Sepp grabbed Loren, but before he could issue an ultimatum, Kerrick shouted, "Down."

Loren sat, sliding right from Sepp's grasp. Kerrick swung his sword and the sharp edge of the dadao sliced right through Sepp's neck, decapitating him. Blood splashed and then pooled on the floor.

And finally, the Death Lily toxin wore off and I slammed back into my body. All the aches and pains in my limbs sprang to life. The skin around my wrists burned as the rope bit deeper. I groaned.

Belen rushed over and untied me. Then threw me over his shoulder. "Let's go."

Flea supported Kerrick and the monkeys held swords at the ready. The reason for the tension and their fighting stances stood beyond the shredded fabric of the tent. Hundreds of soldiers surrounded us.

"What's the plan?" Quain asked.

"Attack the weakest section and create a gap," Loren suggested.

"Surrender," I said. "We're outnumbered. Besides, Sepp and Wynn are gone. Wynn and Sepp's troops won't kill us until the Skeleton King arrives. We'll have a couple days to escape."

No response.

I tried again. "If we attack, we'll be injured or killed. We're all together and we're all alive. Let's stay that way for a while. Please?"

Belen chuckled. "No one is presumed dead."

The others looked to Kerrick. He just about swayed on his feet. "She has a point. I doubt we'll be allowed to stay together, so if you get a chance to escape, take it and find Ryne. Don't try to free the rest of us. Otherwise, sit tight."

Of course, no one would leave anyone behind. And their expressions said as much.

Belen lowered me to the ground. I hugged him close. "It's so good to see you. I missed you so much!"

He squeezed me back. "Let's hope we survive this so we can catch up."

I laughed at his comment—let's live so we can chat.

"Put your weapons down and come out of the tent with your hands on your head," a male voice ordered.

"And so it begins," Quain said, laying his sword on the ground.

I slid my shoulder under Kerrick's arm, helping Flea.

Kerrick kissed me. "Don't do anything stupid."

"Who, me?" I batted my eyelashes at him.

He ignored me. "No giving your word to help them if they let us go. Or anything similar to that. Promise?"

Drat. He knew me so well. I didn't answer.

"Promise or I go out there swinging my sword," he threatened.

I huffed. "Oh, all right."


After we were frisked for weapons and our hands manacled—mine in front, thank the Flea—the soldiers escorted us to separate tents as Kerrick had predicted. Two armed guards remained inside with me, blocking the exit. Exhausted and famished, I sprawled on the floor until a young soldier brought me a bowl of food with a spoon.

"Sorry," he said, dipping his head. "Major Wynn wouldn't let us feed you before."

"That's okay, you're feeding me now." I held my hands out.

He hesitated, staring at my fingers. "Uh…"

I dropped my arms. "Just put it on the ground."

A quick smile. The soldier placed it by his feet, then shuffled back near the guards. I pounced on the bowl, shoveling the warm gritty mash into my mouth even though the short chain hampered my range of motion. The mash tasted horrible, but my stomach didn't care.

He waited while I ate. When I slowed, I asked him about my friends.

"Oh, they're all…cooperating." He sounded surprised. "We fed them, too, but the one guy passed out soon after you all were captured and hasn't woken since. Did he sustain a head injury?"

*Sustain?* Perhaps there was more to this kid than I'd assumed. "Well, there was that big rescue attempt." And Kerrick had been at the very end of his strength. But I didn't want to let him know about Kerrick's magic.

"Rescue attempt? Are you sure you don't mean assassination plot?"

I studied him, seeking signs of hostility or duplicity. "Sepp's death was pure serendipity, a bright spot in an otherwise failed rescue."

"Oh."

"Who's in charge now?"

"Of the battalion?"

"Yes."

"Lieutenant Colonel Horace."

"Until the Skeleton King arrives?"

"Yes."

Lovely. At least Sepp was gone. That was worth…well… pretty much everything as far as I was concerned.

"When will he be here?"

"That's classified."

"I should check on the unconscious man, just in case," I said.

"That would be the LC's decision."

When I finished eating, I placed the bowl on the ground and scooted away. The young soldier gestured to the guards. "If you give them any trouble, they have orders to put gloves on you and secure your wrists behind your back."

Good to know. "Will they read me a bedtime story?"

"No," the guard on the left said.

The soldier scooped up my bowl and dashed off. Probably to report back to his commanding officer.

I didn't get my bedtime story, but a woman delivered my bedroll and blanket. Other than that, not much happened. The next day on a trip to the privies, I noticed a fair amount of activity and soldiers buzzing about the camp.

Despite searching, I didn't spot my friends or Kerrick. I considered tricking my guards and zapping them, Instead, I decided to make my escape in the middle of the night.

Of course, I imagined Kerrick and the others had already escaped with ease. They were probably all standing around the horses wondering what was taking me so long.

Early that afternoon, four female soldiers arrived to escort me to the bathing area. I had a meeting with, I guessed, the lieutenant colonel. They provided me with a clean uniform, but made me promise not to attack them if they unlocked the cuffs so I could wash myself.

For a bath, I'd have promised almost anything. Kerrick would understand. And this wasn't a perfect opportunity for me to bolt, so I wasn't breaking my promise to him. After washing in a nearby stream—the cold air and water ensured I didn't linger—and changing, my skin tingled and I reveled in being clean.

With the manacles on, my wrists hadn't healed all the way and the still raw flesh stung from the soap.

Unfortunately, the ladies recuffed my wrists.

"Orders," one woman said when I grunted in pain.

They led me to a big, olive-colored tent near the southern edge of the camp. Guards ringed the outside of the structure. It appeared Horace was worried about an assassin cutting through the fabric. Smart. The two soldiers on either side of the entrance pulled the flaps back as we approached.

It took a moment for my eyes to adjust to the dim interior. A thick center post held up the roof. Cots lined up along the left side and a table and chairs occupied the right. A handful of men and women sat around the table with a few standing behind them.

One of my ladies pushed me farther inside.

The man at the head of the table rose and I stopped. He wore armor crafted from bones. A crown of rib bones adorned his head.

The Skeleton King.

# KERRICK

The soldiers had been quick to cuff Kerrick's wrists behind his back. They'd done the same to Flea, the monkeys, and Belen. Poppa Bear met Kerrick's gaze, giving him a silent signal with his bushy eyebrows before being escorted away. Kerrick passed the information on to the others before they were all separated.

Belen's eyebrows had warned them he planned to cause trouble tomorrow night. Kerrick hoped a day's worth of rest would give him the energy to take advantage of the ruckus.

As his guards led him to a small tent, Kerrick focused on the effort needed to walk. Everything ached and fatigue dragged at his body as if he wore a blanket of chain mail around his shoulders. When they swept aside the flaps, Kerrick merely ducked inside and collapsed on the ground, not caring the men had taken positions blocking the entrance. He'd deal with them when the time came.

He slept all afternoon, rousing only for a meal, but even then he had to force the food down, hoping it would provide a bit of energy. It didn't.

The living green called to him.

Time for quiet.

Time for rest.

Time to sleep.

Time to wait.

Kerrick fought the summons. He would not go...dormant. Gathering the remaining bits of his magic, he pushed against the living green's command. And to think he'd complained about not being able to leave the forest. Compared to this, he'd gladly go back to those early fall days.

Memories of lying in the colorful leaves with Avry swirled. He concentrated on her. She needed him. Sepp and Wynn had been neutralized, but Tohon, Cellina, and the Skeleton King had to be stopped.

He doubled his efforts to wake up. Opening his eyes, Kerrick scanned the tent. Nothing had changed, except he'd depleted all his magic.

With nothing left, he could no longer resist the call and break free of the darkness. The living green welcomed him as he nestled in deeper. He'd wake...later.

# CHAPTER 20

The Skeleton King smiled, revealing brown teeth that had been sharpened into points. The crown of bones rested on a nest of messy black and gray hair. Light green eyes studied me from a pale, gaunt face. Fear ignited in my chest. Heat flashed over my skin as sweat beaded.

"Such a fuss over you," the Skeleton King said, moving closer. "Sepp is dead and Wynn is frozen. Such a surprise."

A rancid odor filled the space between us. I suppressed the urge to gag. He reached for my hair with thick skeletal fingers—his hands the only part of him not protected by his bone armor. Revulsion coated my throat with bile. Stepping back, I bumped into one of my guards. She grabbed my shoulders, anchoring me in place.

The king stroked my cheek; I batted his arm away. His smile faded as he gazed behind me, tilting his head a fraction.

The guards pushed me against the big center post and yanked my arms up. In a heartbeat, they had secured the manacle's chain to a hook above my head. I stood on tiptoe. The other officers in the tent exchanged queasy glances. Not good.

He pulled a knife with a bone handle from his belt. "This will be simple. I have questions. You have answers. Play nice and you'll be able to walk back to your tent."

My gaze jumped from the weapon to him. He was at least six inches taller than me. A crazed gleam lit his eyes. "And if I don't?"

"You'll be dinner." The Skeleton King flashed his sharp teeth, exposing black gums.

Just when I thought no one could possibly be worse than Tohon, here stood the Skeleton King to prove me wrong.

"First question. Who froze Wynn?"

Oh, no. I wouldn't endanger Flea. "Sepp did before we killed him."

"Wrong answer."

I braced as his knife slashed toward my left arm. But no pain burned. Instead, ripping fabric sounded. The Skeleton King had cut away the sleeve of my shirt, exposing my skin. He leaned forward and bit my forearm.

I gasped with surprise. His teeth sank into my skin, stopping only when he reached bone. Pain shot up my arm along with nausea. He sucked the blood, slurping as if enjoying a juicy steak. My stomach churned and every inch of me shuddered with revulsion.

Releasing my arm, he licked his lips. "You taste like vanilla and anise. Yum. Who froze Wynn?"

When I refused to answer, he bit me again. This time near my elbow. Unable to contain the horror over such a vile act, I yelled. And I continued to shriek as he kept asking and I kept refusing to answer. Each bite increased my terror.

A small part of my mind viewed his torture logically. It was just pain. Nothing else. However, the rest of my senses scattered in a primal panic, and I knew I'd cave in eventually.

After the Skeleton King finished my left arm, he started on the right. When he reached my shoulder, I shouted in desperation, "Ask me another question."

He paused. My blood stained the chest of his bone armor. "Can you kill Tohon like Wynn claimed?"

An easy one. "No. He knows all my tricks."

"Correct. How do you stop his dead soldiers?"

Was this another test? "With Death Lily toxin."

He squinted at me as if trying to read my thoughts. "And only you can harvest this toxin?"

"Yes."

"Will you harvest it for me?"

"No."

"Why not? I will stop the dead. Good for all."

"But you can also use it against us."

"What if I promised not to?"

I coughed out a laugh. "I trust you about as much as I trust Tohon."

"No need to worry about Tohon. His days as king are nearing the end."

Doubtful. But I kept that thought to myself. No need to upset the psychopath.

"Next question. Where is Prince Ryne?"

"I don't know."

"Wrong answer." He sliced my shirt, ripping right through the buttons. Tugging my undershirt away from my skin, he rested the knife on the collar.

A vision of the bite marks on Private Tori's breasts flashed in my mind. "In the north," I blurted. "He went north. I don't know where."

The Skeleton King smiled. "Chasing Cellina's skirt. Good. Now, back to the first question. Which one of your five friends is the death magician?"

"Uh, sire?" one of the officers interrupted. "It won't be difficult to determine that on our own."

"Difficult, no, but not as much fun." In one swift movement, he pulled the blade through my undershirt. The Skeleton King cupped my right breast. "Last chance."

Determined not to expose Flea, I closed my eyes and concentrated on an image of Flea shooting me one of his lopsided grins. Agony from the first bite shattered the vision. All the others that followed erased every last piece. My throat burned from screaming as my skin crawled. I pressed against the wooden post and twisted, but was unable to escape the torture.

The torment stopped…sometime. Pain pulsed throughout my chest, stomach, and arms. My body felt like a chew toy for an ufa.

Having no desire to see the damage, I kept my eyes squeezed shut. Whispers sounded and a rustling of footsteps. Dizzy from blood loss, I drew in deep breaths. Waiting for the next attack proved difficult. To keep sane, I debated if this had been worse than when Tohon had zapped me with his magic. I decided that while the pain was equal, the whole biting thing made this intolerable. Who would have thought I'd miss Tohon? Not me.

Time passed without another question. Perhaps he'd given up.

Harsh voices, boots scuffing the dirt, and a rattle of chain snapped me from my daze. The flaps of the tent snapped and then grunts followed a growl.

Belen.

I peeked through slitted eyelids, glancing over my shoulder. Sure enough, Belen stood in the middle of six guards—three on each side. His hands had been manacled behind his back.

"What the hell! Are you all right, Avry?" Belen asked.

"She's fine," the Skeleton King answered. "I just had a taste."

I shuddered at his possessive tone.

"I wasn't talking to you, you filthy cannibal."

The king strode to Belen. "You have no right to judge. I'd like to see what you'd resort to to keep your family from starving to death."

"Everyone was hungry after the plague and they all managed without becoming cannibals."

So the Skeleton King was an actual cannibal. It explained… a lot.

"Managed? You call dying by the thousands managing?"

Belen just shook his head. "Avry, are you all right?"

"I'm—" what to say that wasn't a lie? "—here."

"What did you do to her?" Belen demanded.

"She did it to herself. She refused to answer a question. Maybe we'll have better luck with you."

I met Belen's gaze. "Don't."

"Who is the death magician?" the Skeleton King asked Belen.

"Me," Belen said without hesitation.

"Prove it."

"Okay, take off these cuffs."

The king's cackle set my nerves on edge.

"I have a better idea." He rummaged in a pack on the conference table and withdrew a syringe filled with a clear liquid.

I sagged against the post. He was going to threaten to infect Belen with the new plague and I'd have to decide between him and Flea.

Sure enough, the king held up the syringe in front of my face. "Sepp claimed he was immune. Do you want to test his theory?"

I tried delaying the inevitable. "Did you get that from Wynn?"

"Yes. Her sister was too squeamish to use it against her enemies. Wynn was smart to bring it to me."

"And you've been busy using it to send a message to Prince Ryne."

"Exactly. He needs to know who is going to be in charge. Plus it's a good idea to mark the victims. I wouldn't want my people to accidentally eat an infected person. That wouldn't do." He waggled the syringe. "Now, about that test—"

Belen roared. The guards shouted as Poppa Bear charged. The Skeleton King backed up, holding the needle out like a weapon. But the king wasn't his target.

Instead, Belen dipped his head and rammed into the wooden post with his shoulder. The impact rattled my teeth. The post creaked and leaned. Belen grunted, digging into the dirt. With a crack, the post fell over, dragging me and the tent fabric with it. The material collapsed on top of everyone.

My manacles popped free of the hook when I slammed to the ground. Belen landed next to me. The rest of the occupants were obscured by the olive-green fabric, which muffled their shouts and curses.

"Don't stand," he said to me. "Roll until you're clear."

"And then what?"

"Run."

At least the plan was easy to follow. I rolled to the right until I reached the conference table. It remained upright and underneath was the syringe. Unbroken. I palmed it, careful not to prick my skin even though I was immune.

A few guards regained their feet and yanked the fabric up, exposing my hiding place. Right as I resumed rolling, a pair of black boots with scapulas stitched on them blocked my path. I stopped and stared at the boots to keep from panicking. The flat triangular shoulder bones worked well as shin guards, reminding me of Tohon's comment about using all your resources.

"Going somewhere?" the Skeleton King asked.

I glanced around. More pairs of boots surrounded the king. At least Belen had escaped for now.

"Not anymore." I pressed my arms to my chest, covering my raw and bleeding flesh. The thought of being tortured again almost pushed me over the edge.

"Get up," he ordered.

And then I remembered. "I need help."

When he reached under to clasp my hand, I jabbed the syringe's needle into his palm at the same time as I grabbed his wrist with my other hand. He tried to jerk back, but I held on tight and depressed the plunger, sending the plague into his body.

He screamed and dragged me out from under the table. I released him as the guards pulled their swords while still keeping the fabric off the Skeleton King's head. Impressive.

The king yanked the needle from his hand and slammed his palm down on the conference table. "Cut my hand off at the wrist," he ordered. "Now!"

Smart. Too bad his confused guards didn't catch on. They hesitated over his alarming request, allowing the plague to spread up his right arm.

The Skeleton King snatched a sword from one of his men.

"Elbow by now," I said.

The king swung the blade down on his elbow. With the awkward angle and limited range of motion, he didn't have enough force to sever the arm. All he managed was a nasty gash.

Frantic, he pushed the sword back into the guard's hands. "Cut my arm off at the shoulder or I'll die." He knelt next to the conference table and stretched his arm across the top.

Finally catching on, the guard brought the weapon down on the king's shoulder. An awful scraping noise and a loud crack sounded. However, the king's arm remained in place.

"Wow, that bone armor really works," I said.

He stood to pull off his chest protector.

I shook my head. "Too late."

When he rounded on me, I knew I should have kept my mouth shut. The Skeleton King seized my upper arms and yanked me to my feet.

He leaned forward, his nose almost touching mine. "I'm. Going. To. Eat. You. Alive." He bared his teeth. "I've learned so much. You'll linger for days before I stop your heart."

This time I clamped my lips together. No need to remind him that he might not be feeling well in a few days. Although, he might have ingested enough of my blood to protect him from the plague. Unless the acid in his stomach destroyed it. If I survived this, I'd have to experiment. Big if.

The soldiers who had been stationed outside the tent finally cleared off the fabric. Sunlight and fresh air flooded the area. I blinked, letting my eyes adjust. The sun hung low in the west. Had the torture only lasted an afternoon? It had felt like days.

Another soldier ran up. "Sire, we are under attack!"

The Skeleton King glanced at the man in surprise. "Tohon's soldiers?"

"No, sire."

"Dead soldiers?"

"No, it's an army of women, sire."

Now I was surprised. I'd thought Fydelia's troops had gone north with Ryne. He'd lied to me again, but I was too happy to be upset.

The king shoved me toward his guards. "Take her back to her tent. Watch her very closely."

"Yes, sire," they said in unison.

As they towed me through the camp, I scanned the woods, looking for Belen and the others while also seeking signs of the attack. Nothing except the Skeleton King's men rushing off to the southeast—the makings of a perfect distraction.

Hunching inward, I slowed my steps.

"Come on." The guard on my right tightened his grip.

I hissed in pain, because it hurt like hell.

"Don't worry, sweetheart, you'll heal," he said.

I'd do more than that, I promised, but kept that to myself. After we entered the tent, I rummaged in my pack for my other shirt. Huddled on the ground, I acted pathetic, fumbling at the buttons while trying to keep the tattered, blood-soaked remains of my shirt over my breasts.

Finally, I huffed in defeat and stared up at the guards with, what I'd hoped, was a helpless expression. "Can you take these off for a moment so I can change?" I stood, holding out my arms. "Please?"

The guards exchanged a look. The one on the left shrugged. When he approached, he said, "Make it quick." He unlocked the manacles and removed the heavy metal cuffs.

"Oh, my," I said, swooning. I clutched his arm. "I think… I'm going…to…"

He automatically stepped closer to support me. I rubbed my free hand on my chest and coated my fingers with blood. I waved them in front of the guard's face.

"Look at this!" I shrieked as I slid my grip up his arm and to the back of his head.

One shot only. Better not miss.

I touched his neck and zapped him, rendering him unconscious. He keeled forward.

"He fainted," I cried. I knelt next to him, rolled him over, and fanned his face.

"Move away from him," his friend ordered, keeping the guard between us.

I backed up as the soldier checked his pulse.

"Come on, Trey, it's just a little blood," he said.

Relief eased my racing heart a fraction—he didn't know about my full abilities.

"Do you want me to check and make sure it's not something else?" I asked. "I felt a cut on Trey's arm, it could be infected." I dangled one of the common worries for foot soldiers—infection which could lead to gangrene.

"Uh…"

I returned to Trey's side. Lifting his right arm, I tugged his sleeve down, but it was awkward. "Here, hold his arm." I thrust it at the other man.

Instinctively, he grabbed it. Big mistake. I covered his hand with mine and zapped him, pushing the full strength of my power into his body.

He cried out and hunched forward against the pain, exposing the back of his neck. One quick touch and he collapsed over Trey.

Yes! I ripped off the bloody rags and changed into a clean undershirt. Then I stripped the second man's shirt off and donned it. The long sleeves hid the bite-shaped wounds. I kept my pants as they resembled the ones worn by the king's troops, but I rifled through the guards' pockets and helped myself to a few other items, including a sword.

Slinging my pack over my shoulder, I paused for a moment as a wave of pain radiated. I hoped the Skeleton King suffered greatly before he died from the plague. When the sharp pain eased back into a steady throb, I peeked through the flaps of the tent. The sun's final rays painted the sky with yellows and oranges. I debated waiting until full dark to make my escape, but the camp appeared to be deserted.

Glancing at the woods to the north, I figured Belen, the monkeys, and Flea had all escaped by now. But I worried about Kerrick. He had used much of his energy during the

attempt to rescue me, and that first guard mentioned someone collapsing after being escorted to another tent. I scanned
the encampment again, this time seeking signs of a guarded
tent before realizing that if Kerrick was awake, he'd have
slipped pass his guards by now, and if he wasn't, then why
would they assign men to watch an unconscious man when
they were under attack?

Now or never. I strode from the tent and moved through
the camp as if I belonged there. Peeking inside every tent I encountered, I discovered they all were empty except for messy
blankets and scattered personal items.

I spotted a prone form in the tenth one I checked. Even in
the dim light, I knew it was Kerrick. Rushing to his side, I
called his name. No response. I felt for a pulse, pressing my
fingers on his cold neck. After a moment, I pressed harder. A
faint throb pushed back. I shook his shoulder and, not caring
who heard, I yelled, "Wake up," in his ear.

Nothing.

I put a few clues together and gasped.

Kerrick had gone dormant.

# KERRICK

Some…thing…

Tugged…

Called…

Wouldn't…stop…

Energy flooded him, buoying him back to the surface. He opened his eyes. A dark shape bent over him. A warm hand pressed against his frozen cheek. The smell of vanilla filled his nose.

Kerrick blinked. "Avry?" He struggled to sit up. His hands were still manacled behind his back.

She pushed him down. "Easy."

"Don't waste—"

"Hush. I'm not letting you hibernate."

He smiled at her. "I don't think I have a choice."

"You won't survive until spring."

"But the forest…I survived before."

"That was only for three weeks. I'm not taking any chances."

A wave of vigor infused him. His protest died with one look at the stubborn set to her shoulders. After a few more minutes, he felt better.

"Ah, there's some color," Avry said, removing her hand. She

searched her pockets and produced a small key with a flourish. "Good thing I found this because *someone* hasn't taught me how to pick a lock yet."

The pressure around his wrists eased as the cursed cuffs popped open. His stiff muscles ached and Kerrick groaned as blood rushed to his hands. This time Avry let him push into a sitting position.

"Where are the others?" he asked, rubbing his wrists.

Avry sat back on her heels. "I hope they've all escaped. I'm pretty sure Belen is long gone."

"Not without you."

"But he would be violating a direct order."

Kerrick stared at her. They were talking about Belen after all.

She sighed. "Yes, well, the camp is deserted. Seems the Skeleton King is being attacked by Fydelia and her lady warriors."

Ah, some good news. "Belen and the others most likely joined the fight." He considered. "Didn't Fydelia's women go north with Ryne?"

Now it was her turn to give him a don't-be-stupid look. Right. They must have looped around to the south, which meant Ryne had lied to Avry, the infirmary workers, and the soldiers left behind to protect them.

He surged to his feet as fury pulsed through him.

Avry hopped up and clutched his arms. "Relax."

"Relax? That son-of-a-bitch used you for bait again. I'm going to kill him."

"After the war, he's all yours. But right now we should find a safe place before the soldiers return."

Kerrick spotted a sword tucked in Avry's belt.

"Don't even think about it," Avry said. "You're in no condition to fight."

He opened his mouth to argue, but a shrill cry tore through the air.

"That's our cue to leave." Avry stepped close to him, tucking her shoulder under his armpit.

He refused to lean on her for support, but after a few steps, he abandoned his pride. His weak legs threatened to collapse under him. Damn legs.

In the fading twilight, they headed north, aiming for the woods. Shouts mixed with the clangs and scrapes of metal as the battle sounds grew louder. About halfway to their destination, victory yells echoed along with a stampede of boots.

They paused. Kerrick glanced back. Hundreds of soldiers raced toward them.

Avry tugged on his arm. "Come on. Once we reach the forest—"

"I can't do a damn thing." He yanked the sword from Avry's belt and spun, sliding his feet into a fighting stance.

The soldiers stopped in the middle of the camp and stabbed their bloody swords into the air as they celebrated. Almost all of them were women. Relief coursed through him.

Fydelia approached. "And what exactly do you plan to do with that?"

Kerrick lowered his weapon.

Avry embraced the woman with a whoop. "Did you—?"

"Yep, we captured the Skeleton King. Prince Ryne has him under guard."

Ryne was here? Kerrick straightened.

Touching his arm, Avry said, "Easy."

He shot her a look, but his murderous plans would have to wait. Another cry pierced the air and, in a blink of an eye, they were surrounded by Belen, Flea, and the monkeys all talking at once.

"...so cool, you should have seen the look on their faces."

"…not expecting a battalion of very pissed-off women."

"…or a death magician…"

"…and then Belen comes roaring in, I swear the guy I was fighting peed his pants when he saw him." This from Quain.

Kerrick held up a hand, stopping the excited chatter. "Report."

Fydelia filled him in. "We looped in behind the Skeleton King's forces and waited for Prince Ryne to give the signal. After that, it didn't take long to overpower them."

"What about Tohon's forces in the north?" he asked. "He probably sent Cellina and a bunch of troops over the Nine Mountains to use the Milligreen Pass to ambush us."

"Noak and his warriors are en route to intercept them. Everything is covered."

So Ryne had already figured it out. Kerrick shouldn't be surprised. He glanced at Avry, but she gnawed on her lower lip as if deep in thought. Belen and the others sported cuts and bruises. Wet muck coated Flea's back as if he'd been wrestling in the mud.

One of Fydelia's officers rushed up. "The camp is secured. Prince Ryne wishes to speak to you." She swept her arm out. "All of you."

"Come on," Fydelia said.

"We'll catch up in a minute," Avry said. "I need to check my guys, make sure no one is hurt."

The monkeys protested, but Avry glared them into silence.

When Fydelia hesitated, Avry said, "Can you tell Ryne that the Skeleton King has been infected with the plague? No one should touch his blood."

That stopped Fydelia. "Blood?"

"Yes. Just keep your distance from him. I'll explain everything to Ryne."

With a queasy expression, Fydelia nodded and left.

"How did the Skeleton King get the plague?" Kerrick asked Avry.

She smiled sweetly. "I gave it to him."

"How?"

"Long story, I'll tell you later."

"At least tell me what's going on."

"We're not joining Ryne," she said.

"We're not?" Belen asked.

"No." The steel in her voice dared anyone to question her.

"Fine by me. Where are we going?" Belen asked.

"North. Let's get moving, I'll fill you in on the way," Avry said.

"Okay." Belen handed him his dadao sword. "I found this with ours. Nice weapon, Kerrick, I want one for my birthday."

"I'll see what I can do. Er…when is your birthday?"

Belen muttered under his breath as they walked. It had been a recurring joke between them that Kerrick could never remember Belen's birthday. Yet somehow an anonymous gift would appear on the correct date.

They continued toward the forest and stopped at the place they had hidden their packs and the saddles. The horses waited there, as well. Kerrick marveled at Hux's loyalty as he scratched him behind the ears. He dug out the feed bags. Hoping to have the horses saddled and ready before full dark, Kerrick hustled and barked orders at the others to help him.

After one snide comment about weed boy, they were on their way. Flea and Belen on Tea, the monkeys riding Coffee, and he and Avry on Hux. Energy flowed into him as she wrapped her arms around his waist and snuggled against his back. The effort to prep the horses had drained him and, while he'd like her to save her strength, he'd need to stay focused.

"How did you manage to infect the Skeleton King?" Kerrick asked.

Her arms tightened around him for a moment before she relaxed. "He had a syringe full of the horrid stuff and threatened to use it on Belen." She chuckled. "That was until Belen rammed the post and knocked the tent down."

"All right!" Quain high-fived Belen.

Poppa Bear's queasy expression didn't match the gesture.

"…in the confusion, I found the syringe and stabbed him." Avry finished her story.

"That filthy cannibal needs to die," Belen said with such vehemence, Kerrick studied his friend.

"Won't the plague kill him?" Flea asked.

"I don't know," Avry said. "He ingested some of my blood and that might protect him."

Alarmed, Kerrick turned to glance at her. "How?"

"He bit me. It's nothing."

Kerrick doubted that was the full story.

"Do you think Prince Ryne will send soldiers after us?" Flea asked. "He probably thinks we're deserting him again."

Kerrick considered. "He might. It would depend on what he planned for us to do after the attack on the Skeleton King."

"I don't care about his plans anymore," Avry said. "I'm tired of being used as bait."

"Is that the reason we left so fast?" Quain asked.

"One of them. But think about this… With Ryne's forces split to the north and south, what's left?" she asked.

Following her logic, Kerrick said, "The middle."

"Right. And who's going to fill that middle, keeping Ryne's troops divided?"

Kerrick cursed under his breath. "Tohon."

"Exactly."

Loren said, "Prince Ryne has troops at HQ."

"Not enough," Belen said. "Tohon's been amassing his dead armies in Vyg. Probably just waiting for the right moment."

"Are we going to warn the soldiers at HQ?" Quain asked.

"We can, but that's not the reason we're going north," Avry said. She drew in a deep breath.

Unease rippled through Kerrick. He braced for Avry's next sentence, knowing it would be big. She didn't disappoint him.

"Warning them won't help in the long run," she said. "We need to assassinate Tohon and stop this war."

# CHAPTER 21

Stunned silence.

Only the soft steps of the horses sounded in the dark forest.

Kerrick recovered first. "Shouldn't assassinating Tohon be Ryne's job?"

"It should," I agreed.

"But?" he prompted.

"But no one can get near him. I've thought about this. Wynn and Sepp were right, I'm the only one he won't kill right away. I'm the only one who can get close."

"He's not going to underestimate you again," Kerrick said in a quiet tone.

"True. That's why I need all your help."

"Do we even trust Wynn that Tohon is awake?" Flea asked. "That could be a ruse to get us to storm his castle in Sogra and be ambushed."

"Storm the castle?" Quain huffed. "You and what army? It's more like sneak in and hope for the best."

Ignoring Quain, I mulled over my dreams with Tohon, Wynn's and Sepp's palpable fear, and the increase in attacks by the squads of dead soldiers.

"He's awake," I said. "And his castle's a trap. That's a given.

He's probably in Vyg somewhere near the action, but not too close to the danger."

"What about Zila?" Kerrick asked in a subdued tone.

"If she survived, then she's either at the castle or with Tohon."

"And the chance that she's alive?" Flea asked me.

"It'd be a miracle."

No response. We rode on in silence.

"How do we find Tohon?" Belen asked. He'd been quiet during most of the discussion. "Vyg is a big place."

A nervous tingle shot down my arms and legs. "Uh…" Reluctance blocked my words.

Kerrick stiffened. "I'm not going to like it, am I?"

"No."

"Just tell me."

I explained about the dreams. "…and I think I can discover his current location."

Kerrick twisted to look at me. His face a mask of hurt fury. "And you're just telling me this *now*."

"After you returned, the dreams stopped until I was in the monastery. At the time I believed they were just nightmares." The words rushed out. "Once we escaped, they disappeared again. I didn't dream of Tohon until you left for Mom's. That was when Noak told me about the bond. Besides, it's not like we've had a lot of time to talk since then."

"But why didn't you tell me you've been dreaming about Tohon?"

"Kerrick," Belen said. "She already covered that. Plus Tohon's the stuff of nightmares and she probably didn't want to worry you."

"Or hurt your feelings," Flea added.

"Which isn't hard to do—he's the sensitive type," Quain teased.

"The good news is we can locate Tohon," Loren said.

"And the bad?" Quain asked.

"It will be almost impossible to get to him without being killed."

"What's the next step?" Flea asked after a couple hours of hard riding.

"We don't want to cross into Vyg," Kerrick said in a gruff tone—probably still angry. He faced forward. "At least, not yet."

"How about I find out where Tohon is first and then we can plan our route," I said.

"We need to keep moving. I don't want Ryne catching up to us," Kerrick said.

"Then let's keep going north," I said. "If Tohon is in Vyg, maybe we can pull the same stunt as Cellina."

"By sneaking in behind him?" Belen asked.

"Yes. We can cross the Nine Mountains by using the main pass, then go west and cut back over the Orel Pass to drop in behind Tohon."

"Except we'd have to wait until spring," Quain said. "And if Cellina plans to cross Milligreen, then her trap is also poised to strike at that time."

"Poised? That's a pretty impressive word, Quain," Loren teased.

Quain showed remarkable restraint in ignoring the jab.

I searched my memory, trying to remember one of the maps Ryne had at his HQ. The one with the red Xs marking the enemy positions in Vyg. "Maybe Tohon's forces aren't that far north. We could slip through Peti and loop around that way."

"But how can we be sure they're not there?" Belen asked. "Kerrick can't sense them, and if they're camouflaged we could walk right into them."

He had a point. I mulled over the problem. Perhaps when we stopped at HQ, I could take a look at those maps—I gasped as an idea flashed. When I glanced up, Quain stared at me from Coffee's back.

"Oh, no," Quain said. "I recognize that look. It means trouble."

"It means she has a plan," Loren corrected.

"Same difference," Quain muttered.

"Are you going to share?" Flea asked me.

"We'll meet at Ryne's HQ," I said.

Kerrick jumped on that. "Meet?"

"Yes, meet. I can't connect with Tohon if I'm with you. We'll split up into two groups." I touched his shoulder, stopping Kerrick's outburst. "We should be safe. As long as we avoid Grzebien, there's nothing between here and Victibus."

Clearly not happy, Kerrick asked, "Why can't we travel together and just sleep apart?"

"I think there needs to be some distance between us."

"Won't that strengthen his bond with you?"

Ah, the real problem. "A little, but we need to know where he is."

"It'll only be five days on horseback," Quain said.

Kerrick glared at Quain.

"Hush," Loren said to Quain. "Let Mommy and Daddy fight."

"Will you be able to keep our secrets from him?" Kerrick asked.

A good question. "He lied to me in the dreams, so I should be able to lie to him, too." I hoped.

"How about we just separate the last night?"

"The dreams usually start a couple days after you're gone." I shifted closer to Kerrick. "It'll be fine."

His shoulders sagged. "All right, but I decide who goes with you."

"Custody battle," Loren quipped.

I scowled at him, but Loren just smiled. Squeezing Kerrick's waist, I said, "All right."

"Belen and the monkeys will go with you. Flea stays with me."

A protest died in my throat. Hard to split three horses evenly. "Okay."

"We'll split up after our first rest stop."

"Yes, sir."

Loren beamed. "Aww—"

Kerrick woke me before checking on the horses. It took me a moment to remember where we were—in the woods. My arms and chest muscles had stiffened while I slept. I pushed up my sleeve and took a quick peek. Purple and red welts ringed the still-tender bite marks. The wounds should have been further along in the healing process, but I'd given most of my magical energy to Kerrick.

Belen approached and I tugged my cuff down, covering the bruises.

He inclined his head at my arm. "Is there a reason you haven't told anyone about those?"

"I mentioned it yesterday."

"One bite is a far cry from what he did to you."

"It's in the past. No need to worry anyone. They'll heal." I stood and rolled up my blanket.

"You mean, no need to worry *Kerrick*," he corrected.

"Yes."

"He'll find out eventually. Just like the dreams."

"But if I tell him now, he'll refuse to let us split up."

Belen raised a bushy eyebrow. "Are you sure about that?"

Before I formed an answer, he turned and joined Kerrick at the horses, helping to saddle Tea, who wouldn't stand still for anyone except Poppa Bear—the annoying man who had a good point.

Before we mounted, I pulled Kerrick aside. "I need to talk to you…in private."

He nodded and we walked deeper into the forest.

"What's wrong?" he asked as soon as we were out of hearing range.

How to tell him? I leaned my back against a tree and closed my eyes.

"Avry? What's the matter?"

His voice held worry, alarm, and a softness—love.

Opening my eyes, I met his concerned gaze. "Remember when I'd said the Skeleton King bit me?"

Kerrick nodded.

"The reason… Well, he asked me a bunch of questions, and when I refused to answer…" I yanked my collar down, exposing a couple of the half-moon-shaped teeth marks. "He'd bite me. And you know me… Stubborn."

The horror of the torture slammed into me anew. Kerrick drew me into his arms and held on as shudders racked my body.

When I calmed, he asked, "How bad?"

"Most of my upper body."

He growled low in his throat. "If he doesn't die from the plague, I'm going to chop him into a million little pieces and feed him to a pack of ufas."

I smiled at the image. "I'll help."

Kerrick pulled back to look at me. "That's my girl."

"Yours?"

"Oh, yes. After this is all over, we'll make it official."

While a warmth spread throughout my body, I couldn't resist saying, "Are you asking or telling me?"

He groaned. "Oh, no, I'm not going to answer. I'm not falling for it."

"Falling for what?"

"The trap. If I say I'm asking, then you'll tease me forever about my horrible timing. And if I say telling, then you'll automatically do the opposite."

"Come on, lovebirds," Quain called. "We're burning daylight."

Kerrick grew serious. "My first reaction to your...news was to insist we stay together. But I'll never get that chance to propose until we stop Tohon. So I'll have to settle for saying, be very careful."

"Belen and the monkeys will be with me. What can go wrong?" Not the right answer if I interpreted his flat stare correctly. "I will."

"Good." He kissed me.

We joined the others and I mounted Tea, settling in behind Belen. Even with all the weight he'd lost, he still blocked my view. Kerrick insisted we take the northeast route around Grzebien while he and Flea headed northwest and closer to Vyg's border. Worry about Kerrick hibernating without me near him flared. Flea should be able to share energy with Kerrick and keep him awake. *Should,* which didn't mean he could—hence the worry.

With a wave goodbye we set off. I wrapped my arms around Belen, glad for this time with him. Glad he forgave me for letting him think I'd died back in the spring. From enduring the burning heartache when I'd believed he'd been turned into one of Tohon's dead, I realized how cruel it had been for me to pretend to be dead. And then with Kerrick... I shuddered. No, I wouldn't dwell on that horrible time. Instead,

I would enjoy these five days with Belen and the monkeys. And I vowed to treat each moment as a gift.

*"So nice to see you again, my dear." Tohon said, sitting across from me.*

*I glanced around his forever garden. Nothing was different. Greenery glowed with life and steam curled from the teacups.*

*Tohon gestured to the chair opposite of his. "Sit down and rest. You've been so busy. Tell me what you've been up to, my dear."*

*Perching on the edge, I reached for my cup. Warmth soaked into my fingers. "Why bother? If we're...linked as you claim, then you already know."*

*He laughed. "True. Lots going on—Sepp dead, Wynn frozen, and the Skeleton King captured. Just marvelous. You saved me a lot of time and effort. Revenge can be tiring work." He sipped his tea.*

*"Since I saved you time, can you tell me what happened to Zila?"*

*"Ah, the lovely Zila. Such a dear child, giving her life for mine." He gazed out the window.*

*Ah, hell. Pain ringed my chest, squeezing tight.*

*"I just couldn't watch her die," he said.*

*Poor Zila, left alone in her final moments.*

*"Oh, my, you do have a low opinion of me, my dear. I shared my life magic with the girl. She's alive and well and living like a princess. In fact, I'm going to adopt her so she will be a princess."*

*I stared at him. Did he just say...?*

*"Why so shocked? You could be living like a queen right now if you hadn't been...corrupted by nasty Kerrick and his goons."*

*Recovering, I jumped on the opening he'd given me. "So you're saying I'd be here at the castle with you instead of on the road?"*

*"You're really not cut out for deception. It's sweet that you want to know my location, my dear."*

*Time to wake up. I pinched the skin on my arm, drawing blood with my fingernails. Nothing.*

*Without warning, Tohon stood and put his hands on my shoulders. I startled.*

*"Look out the window," he whispered in my ear.*

*The rolling valleys and farm fields of Sogra Realm transformed into forest surrounding a large ruin. Toppled stone columns and the remains of three once magnificent buildings littered the ground—their interiors burned and their walls shattered. A handful of smaller structures had also been destroyed.*

*"You're at the Healer's Guild headquarters." A surprise because it was located in Pomyt Realm and not Vyg. "Why?"*

*"It all started here. Fitting that it should all end here."*

# KERRICK

"I've been thinking," Flea said from behind him as they rode Huxley. "That a small group, no matter how talented, won't be able to get near Tohon even if we know where he's hiding."

Kerrick agreed. "He's probably surrounded by his dead soldiers and a dead-ufa pack or two." He suppressed a shudder. Ufas were bad. Dead ufas haunted his nightmares.

"So why does Avry think we can get to him?"

"Because he needs to be stopped."

"I get that, but if we can't reach him, we can't stop him."

The hard knot in Kerrick's stomach that had formed when Avry had told him of her dreams tightened. "Tohon won't kill Avry. He's had ample opportunity in the past." Another painful jab twisted his guts. "She can reach him and use that reluctance to her advantage. And it's our job to make sure she does."

"Oh…but that's suicide."

"Yes."

"No. We won't be doing that."

Kerrick glanced back. "We won't?"

"You're not thinking clearly. If all he wants is Avry, then she can just ride Hux right into the enemy camp and no one will touch her. No. He wants everyone. So we should give him *everyone*."

"What are you suggesting?"

Flea explained his idea. "…and we can't tell Avry. This bond thing between them can't be good. We should assume what she knows, he knows."

"She'll be angry if she finds out we're keeping secrets."

"Better to be angry than be Tohon's."

"Good point. Flea, you've come a long way from the boy we rescued."

"I've been paying attention, listening to you, Avry, and Prince Ryne discuss strategy and follow the logic."

"I missed it this time."

"You're acting more like Belen, being all Poppa Bear about Avry. Not a bad thing."

But not a good thing, either. He'd let his emotions make decisions, which was the reason Belen hadn't been in charge of their group. "Duly noted."

Flea chuckled.

"Now what?"

"Oh, I'm just thinking about how the sparks are gonna fly between you two."

"I'm glad I can provide you with some entertainment," Kerrick said drily.

Anxious to reach HQ, Kerrick kept their stops to a bare minimum. Flea dozed in the saddle, leaning forward on him. The boy could sleep all he wanted once they arrived. But calling him a boy wasn't quite right. Flea might be young, but he'd matured since accepting his magic. While glad Flea no longer refused to use his power, Kerrick lamented the boy's loss of innocence.

Expecting to be a day ahead of the others, Kerrick stopped

Hux in surprise when he spotted Coffee and Tea outside Victibus. Not able to enter any of the buildings without expending lots of energy, Kerrick sent Flea to find the others. While
he waited, he unsaddled the horses and groomed them.

Not long after, Flea returned with Avry. She dashed toward
Kerrick while Flea retreated inside. He waited for her, growing
alarmed as she neared. Dark circles hung under her eyes and
most of her auburn hair had escaped her normally neat braid.

Avry slammed into him, wrapping her arms tight around
him.

"Easy." He hugged her. "What's wrong?"

"The dreams... I don't want more dreams." She shook. "I
haven't slept...in days."

"Hey, it's okay. I'm here now. I'll block them."

"I...couldn't... He knows about Wynn and Sepp and the
Skeleton King. I didn't want him to learn anything else."

Avry dropped her arms, but Kerrick wouldn't let her go.
"It's okay."

"I found out Tohon saved Zila's life and wants to adopt her."

One small but tight knot in his chest eased. "Great news
about Zila, but there is no way I'll let him keep her. We'll
rescue her once we figure out another way to locate him."

She pulled back slightly. "He's at the Healer's Guild."

"Are you sure?"

"He could have lied, but deep down I don't believe he did."

His skin prickled and he scanned the woods, searching for
hidden soldiers. "The guild is only three days away. How long
ago did you dream his location?"

"Two days. Why?"

"He could be on the way here."

"He said he'd wait for me there."

Smug little snot. "Flea and I can go scout the Healer's Guild,
see if anyone is there."

"And run right into a dead ambush? I don't think so."

"But Flea's a death magician. He can sense the dead."

Avry rubbed her face. "I forgot about that. But his power isn't exactly the same at Sepp's."

"Then test it. Is Yuri still here?"

"I don't know."

"Find out. Did Ryne leave soldiers behind?"

"Yes." Still she hesitated. "But you're weak, Kerrick."

"It's a reconnaissance mission. We won't engage the enemy. We'll just take a look around, but we'll have to leave the horses so we'll be gone six days max."

She broke from his grasp and put her hands on her hips. "I've heard that before."

"How about, we'll be back in six days *unless* I learn a good friend who we thought was dead is alive and in trouble?"

His nose crinkled as she smiled. "Better, but I'm still not happy."

"Do you have another idea?" he asked.

"Actually…" Avry glanced at the wide mining building Ryne had converted into his HQ. "I might."

Surprised, he said, "Let's hear it."

"I'm not sure it'll work. I need to check a few things first."

Her classic dodge. It meant he wasn't going to like her alternate plan. And she would be correct. Since he'd rather she remained safe at HQ until Tohon was gone for good.

"All right. But don't be too long. You're exhausted."

"You don't look any better. When's the last time you ate?"

He held up his hands. "Let's call a truce." Kerrick earned another smile.

"All right. I'll be back with food and bedding. You build a nice hot fire."

"Yes, sir."

Her laughter warmed his heart. After she left, he gathered

firewood. The cold air dragged at his limbs as if he moved through mud. And it was only three weeks into the season. What would happen to him in the middle of winter? He couldn't leech energy off Avry or Flea all the time or they'd be useless. Like him.

When Avry returned hours later, she brought more than food. Belen, Flea, and the monkeys followed her, carrying cots, blankets, and wood for the fire. A squad of soldiers also trailed after her.

"We're having a cookout," Quain chirped as they set up the cots.

Avry drew one of the soldiers over to him. "Kerrick, this is Sergeant Saul. He disobeyed Estrid by remaining with Ryne's army. Just like Odd."

Kerrick shook Saul's hand, hoping the man wasn't like Odd. He didn't need to deal with another jealous man. But Saul appeared friendly. A few gray hairs mixed with the blond strands of his buzzed hair. Kerrick guessed he was about five years or so older than Loren.

"Thanks for your help down in Zabin," Saul said. "We'd have run right into that blockade."

Kerrick nodded, wondering where Saul had been during Estrid's rescue.

"He offered to patrol around HQ tonight so we all can get a good night's sleep," Avry said.

Nice.

"I'm gonna take a loop or two with them," Flea said.

Kerrick exchanged a glance with Avry. "It worked?"

"Yes. Flea spent some time with Yuri this afternoon."

"And what about your other plan?"

"I'm still working on it. But in the meantime, I think you and Flea should check the Healer's Guild to see if Tohon is really there or not."

Her resigned expression said more than her words.

"What about your dreams?"

"I'll take a strong dose of sleep powder. That should prevent him from invading my mind."

"Are you sure?"

"Yes."

"All right. We'll leave in the morning," he said.

Saul and Flea left to start their sweeps. The monkeys and Belen settled near the fire.

"So it's our last night together in a while and you brought the boys," Kerrick said.

"There's safety in numbers."

"Uh-huh." He waited.

She huffed. "They refused to stay in HQ."

Figures. He pouted.

"This just means we'll take an extralong honeymoon."

"Are you asking or telling?" he asked.

"Telling. You're better at following orders."

He couldn't argue with that. Happy she didn't preface her answer with an "if we're alive," Kerrick kissed her. And with that kiss, he promised to do everything within his power to ensure they had that honeymoon.

# CHAPTER 22

"Are you sure Sergeant Hogan isn't here?" I asked a private with bright red hair.

"Yes, sir. He accompanied the battalion that went northeast. Prince Ryne only left a few squads behind."

Shoot. "Any reports from the battalion?"

"They reported that the enemy hadn't crossed the pass before the winter snows closed it."

Good news. "Are they coming back then?"

The private's young face creased with confusion. "No, sir. Prince Ryne ordered them to remain there to ambush the enemy when the pass opens."

"Why?"

"Sir?"

I'd exceeded the girl's knowledge base. "Never mind. Is there anyone else here who knows how to navigate the mine shafts?"

"Private Beau has been helping Sergeant Hogan."

"Can you find him, please?"

"Yes, sir." The girl saluted and bolted.

I mulled over the information I'd gleaned so far. It would be two months before the pass opened. Why keep the battalion there when the enemy still occupied Vyg? Unless Ryne believed Tohon had sent all his forces to the south and north. It didn't sound like Ryne would be that…gullible.

My head ached. I rested it on the table, glad the mining machinery all around me remained silent. The maps Ryne had left hadn't helped me discern the enemy's western positions. Which made Kerrick's mission all the more vital. He'd been gone for two days and I missed him so much.

"Are you all right?" Belen asked.

I sat up. "I'm fine."

He set a large box on the table. "I found the maps of the mines."

"Great."

Belen set the lid aside. "Don't get too excited." He pulled one from the box and unfolded it. "They're written in code."

"Code?"

"Yeah, you need a key to figure them out."

I spread the map out. It appeared to be normal except strange symbols had been written along the lines at intersections, starting points, and ending points.

"Do you think these are marked on the mine shafts?" I asked. "I remember seeing numbers and words on the walls."

Belen rubbed his hand over his scar. "Could be. Guess we can check. But with which map?" He tossed a couple more on the table. "There's a ton of them."

Hopefully, Private Beau would know. Rolling up the area maps Ryne had left, I cleared a space. "Let's open them all and see if there's a pattern."

While Belen opened them, I studied each one.

Belen tapped a finger on a map. "You do know the odds of one of these going straight to the Healer's Guild are low, right?"

"Yes, but maybe we can get close. It's worth checking."

"Oh, yes. No doubt. Just didn't want you to get your hopes up."

The sudden desire to hug him filled me, so I did.

He hugged me back. "What's this for?"

"Because you're here and I can."

"I missed you, too."

"Don't disappear again."

"I won't if you don't," he said.

I pulled away and gazed up at him. "You'd think that would be an easy promise to make."

His deep rumbling laugh rolled through me like a cup of hot tea.

"How about no misleading the other over one's death?"

"I'm sorry about that, Belen. I should have trusted you."

"I've a lousy poker face. Besides, you were worried about Tohon. With good reason."

I tapped my chest. "He still has a hold on me."

Belen wrapped me in one of his bear hugs. "Not for long."

We returned to deciphering the maps, but no pattern emerged. The monkeys arrived a few hours later.

"We checked everywhere and couldn't find a legend for those maps," Loren said. "It makes sense not to have a key lying around if you're going to use a code. That would defeat the purpose."

Plopping in a chair, I rubbed my stiff neck. Quain picked up a map and studied it. I didn't have the energy to tell him it was a lost cause. Unless Private Beau knew the codes.

"Have you seen a young private?" I asked the monkeys.

"They're all young," Loren quipped.

"One with bright red hair?"

"Yeah, she was looking for someone," Quain said, sounding distracted.

"I need that someone—Private Beau. Can you see what's taking her so long?"

"Sure." Loren glanced at Quain. He put the map down and followed Loren.

Now what? If we couldn't sneak up on Tohon, maybe we could attack him. I sorted through the rolls of maps and found the one of northeastern Pomyt. Unrolling it, I weighed down the edges with the rocks that littered the entire building.

Belen gave me a questioning look, but I ignored it. Guessing Noak's army waited in the foothills below the Milligreen Pass of the Nine Mountains, I calculated it would take fifteen days for his army to return to HQ. Plus the time it took to send a message via horseback, adding seven days. Twenty-two total.

Could I last that long? Would Tohon wait that long? He had to know our location. If he attacked, we could hunker down in the mines until Noak arrived. Military strategy was not my thing. Maybe Belen had a few ideas.

"Recalling Noak's army could ruin Prince Ryne's plans," Belen said.

"Too bad. So sad. Ryne's just as bad as Tohon."

"Now, don't go jumping to conclusions. There's more going on than you think. We need to trust Prince Ryne."

"Easy for you to say. You haven't been used as bait when he promised he wouldn't."

"Did he know about your dreams?"

"Yes, but—"

"Did Noak tell him about the bond?"

"Maybe, but—"

"Did you consider he might be feeding Tohon false information through you?"

"Uh…"

"Thought so." Belen lifted his chin, giving me a smug smile.

And then I remembered Ryne's four *D*s he'd learned in boarding school for future realm leaders—diplomacy, defense, deception, and disinformation. He'd certainly mastered the deception and disinformation part.

The monkeys returned with Private Red Hair. The private fiddled with the hem of her shirt. I braced for bad news.

"Go on, tell her," Loren prompted the private.

"Private Beau has disappeared. I can't find him anywhere."

"Is he out on patrol?" I asked.

"No. The rest of his squad is inside."

"Do they know where he is?"

"He doesn't hang out with them during down time," Red Hair said. "They had no idea he was missing."

"Lost in the mines?" Loren asked. "Or absent without leave?"

Frustration boiled. "I'd send search parties, but no one can read the maps."

Quain and Loren flipped through the stack.

Out of ideas, I said, "We'll wait for Kerrick and Flea to—"

"It's a symhextric cipher," Quain cried.

"A what?" Loren asked.

"The maps. It's been driving me crazy, trying to remember where I'd seen this before. Prince Ryne used this symhextric code to send messages to his scouts. It uses symbols, numbers, and hexagons."

"How do you know all this?" Loren asked.

"Back when we were camped in Zabin with Estrid's army, he showed it to me."

"Can you decipher these?" I asked.

Quain picked up another map. "I can try."

"What do you need?"

"Uh…a few sheets of blank parchment, a ruler, and a piece of charcoal."

I scrambled to assemble the supplies while Loren helped him organize the maps.

After I finished, he shooed me away. "No need to hover. I'll let you know if this works."

I pulled Belen aside. "Seems a big coincidence that Quain knows this code."

"Coincidence or part of Prince Ryne's grand scheme?"

Too tired to argue, I said, "I'm going to bed. Wake me if there's any news."

Grabbing an extra lantern, I walked through the oversize loading doors into the next room, skirted the piles of dirt, and descended into the living levels of the mines. I'd been sleeping on the cot in Ryne's office. My blankets smelled of spring sunshine and living green. I debated about taking the sleep powder. Would Kerrick's scent keep the Tohon dreams at bay?

A light tapping sounded on the door. I answered. A man in his late twenties stood at attention.

"Private Beau, sir. I heard you wished to see me?"

Rather old for a private, but he could be a new recruit. "Yes. Where have you been?"

"Scouting in the tunnels, sir."

"Are you supposed to be doing that?"

He blushed. "No, sir. Not without Sergeant Hogan, but I... was... I wanted to show a colleague this...rock formation... and..." Beau squirmed with embarrassment.

Ah, the old let-me-show-you-this-rock-formation move. Beau probably had a lady with him.

"That's okay, you're here now. I need you to help decipher the maps of the mines. We're looking for an underground route to the northwest. One that will get us close to the Healer's Guild."

"No problem. That's the three-triangle route. It'll get you about two miles west give or take a mile," he said.

Excited, I asked how to find this route.

"I'll show you the entrance and the symbols you need to follow." He picked up my lantern.

I hurried after him. We descended two levels and he headed to a tunnel on the far left. Shining the light on the wall, he illuminated a symbol that resembled three blue triangles in a circle with their tips touching. There were other symbols painted on the wall as well.

"This tunnel branches in different directions," Beau said. "Just down here…" He walked farther in, gesturing for me to follow him. "Here's an intersection. As you can see, the three triangles are painted on this branch, but not this one. All you need to do is follow them, and make sure you keep the symbol on your right, that means you're moving away from the center. If they're on the left, then you're heading back. It can get confusing down here."

I agreed. Too bad the shaft wasn't big enough for horses. "How long does it take to get to the guild?"

"It's not a straight shot. Four, maybe five days. Let me see…" Beau continued down the three-triangle tunnel until he reached another junction. "Ah, yes." He pointed to a symbol that had four circles side by side. "This shaft is a shortcut and will eliminate a couple days. Hmm…three days total."

"Sounds like you know this area well. We might need you to guide us."

"Oh, sure. I've done this route a couple times." He smiled, revealing yellowed teeth.

An uneasy chill zipped through me. No one knew I was down here. We had gone farther into the mines than I'd expected. Too far for anyone to hear me yell.

"Great." I turned to go back.

"Wait," he said.

I glanced over my shoulder. He'd hung the lantern on a hook and reached into his breast pocket. Beau pulled out a slender object. A blow gun? I shifted my weight to the ball of my feet, ready to flee. Then he dipped his hand in his pants pocket. Was that a dart filled with Death Lily toxin?

He yanked a piece of folded parchment from his pocket. "I just want to write down these other symbols so I can double-check the directions on the maps." Beau smiled again. "I don't want to get us lost. My sergeant would kill me."

A mixture of relief and chagrin calmed my heartbeat. It wasn't foolish to think he might be a spy for Tohon; it was very foolish not to consider it until after it was too late.

After Beau wrote down the symbols, we returned to the surface. He joined the monkeys. Quain had found the right quadrant, but not the correct tunnels. Beau helped.

Belen followed me back to Ryne's office. "What's wrong?"

"How did—"

"Poppa Bear, remember?"

I explained about my moment of panic. "I'm not cut out for all this...subterfuge."

"It's not one of your strengths," Belen agreed with a broad smile. "How about we keep a guard nearby just in case?"

"All right."

He peered at me in suspicion. "That was too easy."

"As I see it, I'd rather go to Tohon on my own terms than be dragged there by one of his spies."

"Ah, that's our girl."

I mixed a teaspoon of sleep powder in a glass of water and gulped it. One way to keep Tohon guessing was to block him from my dreams.

Belen tucked me in, pulling the blanket up to my chin.

Then he turned the lantern's light down low, dragged Ryne's chair over by the door and sat with his sword across his lap.

"Belen, you don't—"

"Hush. Go to sleep."

"Yes, sir."

His chuckle sounded like the sweetest lullaby.

Kerrick and Flea returned in the evening of the sixth day. I rushed out to meet them with Belen and the monkeys right behind me. Too pale and too skinny, they both appeared in serious need of a month's worth of Mom's cooking and a week's worth of sleep.

I embraced Kerrick, sharing my energy. Instead of stopping me, he drew me closer. Not a good sign.

Eventually, he pulled away. "Thanks."

"I thought Flea could share his strength with you."

"He can, but we kept moving and I didn't want to slow him down."

"What did you find out?" Belen asked.

"Give the man a break," Quain said. "Let's get a fire started and heat up some food."

"Trust Quain not to miss a meal," Loren said.

Quain bumped Loren's arm hard as he issued orders. In no time, a warm fire blazed and a pile of dirty dishes grew. I snuggled next to Kerrick, anxious to hear his report, but also afraid.

"I can't wait any longer—was Tohon at the Healer's Guild?" Belen asked.

"Yes," Kerrick said. "He set up camp right in the middle of the ruins. Big fancy tent with a rug."

I straightened in alarm. "You got that close?"

"No, I caught a glimpse when the flaps opened."

"How many troops does he have with him?" Loren asked.

Kerrick glanced at Flea.

Flea said, "Approximately five hundred living soldiers, and about eight hundred dead protected with neck armor. And a dozen dead ufas that guard Tohon's tent."

"And we have—" Quain pretended to count heads "—the six of us."

Sinking back against Kerrick, I closed my eyes. Tohon was too well protected.

"We have an idea," Kerrick said.

I opened my eyes in time to see Flea nod.

"Yeah, we're thinking we can stay downwind of the camp, Loren can shoot a flaming arrow at Tohon's tent, setting it on fire, and when he runs out into the confusion, Loren puts another one into his heart."

"And there's also Saul's squad and a few others Ryne has left behind so we can create a nice distraction," Kerrick added.

"You really think Loren can get that close?" I asked.

"Well, there's a slight chance of success."

"How about if Loren comes in from another direction?" I asked.

"What are you suggesting?"

I told him about the mine shafts. "If you create a distraction to the east, we could sneak in from the west."

Kerrick and Flea exchanged a significant look.

"Yes, that could work," Kerrick said.

"And if it doesn't?" Quain asked.

"Plan B," I said.

Everyone looked at me.

"And that would be…" Quain prompted.

"Retreat through the tunnels."

"Not bad." Quain pursed his lips.

"When are we implementing this plan?" Loren asked.

"Wait," Quain said. "Why rush? Why can't we send a message to Prince Ryne and have him send a thousand troops to back us up?"

Kerrick inclined his head. "Tohon knows we're here. He won't wait much longer. The sooner we move, the better. How long did Private Beau say it'll take to navigate the tunnels?"

"Three days, and we'll come out about two miles west," I said.

Kerrick drew a circle in the dirt with a stick. "The enemy is about a mile deep, but I'm sure Tohon has patrols going farther out. It'll take the overland and underground teams the same amount of time to reach the Healer's Guild, so that fourth day will be our action day." He tapped the stick on his boot. "Do we want to strike at dusk or the middle of the night?"

"What's the advantage of dusk?" I asked.

"It's like catching them with their pants down," Quain said.

"Not quite," Loren said drily. "They're settling down for the evening, eating supper, and washing up."

"That's what I said. And middle of the night means we have to be extraquiet—any sound is amplified."

Loren leaned forward. "But the enemy is confused and disoriented from being woken. Plus the darkness will help hide us, which will work in our favor since our teams will be—"

"Tiny, petite, minuscule, infinitesimal." Quain pinched his finger and thumb together.

"Mobile, fast, flexible," Loren countered.

"The darkness can also make it hard for *us* to see," Belen said.

"Unless the moon is bright," Flea added.

"If it rains, we'll have to wait until it stops. Hard to have flaming arrows in the rain." Loren lined up an imaginary bow.

The discussion continued and everyone offered their opinions and advice.

In the end, Kerrick decided our course of action complete

with contingencies in case it rained and set the time of attack to a few hours after midnight.

"The overland team will be led by me and consist of Flea, Belen, Sergeant Saul, and his squad. The underground team will be led by Avry and consist of the monkeys, Private Beau, and the rest of his squad. We'll leave in the morning," Kerrick said.

The others rushed off to gather supplies and prepare for the mission, leaving me alone with Kerrick. No cookouts tonight.

"Well, that was rather convenient," I said.

He smiled. "Nice of the boys to clear out."

But my mood soured thinking of Belen and the others. Had I just condemned them all to death? Or worse?

Kerrick brushed a hair from my face. "What's wrong?"

"Quain has a point. Why don't we just go hide until Ryne and his army catches up? He has plenty of personnel now and we're a small force. It's suicide."

"No. It isn't." He turned so he faced me. Taking my hands in his, he met my gaze. "Trust me. This is exactly what we need to do. Okay?"

Understanding mixed with frustration. Kerrick hadn't told me everything. He didn't want Tohon to discover it through me. Smart.

"I trust you."

"Good." A slow smile spread on his face. "Besides, I'm feeling…energetic."

"You shouldn't waste your energy."

Pushing me back until I was on the ground, Kerrick leaned over me. "This is *never* a waste of energy." His lips found mine.

After that, it didn't take me long to agree with him. And for a few hours, all thoughts of battles, ambushes, and assassinations disappeared. Replaced by every aspect, detail, and scent of Kerrick.

★ ★ ★

In the middle of the final preparations the next morning, Flea pulled me aside. "Avry, I need you to do something for me."

Just by his queasy expression, I knew it involved magic. "I'm not going to like it, right?"

"No, but it's important. And believe me, I'm not happy about it, either."

Curious. "What is it?"

"I need you to tell Yuri to listen to my orders."

Yuri? Oh, no. "You want to take him along."

"Yes."

"Why?"

"I can't tell you."

Kerrick's words *trust me* repeated in my mind. "All right."

Flea tried to hide his surprise with a familiar smoothing of his features. All that time spent with Kerrick was rubbing off on him. He grabbed a lantern and led me down three levels to a small dark room. Inside, Yuri lay on a stone slab.

Guilt rushed into my heart. I'd been avoiding facing my horrible mistake since I'd arrived. And the poor man had been left all alone. "No light?"

"He doesn't need it, Avry."

I approached the young man. "If I'd been smarter, I could have cured him."

"He was part of the learning process. Without him, you wouldn't have cured thirty others."

I glanced at Flea in suspicion. "Did Kerrick tell you to say that?"

Flea ducked his head. "He knew you'd be upset and I…" Now he met my gaze. "I was awful to you, Avry. I'm sorry. It just freaked me out and I couldn't deal. At that time, refusing to use my magic made perfect sense."

"And I pushed you too hard."

"You had to, we're at war."

"What changed your mind?"

He gave me his lopsided grin. "Belen. Helping him, but even before when I caught a whiff of burned flesh…" Flea hugged himself.

"Yeah, horrific things can really motivate a person. Tohon's dead soldiers convinced me to heal Ryne."

"And not Belen's school stories?"

I laughed. "No."

"Quain owes me big!"

Trust the boys to bet on that.

"Are we friends again?" I asked Flea.

"Yep."

My smile died when I returned to the task at hand. I approached Yuri and asked him to sit up. He didn't move. I ordered him. Still nothing. It had been so long since I'd awoken him with my touch, perhaps he didn't recognize me. Plus I'd avoided touching him since.

I pressed my fingertips to his forehead. "Yuri, stand up."

He complied.

"Yuri, I want you to obey Flea's orders from now on," I said.

"How do we know if it works?" Flea asked.

"Tell him to do something."

Flea set the lantern on the floor. "Yuri, pick up my lantern."

Yuri walked over and grasped the handle, lifting the light.

"Wow," Flea said.

"That's one thing to go right," I said.

"The first of many. Come on, Yuri, follow me."

We returned to the surface to join our teams.

"How much toxin do you have?" I asked Saul.

"We're out. Prince Ryne took the last of it when he left. I was hoping you had more," Saul said.

I cursed under my breath. "I have two sacks left." Rummaging in my pack, I withdrew them. "Here."

"You keep one."

My gut reaction was to refuse, but there was a chance of running into a dead patrol when we crept in from the west. "All right."

After a quick review of the plan, we split up. Kerrick and I had said our see-you-laters last night, but I still hugged him tight. Then I hugged Belen and Flea, making them both promise to be careful.

My team descended into the tunnels and I asked Private Beau to take point with Quain assisting. Quain had found the maps for this shaft and they were tucked into his pack just in case Beau lost his way. I followed them while Loren assumed the rear-guard position. Beau's squad, led by Sergeant Walmer, stayed behind me. Fourteen people total, including Private Red Hair.

While not under the most ideal conditions—hard rock, mucky puddles, damp air, clammy walls—our trip went well. Keeping track of the days proved the most difficult task since the lanterns provided the only light. And I had to be careful how much sleep powder I mixed since I didn't want to waste time by oversleeping.

Beau stopped us about a quarter mile from the exit. "Do we want to make sure the way is clear before we all go?" he asked.

Good idea.

"We'll go," Loren said, volunteering Quain.

"No lanterns," I said. "There should be daylight outside. Just take a peek and report back."

"Yes, sir." Quain saluted me with his dagger.

"The shaft veers to the right and there's a steep slope to the exit," Beau explained. "Just keep a hand on the wall."

The monkeys nodded and soon disappeared into the darkness. Unable to keep still, I fidgeted with the straps on my pack and checked my knives. I counted seconds in my head, calculating how long it would take for them to travel a half mile.

When they failed to return by my estimate, I pulled my stiletto and mentally gave them another five minutes before we'd investigate.

To my vast relief, they returned with a minute to spare. However, their serious expressions meant bad news.

"Well?" I asked.

"The way out is blocked," Loren said.

"A cave-in?" Beau asked.

"No, but something that's almost as impenetrable."

"Just tell us," I ordered.

"The exit is blocked by thirty dead soldiers."

# KERRICK

He hated keeping secrets from Avry. But in this case it'd been vital to the success of their mission. And she had understood.

After Avry's team left, Kerrick asked Flea about Yuri.

"It worked, but it might have been too subtle. It'll all depend on what she remembers."

"And where is Yuri now?"

"Back in his room."

"Good."

As he led his team through the bare woods, Kerrick marveled over the sheer genius that had brought them all to this point. Amazing. He also wanted to throttle that same genius for putting Avry through so much pain. But if everything went as planned, then it would be over for good and they could live their lives. Provided he didn't go dormant in the meantime.

His team followed him in silence. Avry had trained Saul and his squad well. They easily kept up without making a sound. And Kerrick set a fast pace. He limited rest periods and stops. His goal was to arrive near the Healer's Guild well before Avry's team.

After a day on the road, Kerrick slowed and allowed Flea to scout ahead. Flea navigated them around pockets of dead soldiers who had been ordered to hunker down in the dips of the terrain. Flea also shared a bit of his energy with Kerrick. Each day dawned colder than the last, draining his magic.

As the sun set on the second day, Kerrick prodded the sluggish living green. With Flea's help, he sought the intruders surrounding the Healer's Guild, committing their locations to memory because this would be his only chance. The effort exhausted him more than he'd admit to his team.

"We need to head northeast," he told the others.

"But you told Avry we'd attack from the east," Belen said.

He didn't have the energy to explain, but Flea quickly informed Poppa Bear that everything they had told Avry was a lie for Tohon's benefit.

"I thought Prince Ryne fed her bad information on purpose, but she wouldn't listen to me. She'd rather hate him. Again." Belen chuckled.

"She's supposed to hate Ryne," Kerrick said. "It's for the best."

They spent the rest of the night skirting the outer ring of Tohon's army.

"Are we still going to provide a distraction?" Belen asked him when they stopped for breakfast at dawn.

"We're going to do more than that. If all goes well, Tohon will be taken care of before she reaches the Healer's Guild."

"Nice." Belen slapped him on the back.

Kerrick clamped down on a cry of pain. When he recovered, he noticed Flea studying him. He waved off Flea's help. Flea needed his full strength. The boy's magic would be invaluable when the action started. By then, Kerrick would only be able to direct from a safe distance.

A few hours later, Kerrick led the team to the location he'd zeroed in on earlier. Shuffling his feet, he crunched a few dried leaves and snapped a twig. Belen shot him an annoyed look.

However, Belen was the least of his troubles. Soldiers

jumped from hiding places and swung down from the trees. It happened so fast that the ambushers' swords pointed at his team's exposed necks before they could react.

Kerrick held his hands up, showing he was unarmed. "I know this is a cliché, but take us to your leader."

They traveled until the early afternoon when they reached a small valley. There more soldiers joined them.

"Kerrick, are you going to explain what the he—" Belen gaped at the tall muscular man who strode toward them.

Kerrick stifled a laugh at Belen's expression. Poppa Bear had probably never met his match in size and strength.

"Magic Man, this is unexpected," Noak said. He waved off the warriors. "Did Prince Ryne send you?"

"Sort of."

Noak waited.

"He arranged for this to happen, goading Avry into not trusting him and doing what she thought was the opposite of what he wanted," Kerrick explained. "How soon can you be ready to fight?"

"We go now."

"Not necessary. We plan to attack at dusk."

Noak gestured to his warriors, giving them the information. "We will be ready."

"There are soldiers with metal collars. They—"

"Unnatural abominations. We cut off their heads." Noak sliced the edge of his hand across his throat.

"But the collars are—"

The tribesman yanked his dadao from his sash. Brandishing the weapon, he said, "One chop. Gone." He pointed to the dadao hanging from Kerrick's belt. "Yours, too."

Sweet.

Kerrick introduced Noak to the others. Serious and formal, Noak shook all their hands. When it was Flea's turn, he gazed at the big man in awe. "Was the ambush at Milligreen Pass just a ruse?"

"Yes. That army is not a threat until snow melts." Noak kept Flea's hand. "You Magic Man, as well. You touched by autumn."

"We call it death magic," Flea said.

"A part of life. Same thing." He released Flea's hand.

Flea rubbed his fingers, looking thoughtful. Kerrick ordered his team to rest while he discussed strategy with Noak.

But Noak wouldn't talk tactics. Instead, he held out his hand. "Something is not right."

"I'm fine."

"Magic Man losing his magic."

That alarmed him. Kerrick allowed Noak to take his hand. A cold shiver raced down his back.

"Healer bond within you is thin, breakable," Noak said. "Your bond with winter is stronger."

"Tell me something I don't know."

"*You* must break the healer's other bond, no one else. Otherwise she will die with him."

# CHAPTER 23

"Thirty dead soldiers?" I asked the monkeys. "Are you sure?"

"Yep," Quain said.

"They had the collars, that dead gaze and stood as still as… well…death," Loren added.

Not good. I glanced at my team. With fourteen of us, disabling two each wouldn't be that difficult, but the narrow confines of the tunnel made it tough. Did we retreat? No. Kerrick said we needed to be here. And enough was enough. It was past time for Tohon to be stopped once and for all.

"Has everyone treated their weapons with Death Lily toxin?" I asked.

Nods and "yes, sirs."

"Who has the blow gun?" I asked.

Private Red Hair stepped forward.

"Loren, are your arrows—"

"Yes, they're covered."

And my throwing knives had been dipped in the toxin. "Loren, you take point, followed by Private…"

"Judi, sir."

"Judi and me. The three of us will do as much damage as possible from a distance. When they close the gap, we'll try to push through so you can engage the enemy. Don't forget there's a delay before the toxin works. Do you all know the skull jab?"

More nods and "yes, sirs."

"Questions?"

"What if there are more outside the shaft?" Beau asked.

Good question. "Once we start the fight, there's no going back. We'll keep pressing on until we run out of opposition." Or they stopped us, but I kept that to myself. "And keep to the plan if anything happens to me. Loren's the one who needs to get close to Tohon's tent. I'm just here as backup. Understand?"

Unhappy agreement.

Beau extinguished the lantern, and Loren led us through the darkness. We formed a line, keeping a hand on the shoulder of the person in front of us.

As we neared the exit, the blackness diluted in subtle hues. Loren solidified into a dark figure and shadows defined the rough contours of the walls. The shaft veered to the right. Loren fitted an arrow into his bow, signaling us to be ready.

I pulled two knives, while Judi primed her blow gun. We fanned out to each side of Loren. Light shone beyond the bend.

Loren counted under his breath, "One, two, three."

On three we stepped into view. The bow twanged and a puff of air sounded. Squinting in the brightness, I aimed at the closest figure on the right without an arrow sticking out of his or her chest. Judi aimed left so we didn't waste our weapons. I managed to hit another before the first wave of dead reached us.

We were armed with swords, but the tight space limited their effectiveness. Instead of throwing my knives, I poked the thin blades into the enemy as I shoved through them.

The stench of the dead filled the tunnel along with shouts, curses, and the ring of metal. After I used my last knife, strong hands clamped on my wrist, tugging me toward the exit. I glanced back to see the gap between me and my team widen.

Fear and revulsion fueled my efforts to break free. Frantic I pressed my hand on one man's face, zapping him. Of course, it didn't slow my progress. I covered another's eyes. No effect.

If only they obeyed me like Yuri. But he didn't obey me until I touched him again. Why not? I gasped. Flea! Flea had checked Yuri's pulse after I awoke him to confirm Yuri's status. That was why Yuri didn't listen to me until after I touched him the second time.

I reached for the closest dead flesh and yelled, "Stop!"

He did. Ecstatic, I touched the ones near me, ordering them to stop. However, others pressed in, trapping my arms. They passed me up the steep slope and right into the waiting arms of Tohon.


Tohon smiled. "Fancy meeting you here, my dear."

I grabbed his throat, intending to squeeze the life from him. But two living soldiers pulled me off him and yanked my arms behind my back. At least two dozen others fanned out around the tunnel's exit along with a half dozen dead ufas.

"Bind her hands," Tohon ordered. "You try my patience, my dear."

Cold metal bit into my wrists—an all-too-familiar feeling.

"How did you know?" I asked.

"Your sleep powder actually worked in my favor. I could rifle through your thoughts without your waking or remembering my presence." Tohon gestured to his guards. "Take care of anyone who makes it out of the tunnel."

"Yes, sire."

"No!" I said.

They all ignored me.

"Don't, Tohon, I'll..."

"You'll what?" Tohon asked. "Cooperate? Promise not to kill me? Agree to be my queen? It's too late for that." He stepped closer to me. "No doubt you're smart. It's no surprise you figured out that the dead obey whichever magician touches them last. So let's not pretend you don't know what else is going on between us."

"You can't claim me, Tohon. You tried before and failed."

"And now I know why. With two magicians, one can't force it on the other. It grows with time and the use of magic. That's the beauty of this...bond." He savored the word.

My stomach churned with bile.

"Do you remember the first time we met?" Tohon asked.

"Unfortunately." It had also been my first run-in with his dead.

"During our brief encounter, I imprinted on you and started the process. Sheer happenstance." He swung his arm wide. "I've been learning all about this wonderful quirk of our magic while waiting for you."

Ah. The real reason he'd been camping in the ruins of the Healer's Guild—the underground storage room with all those crates full of research notes.

Tohon linked his arm through mine. "Now, let's go get into position so we're ready for Team Kerrick. I believe they're attacking two hours after midnight."

I glanced back. No activity at the mouth of the tunnel. Pain clamped around my heart. Maybe the quiet meant my team had retreated deeper in the mines. Beau did know his way around. I clung to that bit of hope.

The hope expanded a smidge when half of Tohon's men followed us to the guild with the dead ufas trotting beside them, leaving only a dozen soldiers behind. From the angle of the sun, it was just past midafternoon. I also clutched the fact Kerrick knew about my dreams. Never had I been so glad to be lied to.

Tohon chatted about what he'd learned about the bond. Half-distracted with worry for Kerrick and my team, I didn't fully listen. Noak had told me Tohon's death would break the bond and that was all I needed.

"...will result in the immediate death of the other," Tohon said.

That caught my attention. "Even if the other isn't hurt?"

"Yes. So it'll be in my best interest to keep you alive, my dear. And vice versa."

A tightness ringed my chest. Breathing became difficult. *Don't panic,* I repeated in my mind. "Except we're not... We haven't...completed the process."

"Not yet. Kerrick must die or go dormant. After that, we'll be bonded."

"And I'll have an excellent reason to commit suicide."

"Now, now, my dear. Don't be nasty. Do you remember how your body reacts to my touch?"

"Unfortunately."

"I believe your words were *scatterbrained* and *swooning.* Well, I tried *clearheaded* and *cooperative,* and was tricked. Then I tried threatening you, scaring you, and killing your sister. Yet, you resisted every effort and almost killed me in the process." He tsked. "Once we're bonded, I will ensure that quick intelligence of yours is turned to goo. I will enjoy scatterbrained and swooning Avry very much."

Even more motive to commit suicide, but I clamped my mouth shut for the remainder of the trip to the Healer's Guild.

When we arrived, Tohon shook his head. "Such a waste. The buildings were magnificent. Perhaps I'll have them rebuilt. Would you like that, my dear?"

Actually, I would. Very much. "Yes."

"Don't sound so surprised. I do care about the Fifteen Realms. So much so that I want to unite us all so we can prosper and grow."

Again, I refrained from commenting. While his goal was admirable, his methods were not. No amount of arguing would change his mind. He'd convinced himself that his actions had been with the purest intentions. That murdering six million people wasn't a crime when you called it biological warfare. That reanimating the dead was making the most of your limited resources and not morally repugnant.

Instead, I asked, "How did you protect your…er…friends from the first plague virus?"

"Ah. I wondered when you'd ask me that. Although, I think you've already figured it out."

I had? "You had the cure and managed to give it to Ryne and the others during your school reunion before spreading the plague."

"Correct. And you already know what the cure is."

I mulled it over. My blood cured the new plague, so following the logic… "Your blood!"

"Correct. I discovered my life magic infused my blood with curative properties while doing my research at the Healer's Guild. Along with the fact that about a third of the people didn't contract that plague either by avoiding exposure or just a natural resistance—a happy side effect as a king needs subjects. Besides, it would have been incredibly stupid to release the plague without a cure."

"Do you have a cure for the new plague? The one Wynn stole?"

"Of course. However, I developed that one to be more difficult to spread—to use more for assassination than mass exterminations. Your death magician was kinder to that traitor than I would have been. I'd planned for Wynn to experience a great deal of agony before she died."

My thoughts spun. He'd gone to such lengths to be a king—the more I learned, the sicker I felt. At that moment, I gave up trying to figure out this horrible business of war. Spies, double crosses, ambushes, and strategic military positioning; how did anyone keep it all straight?

Then I realized it wasn't my job to keep track. It was Ryne's and maybe I should have just trusted him to do his job and I should have focused on my job—healing patients. Interfering with Ryne's strategy had only landed me here with Tohon.

Tohon guided me inside his tent. The fabric hung low on its frame and water dripped from the edges. They had soaked the material to keep it from burning. Lovely.

He pushed me into a chair then ignored me as he sent for his officers. No one, except the guards at the entrance, paid me any attention. Even if I slipped past them, I doubted I'd get far.

"Any signs of Prince Kerrick's team?" Tohon asked one of his lieutenants.

"No, sire."

"Keep vigilant, they could strike at any time. And spread the word, all patrols are on duty. No one sleeps tonight."

"Yes, sire!"

Tohon noticed my interest. "You don't really think I believed *all* your information? I was pretty confident about you, but once you told Kerrick about our dreams, I'd be a fool to trust anything he said."

Yet he had soaked the fabric of his tent. I listened as Tohon positioned his troops and dealt with the various problems and questions from his men. Fear simmered in my chest, but a numb sense of inevitability settled over me. Events had been set into motion; I would either get an opportunity to act or not. Ideally, I'd kill Tohon. Worst case... I shied away from that line of thought. As Ryne had once said, positive thoughts led to positive results.

After three nights with little sleep, I dozed in the chair.

"Am I boring you, my dear?" Tohon asked, waking me.

"Has anything happened?" I asked.

"Not yet, which is why we need to leave. But first you need to change." Tohon grabbed my arm and helped me stand. He gestured to two women waiting nearby. "Don't touch her skin."

The ladies towed me behind a screen.

"What's going on?" I asked.

They ignored me as they removed my cloak and uniform. With a quick no-nonsense efficiency that would have made Mom proud, they dressed me like one of the dead soldiers, complete with metal collar. Instead of my hands clamped behind my back, they secured a wide leather belt around my waist and cuffed my arms to my sides. They wound my hair into a bun and covered it with a knit cap.

When we returned to the main area, Tohon had also changed from his silk tunic and black pants. He, too, resembled one of the dead.

"Ah, there're our doppelgangers," Tohon said.

I turned. A woman with long auburn hair pulled into a single braid and green eyes arrived along with a handsome dark-haired man. The woman tied my cloak around her and the guards manacled her hands behind her back. The man stepped behind the screen and returned wearing Tohon's clothes.

"Nice." Tohon beamed. "Do you remember the plan?"

Both nodded.

"Very good." Tohon gestured to the flaps. "Shall we, my dear?"

Not like I had a choice. We ducked outside. The sun hung low in the sky. It was about two hours before dusk. As we strode through the camp, I scanned the soldiers. No one appeared to be settling down for the night. No "catching them with their pants down." Another group of guards followed us, as did the dead ufas, of course.

"You're rather quiet. What are you thinking?" Tohon asked.

"The doppelgangers are a smart move." Unfortunately.

"A compliment? You must be feeling ill, my dear."

The thought of being bonded to him went way beyond ill into the domain of nauseating, foul, repulsive, and vile. A sarcastic comment died in my throat. No sense upsetting Tohon unduly, and if he believed I was resigned to my fate, then all the better.

We left the guild's compound and entered the forest. After an hour, I recognized the area. I slowed.

"Something wrong?" Tohon smirked.

"Is that—"

"Yes. Ryne's first headquarters. Do you have fond memories of that cave?"

"I don't like caves," I said.

"Really? Yet you spend so much time in them."

"They provide protection for my patients."

"Yes, they're handy for protection." Tohon led me straight to the entrance.

I hesitated. Once inside, the chances of my rescue or escape bottomed out at zero. The soldiers behind us moved closer.

"Go on, my dear. Make a break for it. It might make you feel better. Frankly, this docile act is rather boring."

I'd get two steps before being tackled. No thanks. I walked toward the cave. Right before I entered, an icy chill brushed my skin, raising goose bumps on my arms. An omen? Or something else? A memory stirred and then slipped out of reach.

Instead of a damp, cold cavern, warmth pulsed. A fire had

been started and comfortable chairs set around it. In fact, the place had all the trappings of Tohon's lavish tent. Most of the men followed us inside, but the ufas remained outside.

"Impressed?" Tohon asked.

"Yes. I'd like caves a lot more if they were all like this."

He laughed. "Stick with me, my dear, and you'll never have to sleep on the ground again."

"If you're giving me the choice, then I'll take the ground."

"And there's the sarcasm. Good, I was getting worried." Tohon yanked off his metal collar and tossed it aside.

When he approached me, I recognized the gleam in his eyes. I backed away until I bumped into the wall. He un-hooked my collar and dropped it, and then removed the knit cap. Untying my bun, Tohon let my hair down. He placed his hands on either side of my head and leaned in as if to kiss me.

I ducked.

With a growl, he hauled me to my feet. "Cute." He put his hand over my mouth and shoved my head back. Hard.

Pain exploded as my skull connected with the stone. He let go and I slid down. My vision blurred and the cave spun, but I held on to consciousness. I remained on the ground as Tohon settled in a chair and directed his men.

Soldiers arrived from time to time with news. Eventually the sharp pain dulled into a throb. I struggled into a sitting position.

One man ran into the cave and announced they were under attack.

Tohon huffed in amusement. "Under attack? With such a small force, it's more like a nuisance than an attack."

"But, sire. There are hundreds of them! Coming from all directions."

Tohon hopped to his feet. "Details, now!"

The man explained, his words tumbling out with a rush.

"They don't look like Prince Ryne's troops. They have strange curved blades and colorful sashes."

Noak and his men! I suppressed a shout of joy.

"We have plenty of troops. Send them where they need to be," Tohon ordered.

"Yes, sire." The man bolted.

Tohon stormed over to me. "Did you know about this?"

"No."

"They're the tribesmen from the north. They're supposed to be guarding the Milligreen Pass. My men confirmed it."

I kept quiet.

He pulled me upright. "This changes nothing. I've over a thousand troops."

"Are you trying to convince me or yourself?" The words slipped out without thought. Big mistake.

Fury blazed in his eyes. I braced for pain. Tohon didn't disappoint. He wrapped his hands around my throat and his power slammed into me like a lightning bolt. I cried out as every inch of my body burned. Even my bones pulsed with an unrelenting pain.

Through the haze of torment, I struggled to counter his magic. To zap him back. I sensed the bond between us and used that to channel his onslaught into him.

He yelped and let go. "You dare attack me!"

"Vice versa, Tohon. You're only hurting yourself."

"The bond's not complete yet. I can kill you without consequence."

"Go ahead, test your theory." Because of my little stunt, I'd strengthened the bond and I believed I'd take him with me.

But he was too smart to fall for the taunt. Tohon drew back to punch me. Howls pierced the air, stopping him. His ufa pack had sounded a warning. He hustled to his guards, barking orders. They raced outside.

I sank down. No sense getting my hopes up. Noak and Kerrick would target Tohon's tent and find fake Avry. Would they even think to look beyond the camp's boundaries? And then I caught that elusive bit of memory triggered by the chill before I'd entered the cave. Had Noak spotted me? The brush of cold matched when he'd used his magic on me at the infirmary. Or was I indulging in more wishful thinking?

More howls and a yelp echoed off the cavern's walls. Then a ruckus sounded and a knot of guards wrestled with a struggling man. They threw him to the ground.

Kerrick! Oh, no. I hopped to my feet. Blood and gore stained his torn clothes. Was that an ufa bite on his arm? His ashen face was lined with strain as he sucked in gulps of air. It must have been an immense effort for him to be here.

Once he met my gaze, he relaxed and remained on the floor of the cave. The guards handed Tohon his dadao. Black ichor coated the blade.

Tohon held up the weapon in triumph. "Perfect. Did he attack the tent?" Tohon asked one of his guards.

"No, sire, he came after the ufas."

Tohon turned a contemplative gaze on me. "How did he know?"

"We share a bond, as well," I said.

"It's too weak. You've been too busy splitting up and playing heroes. Besides, I imprinted on you before him, my dear."

Kerrick pushed up on an elbow. "Imprinted?"

Tohon's eyes gleamed. "Oh, yes. When Avry and I first met. While you were still being Mr. Stony Silence." He hefted the dadao and approached Kerrick.

"No," I shouted and flew between them. "You can't kill him or we'll all die."

"Nonsense," Tohon said.

"Kerrick and I imprinted before I met you. He saved my life when I healed Belen. Kept me from dying."

An ufa howled. Then growls and yelps filled the air. Tohon gestured to his men to investigate before shoving me aside. He knelt next to Kerrick and grabbed his throat.

"You lied again, my dear. He's bonded to the forest and not you. And now I'll pluck—

I yelled and plowed into Tohon, knocking him over. We rolled, but he ended up on top, pinning me to the ground.

"Sire?" A guard cleared his throat.

Tohon's anger transferred to the interrupter. But then he smiled. He stood and smoothed his shirt. I glanced up. Noak and Flea stood amid a clump of guards. A pack of dead ufas slinked inside, surrounding them all.

It appeared Noak and Flea had been captured. I doubted they would be prisoners for long. I slid over to Kerrick. He gave me a weak grin and unlocked my bindings. I wiggled free.

"Report," Tohon said.

"We caught these two trying to sneak in here."

"I do not sneak," Noak said, sounding affronted.

The guard blanched even though he held Noak's huge dadao.

"Ah, the ice giant and a boy," Tohon said. Then his good humor disappeared. "You're Flea."

"Yes. And I'm tired of being called a boy." Flea touched the guard closest to him and froze him in a magical stasis.

"Trap his hands," Tohon shouted.

But it was too late. Noak moved, knocking guards flat before they could reach Flea.

"Attack," Tohon ordered the dead ufas.

They didn't move.

"Protect," Flea said, and the pack turned to join the fight.

446 Maria V. Snyder

Way to go, Flea! He must have touched them all and transferred their loyalty to him. Too bad we hadn't figured that out sooner.

Desperate, Tohon darted in and reached for Noak's bare arm.

"Noak, watch out," I yelled, scrambling to my feet. I ran.

Tohon clamped onto Noak's forearm just as I grabbed Tohon's wrist. Magic exploded around us. Ice, pain, and fire mixed.

"Back off," Tohon said. His voice cracked with strain.

"You first," I said.

"Let go, or I'll kill him," Tohon puffed.

"No."

Tohon tugged at Noak's life. Not if I could help it! I held his life force in place with all my strength. We struggled without sound.

Kerrick hovered at the edges.

"Do it," Noak ordered.

"Will it kill her?" Kerrick asked.

I met Noak's gaze. Pained uncertainty.

But not for me. I knew what needed to be done. "No. Do it now, I'm fading fast."

A swoosh and a flash of light off a wide curved blade. The sharp edge of the dadao sliced right through Tohon's neck, decapitating him.

A wall of energy slammed into me, shattering all thought.

Destroying all sensation.

Erasing all life.

# KERRICK

He kept a vigil by the Peace Lily, refusing to budge. He stayed there day after day after day. Flea and Noak gave him the strength to physically survive the winter, fighting off the desire to go dormant. The monkeys and Belen provided company. They took turns while they chased down the rest of Tohon's dead troops. The living soldiers quickly surrendered after Tohon's death, relieved to be finished with the fighting. Noak and his warriors returned to their positions near the Milligreen Pass, planning to surprise Cellina and her troops when they crossed into Pomyt Realm in the spring. With Estrid locked behind her borders, the war would truly be over.

Emotions twisted inside him. Fury that Avry had lied to him. Utter grief that Tohon had taken her with him. If the Lily didn't save her, he planned to join her. Of course, he wouldn't share that desire with anyone or they'd never leave him alone.

Instead, he chatted and learned what else had happened the night of the attack. Quain and Loren's story provided the most entertainment.

"We retreated into the tunnels, leading the dead on a merry chase," Quain said.

"Beau showed us a shaft that looped around and half of us got in behind them," Loren said.

"Yeah, then it was just a matter of time." Quain snapped his fingers.

"What about the guards waiting outside the shaft?" Kerrick asked.

"Child's play."

"Uh-huh. I heard one of Noak's teams had to rescue you," Kerrick said.

"We were fine, they *assisted*."

"And we did our job. Well, sort of." Loren added another log to the fire. "I did put an arrow through Tohon's heart. Wrong Tohon, but for a moment it felt very fine."

"How did you know they weren't in the tent?" Quain asked Kerrick.

"Noak spotted Avry going into the cave. The rescue went as planned, except..."

They all glanced at the Peace Lily.

Except.

When Belen joined Kerrick one evening a couple weeks after the attack, Belen shooed the monkeys away. Something was up.

"Prince Ryne is here and he wishes to speak to you," Belen said.

Kerrick just stared at Belen.

"Don't be like that. He didn't know what would happen to Avry."

"Don't make excuses for him. He was well aware of what would happen."

"Will you talk to him? Please?"

He could never resist that look. "Only if you stay with us."

"Why?"

"So I don't kill him."

"Good reason." Belen left and returned with Ryne.

The prince was smart to tread carefully. Instead of jumping

right into the night Avry died, he filled Kerrick in on a few bits of good news. Softening him up, Kerrick thought sourly.

"I've received a message from Alga. Your brother and great-aunt are fine, and she says if you don't visit soon, you'll be in *big* trouble—her words exactly." Ryne gave him a wry smile. "From the impression she made on the messenger, she sounds like a formidable woman, one you don't want to disobey."

"She is," Kerrick said. Avry would have loved her.

"I sent a battalion to Tohon's castle in Sogra and rescued Zila. She's in perfect health and with Danny now. He wishes to wait until Noak returns to decide what they'll do next."

"What if Cellina gets word of Tohon's defeat and doesn't cross the pass?" Belen asked. "Her troops could cause a bunch of trouble for the people living in Ivdel and Alga Realms."

"I'm sending a battalion over the main pass, so we'll block her if she decides to retreat. Either way, we'll stop her."

"Stop her or kill her?" Belen asked.

"Depends if she surrenders or not. I'm not executing my enemies. The Skeleton King was a prisoner of war until he died from the plague."

Guess he didn't ingest enough of Avry's blood. Good. It saved Kerrick from ripping him apart for torturing Avry. He glanced at the Peace Lily. *Come back, Avry, please.*

"What about the dead soldiers?" Belen ran a hand over his scar.

"Flea's been helping corral them. We'll prick them with toxin and give them a proper burial."

"And the Skeleton King's army?" Kerrick asked.

Ryne grimaced. "Most of them are highly...unstable. I'm still working on how to integrate them into peaceful society."

Kerrick huffed. "Good luck with that."

"We have a million details to settle and I'm coordinating with all the surviving leaders to reestablish the Fifteen Realms.

That's one of the reasons I wish to talk to you." Ryne steeled himself. "Since your brother is King of Alga, I wanted to offer you Sogra Realm. We need a strong leader there with experience. You can change the name of the realm. Tear down Tohon's castle and build your own in the woods. Whatever you'd like. Please, think about it. I don't need an answer right away."

Once the shock wore off, fury filled the hollow gaps inside him. How dare he—

Belen put a hand on his shoulder. "Easy. You need to think beyond your grief. And you know the monkeys and I will be there with you."

Pain burned deep in the pit of his soul, unrelenting. Belen didn't believe she'd return. That seemed a worse betrayal than Ryne's.

"Kerrick, I'm very sorry about Avry. I knew about the growing bond, but I'd truly thought it wasn't that strong. I thought she had more time."

By pure force of will, Kerrick remained sitting. Hard to believe Ryne didn't know how close she'd gotten to Tohon. Hard not to believe he had planned this from the beginning. Instead of throttling Ryne, Kerrick asked, "Why did you let Avry get taken by Wynn and Sepp?"

"I needed more time for Noak and his army to get into position. Tohon wouldn't have believed a rumor Noak was at the Milligreen Pass or Avry's dreams. He needed to have it confirmed by a trusted officer. Once he knew about Noak, I'd hoped Tohon would go after the Skeleton King's forces in the south to rescue Avry, but he stayed at the Healer's Guild." Ryne raised his hands as if surrendering. "I know I'm horrible for using Avry. But she was Tohon's only weakness."

A smart plan, except...

Except.

"I'll think about it," Kerrick said, hoping that would get rid of Ryne faster.

It didn't.

Ryne talked about fixing all the problems the war and plague had left behind; returning the Fifteen Realms to its prior health would take years and years of hard work and dedication. Kerrick didn't listen, letting Belen ask questions. Instead, he wondered how long.

How long would the Peace Lily keep Avry? Before, the flower had spit her out soon after she died. So far, it had been twenty-five days. To stop the panic, he focused on Flea. A Peace Lily had held Flea for close to six months.

Grief clamped down on his heart when he remembered Avry's limp body and cold, dead eyes. They'd found the Lily map in her pack. Noak had scooped her up and Flea had led him to the closest Lily patch. At that time, Kerrick had been too weak to stand. He still remained sluggish and tired. What kind of leader would he make when he'd have to fight to re-main conscious every winter?

Besides, life had no appeal without Avry.

How long would he wait for her? Growing in this cluster, there were four Peace Lilys, and a few yards away was one Death Lily. The yellow-and-orange firelight flickered on its white petals. Kerrick had memorized the contours of that Lily.

"...new realm should be called Avry Realm," Belen said.

Wary, Ryne stared at Kerrick. If anyone else had said that, Kerrick would have pounded him. But not Belen. Only Belen could get away with those type of comments.

"You should call it the Realm of Belen and make Belen king," Kerrick said.

Belen shook his head. "Oh, no, I'm not a leader. I'm well suited for the role of loyal support personnel. Last time I had to make a decision I got my head bashed in."

"It's a good thing you have such a thick skull," Ryne teased.

"Avry wouldn't want it named after her," Kerrick said in a low voice. "She never liked that type of attention. She'd argue to name it after her sister, Noelle, or... What was that one sergeant's name that you hunted the dead with?"

"Ursan," Belen said.

"Ursan, or her teacher, Tara."

"You can only name the realm if you take the job," Ryne said.

Kerrick stared at him.

"That doesn't work on me. I know you too well."

"Avry would have wanted to build a place for healers to learn," Belen said. "Maybe you could build another guild for Zila and Danny in the new realm."

Now Kerrick turned his ire on Belen.

Unimpressed, the big man smiled. "You can call it the Realm of Healing, or the Healer's Realm.... No, I like the first one better."

Ryne stood. "Think about it. I know you need time to... We all do. You're not the only one missing her. And you know she'd be furious at you if you did anything stupid. Just think of what you'd want her to do if your roles were reversed."

He fisted his hands, but kept them pressed to his legs. "Our roles *were* reversed. I was presumed dead and she refused to believe it. She didn't give up."

"But she did move on." Ryne gazed at the fire for a moment. "I'll be at the old Healer's Guild for the next couple days. Then I'm traveling to Mengels to meet with the other realm leaders. It's a central location and Mom offered to lodge and feed us. For a fee, of course."

"It'll be worth every coin," Belen said.

Ryne patted his stomach. "And every pound, I'm sure." Then he said goodbye and left.

Belen grew unusually quiet.

Kerrick cursed Ryne under his breath because he knew exactly what his friend was thinking. "No. I'm not going to do anything...rash."

"But you were considering it?" Belen asked.

"Yes."

"Did Ryne change your mind?"

"No."

Belen waited. He'd learned that trick from Kerrick, which made it even more infuriating.

Kerrick stabbed the fire with a stick. Sparks flew into the air. "Avry did. By her own actions. She refused to give up on me, so I won't give up on her. Happy?"

"Happier. But not happy."

Belen's comment pierced his hard shell of grief. They all suffered.

Loren and Quain returned to the campfire and soon Flea joined them. He'd just gotten back from a dead sweep in Vyg. They noticed a shift in mood right away. Flea gave Belen a questioning look, but Poppa Bear shook his head. Belen would tell them everything later.

They talked about random, unimportant things like the quality of the whiskey from a local farm and how the dadao's blade had been made with a metal similar to the liquid metal mined under the Nine Mountains. They joked.

Until Quain went too far. "Are you sure Avry's still in there? Maybe she slipped out the back door and is playing dead again."

Loren swatted him on the arm. "It's a flower, there's no back door."

"Back petal, whatever. You know what I mean."

"Why would she do that? The war's over. Think before you speak, Quain."

"She's there," Flea said in a quiet tone. "I watched Noak. And the Lily took her right away." He met Kerrick's gaze. "That counts for something. She wasn't rejected."

True. Kerrick studied the Peace Lily. He'd wait until spring arrived in a month. Then he'd decide his next move.

# CHAPTER 24

Tears streamed down Kerrick's face as he sobbed, holding me tight. I stared at him in confusion. Why was he so upset? My memories swirled and settled on one image. Me, Noak, and Tohon locked together. Did Tohon kill Noak?

Alarmed, I wriggled to break free.

Kerrick tightened his grip, pressing me to his chest. "Just give…me…a moment."

I stilled. Gaunt and haggard, he looked as if he suffered from the wasting disease. But my magic didn't stir, so it must be lack of sleep. I sensed his bond with the living green. From what I'd learned about magical bonds, I planned to fix that little problem.

I glanced around. At least we were no longer inside the cave. Buds spiked the trees and a green fuzz coated a few bushes. Lilys swayed in the warm breeze and the air smelled of fresh grass and spring sunshine. Spring? Or Kerrick's scent?

He stared at me with emerald-colored eyes. Spring. Which meant I'd missed…two months!

"Start talking," I forced the words from my dry throat.

Instead, he kissed me. I returned it, raking my fingers in his hair. Sometime later we broke apart.

"Bad news?" I asked.

"Not anymore." He smiled a killer smile and I had to kiss him again.

Much later, after I'd dressed and eaten a ton of food, I snuggled next to him while he filled me in on the past two months. I marveled that the Peace Lily saved my life again. A faint memory of the Peace Lily telling me it would no longer help and asking to be left alone stirred. I would ensure the knowledge about the flower remained limited to those already in the know. We would not bother it again. Its serum only preserved a body from decaying; it didn't heal. And I would do everything I could to keep another rogue magician from using its serum to create dead soldiers.

"Where's Belen and the others?" I asked.

Kerrick beamed. "They're going to be ecstatic."

"So they are close?"

"Out hunting. They've been keeping me company."

"That was nice of them."

"They were upset, too."

"Gee, this is my third time—you'd think they'd be a bit more relaxed," I teased.

But Kerrick failed to see the humor. "It was a *long* two months."

"I'm sorry."

"Not like you had any control."

"I meant for lying to you. Tohon had to die."

"I know. It took me a month, but I forgave you."

"The good news just keeps on coming." And one of the best parts—the war was over. "Is Ryne going to keep his promise to reestablish the Fifteen Realms?"

"Yes." Kerrick explained about the leaders. "And he offered me Tohon's realm. But I can't accept it."

"Why not?"

"Because I can't leave the forest. Because I go dormant in the winter. Because—"

"What if I told you I can break your bond to the living green?"

"Without killing me?"

"Yep."

"How?"

"By doing this…" I kissed him.

He pulled away. "What's the catch?"

"After spending lots of time together and sharing magic, we'll be bonded. You'll be swapping one bond for another. There are some limitations and the whole 'if I die, you die' thing and vice versa." I suppressed a shudder, remembering my link with Tohon. "I'll understand if you don't want to."

Kerrick crushed me to his chest. "Avry, today you just gave me back my life."

"Does that mean you'll accept the position of King of Sogra?"

"Depends."

"On what?"

"If you'll agree to be my queen."

My heart jolted. "And a healer?"

"Of course. Belen figured you might want to reestablish the Healer's Guild."

"That's a great idea. I can work with the Death Lilys to discover more potential healers. Without harming them, of course! And Danny and Zila can live with us."

"I'd like that."

"And we'll have children?"

"As many as you want. That *won't* be a problem." He leered.

"And we'll have a very long honeymoon?"

"Oh, yes. As long as you wish. It's going to take a while to knock down Tohon's castle and build another."

"Oh, no, you can't knock it down."

"Why not? There's nothing but bad memories there."

"There are good memories, as well. The infirmary is wonderful, there are lots of Peace Lilys, and a rooftop garden that you would love—trust me. Besides, that's where we kissed for the first time. Not under the best circumstances, true, but..."

"All right, we'll keep the castle as long as we can have a huge bonfire and burn all of Tohon's things."

"Agreed."

Kerrick dug into his pocket and removed a ring. "Avry of Kazan Realm, will you marry me?"

"Yes."

He whooped and kissed me.

Warmth spread throughout my heart as he slipped the ring onto my finger. Made of stone, the ring had an intricate pattern of vines on the outside that Kerrick must have carved.

"This is temporary. It kept me busy while waiting for you."

"This is wonderful. No need—"

"Nope, I'm buying you one made of liquid metal. It has to last forever."

I grinned. "Hard to believe I'll be Queen of Sogra."

"You'll be a queen, but not of Sogra. I'm changing the name of the realm."

"Now, that I agree with. What's the new name?" I asked.

"The Realm of Peace. Because it's what we set out to accomplish and even though it'll take many years to achieve, I'm hopeful. Besides, Peace Lilys are my favorite plant."

"What a coincidence. They're my favorite, as well."

★ ★ ★ ★ ★

## ACKNOWLEDGMENTS

It shouldn't be a surprise that my support network grows with every book like ripples on a pond. At the center are my husband, son, and daughter. They are the rock-solid core that I lean on. They encourage me and inspire me and brag about me and even entice me away from my writer's cave from time to time. Thanks so much!

Then there's my editor, Mary-Theresa Hussey, and agent, Robert Mecoy, who like it when I spent lots of time in my cave, creating new worlds and characters. Their help with shaping my stories has been instrumental to my success, and I'm grateful for their insight, humor, and for not letting me get away with lazy plotting.

After all the hard work of writing the book, I'm thankful I don't have to design a cover, write press releases, and deal with the million other details that arise when producing a book. Thanks to all the people at Harlequin who are involved in crafting this lovely book that I can display on my shelf (and my eReader) with pride!

And I must thank all my readers. You have been an unexpected joy. The outpouring of support and encouragement and, yes, even the emails urging me to write faster have been wonderful. I used to write for myself; now I write for you.

# THEY DESTROYED HER WORLD. BUT SHE'S THEIR ONLY HOPE...

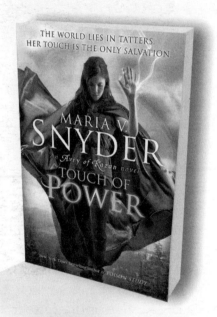

Avry's power to heal the sick should earn her respect in the plague-torn land of Kazan. Instead she is feared and blamed for spreading the plague.

When Avry uses her forbidden magic, she faces the guillotine. Until a dark, mysterious man rescues her from her prison cell. His people need Avry's magic to save their dying prince.

Saving the prince is certain to kill Avry. Now she must choose—use her healing touch to show the ultimate mercy or die a martyr to a lost cause?

# HUNTED, KILLED—
# TRIUMPHANT?

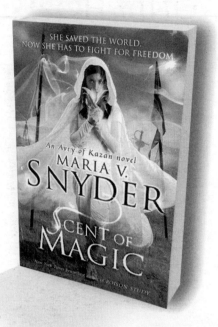

As the last Healer of the Fifteen Realms,
Avry of Kazan is in a unique position: in the
minds of friends and foes alike, she no longer exists.

With her one-of-a-kind powers, Avry must now face an
oncoming war alone and infiltrate deadly King Tohon's army
to stop his most horrible creations yet: a league of walking
dead soldiers—human and animal alike, and beyond any
known power to defeat.

Unless Avry figures out how to do
the impossible…**again**.

www.mirabooks.co.uk

# CHOOSE:
# A QUICK DEATH...
# OR A SLOW POISON...

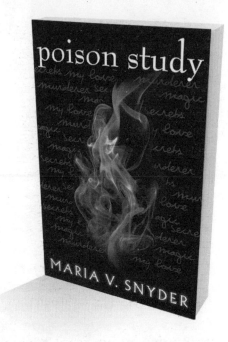

About to be executed for murder, Yelena is offered the chance to become a food taster. She'll eat the best meals, have rooms in the palace—and risk assassination by anyone trying to kill the Commander of Ixia.

But disasters keep mounting as rebels plot to seize Ixia and Yelena develops magical powers she can't control. Her life is threatened again and choices must be made. But this time the outcomes aren't so clear...

www.miraink.co.uk

BL_290_PS (C)